The Infinite Tides

The Infinite Tides

A Novel

Christian Kiefer

BLOOMSBURY

New York   Berlin   London   Sydney

Published by Bloomsbury USA, New York

All papers used by Bloomsbury USA are natural, recyclable products made
from wood grown in well-managed forests. The manufacturing processes
conform to the environmental regulations of the country of origin.

LIBRARY OF CONGRESS CATALOGING–IN–PUBLICATION DATA

Kiefer, Christian, 1971–
    The infinite tides : a novel / Christian Kiefer. — First U.S. edition.
        pages cm
    ISBN 978-1-60819-810-8
    1. Astronauts—Fiction.   2. Immigrants—Fiction.   3. Ukrainians—
United States—Fiction.   4. Male friendship—Fiction.   5. Suburban
life—Fiction.   I. Title.
    PS3611.I443I54 2012
    813'.6—dc23

                                                        2011045534

First U.S. Edition 2012

1   3   5   7   9   10   8   6   4   2

Typeset by Westchester Book Group
Printed in the U.S.A. by Quad/Graphics, Fairfield, Pennsylvania

The Dark Matter

THE AIRLOCK OPENED. He knew there would be no perceptible change in pressure but now that the moment had arrived he somehow expected the transition of atmosphere to be audible, for the brief symphony of thumps and clicks between the shuttle and the docking node to include the hiss or shush or sigh of oxygen exchange and yet, despite the absence of such a marker, the swing of the hatch felt to Keith like a sudden outrushing of the tide, a sensation that remained with him as he floated through the opening and entered the Harmony Module where the crew they had come to relieve all smiled expectantly back at him. It was a moment as glorious and transcendent as any he could have imagined and he would realize only later that it represented the single coordinate point in which he understood that he had done it, that at last he had entered the long incredible upward-turning arc that had been the trajectory of his life, and that he was, finally and undeniably, an astronaut.

In the days to follow he would try to describe the experience but

what words were there for such a moment? He thought first of numbers, not of words, but then he always had. The seemingly infinite
parallels that extended off the edges of the grid forever in their ongoing x and y coordinates had finally intersected on some z plane that he
had thought about since his earliest days and yet had never been able to
truly understand or plot or calculate. He had stared at it through the
window of the shuttle on their approach: the interconnected tubes and
the fanning wings of the solar arrays stretching out like some magnificent metal flower above the blue swirl of Earth. And even then he
was thinking of the numbers: the average speed of 17,239 miles per
hour in an orbit very nearly that of a perfect circle, the apogee and
perigee perhaps ten kilometers in difference and inclining to 51.6459
degrees, the angle of its motion, the angle of its helixed continuance.
The feeling of weightlessness itself so familiar and comfortable it was
as if he had lived within that condition for the entirety of his life. And
in many ways he had.

   He would ask himself if this had been his destiny and each time he
would answer yes. He would answer yes yes yes as if the weightlessness of his body was itself the vindication and proof that a life spent
huddled over papers scratched through with the symbology of mathematics had indeed been the true vector, the numbers themselves extant
in a universe that was this universe and no other: days and nights
spinning past in forty-five-minute increments, continents and oceans
and weather patterns unscrolling under the round porthole windows, the lit webwork of cities and roads on the black sphere of the
planet below. And the flow of the numbers, his numbers, in everything, always.

   In his memory, that moment of passing through the hatch would
resolve itself into an unambiguous image of triumph. But there had
been something else as well, a sensation so fast and intense and so
quickly gone again that it had been easy to forget. There had been
that feeling of pride, the rush of his success, of all the years of his labor coalescing into this finally solved equation, but for one instant

there had also been the clutch of an impossible helplessness so complete and staggering that it seemed to seize at his heart. A flicker and then gone. In its wake only the after-echo of a distant high-pitched ringing that vibrated through him even as it returned to silence once again, as he stared into the smiling faces of the crew and told himself that yes he was meant to be here, that it had been his destiny to succeed and so he had succeeded, the sense of panic already replaced by the pride of his accomplishment, replaced so completely that he would not remember that flicker, would not allow himself to remember, even after everything else had happened. In his memory of that moment, he was an astronaut and they were welcoming him aboard the space station. And in his memory he was smiling.

Is this not what he was meant to do? Is the answer not as fixed and indisputable as any equation he might have been tasked to solve?

Watch them now: the numbers as if stretched upon a wire. The sixes stacked astride the decimal. The seven and three and zeroes behind them. Study them all your days and then ask yourself how any such equation could describe anything at all: the water rushing across the sand, the tiny stars, the way her hand curled into his. They could not even describe the way he felt about the numbers themselves, what they had meant to him, what they would continue to mean.

Such equations to imagine. Now watch them vanish into the spiraled lemniscate of what is to come. This the black firmament. This the dark matter flowing into and out of your heart.

Part I

One

THERE WAS NO sound at all and what sense of movement he generated upon entering returned to him from every surface as if the house
had become some kind of empty museum, his footfalls echoing off
the tiles and the clunk of the closing door behind him so abrupt and
alien that he actually shivered as he moved forward into the entryway, setting the two black suitcases by the door and flipping the light
switch, the tiles and the carpeted room before him illuminating all at
once: dull, white, empty. He stood there as if his delay might somehow undo what he had already seen but his hesitation only confirmed
the silence and vacancy. She had left the coat hooks hanging by the
door but the coats themselves were gone. Through the squared arch-
way leading into the living room he could see the enormous sofa but
there was no other furniture visible whatsoever. He had known this
would be the case, that the house would be empty, and yet he had not
expected the totality of it, the sofa's singular presence there a grim and
ironic goodbye in the guise of overstuffed gray leather.

Empty. Absolutely empty.

He moved through the downstairs with military precision, flicking on each light as he passed. The refrigerator continued to hum in the kitchen but he did not open its door. Instead, he went to the cabinets and inventoried each one in turn. A few boxes of cereal, undoubtedly stale, and various cans of odds and ends. Peaches and fruit cocktail. String beans. Canned yams. He did not even know who ate these things. Himself? His wife? His daughter? Items not worth moving or at least not worth moving for her. An extra key to the house on the countertop and a smaller gold key for what purpose he did not know. No note left behind; instead, canned yams.

How much of her had he simply and completely misread? The insistence and expression of her care for him, her interest in his career, and, later, her various moments of weeping and the desperation with which she had told him, finally, that she had moved out of the house and would not return: all of these now trembled upon the threshold of each empty room. She really had taken it all, and when he found that his bed—their bed—remained in the upstairs bedroom, although without sheets, blankets, or pillows, the sight struck him as such a feeble presentation of his former life that he actually laughed aloud. His dresser, and, in the corner, the small television in its wooden armoire. There were holes in the walls where pictures had hung but he could not recall what those pictures had been. Family photos or framed art or something else, and in the closet a single overhead bulb lighting a bleak arrangement of slacks, jeans, collared polos, and a handful of dress shirts, most light blue, all of which huddled against the left wall of the closet as if to underscore the emptiness of the opposite wall or the obvious fact that this was what remained.

"Fantastic," he said, his voice ricocheting off blank walls and square angles.

Down the hall, Quinn's bedroom door yawed open revealing a bare gray space: dirty carpet, a few tacks remaining in the walls, empty electrical sockets, phone cord dangling limply. A room he might have entered but which he did not, instead lingering in the doorway. There would be time to enter that room later. This was what he told himself. Maybe tomorrow. Maybe later in the week. For the moment it would remain a room defined only by the fact that whoever had once lived in it no longer did and he was a man standing before a vacancy, holding only the dull colorless waste of his fatigue, an equation the sum total of which was zero.

He returned downstairs to the doorway, hefting the suitcases and mounting the stairs again and then setting the suitcases at the foot of the bed and opening his dresser drawers to extract clean socks and boxer shorts. Then he returned to the closet and pulled a pair of pants and a polo shirt from their hangers. There was a set of yellow towels under the sink in the master bath—at least a towel then—and he undressed and folded his shirt and slacks on the bed and coiled his belt and then turned the shower on. A half-used bar of soap remained and a bottle of nearly-empty shampoo and he waited for the water to move from frigid to warm and stood cold and shivering. For a moment he had thought she actually had had the foresight to turn off the water heater but the shower temperature began to turn and he entered it and stood for a long moment as the water scalded him. His mind felt soft. A dull ache behind his eyes.

When he returned downstairs he was wearing the tattered bathrobe he had found hanging on its hook in the closet and had retrieved the amber bottles of Vicodin and Imitrex from the smaller of the two suitcases. He swallowed each tablet with a handful of water from the kitchen sink. Then he removed a box of cereal from the pantry and opened the cabinet but like everything else the plates and bowls had been removed and when he reached into the box his motion was met with a flurry of tiny brown moths that fluttered up out of the dark and circled his head in a chaos of arcs and lines. No cereal, then. And upon opening another cabinet: no pots or pans either. A few chipped glasses and coffee mugs left behind. Had the walls been pale yellow when they had first purchased the house or had she painted them while he was away? There was an eye-level hole in the wall large enough to fit a finger and he wondered what had hung there, what they had owned that was large enough to require such a bolt-hole.

The sliding glass door: a black wall reflecting his ghost. An exhausted rag of a man in a sagging purple robe, clutching a coffee mug that he did not even remember removing from the cabinet. No astronaut but a patient escaped from some hospital. He straightened his back and faced the glass and stood at a kind of attention for a moment, shoulders square and legs tight together as if he might be preparing to salute, but the posture did nothing to make him look more like himself, the flat white glow of the kitchen rendering him a ruined silhouette.

Around him the walls blank and empty. A huge space where the dining room table once stood. The kitchen island in the middle of the room like a geologic formation.

Sleep like a promise. This the only clear thought he had.

He did not even remember lying down, instead opening his eyes to a bewilderingly bare room and remaining there, unmoving, prostrate on the mattress for a long silent moment. He had been dreaming of the ISS but had awakened into a sense of gravity so thick and heavy that he briefly wondered if it would be possible to move at all. Sunlight slanted through the windows, but whether it was early morning or early evening he could not tell. And there was a sound: the buzzing of his phone somewhere in the room, which paused just as he identified it and then started up again.

The third time the phone began to vibrate he sat up slowly and dropped his feet off the edge of the mattress but made no further press into motion, rubbing at his face and the back of his neck and continuing to listen as the buzzing continued in its short bursts—nine, ten, eleven—paused and then resumed once more. He leaned forward and lifted his crumpled pants from the floor and at last fished the phone from the pocket, lowering himself to sit at the edge of the bed as her voice came through the tiny speaker.

"Hi, it's me," she said.

He breathed. "Christ, Barb," he said.

"You're in a good mood," she said.

"There's not even a vacuum here."

"Where?"

"At the house."

"You're at the house?"

"Yeah."

"Are you OK?"

"Yeah, I'm fine."

"You don't sound fine."

"I'm fine," he said again. "I was asleep."

"Oh. Sorry. I guess it's early there."

"Probably," he said. He pulled his fingers through his hair. Rubbed at one eye and then the other, then pressed his fingertips against tightly closed eyelids. Everything red for a brief moment.

"When did you get there?" she asked.

"Last night."

"I thought you were maybe still in Houston."

"We finished up a couple days ago."

"Good."

"I guess."

He could hear her breath. "What do you want me to say, Keith?" she said at last.

"I don't want you to say anything," he said. "You called me."

"You're not being fair."

"Fair?" He breathed. Waited. Then he said, "What am I supposed to do here?"

"Just get your stuff and put the house up on the market."

"It needs some work first. Cleaning at least. And probably paint."

"The new owners can do that."

"I don't think it will sell like this."

"Just sell it, Keith. OK? That's all you have to do."

"That's all I have to do?" he said. "Really? That's all?"

There must have been an edge in his response for when she spoke again her voice was high-pitched and soft. "Don't be mean," she said.

"You left the sofa here, Barb. Of all things, you left the sofa."

"I couldn't fit anything else in the U-Haul," she said, the words wobbling on the verge of tears now. "I have to start over. I'm sorry. Just take your stuff and go."

He sat for a moment in silence. Then he said, "Don't cry. I just don't know what you want me to do, Barb. What do you want me to do?"

"I don't care. Just sell it," she said, breaking into full sobs now. "I can't go back there. I just can't."

He listened to her weep, his voice making a quiet and automatic *shhh* into the phone. Her grief might have brought him to tears as well but in that moment there was only the simplicity of her distress and his automatic attempt to comfort her. He listened as her breathing slowed once again. "OK, OK," he said, repeating it over and over. "I'll take care of it."

"Thanks," she said at last.

He stared at the blank white wall before him. The slashes of light through the window. Then he said, "I need to go."

"Don't be mad."

"I'm not mad."

She broke into sobs again.

"Don't cry, Barb. It's OK. It's fine. I'm just tired."

The rasp of her breathing. "Tell me when you want to come out here and I'll go with you."

"I don't know when that will be," he said.

"I'm sorry, Keith."

"I know."

"I didn't mean for this to happen."

"I know."

"Listen, call the realtor, OK?"

"Yes, I'll call a realtor," he said.

She was quiet for a moment and then she said, "I'm glad you got back OK."

"Thanks."

They said their goodbyes, her voice feeble and quiet and far far away. Then a sharp click and the line was dead.

He set the phone on the mattress beside him. He had slept in his clothes, for he had found no bedding in the house apart from a half-size child's blanket featuring Mickey Mouse's grinning face and he had used that for what he could, bunching it around his neck to create an illusion of comfort.

Above him the ceiling fan rotated slowly in the cool morning air. If there was some appropriate emotional response to the phone conversation he could not find it now. Instead there was only the ever-present sense of fatigue, the heaviness of his body that he had felt so keenly since returning to Earth's gravity six weeks ago. Nothing else. And as he lay there the only thought he could muster was a vague confusion as to what he was to do next. It had never been his intention to stay at the house for any significant length of time. The garage was likely filled with whatever she had decided was his. His personal effects, whatever they were. Maybe he could simply leave the sofa and the bed and his dresser and the little television all behind and he could move into a hotel, at least for the next few weeks or months or whatever it turned out to be. The real estate listing could read: "Three-year-old house, comes with leather sofa and mattress. Random other pieces. Stale cereal a bonus! Canned yams! Mystery garage!" The sofa, of all things. That had a sting that could not have been accidental.

When he opened the front door he thought the blinding light might set off another migraine. Despite the medication, the thin keening whine of that condition floated somewhere in the back of his mind. He tried not to think of it, tried to will the moment away, all the while knowing that neither force of will nor ignorance could divert the tide of pain if such a tide was indeed coming to claim him. He briefly pawed at his shirt for his sunglasses before remembering that they were in the rental car, and then stood for a long silent moment, his eyes staring at the blank square of the garage door as the feeling of pain or of panic wobbled and at last faded. There remained a sense of unease in his chest, a feeling that had been present upon waking as if he had been delivered out of some obscure and mysterious and already forgotten dream, the trappings of which still clung to him everywhere in thin silvery strands.

He wanted more than anything to be back in the microgravity of the ISS, back in that series of interconnected oxygen-filled tubes, but the mission was over and there was nothing he could do about that now. At least they might have simply left him alone to work at his desk in Houston. During the weeks after returning from the mission he had become involved in a variety of projects at the Space Center. But in the end the Astronaut Office could not even allow him that. The only question remaining was when he could return and what he was to do in the meantime.

Around him, the cul-de-sac appeared much as it had when he had left for the launch, as if it had become frozen upon his departure. Diagonally across the street, a skeleton of two-by-four boards framed the shape of a house, the surrounding lot overgrown with weeds. Next to that ghost, directly across from him, was a home so complete and perfect it might have been an advertisement for the American suburban lifestyle. Slightly farther away, the nether end of the cul-de-sac opened into a completely empty lot mottled with golden grasses and the light green of thistle. Yet more distant, an endless flow of rooftops swung over the low hills and disappeared into the fractal maze of freeways and subdivisions beyond.

He stumped past his neighbor's house—apparently empty, the

lawn yellowed and dead—and followed the curve of the sidewalk, his body like a lead block being dragged through water. When he reached the edge of the vacant lot he stopped, peering across its thistled expanse to where the land curled out of sight into a drainage ditch and then rose again to meet a cinderblock wall that broke up out of the earth, dividing that vacancy from the backyards and rear walls of houses lining some other cul-de-sac. The walk from his front door to where he now stood was only twenty or thirty yards and it did nothing to lessen his feeling of density and weight. The more pressing problem was the faint high-pitched whine that had resumed deep behind his eyes. He felt at his collar for his sunglasses and once again failed to find them there.

And then, all at once, an explosion of movement so unexpected that he leapt backwards in surprise, his voice making a sharp, quick noise comprised entirely of vowels. Even then his mind did not register what it could be, its size and upward motion impossible. And then he saw it more clearly: a huge black bird that rose out of the field not twenty feet away, its wings pounding up out of the dry grass and thistle, already past the rooflines and rising into the flat blue of the sky and then its wings extending into a single flat plane as it began to spiral upwards in slow lazy circles.

He did not know how long he stood watching it, but the circles it described continued, the dark shape so wholly unmoving in its rotation that it appeared as if a shadow cut from darkness or a bird-shaped hole in the sky revealing that black space beyond the color of the sun, that point shrinking so quickly that when he momentarily glanced down to the field and then looked up again he could no longer find it. It was as if the bird had risen into the atmosphere or beyond and was itself in some kind of low orbit. He continued to stand there for a long while, scanning the sky, but now he did not even know what he was looking for. A speck of movement. But nothing would be revealed. The only evidence anything had occurred at all was the quick, rhythmic beating of his heart.

17

At last he returned to the car and pulled into the street and to the end of the court and then turned onto the farther street beyond and turned again. Another court amidst more stunted trees and the occasional empty lot and he followed the curve of that cul-de-sac and exited only to find himself approaching the rounded sidewalk of yet another court. The lawn beyond the windshield: a yellow waste of dead grass. It is true that things turn out this way. One moment you are an astronaut floating high above a space station at the end of a robotic arm of your own design, the next you are driving through an endless suburb. He again swung the car around and cursed to himself. Grass-covered squares and rectangles. Seemingly identical cul-de-sacs appearing and disappearing as he passed, different only in their state of completion: a perfect model home, then the skeletal structure of a wooden frame, then a patch of bare dirt holding an unfinished foundation. Between these states: a fractal landscape of courts and ways that turned inward upon themselves, thin and many-legged spiders that had, in death, curled into their own bulbous bodies, clutching the empty, still air between perfectly manicured lawns.

He found a Starbucks and parked. In contrast to the absurd blinding brilliance and slowly rising heat of the parking lot, it was cool and dark inside and he lifted the bag that contained his laptop and approached the counter as his eyes adjusted to the change in light.

"What can I get started for you?" the girl at the counter said.

He looked up at the menu on the wall behind the counter and as he did his phone began to vibrate in his pocket.

"Just a cup of coffee," he said quickly. He looked at the phone. A Houston area code but a number he did not recognize. "Hello?" he answered.

"What size?" the girl said.

"Chip," the voice said through the phone. "Bill Eriksson."

"Eriksson," Keith said. Then: "How are you?" And then, to the girl: "A medium is fine."

"I'm doing good," Eriksson said. "Doing good. But I'm calling to find out how *you're* doing."

"What?" Keith said.

"I want to know how you're doing," Eriksson said again.

"No," Keith said. "Hang on. I'm at Starbucks." Then to the girl at the counter: "What?"

She told him the price again and he fished out his wallet. "Sorry about that," he said into the phone.

"Hey, no problem," Eriksson said. "So how you doing?"

"Fine. Grabbing a cup of coffee." He handed the girl his credit card and she pulled it through the edge of the register and then handed him the card and the receipt.

"Yeah? You been home?"

"Home," Keith said. "Well, yeah."

"And?"

"And I'm getting the house ready to sell."

"Is that what you decided?"

"Yes, that's what I decided." She handed him a paper cup and he took it and mouthed a thank you and then cradled the phone awkwardly against his ear with his shoulder and carried his bag and coffee to a padded chair at the back of the room.

"She there?"

"Barb?"

"Yeah, Barb. Who else?"

"OK," Keith said. "No, she's definitely not here."

"That's too bad."

For a moment neither of them spoke. Then Keith said, "She really emptied me out."

"How so?"

"There's nothing in the house at all. The whole place is empty."

"Shit."

"Yeah, shit."

"So what's the plan?"

"Well, I'm looking for a realtor."

"Any chance of counseling?"

"Marriage counseling? I don't know. Maybe."

"Is that something you want?"

"I want to sell the house. That's what I want."

"All right then," Eriksson said.

A pause. Then Keith said, "Yeah. That's about it. Get the house sold."

"Then vacation somewhere?"

He looked at his coffee and then stood and walked to the small table near the counter and poured creamer and a packet of sugar into the cup. "Maybe," he said.

"No maybes. Take a break, Keith. We all earned one. Especially you."

"You said that before."

"Yeah, but I feel like you're not really hearing me."

"I hear you."

"All right. All right. Just looking out for the crew."

"Mission's over."

"It's over when I say it's over," Eriksson said. "So how's the processor?"

"Funny. How's yours?"

"Same sense of humor," Eriksson said, not without irony. "Listen, the offer still stands, you know. You're always welcome here."

"I need to get this house thing done. I appreciate it, though."

Keith could hear a child's voice in the distance of the phone and Eriksson said, "Hang on," and then, muffled, "Daddy's on the phone. I'll be off in just a second. No, you cannot have a Pop-Tart. Just wait a second until I'm off the phone." And then, to Keith: "Sorry about that."

"How are they?"

"Running me ragged."

"I'll bet." Through the phone he could hear the sound of a child's voice yelling, whether in joy or terror he could not tell.

"Oh, so that reminds me," Eriksson said after a pause, "my wife keeps asking if you've looked at that book at all."

"Book?"

"Yeah, that thing on the grieving process. She was asking me if it's been helpful."

"Oh yeah, sure. Tell her . . . tell her yeah it's good. It's been . . ." He paused a moment and then added, "helpful." Another pause. Then, "Thank her for me."

"Will do."

"So look, you call me now and then. I want some check-ins."

"You've got my number," Keith said.

"I'm serious. Status updates."

"OK," Keith said. "Can you do me a favor?"

"Sure, buddy. Anything."

"I asked Mullins for some files from my office. Can you see what the status of that is?"

"Yeah, OK. I'll find out but you know you're supposed to be taking a break."

"Just find out. OK?"

"All right, I will."

"Thank you," Keith said.

"You'll check in, right?"

"Yes," Keith said.

"That's all I wanted to hear," Eriksson said. Then: "Talk to you later, buddy."

"OK," Keith said. "Talk to you later."

He pocketed his phone again and then he lifted his bag and removed his laptop and opened it. He looked through his e-mail but there were no messages of note, only some general information about changes to health care, some budgetary updates, a newsletter or two. After a few moments he searched the Internet for local real estate agents and wrote them on the back of his coffee receipt and then found the addresses of a nearby building supply store. Then he closed the laptop and lifted the coffee cup and leaned back in the chair.

There was a discarded newspaper on the small table next to him and he retrieved it and flipped through its pages without any real interest. Fires in some adjacent county. Democrats dumping money into something. Economic downturns and rising joblessness.

The door opened and closed. A scattering of customers arriving and departing. The static of steam jets and the murmur of conversation.

He turned the newspaper over. Some hotel in foreclosure and, on the adjacent page, a claim that commercial real estate was remaining strong. The usual murders and crimes. Sports teams winning. Sports teams losing. A brief note about a comet set to crash into Earth, killing everything.

The door opened again and Keith glanced up to see a thickly built man in a red T-shirt who approached the counter and said, "Hello, Audrey," in a booming voice. Keith could not hear the barista's response but a moment later the man's voice came again: "You look lovely today as usual." He had an accent of some kind. Keith thought it was likely Russian or Ukrainian. His body was low to the ground and squared off as if it had been carved roughly from a block of wood and his face was friendly even though it too was all square angles below a thatch of close-cropped salt-and-pepper hair. He wore a red vest that was stretched over his similarly red T-shirt with a name tag Keith could not read. Coming from work, then. "Time now for morning mocha," he said.

"Of course it is," the barista said, loud enough that Keith could hear her this time and when she came into view from behind the register, he could see that she was smiling broadly.

"And are you having good day today?" the man said.

"Sure," she said.

"Good day for me also," he said. He shifted his eyes toward the back of the shop where Keith sat with the paper and said, in a voice that was near shouting: "Hello! What is big news this morning then?"

Keith blinked. "Oh," he said. "Not much."

"No?" the man said.

"Well," he said, glancing at the paper again, weighing for the briefest moment whether or not the man was actually asking him a question or if he was simply making small talk to the only other customer in the shop. "OK," Keith said, his eyes fixing on a headline, "we're apparently going to be killed by a comet."

"Ah yes, about this I know something. Don't be worried."

"I wasn't," Keith said.

"Good thing!" the man shouted. Then he turned back to the counter again.

The barista worked at her machine of hissing and bubbling and a moment later she handed the man a cup and he paid her.

Keith finished his coffee and stood and lifted his laptop bag, dropping the newspaper to an adjacent table.

As he passed the counter, the barista looked up at him. "See you next time," she said.

Keith nodded, said, "Take care," and was at the door when the Russian man said, "NASA?"

Keith paused and turned back toward him and nodded.

"This is NASA on shirt?" the Russian man said.

"Yes, I work for NASA," Keith said.

"What is work you do?"

He froze there with one hand on the door. Then he said, "I work for the Astronaut Office."

"For Astronaut Office is being astronaut?"

Again silence. Then he said, "Yes, I'm an astronaut."

"You joke on me I think," the man said.

Keith shrugged, thinking momentarily of Eriksson. "Not likely," he said. Then, "I have to go. Good talking with you." Before the man could say anything else he stepped through the door and let it swing closed, continuing off the curb then and into the heat of the parking lot, half closing his eyes until his sunglasses were in place. Two old men sat in wire chairs in front of the store, one of them wearing a ball cap embroidered with the words "US Navy Retired," the other in a battered leather flight jacket covered in patches. Their conversation ceased as Keith passed and a moment later he was too far away to hear if it resumed.

The heat thick and heavy. He returned to the car with sweat cascading into his eyes and sat for a long moment with the vents blowing upon his face. Huge cars everywhere around him, all of them shimmering with sunlight.

When he turned onto the street again, he drove in the general direction of the hotels near the interstate but then pulled into a retail lot and slipped the gearshift into park and stepped once again outside. Moments later he was a solitary shape amidst quiet shoppers with bright red plastic carts, trying to recall the last time he had gone shopping for anything. When he had been training in Houston he had rented a tiny apartment, flying back and forth between it and home whenever there was a break, but it remained unfurnished apart from a cot and an alarm clock and he subsisted entirely on takeout and the JSC cafeteria. Before that, in those few instances when he had tried to help Barb with the household duties, he would end up buying the wrong item and she would later have to return it anyway, his attempt to lighten her workload only resulting in making things more difficult. Now he seemed to be moving ever against the general flow of traffic, red carts coming towards him no matter which side of any aisle he rolled down and him muttering, "Sorry," under his breath in a kind of slow loop as he found himself repeatedly in the way of other shoppers.

The simplicity of his ineptitude was irritating and he found himself once again thinking of his office in Houston. They had asked him to take a vacation but did they understand that this was how it would be, that the only thing he really needed was to remain at his office? Did they expect him to go sit on a beach somewhere and contemplate the sunset? Did they know him no better than that when all he had ever wanted was to be in space and now all he wanted was to return? He had thought that they understood him but he had been wrong. Somehow they believed that being away from his office was the best thing for him, a concept that made so little sense he could not even ascertain the shape of the equation.

He circled the store at least a dozen times and the only thing in his cart was a coffeepot. He did not even know what he would need. A rudimentary particleboard furniture section. Would he remain long enough to need furniture? Again he did not know. When he passed the laundry detergent he realized he had not yet opened the door to the laundry room and did not even know if he had a washer or dryer, then wondered if he would be doing his laundry at a Laundromat. He would be an astronaut doing laundry at a Laundromat. That would be fantastic.

He found a garbage can that was plain and white and plastic and then filled it with ten frozen microwaveable dinners and later found the linens aisle and selected a pillow and a set of white sheets and dark blue blankets. An alarm clock. A cheap set of pots and pans. A table to eat at and a chair of some kind would wait until he determined what he was going to do next.

The parking lots connecting one after another. He managed to snake his way through them and onto the main artery again, the names of various subdivisions flashing by the window: the Stables, Willow Glen, and then, finally, his own: "The Estates" emblazoned in white letters across a low stone wall attached to one of two tall stonework pillars. It had been intended as a gated community, that had been one of the selling points for Barb, but although two pillars flanked the entryway, no gate swung open and closed between them; whatever any such gate would have enclosed or excluded flowed freely through the entrance. Astronauts. Maniacal shoppers. Soccer moms.

By the time he reached his cul-de-sac, the sky was flat and white with haze and the landscape had taken on a feeling of desolation: heaps of dirt and half-completed homes and naked foundations spaced between finished homes with their dwarfish trees and shrubs. His own court no different. He looked into the sky momentarily for the bird he had seen but there was nothing.

He unloaded the trunk of the car into the kitchen and piled the boxed dinners into the freezer, thinking now that he should have bought a radio of some kind. Something to fill the silence all around him. He turned to place the trashcan at the end of the counter but then paused. Not only was there a trashcan already in place but as he looked from one to the other he realized that he had purchased exactly the same kind. It might have been funny but it was not. His breath a long exhausted sigh. He set the new trashcan next to the other and began unpacking the coffeepot.

Such was his homecoming.

Two

IT HAD BEEN just at the moment of his greatness. Of course it had. Were the intersection of vectors to coincide with some other moment, some other instant that was here and then past, would anything have changed? Even now there was no way of knowing what she had been doing when any one of those pinpoints fled, the long spiral unscrolling ever upward and away. This one: when Eriksson's radio voice sounded in his ear, "A–OK, Corcoran?" and his own response came, "OK here." And another: when they tethered themselves to the body of the ISS, their motions clumsy in the stiffly pressurized space suits. And yet another: when the airlock turned and opened in absolute silence and he moved through the black porthole and into the darkness of space and at last into the field of numbers that he had imagined all his life. She might have just arrived at the party then, perhaps had been handed something to eat or drink, perhaps was talking to someone. A boy? Someone else? But of course it was impossible to know. And he did not think of her anyway, not then, because he was already

27

outside, already floating in the dazzling contrast of blazing light and the incomparable distance of the stars. Eriksson's voice again: "Mission Control, we are clear of Quest and are proceeding to the MSS."

"ISS, you are clear to proceed," came the response.

He could see Eriksson's helmet where it appeared over the edge of the truss: a black orb framed in white, his face invisible. Behind him the solar arrays glowing like dark, angular eclipses and beyond that only space itself: black and infinite and stretching out forever.

They would need to reach the base of the robotic arm, the arm he had designed himself and which had been installed on the previous spacewalk a month ago and now would be used to exchange the nitrogen tanks. He would be attached to the nether end of the arm by his feet and would be moved bodily in a huge arc across the whole of the station, from one end of the truss to the other, holding the empty tank in his gloved grip, stowing it on the far side of the station and then bringing a full tank back the same way, performing that long parabolic arc twice. That was the task, but first they would need to reach the base of the arm, and so they moved, hand over hand, the process like crawling sideways over the exterior of a submarine or an enormous floating propane tank, and then to the dark crisscrossing beams of the truss, that structure stretching away beyond him in both directions and the round tubes of the modules in which they lived and worked already below him, toward Earth. He moved slowly, without speaking, his breath a rhythmic and repeating hiss as he moved and each task a focused act: the flexing of his hands inside the huge white gloves, the way in which they curled around the metal handles, the silence of the tether as it slid along with him, the repetition of his breath in the helmet. Each honeycombed panel memorized. The round rivets. The aluminum shield. Everything here named and numbered. The diameter of the moment: two thousand and thirty two millimeters. Fifteen-point-five-eight-three feet, the three extending into some forever of thirds and curving into those thirds as the robotic arm came into view, its structure collapsed into a loose stack of overlapping angles as if some thick white straw had folded in upon itself, the terminal end nearly touching the outer skin of the Kibo Module. Before him, the white base of Eriksson's boots waved in parallel like floating quotation marks as he pulled himself forward over the curve of the Unity Node and across the trussworks, hand over hand, the tether following, up through the white padded girders where the dark interior of the truss opened in shadow like the hidden superstructure of a skyscraper.

An occasional word from Eriksson to Mort Stevens inside the station and the CAPCOM in Houston but otherwise silence. Silence everywhere. Only the sound of his breathing and the occasional click as Eriksson's microphone activated and deactivated. The curves and angles of the structure over which he moved. Perhaps the whole compass still turned in its twisting helix, yet to find its northpoint, all possibilities fluxing out into the darkness around him.

That had only been a season ago and yet was gapped now by a distance he could hardly believe, the curved glass of his helmet replaced by the curved glass of the rental car's windshield so that, instead of the clean compact functionality of the ISS, his current view was of the back of the car that preceded him. He had been home for two days and had awakened with a familiar feeling of weightlessness, a feeling that faded almost immediately but the memory of which continued to cling to him. Even now, parking the car and entering a vast hardware store, he could feel its shape in his mind: a sphere, a lit globe, a clear sparkling star that floated amidst the endless aisles of gray industrial shelving, fading slowly until it was gone.

He returned home with a single five-gallon bucket of satin finish eggshell white and all the related supplies necessary to begin painting the living room and kitchen, a project he began immediately, taping off the cabinetry and the kitchen window and sink. His progress was slow and meticulous but soon the window and the bottom edge of the kitchen cabinets were framed in bright, almost luminescent blue.

29

Then the kitchen island: he unrolled a sheet of clear plastic to drape over that surface and sealed it by taping the circumference of the plastic to the linoleum floor.

The activity was meant to keep himself occupied but already he could feel his mind wandering, not to his memory of the International space station or to engineering tasks but rather to Barb and, yes, to Quinn. In the midst of such wandering thoughts he would pull free the last strip of tape he had placed and would reposition it or would physically grasp the refrigerator to wheel it out or back a few additional inches and then would return to the task before him, each track as defined and precise as a line on a graph: this singular ray pushing out along a trajectory that mapped the edge of one plane against another, the line of blue tape marking out a set of answers clear and simple and predictable, all things reduced to numbers, angles, vectors, equations.

The cabinets rose nearly to the ceiling but there was a short space above them of bare wall too high to reach and so he returned to the hardware store and bought a folding aluminum ladder and several additional rolls of tape and plastic sheeting, placing all these items in the trunk of the car, the ladder extending a foot or more from its interior so that he had to reenter the hardware store once more to retrieve a scrap of plastic string to tie down the trunk lid.

Across the parking lot he could see the green awning of Starbucks. He knew he had passed at least one similar awning nearer his house and it might have been that he had passed many more. The mathematics repeating. Everything here identical to itself, a grandeur of sameness framed by the black asphalt of parking lots and the lighter gray of sidewalks, all things within his sight enormous and clean and new as if the whole of the scene had been here forever and had never changed. No history. No passage of days. Indeed time itself an abstraction the meaning of which had dissolved so that each moment slipped into the next without distinction, change, or possibility.

. . .

When he arrived home he sat for a long moment behind the wheel looking up at the flat front of the empty house. It was difficult now to understand why any of them had ended up here, in this neighborhood that was a plane ride away from his office in Houston, but then he knew that part of the reason, or perhaps all of it, had been his own belief that Quinn's life would be much the same as his, that she would excel in the same way that he had. Was that not an equation the solution of which had function and meaning and importance? Was that not what every father would want for his daughter?

At last he turned off the motor and opened the door and as he did so the garage across the street began to hum open. To his left stood the closed square door of his own garage, a space he still had not entered even though the central reason he had returned to the cul-de-sac was to remove his own belongings from the house. He knew such items were in the garage, boxed and waiting for him, and that he should be loading them into a U-Haul and driving back to Houston to find someplace to rent or buy but he had not done so, instead remaining to paint the house and watch over its sale, although he knew these efforts were not necessary. He knew he should just walk away from the whole thing and leave the empty container behind. That was what Barb had done, after all. And yet he remained, a proposition baffling even to himself, the idea of opening the garage and sorting out its contents something he simply did not yet want to address.

A red sportscar had emerged from the dark interior of the open garage across the street and as Keith turned toward his own house the driver's voice came: "Hey there, neighbor."

He turned back toward the street. The temperature had risen five or ten degrees since he had left the hardware store and the air was thick with heat. "Hey there," he called in return.

She might have been in her mid-forties, oversized black sunglasses and a broad friendly smile framed in the open window of the sportscar, brown hair pulled back from her face. He expected the car to drive away but then she called out to him again: "I don't think we've met," she said. "Jennifer. I live, well, I live right there." She motioned to the house.

"Good to meet you," he said in return. She did not drive away and he stood awkwardly, waiting, and then set the laptop bag on the hood of the rental car and stepped forward into the street. When he arrived at her car she extended a hand out the window and he took it.

"I'm Keith Corcoran," he said.

She smiled and removed her sunglasses and hooked them into the front of her top. Keith found his gaze following them into her cleavage and when he snapped his eyes back to her face she smiled more broadly as if to acknowledge that she had noticed this wayward glance. "You're all moved in?" she said.

"Not really," he said. "Mostly getting it set up to sell." He paused, wondering briefly how much she might already know and what to say next. Then he said, "You probably met my wife, Barb. She was living here before."

She stopped smiling for a moment, staring at him, and the silence that ensued was long enough that he began to wonder what he had said to bring the brief conversation to a stop.

"I'm sorry. Did I say something wrong?" he said.

"Oh, no, not at all." She sounded surprised and looked out the windshield briefly, as if charting her route out of the cul-de-sac. Then she turned to him again. "I thought you both moved out."

He paused before answering. "More or less," he said, looking for more words but finding none. What was he supposed to say? "She moved out, anyway," he said at last.

"Well, you seem to be holding up all right, considering."

Again he wondered how much she knew about Barb. What she had told her about Quinn. Maybe they had been friends. "Uh, yeah, I'm doing OK," he said. "Considering."

"Where'd she go?"

"Barb? Uh . . . she's in Atlanta. At her mom's."

"Atlanta?"

"Yeah," he said. "You were friends?"

She was quiet for a time, looking at him. "Just neighbors," she said at last. Once more she turned her gaze toward the open end of the cul-de-sac, saying nothing for a long while, and then turned to him again, this time a smile on her face. "So you're the astronaut," she said.

"That's right."

"Welcome back to Earth."

"Well," he said, "thank you."

"Gosh, I probably look a mess," she said abruptly. "I'm just off to the gym."

"Oh, no, you look . . ." He paused. Then he said, "Beautiful."

"Oh, you're too sweet." She laughed.

There was a sense of relief that the conversation had apparently righted itself and he smiled.

"So you're probably just here for a few days," she said.

"I'm not sure. Maybe longer than that."

"Well, let us know if we can do anything for you."

"OK," he said, then added, "I'll do that."

"It's great to meet you, neighbor," Jennifer said. She extended her hand and he took it. Her hand was soft and warm.

He glanced at her cleavage again, an act that was almost involuntary. Her face and chest were tan, her breasts swelling inside the confines of her top. It occurred to him that he was essentially single. It was a thought made strange because he had not arrived at that conclusion before. "Great to meet you too," he said.

"I'm sorry about what happened."

"What's that?"

"I saw it on the news. I'm so sorry."

"Oh," he said. He stopped and then, "That's . . . ," and again fell silent. After a moment he said, simply, "Thank you."

"If there's anything you need, you just come and let us know."

"I'll do that," he said again.

She smiled and then the window hummed closed and the car sped to the corner and out of sight.

He felt aroused and actually thought momentarily of entering the house and masturbating but the idea seemed so pathetic to him that he did not enter the house at all, standing instead for a long moment in the heat next to the rental car and then walking to the end of the cul-de-sac. He stopped at the edge of the sidewalk where the length of chain separated the concrete from the dirt and grass and thistle and stared out across the field to the trees on the opposite side. The ground everywhere radiated with heat. Perhaps too hot even for the great, dark bird. Mouse and lizard and whatever else all huddled in their various dens of cool darkness. Already the chill of the air conditioner had faded and his sweat stuck the NASA polo against his back and beaded on his forehead. He scanned the trees. Their leaves blue and shadows deep and dark. Beyond them: the roofs of houses just like his, one after another, stretching on as far as one could see, distant hills with clusters of neighborhoods and curving streets of identical, earth-toned homes. He wondered momentarily what that bird might see from its widest high circle. A landscape like a huge and multicolored intestine. Self-similar. Fractal. Maybe there were empty fields else-where. Eyes searching for death hidden in the close-cropped lawns. Keith looked up, hoping to see the black shape where it spun in a slow-moving orbit against the bright blue of the sky but such a shape did not appear.

For the remainder of the day he continued masking off the kitchen and the exhaustion he felt was surprising and profound. He had been weak upon his return to Earth—they all had—but there had been six weeks of daily physical rehabilitation and conditioning. And yet he felt completely spent, stepping off the ladder at last to survey his work: the kitchen tightly sealed and taped with care and attention. It was night now and despite his fatigue he spent a few moments tidying up the work area and organizing the stack of painting supplies for the next day. It was not until he had completed this task that he realized he had neglected to eat both breakfast and lunch, a situation that had been, at one time, an occurrence so regular that it had become a kind of running joke between him and his wife and which now bit into him with a cruel irony. There had been periods when he would work through meals two or three times per week, his workday eight or ten or twelve hours without stop or rest or break, until he was the last engineer remaining in the office, until only he and the cleaning staff remained and still he would continue to tabulate out his calculations and angles and data. He had never asked Barb to understand because he thought she already did, or rather that if she lacked the understanding it was not something he could justify or explain. He told himself that it was simply who he was and any other choice would have been to deny the very force of his being, each goal clear and achievable because he had worked so hard to achieve those goals and because he had developed the discipline necessary to do so.

He had learned—even as a child—that there was a difference between assumptions and expectations. He had never assumed anything about his success but indeed he had come to expect it. He would make the best grades in his classes because he put in the most time studying. He would be quickly promoted at his first real job because he worked harder than any of the other new hires and later, when he accepted a commission in the Air Force, his OPRs would show his superiority because he performed his tasks with correctness and exactitude. His teachers and peers had called him a genius and he knew he had a gift but that was not why he succeeded, or rather that was not the only reason. He succeeded because he had learned how to work with that gift as a kind of discipline, putting in the time and effort to see his projects or problems or challenges through from beginning to end. This had been his force and his credo. This had been the engine of his forward motion: not only his ability to see the numbers and to feel, as

if intuitively, their relationships, but also the indomitable and inex-
tinguishable power of attention and focus. There had been a time
when his wife had been at his side, helping push that engine forward,
but it was not so long ago—a year, maybe two—that she had called
him "obsessive," as if the time he was putting in to his own destiny was
somehow optional or as if he had changed. But he had not changed
over the course of their marriage. At least not in any way he could
recognize.

Even now he remained the same, if all he could think to do was
paint this empty house. It was an absurd way to pass the time and he
knew that. Of course he did. It was pathetic and it was not even serv-
ing its true purpose. Had he been working on a project—a real
project—the numbers might have been complex enough to consume
him. But there were no such numbers here. And yet there was nothing else to do, so tomorrow he would spread the dropcloth along the
base of one wall and would pry open the bucket and pour the paint
into a tray. If he worked with the same steady determination he could
complete the first coat in the kitchen in just a few hours, a process he
reviewed as he carefully unpeeled the tape and pushed back the clear
plastic to access the microwave and slid his frozen dinner tray inside,
realizing as he did so that he had also sealed off the new coffeepot he
had purchased the day before and the cabinets that held the chipped
mugs, the two or three bowls he had been using for his breakfast
cereal, and the drawer in the island that held the silverware.

That night he stood and looked out the upstairs window at the bight
of dark concrete that was the cul-de-sac. At one point a figure passed
the house, some nightwalker, its shadow cast out behind like an arrow pointing ever away. Keith watched the figure's slow progress as it
bisected that circular space, passing under the streetlights until the
line it made with its motion disappeared beyond the angle of his view
through the window. The street so still that it seemed a photograph
or a museum diorama. He waited there at the window, watching in
the encompassing silence, but the figure, whoever it might have been,

did not return to his view. He might have been disappointed but if so he did not acknowledge it. Instead, he recognized only self-reliance, a position and idea he had always held, even as he turned away from the window and stared down at the faint speckles of eggshell that flecked over his hands.

"Can you hear me?"

"I can hear you."

"Oh, I can see you."

"I can see you too." A pause. Then: "How . . . how are you?"

"I'm OK," she said. Tears were already streaming down her face.

He stared at her. The compartment was so quiet. So terribly quiet. "It'll be OK, Barb. We'll be OK."

And then the phone was ringing and he burst out spastically, still half asleep, and answered it without even really understanding what he was doing, the laptop glowing in his mind, his body falling back into gravity all at once as he sputtered into the receiver: "Wh-what? Hello?"

"Keith, it's Dr. Hoffmann."

"Oh," he said. "Dr. Hoffmann." He was half sitting, the blankets and sheets splayed around him.

"Everything OK?" Hoffmann said. "You don't sound well. Did I wake you?"

"No, no. I'm . . . I'm OK. I was . . . I was asleep." He lay back down, slowly, carefully.

"You want me to call back?"

"No, no, I'm fine. I'm awake."

"You sure?"

"Yeah, it's fine. I'm awake. It's fine." The clock on the floor by the bed glowed faintly in the morning light: 8:17.

"OK, then." A pause. "Well, I'm calling because you missed your appointment."

He tilted his head back to the pillow and closed his eyes. The image of Barb's face remained: a blurred shape on a laptop screen. The gauze of his memory. A haze of ghosts. Even you, Keith Corcoran. Even you. "I have to apologize for that, I guess," he said at last. "I'm not at JSC right now."

"Well, I know that but I had to make a couple of calls to find out. It would have been nice to get a call from you about this."

"It was kind of sudden," he said, his eyes opening slowly to the flat white emptiness of the room.

"You know, when people miss appointments often there's an underlying reason."

Keith paused before answering. "Yeah, that might be but this time I just forgot," he said. "I'm taking a vacation."

"Where to?"

"Well, right now I'm home."

"Oh. How long have you been there?"

"Two days. I've been painting."

"Painting?"

"The place needs a paint job."

"You've got work to do."

"Yes."

"I didn't mean the painting. I'm sure it's hard being there."

"Oh, I guess so," Keith said.

"You want to talk some? I could do a phone appointment tomorrow."

The ceiling was a blank white void above him. "I don't know," he said. "Maybe give me a few more days to settle in here."

"We've made some good progress over the last few weeks. I'd like to keep that momentum going."

"I would too. I'm busy here with the painting, though. And I'm really doing OK."

Hoffman was quiet for a moment. Then he said, "I'd like you to think about why you forgot to tell me you were leaving JSC. We can focus on that for our next appointment, but give it some thought in the meantime. Think of it as your homework assignment."

"All right," Keith said, without conviction.

"Call me in a week and let me know how it's going and we'll set an appointment then," Hoffmann said.

"That sounds good."

"Everything OK with the prescriptions?"

"As far as I can tell."

"Let me know if you need anything adjusted."

"I'll do that," Keith said.

Even after he ended the call, the memory that roiled out of the half sleep in which he had been drifting remained with him as a kind of aftereffect, as if a flashbulb had burst and the shape of its burning still lingered against the black emptiness of his cornea. At least missing the appointment with Dr. Hoffmann meant that he would not have to discuss such topics today, a fact that offered some sense of relief, although in truth he had done little actual talking during the dozen or so meetings they had had in Houston upon his return from the mission. *Do you feel sad?* Yes. *What do you want to do about that?* I can think of no way to answer that. *Do you think the migraines are related to how you feel?* I don't know. *Did you want to talk about anything else?* Not really. Are we done? He could not imagine the purpose of this line of questioning and so could not imagine any words that could provide an answer. The most fundamental information had been lost: trajectory, velocity, acceleration, indeed the pull of gravity itself. All he knew now was that he was unaware where such variables could be located and so he could find no possible solution, not to any of it. But he did not think this answer was what Dr. Hoffmann was looking for.

By midafternoon he had completed the first coat of paint on the largest wall in the kitchen and had begun carefully cutting under the cabinets with a brush. When the doorbell rang his immediate thought was that he would open the door to find a delivery person with the files he had asked Jim Mullins to send from his office at JSC and with this thought in mind he jogged to the entryway, the paintbrush in his hand, and pulled open the door.

The woman who stood there did not appear to be delivering anything. "Hello, Mr. Corcoran," she said. "I'm Sally Erler."

"OK," he said, blinking in the bright sunlight of the open doorway. He glanced around quickly for the box but there was nothing near the doorway and the only item she was carrying was a briefcase.

"I'm your realtor," she said.

"What?"

She wore a navy blue suit and smiled, extending her hand, which he took as reflex. "Your wife called me and said you'd be home," she said. "I was in the neighborhood and thought I'd just drop by. Is that all right? You look busy."

"Busy?" he said.

"Painting?"

"Oh." He looked at the brush in his hand. "Yes, I'm painting. The kitchen."

"Is this not a good time?"

"No, it's fine."

"If this is a bad time we can make an appointment," she said. The smile remained on her face like a permanent mask.

"No, it's fine," he said once more. He stood there in the doorway, looking at her.

"Would you mind if I came in?"

"Oh," he said. "Sorry." He stepped back and waved her in and when she entered he closed the door behind her.

"Nice, nice home," she said.

"Barb called you?"

"She said you were interested in selling. It's a buyer's market, but you know we can always make things happen."

"I'm sure." He did not know what else to say and as he stood there a dull sense of irritation flooded through him and then disappeared. Did Barb think he was somehow unable to call a realtor on his own? What kind of incompetent person did she think he was? "Can I get you anything?" he asked. "A cup of coffee?"

"No, I'm fine," she said. "Can I take a look around?"

"Sure. Is that what you need to do?"

"I have to know what I'm selling, Mr. Corcoran," she said. She showed her teeth again.

He stepped out of her way. "OK," he said.

She opened the black binder in her hands and took notes. Keith wandered behind her into the living room. "You weren't kidding when you said you were painting," she said.

"Yeah, I just started."

"When do you think you'll be done?"

"I'm not sure yet. Four or five days?"

"OK," she said. She wrote something in her notebook. "New appliances."

"I guess so."

She nodded. Then she motioned toward the massive sofa next to them in the living room. "Not quite done moving?" she said.

"That's right."

"Uh-huh," she said. "It might be easier to sell if all your personal belongings were removed from the home. Maybe you could move the remaining items to the garage for now?"

He looked at her. "OK," he said.

Again, the smile. "Mind if I go upstairs?"

"No, but I haven't painted up there yet."

She wandered away and he did not follow. Instead, he set the paintbrush in the tray in the kitchen and retrieved his phone from atop the plastic-covered island and dialed and when Barb answered he said, "You called a realtor?"

"Oh," she said. "Yeah. Is that OK?"

"Is that OK?" he repeated. "I'm a little confused here."

"Confused how?"

"I thought I was doing that."

"Doing what?"

"Calling a realtor."

"I was just trying to help," she said. "Is that OK?"

"No, not really."

"I'm sorry."

He was quiet for a moment. Then he said, "It's fine. I just . . . I'm painting in here so it's not really ready for a realtor yet."

"You're painting?"

"I'm repainting it. It needs paint."

"You should just hire someone and leave."

"Leave for where?"

"I don't want you to be there."

"What? Why not?"

There was silence on the phone for a long moment and then she said, "Never mind."

"I don't know what you're talking about."

"It's OK," she said. "I was just trying to help. Is that a crime?"

He was still confused by the conversation but he did not return to that confusion now. "I don't need your help with this," he said.

"OK," she said again. Then: "It doesn't need to be painted to be listed."

"I know that."

There was a silence on the line. Then she said, "How are you doing?"

"How am I doing?"

"Yeah."

"Fine," he said.

"Really?"

"Yeah, I'm fine, Barb. Everything's fine."

"OK," she said.

"I've got to go deal with the real estate lady."

"OK," she said again.

He said good-bye and clicked the phone closed. There was no emo-tion, not even irritation, just a flat white emptiness.

The realtor's voice was coming from somewhere in the house: "Mr. Corcoran?"

He had been standing at the sliding glass door in his socks, looking out at the backyard, a stripe of green lawn that baked slowly in the increasing morning heat, and he turned from that now and stepped toward the sound of her voice as she appeared in the doorway. "In here," he said.

"I have a few things to go over with you," she said. "It won't take very long."

"OK," he said. He stood there, blinking, waiting for the few things to materialize.

"Or we can do it another time," she said.

"Let's go ahead and do it now," he said.

They moved to the kitchen island and she spread some paperwork before him on the plastic sheeting that encased it and he read, ini-tialed, and signed in the requisite boxes. "And here too," the realtor said. Then: "Is that your daughter?"

"What?" he said. He followed her eyes to the sliding glass door to the backyard. A little girl stood there who looked so much like Quinn at that age that he was actually startled by the sight and he made the same vowel-heavy sound he had made when seeing the bird. She might have been nine or ten years old, her face enshadowed by the cupped shape of her hands as she leaned forward against the glass, apparently peering in at them although the shade rendered her eyes invisible. She was in that pose for only a moment and then, at the sound of Keith's surprise, she bolted, a brief skinny ghost comprised of sharp knees and elbows, disappearing from view.

He turned back to the realtor, his heart thumping in his chest. She stared at him. "I don't know who that is," he said. "Not mine."

She smiled. "Neighborhood kids," she said. "That can be a good selling point to a family looking to buy a home." She packed the papers back into her binder. "Probably kicked a ball over the fence," she added.

He may have answered but there was a sense that something was moving in his chest again, a thin sharp fluttering, and he was relieved when the realtor told him she was done and they both returned to the front door. There was some discussion of price and various details and he stood in the doorway as she finished talking and flashing her toothy smile. Then they shook hands and a moment later she was gone.

There was no sign of the little girl through the sliding glass door, no ball or toy or footprint left behind to signal her presence in the yard, but when he stepped back he could see the marks of her hands where they had cupped her face against the glass and Quinn's face ghosting up between those smudged prints, her age dialed back to the age of the girl he had seen, the age she had been when they still were, for those faint short years, a father and a mother and a daughter in a golden idyll, before the whole thing had, without sound and without violence, spun slowly and imperceptibly into a distance that now gaped open before him. There was so little tangible about the experience, the calculus of loss no equation at all but rather some impossible blur, a field of turbulence so complex as to be blank, like an infinite and ever-moving cloud that could be defined only by a set of equations capable of mapping each individual droplet of suspended fluid, each molecule of vapor.

He stood at the glass door and stared at the smudge of the girl's handprints. Beyond those: a strip of green grass, a small cinderblock wall with some weakly yellowing shrubs, the concrete pad where he rinsed the dropcloths each evening and laid them out to dry, the wooden fence dividing this tableau from nearly indistinguishable ones on all four sides. Past the fence, he could see the edge of the sky over the roofs of adjacent houses. The bird he had seen on the morning after his return had already begun to feel like the memory of a dream, the eagle or hawk or whatever it had been, bleaching into the impossibly new subdivision that surrounded him, the patterned rooflines of nearly identical houses one after another. He could muster no clear sense of grief from such a sight. Perhaps there was a universe not so far from this one where distant birds of prey circled darkly in endless thermal updrafts above perfectly designed and orderly suburban landscapes. It was a pleasant thought but as he turned toward the kitchen island and the paintbrush that lay on its plastic-wrapped surface he knew that the most pressing universe he could think of was the one in which the file box arrived at his doorstep. All others endless and bleak and futile.

Three

ERIKSSON WAS SMILING, his face lit within the glass dome of the helmet. His white teeth. His blue eyes. "Ready for the fun part?" he said.

"Ready," Keith said.

"Mission Control, all clear here."

And the CAPCOM's voice from Earth: "EV-1, we're glad to hear that."

"Lighten up, Corcoran," Eriksson said. "This is supposed to be fun. You made the ride, remember?"

Had he not been smiling before? He did so now, self-consciously. "Eyes on the prize," he said.

"If I had a Magic Marker I'd have you sign the thing."

"Next time."

"I'm going to hold you to that," Eriksson said. "Mission Control, EV-2 is safely connected to MSS and we are good to continue."

"Green light for EVA."

"MS-2, give me a minute to get clear and we'll be good to go."

"I hear you, Bill. One minute to clear."

A long moment of silence then. He watched Eriksson as he slid away and out of sight. Then only the long stretch of the truss where it fled in perspective into weightless distance and the black rectangular mirrors of the solar arrays lifting toward the darkness of space.

"All clear," Eriksson's voice came at last. "You ready, Chip?"

"Ready," he said. Then to ground: "MS-2, we are clear to proceed."

"I hear you, Keith. Stand by." Again silence. Then, "Here we go."

And so here it was. He had designed the arm, had supervised its installation and had tested it repeatedly over the preceding weeks, but this was the moment where it would all come together at last. The sensation was clear and smooth and silent, the body of the ISS moving alongside him as the mechanism pushed him along the truss, open areas of darkness yawning up at him where the superstructure lay exposed and then disappearing under closed white panels reflecting sunlight. To his right, the distant blue ocean flecked with white clouds and to his left the endlessness of the stars, like images from a film or a still picture on the periphery of his vision, unreal, impossible, the white and black surface of the station and the crisscrossing beams of the truss flowing past him. Bisected boxes, planes and angles, all of which aligned in perfect symmetrical structure that was no less than a tangible, physical manifestation of the numbers themselves, so close he could have reached his gloved hand out and touched these things as his body passed them: this panel of the aluminum meteoroid shield, this padded trussbeam, this line of rivets, this long and beautiful machine.

The task itself was not unlike removing a huge dishwasher from between countertop and floor and cabinetry, the power driver in his gloved hand turning the bolts and stowing them in the bag again and again, Mission Control occasionally relaying instructions as he worked, the process tangible and solid and continuous, the bolts unscrewing from their housing, floating in the microgravity as he pawed them with his gloved hands, then transferring them to the mesh bag attached to his wrist. Then another. And another. As clear and straightforward as a simple equation: moving each variable to zero until the whole tank was free of its housing. Then at last he pushed his gloved hands through the scoops he had attached there and pulled his fingers tight against the handles. "OK, Mort, let's pull this out nice and slow," he said.

"Affirmative, EV-2," Stevens said. "Slow and steady wins the race."

He felt himself drifting back, the huge white block of the nitrogen tank coming with him in perfect and absolute silence, its five hundred fifty pounds rendered close to zero in the microgravity, the robotic arm pulling him backwards so that he was lifted up and away from the truss, away from the station itself, out into the plane that was parallel to Earth and was itself a kind of orbit, a parabola extending from yet another parabola which was no parabola at all but a circle.

"MS-2, we're looking good here," he said. "We're just about clear of S1."

And a moment later the tank was indeed clear, leaving behind a square gap where it had once been housed, the empty nitrogen tank a rectangular box the size of a refrigerator, held now by two simple handles gripped by his gloved fingers, his space-suited body standing straight and tall at the end of the robotic arm, his boots the only direct attachment to the machine he had designed to carry him.

"Ready to wipe some windshields?" Stevens said in his ear.

"Affirmative, MS-2. All ready here," Keith said.

Then Stevens again: "EV-1, we are ready to proceed to ESP-3."

And Eriksson: "Affirmative, Destiny. All clear." Then to Keith: "Have fun, Chip."

There was a brief pause and then he began to turn, slowly, the huge segmented arm twisting until he was tilted at a slight angle, the tank moving with him as the scene shifted in the helmet glass: the long stretch of the truss and the more distant Russian module and the radiators blazing in the sunlight and then the solar arrays and the whole of the ISS as he continued to move up and away from it all, the motion of his lifting and the distances below him seeming to shift as he watched. One zero eight-point-five, this line he moved along, the axis of the truss line crossing the modules at seventy-three meters and the point of motion that was himself and the full nitrogen tank he held in his outstretched hand, that point moving along the parabolic arc, mapped along a path he could see as if it existed only as a graph on a sheet of paper. One zero eight-point-five, each number before him, not just the total but the graduated divisions that marked off the measurements as if some enormous thermometer marked by regularly spaced red lines.

"How's it look up there?" Stevens said.

He paused before answering. Then he said, "MS-2, visual clean and clear."

"Yeah, but how does it look?"

"It looks . . . ," he said. Then he paused again. There were no words. The whole of the station like an enormous winged insect and the arm swinging him backwards above it so that the farthest reaches of the truss and the huge black rectangles of the solar arrays flashed and reflected their darkness to him, diminishing as he moved, knowing what was below even when he could not see it, as if points on a map or a grid, points denoted clearly and plainly by their coordinates. The names shuttled by—the Mobile Servicing System, the S0 truss segment and then the Unity Node, the Columbus Module, the Destiny Lab—objects named to denote the idea of their most perfect state of being, as if already clarified by their purpose or by the purpose they had been set forth to fulfill and all of them designed by other engineers, other mathematicians. He moved above them, pressing toward the apex of that motion where the parabolic curve would shift from zero to one, all of it visible now: the various modules where they clustered below him and the black mirrors of the solar arrays where they connected to the long crisscrossing trusses, each shape outlined and ringed in blue lines and arrows, the numbers circling and ringing and indicating and denoting their symbolic values. The numbers of the machine. The perfect machine.

Then Mort Stevens's voice in his helmet: "You still with me, Keith?"

"Hang on," he said. Then, "I wish . . . I wish you could see this. It's amazing here." Not even aware of whom he was addressing. He thought he would actually tear up, that he would actually cry. Not because of the mission or because he had accomplished everything he had set out to do but because what he could see in that moment was so stunning in its beauty and purity and complexity that it could not be believed. Everything within the angle of his vision rendered infinite. My god. Below him spun the bulge of South America where the brown and muddy Amazon emptied into the Atlantic and a swirl of clouds that ran under the Destiny Module like a dust mote swirling under a piece of furniture: green and brown continents and blue oceans and white clouds and above it all: the clear and precise white and black of the station and the robotic arm itself where it moved in umbilical perspective down to the Kibo Module, the ISS, those oxygen-filled tubes in which they worked and lived. And Keith Corcoran: floating above it all.

Already Earth returning to its forty-five minutes and thirty seconds of night as he moved in the orbit path, the coming of darkness like some lightning eclipse, and he pulled one hand free—not even thinking now, for perhaps the first time in his life completely without thought—and clicked off the light of his helmet and peered into the multicolored glow of space itself. All his life the numbers in his mind arrayed in some black substance that was this substance, this dark matter, and now here it was and he stood on a platform and was raised up into it as if into some pool that drifted not below him but above, his body cresting into that surface and breaking it and finding no numbers there whatsoever, instead only the stars, not on the flat dome of the night sky but actually in perspective and distance and in color and not a one of them twinkling or blinking but steady and solid and so clearly at different distances and sizes and locations and of varieties staggering to behold. A universe comprised of radiation and light and gravity and energy and mass. What equation to describe such a reckoning? What set of numbers? Only the dark matter and the resplendent and glorious universe itself spinning out all around him. Around us all.

It was only a single moment and then the numbers fell into their places once again. His heart ascatter in his chest. The robotic arm he had designed. The tangent of theta. Pi over two. Sine equals one. The apex had been reached and he was descending down the other side of the long arc and the radians moved through his mind—two pi over three, three pi over four, five pi over six—and it already seemed like something that had occurred in a dream, as if he had been sleeping or had slept and had imagined the thinking of some other man, of some other astronaut. His mouth dry. His heart racing as if he had been startled awake. What was he doing here? What were any of them doing out here at all?

And then it was over. You are here. Nowhere else.

Stevens's voice in his helmet: "Looking good, Keith."

He blinked quickly behind the helmet glass. "Uh . . . ," he said, the sound as if from somewhere else, as if someone else's voice, someone distracted. "MS-2, I read you. Smooth and steady."

"Five meters," Stevens said.

And Keith said: "All clear."

Then he could see Eriksson on the more distant P3 truss, the long black rectangles of the solar arrays spreading out from his tiny shape like the petals of some metallic flower. He shook his head inside the helmet. Eriksson before him on the truss, moving in his own awkward spacesuit. He had already pulled the full nitrogen tank from its storage site, had stowed it on the opposite side of the truss so that Keith could place the empty tank in his hand directly into the gap left behind and Mort Stevens was moving him into position to do so.

"That looked like a good ride," Eriksson said.

"It was," he said. His gaze had settled upon a shape behind Eriksson, out past the black empty bowl of Earth, the curved distance of which was illuminated in a glowing blue arc. There, just at the horizon, rode the smaller sharp sickle of the moon, drawn in a thin white line as if the closed half of a perfect empty circle and holding there for some uncountable moment as he watched, its shape appearing to pause in orbit, unmoving and suspended against the edge of the earth. It might have held there only a moment. It might not have held there at all. In the next instant, the whole of that shape seemed to shudder and plunge into the dark surface of the planet and was gone.

"Everything all right?" Eriksson said.

"Of course." His voice was faint and weak. He cleared his throat and spoke again, more firmly this time: "Everything's A-OK."

"How's about you turn on your helmet light so I can see you," Eriksson said.

"Right." He reached up and flipped on the light. There was a flutter inside his chest as if a hollow there had opened: a cabinet, an emptiness, a vacancy. And a strong feeling that he had lost something. Something tangible. The toolbag. His helmet. The wrench. The instructions tethered to his wrist. But everything he had when he pulled himself through the airlock was accounted for. And yet the feeling remained.

When he and Eriksson reentered the module, Tim Fisher, Mort Stevens, and Petra Gutierrez were all there waiting for them and he shook each of their hands in turn, their faces smiling. He too, smiling now.

"Well done, gentlemen," Stevens said.

"You too, Mort," Eriksson said. "Thanks for the piloting work."

"Glad to be a part of it," Stevens said.

Eriksson had finished shaking Stevens's hand and now Keith did so, still half smiling. "Feel about the same?" Keith said.

"Yeah. Works perfectly," Stevens answered.

"Smooth?"

"Yes. How was it on your end?"

"Fine," Keith said. He paused. Stevens was looking at him, waiting. "What's the draw?"

"I'll get you the data. Super minimal, I'm sure."

"Within the test parameters?"

"As far as I could tell. No fluctuations."

"I'd like to see the data."

"I can start the analysis in the next hour," Stevens said.

Eriksson laughed at his side. "Christ, Chip," he said. "Power down, already."

Keith looked at him, then back at the crew, and tried to smile.

"It worked great," Eriksson said. "Just like you designed it."

"All right, all right," Keith said. He glanced up at Stevens and nodded and Stevens shrugged.

Then Petra: "Sure looked like a fun ride."

"It was," Keith said. "Amazing."

"I got a couple of good pictures of it with the Nikon," Fisher said. "Through the window."

"Fantastic," Keith said. "I appreciate that."

"Well?" Petra said. "What was it like?"

He looked at her, her eyes expectant. All of them waiting for his response. "I don't know what to say about it. It was like . . . floating." They waited for him to say more but no more words would come to him. Inexplicably, he thought of Quinn.

"Looked pretty amazing through the window," Fisher said. "You were pretty far away."

"Yeah," Keith said. "Seemed like it too."

There was a pause in the conversation and then Fisher said, "Hey, Bill, CAPCOM is waiting to hear from you."

"About what?"

"I asked but they wouldn't tell me," Fisher said.

"Seriously?" Eriksson said.

"That's what they told me," Fisher said. He shrugged. "Private mission commander stuff, I guess."

It was quiet for a moment. Then Eriksson said, "Well, OK. Let's go find out what they want." He moved away from them then, through the round opening into Node 1 and out of sight.

"That's odd," Petra said.

And then Keith: "What was that about?"

"You know as much as I do," Fisher said.

"What did they say?" Petra said.

"They said to have Bill call in when he was back inside. That was all. Jeez, guys, it's not a conspiracy."

"Weird, though," Petra said.

"I guess," Fisher said.

It was silent again. Then Petra said, "Hungry?"

"Starving," Keith said.

"Good. You're just in time for dinner."

Both Petra and Fisher joined him at the table in the Service Module. They might have continued to discuss the possible reasons for the communication but there was little use in such speculation. Instead, Petra asked him questions about the EVA he had just completed and he tried to describe the sense of awe he had felt but again it sounded so feeble when put into words that he gave up entirely.

By the time Eriksson arrived in the galley, Keith had finished his tortilla-wrapped canned ham and was sipping juice from a foil bag. Fisher had just completed a lengthy argument for the culinary superiority of the canned sturgeon brought in by the Russian Space Agency, a controversy on which Keith had no opinion.

"Ready to eat something?" Keith said as Eriksson entered.

"In a minute," Eriksson said. "Listen, Keith, we got some news."

"What kind of news?"

Eriksson glanced at Petra and Fisher and then turned toward him once more. "Let's talk about it in your quarters," he said.

"Really?" Keith said. He looked at Eriksson. If there was some expression on the mission commander's face he did not recognize it.

"Everything OK?" Petra said.

Eriksson looked at her but said nothing.

"What's going on?" Keith said.

"Come on," Eriksson said. And then, to the other crew members: "Can you guys clean up?"

"Uh . . . yeah, sure," Petra said. Her face in that moment: a mask of concern and confusion.

"Thanks," Keith said.

They pulled themselves through the modules, Eriksson leading the way and Keith following close behind, and then into the closet-size space that was Keith's crew quarters and they drifted there as they talked, Keith in the tiny compartment and Eriksson in the curtained doorway.

"So what's going on?" Keith said.

"Look," Eriksson said. He paused. Cleared his throat. "I don't know how to tell you this so I'll just come out and say it. We got a call from ground. Your daughter has been in an auto accident."

"What? What happened?"

"We don't know yet."

There was a moment of silence between them and then Keith said, "I don't understand."

Eriksson looked at him. "She's gone," he said.

"Gone?"

"Yes," Eriksson said. Then: "I'm sorry, buddy."

"Gone? What do you mean 'gone'? Gone where?"

"Gone, Keith. She's gone."

"I don't understand what you're saying."

Eriksson looked at him, not responding at first, only staring. Then he said, carefully and slowly: "Your daughter was killed in an accident."

"What? Are you . . . you're joking?"

"Not this time, buddy," he said. "I wish I was."

"This isn't funny, Bill."

No answer now.

"Quinn?"

"I'm sorry."

"I don't understand what you're telling me," Keith said. He was filled in that moment with a blinding and all-encompassing rage that flooded through him all at once and was just as quickly gone. "Jesus Christ. What . . . what are you saying, Bill? Jesus Christ."

"I'm so sorry, buddy. Houston is waiting for your call. They probably know more."

"Oh my god," he said. His mind was blank. Then again: "Oh my god."

"It'll be . . . ," Eriksson began but he did not finish the sentence.

Keith looked at him. If there was some emotional response expected he could not find it now. There was an equation forming all around him but what the variables were, where the starting point was, he did not know.

Eriksson continued to stare back at him as if waiting for him to say something. "You want me to call in?" he said after a time.

"What?" Keith said.

Eriksson reached to the intercom and pulled it down from the wall and clicked the button. "Houston, Eriksson here."

A moment later came the reply: "We read you. Go ahead, Bill."

"I'm here with Keith," he said.

"OK, stand by." There was a pause and then the intercom crackled and the voice of Mission Command returned. "Keith, we have your wife standing by. Can you connect via laptop?"

"Where is she?" he said.

"He wants to know where his wife is," Eriksson said into the intercom.

"Stand by," the response came. Eriksson was looking at him. He could feel Eriksson looking at him. Then Mission Control again: "We don't know the answer to that."

"They don't know where my wife is?"

"Look, they'll connect her," Eriksson said. "Where was she before? At her folks' place? She's probably there."

There was a wave of confusion. He nodded but said nothing.

Eriksson pressed the intercom button again. "OK, we're standing by," he said.

"We read you. Standing by," the voice said. There was a moment of silence and then the voice returned: "Keith, we don't know what to say. We're all . . . we're all wishing you the best down here."

"The best?" Keith said. He had not reached for the intercom nor depressed the button to be heard and so Eriksson said, "Understood." And then, "Standing by."

Eriksson left the intercom floating in the air before them. The two men adrift, neither speaking, not even looking at each other.

"This doesn't . . . ," Keith said. And then, "This doesn't make any sense."

"I know," Eriksson said. It was quiet between them and then Eriksson said, "Do you want me to get your laptop ready for Barb?"

"Barb," he said. "No, I can do that." As if to show that this action was indeed possible he opened the laptop and clicked on the appropriate icon to initiate the link.

"You'll get through this," Eriksson said.

"OK," Keith said, simply. His voice was clear and he felt composed and ready, as if for some component of the mission that he had only just learned of but which nonetheless needed completing.

"Don't worry," Eriksson said.

"I'm not worried," Keith said.

Eriksson looked at him carefully.

"What?" Keith said.

"Let's talk after."

"All right."

"I'll be just past the hatch if you need me," Eriksson said.

"Got it."

Eriksson looked at him again, his expression one of concern. "You all right?"

"Fine," Keith said.

Eriksson nodded, turned, and pulled himself to the other end of the module. In a moment he was gone from sight.

The laptop before him was open and he stared at it for a long time before his eyes focused on its glowing background image, an image of himself and Barb and Quinn taken a few years before, a snapshot from a trip they had taken to Houston, one of the few actual vacations they had taken together. He was smiling awkwardly but both Barb and Quinn looked beautiful. How old had she been when the photograph was taken? Fifteen? Slightly younger?

He might have continued to stare at the image as he waited but his eyes blurred and when they refocused a point of light drifted in the air before him, a faint luminescence like a distant star. Like a diamond. His first thought was fascination. Then confusion. Then he recognized it at last as a drop of fluid, a liquid of some kind suspended in the recycled oxygen of the compartment. Then he could see another and then another, as if a collection of tiny stars were forming in the air a few scant inches from his face, a new and unknown constellation which he watched with curiosity as if the individual points of light had originated from some other source. Not from him. Not from the tears that floated out and away from him as if drawn toward the image on the screen. Look at those, he was thinking. I'll have to tell her about this. Another, this large enough to wobble slightly until it settled into its silent shining orb. I'll have to tell Quinn. Adrift then. Adrift.

The chamber filling slowly with tiny stars. Count them now and they will equal some infinity of zeros.

My daughter. Oh my god. My daughter is dead.

Four

SHE MUST HAVE been waiting for him because her high-pitched voice came almost the very moment he swung open the door: "Hey! Hey you, astronaut guy! Hey!" He might have simply swung it closed again but he did not and she continued to shout as she trotted in his direction from across the street.

He was embarrassed that he had opened the door yet again but he had come to hear the sound of a delivery truck in every low-frequency hum that wobbled through the empty rooms. Each time he waited for the doorbell's ring or the sound of the driver's knock and when no such sound came he would set down the paint roller and walk to the door in his socks and open it to find nothing—no package, no driver, no truck—instead only the emptiness of the cul-de-sac, the day coming to a close and darkness once again falling over the house like a shroud.

But this time he had opened the door not to silence but rather to the sound of the little girl who had run across the street from the direction of Jennifer's house and now stood before him, bouncing slightly on the tips of her toes and smiling with excitement. "You're the astronaut guy?" she said.

He sighed and glanced around the entryway for the box even though he already knew that there was no box to be found.

"Hello?" she called up to him. "Anyone home?"

"Yes," he said at last, "I'm the astronaut guy." He looked at her. She was perhaps nine or ten years old with brown hair pulled back in a tight ponytail. "Do you need something?" he said.

"Yep," she said and when he did not respond she asked: "Is it fun?"

"Is what fun?"

The little girl rolled her eyes as if exasperated by his apparent lack of intelligence or insight. "Being an astronaut," she said.

"Oh." He thought for a moment. His throat felt tight. He tried not to think of Quinn. "Yes, it's fun," he said.

"What do you get to do that's fun?"

"Do your parents know you're out here?"

"My mom knows," the girl said quickly, as if it was necessary to get this information out of the way so she could focus on the more important question at hand: "So what's the answer?"

"Oh, let's see," he said. "I get to wear a space suit."

"That's the fun part?"

"Sure."

"Is that the funnest part?"

"I don't know. Maybe."

"Really? I don't think so. What's the funnest part?"

He looked at her. "You're kind of demanding," he said.

She smiled and nodded. "Precocious," she said.

"Who calls you that?"

"Grandpa."

"Ah," he said. "What's the funnest part?" He paused and then said, "When the rocket blasts off."

"What's fun about that?"

"I don't know."

She looked at him as if confused or irritated; he could not tell which. Then she said, "You're not really good at this."

"Good at what?"

"Telling about being an astronaut."

He stood looking at her, blinking, then glanced at the house across the street, then back to the girl, realizing as he did so that she was the same child who had looked through his sliding glass door when the realtor had first been to the house. "Does your mom let you talk to strangers?" he said.

"You're not stranger danger. You're an astronaut. It's like talking to a policeman or a fireman. Plus my mom's the one who told me to come over." She smiled at him: a big, goofy smile that was totally fake and yet somehow endearing.

"What's your mom's name?"

"Jennifer." She pointed behind her, across the street. "We live right there."

"Yeah, I thought so," he said. "Why did your mom tell you to come over here?"

"Because of my school report."

"Aren't you out for summer?"

"My school goes all summer long."

He looked at her, then up at the house, then back at her again. "OK," he said. "I probably shouldn't ask, but what's the report?" He glanced past the little girl to Jennifer's house again. He had seen her only once since their initial meeting three days earlier, had waved to her just as her car disappeared into the garage. Now that garage door remained closed. He wondered if she was watching him from some upstairs window but if so he could not see her.

"It's on someone in our neighborhood. Someone who does stuff."

"Stuff like what?"

"You know. Like firefighters and people like that."

"Right," he said. "So I'm your report topic?"

61

"Yep."

"Don't you think you should ask me first? Maybe I'm really busy and don't have time to be in your report."

"I don't think so," she said. "You don't really do anything."

"How do you know?"

"I'm not stupid."

"I didn't say you were."

"You don't have any furniture."

"So?" He wondered if that was all he could have come up with, wondered why he was being run aground in a conversation with a ten-year-old and then tried to remember what Quinn had been like at this age. Would she have spoken to a neighbor with such authority? He thought it unlikely.

"It's not good. All you have is a couch. My mom says that's weird."

"Your mom's right. It is weird."

"So why don't you have any furniture?"

"Did you figure this out by peeking through the window?"

She looked embarrassed.

"It's OK, but you probably shouldn't do that," he said.

"I know," she said.

He thought she might cry but she did not, instead standing there and looking up at him from the concrete. Then he said, "To answer your question, my wife took it all when she moved out."

"Why aren't you with her? Did you have an affair?"

"An affair? Do you know what that means?"

"It means when you go be in love with someone else and you want to marry someone else. It's what my uncle did. I heard my mom talking about it."

He leaned against the doorframe, wondering if he should step outside but he had removed his shoes while he was painting and now stood in his socks between the interior of his empty house and the seemingly less empty exterior of the cul-de-sac. His thoughts went

again to the neighbor across the street, the tan woman who had sent her daughter here. "What's your name anyway?" he said.

"Nicole," she said.

"I'm Captain Corcoran."

"Hi, Captain Coco-ran."

He smiled. "Maybe Captain Keith would be easier."

"Captain Keith," she said. "Hi, Captain Keith."

"Hi," he said.

Across the street the garage door hummed open. He might have expected the neighbor's red car to slide out onto the street but instead the neighbor herself appeared out of the shadows and stepped toward them. She was not dressed in her workout clothes this time but her T-shirt was tight across her chest, the neckline low enough that her tan breasts nearly spilled out of it.

"Does that mean I can do my report on you?" Nicole said.

He stared at Jennifer as she approached. It was not unlike watching some jungle cat. A panther. He glanced down at his shirt and pants, both of which appeared clean but for a few flecks of eggshell paint, and at his shoeless feet, gray socks on the threshold of the open door. Behind him lay the vacant entryway, tiles smeared with dust and dirt and littered with curls of masking tape. Beyond: the living room he had been in the process of painting. He glanced in that direction only briefly before stepping forward and closing the door behind him.

"What?" he said.

"I said," she repeated, clearly impatient with his lack of attention, "can I do my report on you?"

"OK," he said, "but it might have been better if you had asked me that first."

"Why?"

He paused. "I don't know," he said. Then: "That's just usually how it's done."

Jennifer had arrived by her daughter's side, smiling widely. He had initially thought she might be slightly older than he was but now, with her standing before him, it was impossible to tell, her body uniformly smooth and tight and tan as if she was a being constructed entirely of suede.

"Hey neighbor," she said.

"Hey," he said.

"Is she bothering you?"

"No," he said. "She asks a lot of questions."

"Jennifer," she said, extending her hand and shaking his.

"I remember," he said. Then he added, "Keith." Her hand felt smooth and warm.

"I'm afraid I put her up to it," Jennifer said. "She had this report to do and I just thought you'd be perfect. I mean you're so close. Right across the street."

He nodded but did not answer. Smiled.

"The other kids will all have their local mailman or something and Nicole will have our astronaut. That's pretty special, don't you think?"

He smiled again, turning his eyes toward the sidewalk. "I guess so," he said.

"You're a bit bashful about being famous."

"I'm not famous."

"It's not a very big town."

"Seems pretty big to me."

"Well, you're still new here," she said. "Small town with big shopping."

"I guess so."

"It's cute that you're bashful."

He wondered if he was blushing, hoped in fact that he was not. He glanced down at Nicole, who looked up at him expectantly.

"We're just headed out so I won't keep you," Jennifer said.

"OK," he said. Then he paused and stammered, "I mean, it's OK. It's not a problem."

She held eye contact with him and he only broke it when Nicole called up at him from the concrete, her words punctuated by a short hop as if the sentence caused a physical reaction: "Will you be here later?"

He wondered if her mother might intervene but Jennifer said nothing. "When later?" he said.

"Mom, when?" Nicole asked.

"Maybe it would be more convenient if we invited Mr. Corcoran over to our house for dinner," Jennifer said. "That way you can ask him your questions and he can eat something and everyone's happy."

"Yeah, Captain Keith can come over!" Nicole said.

"What do you say, Captain Keith?" Jennifer said. "We can't do tonight. Homeowners association. Maybe you're going to that too?"

"No, I didn't know about that."

"You're welcome to come, you know. You're a homeowner, after all, even if you're selling."

"Oh," he said. "No, I don't want to go to that."

"I don't blame you," she said. "A lot of busybodies mostly." She giggled, the sound of a much younger woman, a girl. "I do like your honesty," she said. Then she giggled again.

He looked at the ground in embarrassment. No words would come.

"How's Thursday?" She looked at him and smiled and once again did not break the contact and he felt a short surge in his lower gut. The concrete felt warm under his feet even though the air around him was still cool and there was the faintest hint of a breeze. He could feel the little girl looking up at him but he continued to stare into Jennifer's eyes and she stared back at him, her smile closing into a mischievous grin. He did not know if he should break the contact, knew only that he did not want to do so.

"Thursday?" he said at last. "I think that sounds fine."

He tried to resume painting but the attention to detail that was nearly automatic when he had first begun the task had become difficult to find, his strokes wobbling and sloppy. At first he was merely distracted because he was thinking of the woman who lived across the street. But there was something else too: a kind of intrusion that overlay those thoughts and would not be ignored. When his phone began to buzz and he looked at it and saw that it was Barb—her timing perfect as always—his irritation reached a pinnacle and he clapped the phone closed and returned it to his pocket. She had continued to call him every day or two, although he could not determine to what purpose. It had not been to share her grief, or at least if that had been her purpose it was unclear. Instead she would simply engage him in some variety of small talk, asking about his day, telling him about her own. At first, when he was still in Houston, he welcomed the calls because her voice was familiar and even though she had already told him that she had moved out of their home and would not return, he needed that familiar contact. Now, though, her telephone calls had come to feel like increasingly futile exercises. Why call him every day if only to remind him that she was gone and that it was, in some way he could not identify, his fault?

"Shit."

He had dragged the roller against an outlet and stood there surveying the chaos of new paint on the living room wall, a ragged block of eggshell in a field of yellow. Guilt. That was what the intrusion was: simple guilt. It was as if his wife—or ex-wife or whatever she was now—was somehow peering into his thoughts, watching him as he secretly fantasized about the woman across the street. There was no logic to the feeling at all. She had been the one to leave, not him. He had asked her to stay long enough to at least discuss what had happened and how they might proceed into some future neither of them could imagine, but she would not wait for him to return from the mission. Her own return to the house—this house—would be only long enough to collect its contents into a U-Haul to drive back to the Atlanta suburb where she had grown up and where her mother still resided, and this she had done while he was still in orbit, two hundred miles above the surface of Earth. And now a woman had asked him to dinner, a woman who was not Barb. He should have felt elation, triumph, a sense of release from his marriage, but what he felt was guilt. To compound his irritation, there was also a small dull lump of pain at the base of his skull, a fact that he tried not to focus on but which was present nonetheless.

He knew the marriage had been far from perfect. Had it not been for Quinn they might have dissolved their partnership long before. But it could not be denied that there had been a time when she had been by his side, that she had helped press him in the direction of his goals, of their goals. Even what he thought of as their honeymoon—their real honeymoon—had been part of that progress, her excitement at the adventure of their move to Palo Alto for his graduate work fueling his desire to choose that school over MIT. That drive—from Georgia to California—had been a lovers' journey filled with tiny hotel rooms and gas stations and roadside attractions and Barb paging through the AAA guidebook incessantly, circling things to see, hotels to stay the night in, restaurants that were good and were near enough to the freeway to actually stop at. There had been a trip to Hawaii funded by Barb's parents but he remembered the road trip as the real honeymoon, and somewhere amidst those long days of gas stations and fields and farms and deserts they had conceived their first and only child, although they would not know that Barb was pregnant for another month, after they had settled into their tiny Palo Alto apartment and Keith's first semester of graduate school had begun.

The whole of it comprised one long moment in his memory now, the moment after Quinn had been born and the three of them had been a family at Stanford and Quinn was an infant and then a toddler and his marriage to Barb was still new. They were broke and there had been arguments about money and, sometimes, already, about the workload that kept Keith so often away from their apartment. And yet what he remembered was an overriding sense of contentment, each day dawning on a California that seemed as blessed and magical as any place they could conceive of, the sun slanting crossways through the wild golden grasses and red-tiled roofs of Stanford's architecture, the arcs and lines and towers of which were decorated with tiny and innumerable mosaic tiles. They woke in the early morning when Quinn climbed into bed between them, the three of them radiating the golden glow that was the glow of his memory, magnificent and endless, and Keith would ride his squeaky ten-speed bicycle from their apartment to the campus as he settled into a world filled with research facilities that were among the very best in the world.

Perhaps his marriage had already begun its slow stumble into entropy. Perhaps it had been crumbling from the very first moment and he had been unaware of it or had been unable to see it. He wondered sometimes if he might have forestalled her leaving had he been able to return from the mission, wondered this even though he knew she was already gone. But of course he had not wanted to return. In the days after Quinn's death Houston told him that it was their intent to get him home and his response had been to refuse, explaining that while he appreciated their concern he intended to complete the mission he had been trained to do. They might have left him alone then had the migraines not begun but this medical reality made his return to Earth a priority for the agency, or at least this was what they had told him. But then his return had been delayed by weather and then by a technical problem and then by weather again and so he had remained on the space station with the rest of the crew and had continued with his tasks and experiments, such as he could between the agony of the migraines. In that time his anger at Barb had faded into a kind of liminality that was a reflection of the situation itself: he could do nothing but ask her not to leave and he did so and she told him she was already gone. All the while he continued to float in that low orbit, working when he could and huddling in the dark pain of his shattered mind when he could not.

She told him she was sorry but that he had been absent from their marriage and their family for so long and that she simply did not want to be alone anymore and when he pressed her she finally told him the truth about what she had done, about what she had been doing. Even now his body shivered at the memory of it, that mixture of confusion, panic, anger, and grief flooding through him once more, the paint roller trembling in his hand. At the time he had been too shattered to do much more than float in the microgravity and listen without real understanding. He had suffered a migraine just before and was in that long period of recovery, his mind feeling soft, the numbers it held a jumbled collection of broken symbols signifying quantities that held no real import or meaning at all. When he had received the video call it had been as if he were watching a kind of static scene that included someone who looked like him and someone who looked like his wife: a man suspended in the closet-size compartment, staring at a computer in silence as a woman's face spoke from the screen. "I need you to understand that it's over," she said to him.

"You keep saying that. Just wait until I'm home and we can talk about it."

Then she said nothing for a time. She had been saying essentially the same thing for the course of the conversation and he had responded the only way he could think to respond. Their daughter was dead and now she was telling him—trying to tell him—that she did not want to be married to him anymore.

And then her voice returned from that silence: "I'm seeing someone else, Keith."

"What?"

"I'm seeing someone else. I've been seeing someone else for a while."

He drifted. He had been drifting. "You're having an affair?" he said.

"Yes, I'm having an affair."

The quiet that came seemed to have no beginning or end, as if it had existed forever and he had merely slipped into its flowing stream. What had she said? Could he have heard her wrong? Could she be making some kind of weird joke he did not understand?

"Say something," she said to him at last.

"What do you want me to say?"

"Anything."

And then not speaking for so long, his body floating in the compartment.

"You don't know how lonely I've been," she said. "You never talk to me."

"I talk to you."

"No, you don't."

Again the silence. Then: "You had . . . you had an affair?"

"I didn't mean for it to happen."

"Jesus Christ. Jesus Christ. You had an affair?" His voice—the voice of this man who looked like him and who was him but somehow was not—this voice not even angry but flat and emotionless, as if discussing something tedious: a policy, a simple string of numbers, a procedure.

"I'm sorry."

"You're sorry?"

"Yes, I'm sorry. I didn't plan it."

"Does that even matter?"

"Yes, it matters," she said.

"How?"

She did not respond.

"Who is it?" he said.

"You don't know him."

"That's not what I asked."

"You don't know him and you won't ever know him. I'm not going to tell you that."

Silence. Silence everywhere.

"I'm sorry but I thought you should know," she said.

"Jesus Christ, Barb."

"It isn't working anymore."

"Obviously."

"You're not being fair."

"I'm not being fair? You're sleeping with someone else."

"Don't."

"It's true, isn't it?" Even though his words were angry, his tone was resigned, disappointed, as if he was reading the script of an argument, reciting the words he knew he was supposed to say and he did say them but without feeling or emotion.

"You're never around," she said.

"I wanted you and Quinn to move to Houston with me—"

"Don't. Don't even say her name. That's not what this is about. This is about me getting my life back."

"I wanted you both to move to Houston with me but you wouldn't do it."

"It wouldn't have made any difference," she said.

"Yes, it would have."

"No, Keith. It wouldn't have mattered because you still don't really talk to me about anything."

"Yes, I do."

"No, you don't. It was the same with her. You pushed and pushed and pushed. And you didn't listen to her. You made her miserable."

"Don't do this."

"Don't do what? You just sit there thinking about math. That's all you ever think about. I need someone to think about me, goddammit. I need someone to think about me."

"Is that what this other man does for you?"

"Yes, since you asked. That's what he does. He thinks about me."

He said nothing for a moment. Then: "After all we've been through. Now this?"

"This started before . . . before Quinn . . . ," she said, and her voice cracked when she said their daughter's name.

"Fantastic," he said. "Even better."

She was silent, staring at his face from the laptop screen. Then she said, "I told you because I want you to understand that it's over."

"What is?"

"Our marriage, Keith. Our marriage is over."

He closed his eyes and then opened them slowly and as he did so it felt as if he was shifting into his own body, as if he had been away and now returned. "Jesus Christ, Barb," he said. "Jesus Christ, can't this wait? Can't this just wait until I'm back home?"

"No, it can't wait."

"Really? It has to be right now?"

"Yes, it has to be now."

"What do you want me to do about it? It's not like I can just come down."

"I know and I don't want you to."

"You can't do this," he said.

"I already have."

"No, you can't do this. You'll be home when I get there and we'll figure this out."

"I'm sorry," she said. "I didn't want it to be like this."

"Christ, Barb. Don't do this."

"I'm sorry," she said.

"Yeah, so am I," he said.

She had called him days later, also on the laptop, to tell him that she had already removed all her belongings from the house and that he would need to collect his own and then it could be put on the market and sold, told him this as if it was a simple business transaction. At the time, he found himself wishing that he could somehow remain on the space station but then another migraine would send him into a red jagged tunnel of pain and it would take days for him to recover and he knew, even then, that he was failing his first mission, perhaps the only mission he would ever have.

Had she not married him for his ambition, because he was going to achieve something beyond the range of most men? Had she not understood that reaching his own destiny would take time and discipline? And now she felt he had put too much time into his work and not enough time into his family. He was an astronaut and his daughter was dead and then his wife had told him that she was leaving him and would not return. What kind of universe would allow such a thing?

By the late afternoon he gave up painting entirely. He had followed a single wall from the kitchen to the living room and then halfway up the stairs, dripping paint all the while so that the carpet and stair rail were flecked with white spots. It was a mess and he knew he should have simply stopped painting long before but of course he had not done so. When he left the house he was so distracted and frustrated that he did not even clean the brushes, merely dropping them onto the plastic-wrapped kitchen counter and walking out the door.

He ended up at Starbucks again, mostly because he could think of no other place to go, taking a padded chair in the back of the room and listening to the quietly piped-in classic rock while he sipped his coffee from its paper cup. His anger had not subsided and he tried to direct his thoughts back to Jennifer but instead found himself wondering how well she had known Barb. And so there she was again, intruding upon his thoughts and bringing with her the unwarranted feeling of guilt that settled into his chest, as if he was keeping a terrible secret from her. Perhaps he was. He still did not even know the name of the man his wife had been sleeping with, as if knowing his name would change what had happened. He wondered if Quinn had known him, if Barb had brought him into their house, into their bed. My god.

On the adjacent table was a newspaper and he reached for it for no reason other than to divert his mind, staring at headlines on foreclosures, the imploding real estate market, the rising price of oil, the

increasing unemployment rate. Servicemen captured in Iraq. Bombs
in Afghanistan. It might have been yesterday's paper or the week before
for little seemed to have changed. As if to confirm this fact he found a
brief article on the comet on page four, apparently somewhat more
important than it had been but still not quite worthy of the cover.
The tagline read: "Comet Set to Hit Earth?" Perhaps when scientists
removed the question mark from their sentences the paper would
move it to the front page. The story noted that it would take nearly
two months before it would make impact, if it was indeed on an earthbound trajectory. It simply might have been too many weeks away for
page one.

He had sat there for perhaps thirty minutes in the calm quiet semidarkness when the door opened and the loud Russian man entered.
Fantastic. He was the same man Keith had seen and briefly spoken to
the morning after he had first returned to the cul-de-sac and he made
a mental note to try a different Starbucks next time, lest he continue
to overlap with what was, apparently, this man's break from work.

The blonde barista—Audrey, he remembered—looked up from
the counter as the man came through the door and greeted him and
immediately the man looked around as if the source of the greeting was
somehow inexplicable. "Who said this to me?" he said. He mocked
looking around the room the way a parent might to entertain a very
small child. In his hands: a white department store box.

"It's me, Peter," she said. She was clearly playing along with a kind
of strange, childlike flirtation.

"I hear beautiful voice, but I see nothing," he said.

"I'm right here," she said again. She was smiling.

The man, Peter, jumped back, his face appearing startled, eyes wide.
"My goodness! Audrey! How you sneak up on me!" Peter glanced toward the back of the shop, to where Keith sat with his paper. "Hello,
famous astronaut Keith Corcoran!" he boomed.

"Hello," Keith responded, trying to suppress both his surprise and his annoyance. Had he told the man his name? If so he did not remember it. Unlikely.

"I would speak to you soon but first my attention is diverting here to counter," Peter said.

As if on cue, Keith's phone began to ring. He fished it out of his pocket. Eriksson.

Audrey laughed. "You're so weird," she said to Peter.

"Hello?" Keith said into the phone.

"Not weird. You mean charming," Peter said. "This word I am learning in English class."

Audrey laughed.

"Chip, Eriksson here."

"Look here what I have got," Peter said to Audrey. "Like a present maybe. You open."

"Hi, Bill."

"Where are you? At the airport?"

"No, I'm at Starbucks," Keith said. He glanced up from the paper again. Audrey took the white box slowly, as if handling something dangerous. Chemicals. Something that might explode. She said something but Keith could not hear it.

"Starbucks again? Is that how you're spending your time off?"

"No," Keith said.

Eriksson laughed briefly.

Across the room, Peter's voice continued to boom: "You are so sweet to me. You deserve something nice. Is that not right, famous astronaut Keith Corcoran?"

Keith waved him off, pointing at the phone. Peter bowed to him. "Hey, have you checked with Mullins about those files?" Keith said.

"Well, yeah, that's what I'm calling about."

"OK."

Across the room, Audrey opened the box. Her "Oh" was audible even through Eriksson's voice but her face revealed no emotion.

"So it doesn't sound like he's going to send them," Eriksson said.

"What?"

"He says it's against protocol. It's hard to argue because he's techni-cally right about that."

Keith was silent for a moment. Then he said, simply: "Crap."

"Yeah, probably not what you wanted to hear, but I thought I should let you know what was going on."

"OK."

"Sorry about that, pal."

"Sorry about what?"

"Just sorry he won't do it. No big deal though, right? You're sup-posed to taking a break."

"Yeah, I'm taking a break."

"At Starbucks."

"At Starbucks." A series of ones and zeroes crossed through his mind, affixed themselves to the surfaces of the visible world before him, and then faded from view. "Is that all?" he said into the phone.

"Well, yeah," Eriksson said. "That's all. Just wanted to give you a quick call to let you know what was happening."

"OK," Keith said.

They exchanged a few more brief words and the call was over. He snapped the phone shut and sat staring into the air-conditioned atmo-sphere before him. He should be in Houston right now. This was what he told himself. He should be in Houston.

Across the room, Peter was mid-monologue and his voice was loud enough to bury all else under the onslaught of volume: "I think of you when I see this. I know it is hot, it is hot outside, but in here always so cool and quiet. I think of my Audrey."

In a voice that was, by comparison, the chirping of a tiny bird: "That's really sweet, Peter. Thank you."

"And now," Peter said, half turning toward Keith, "I visit famous astronaut Keith Corcoran." And with these words Peter turned and crossed the room quickly, his hand already extended. "I want to shake hand of famous astronaut," he said. He grasped Keith's hand in his own and shook it vigorously twice before letting it drop again. "I look up pictures of astronauts on Internet until I see you," he began, his voice trailing off as if looking for the correct word and then finding it: "Magnificent."

"Oh . . . thank you," Keith said.

"You are famous man."

Keith looked at him but said nothing.

"I have much to ask you but now I must work," Peter said.

Again Keith did not answer, only looking back at him without words, without expression.

"Peter Kovalenko. From Kiev. Ukraine."

And now Keith said: "OK." And then: "Keith Corcoran."

"Of course this I know," Peter said. "We're like old friends already."

Keith did not say anything in response. He thought perhaps he should dissuade this man of such a notion but could think of no method that would not sound abrupt or cruel so he simply sat there, quietly waiting for Peter Kovalenko to leave.

"Astronaut. And right here," Peter said at last.

Keith nodded.

"You cannot resist Audrey either," Peter said. "But she is all mine." He said the end of the sentence loudly and turned toward the front of the store. Audrey looked up from the box and smiled, that smile turning to something else as Peter turned back around. Pain or confusion, Keith could not tell.

"Now I go," Peter said. He rubbed his hands together as if he were brushing off flour. "Very nice to meet you," he said.

"OK," Keith said. They shook hands a second time and Peter nodded at him and then turned on his heel. Audrey was staring at Keith and when he looked up at her she turned to Peter and said something quietly and Peter's voice boomed back at him again: "Yes, he is astronaut. Famous astronaut. Look on Internet."

Audrey looked back at Keith and smiled. "Neat," she said.

Keith nodded toward her.

"Don't get any ideas!" Peter said, yelling down the length of the narrow room even though it was small enough to render such volume unnecessary. "Famous astronaut! Magnificent!" He looked at Audrey one last time and then backed through the door and out of the shop.

The door swung closed. Silence. Christ.

Audrey looked at him. "Wow," she called to him. "That's true?"

"It's true," he said.

"Cool." She looked again into the white box and then reached inside, pawing through colored tissue paper and finally extracting a large snow globe that was set upon a bright pink base. Within the glass sphere stood a castle tower upon which was mounted a clock. There were figures around the base but Keith could not make them out from where he sat. Perhaps a prince and princess or something similar.

"I guess you have an admirer," he said.

She looked up at him briefly, an expression of concern or of confusion appearing on her face for an instant. Then she shrugged, as if dismissing his observation entirely. "Peter's all right," she said. "He's been coming here forever."

He watched her as she shook the globe and then set it on the counter, peering into its watery interior in silence as flakes of white plastic swirled across the clock and across the figures.

Keith returned to the newspaper on the tabletop. Everything was as it was: sitting at the coffeeshop, not really reading, his hands covered in tiny dots of eggshell. Eventually he would rise and move back out to the car and would feel the air conditioner against his face and he would return to the house in the cul-de-sac where there would be no package waiting for him, only a span of days that could not be counted by any system he could devise.

Five

BY THE TIME evening came, he had been pacing for the better part of an hour, moving upstairs, walking sometimes halfway down the hall toward her room before returning to the first floor, to the living room, to the kitchen, and then rotating in the direction of the stair-well once again. He was not thinking of that room in any specific way, not even in avoidance. Instead his thoughts centered on that last morning in Houston when he had awakened at his desk after cele-brating with the crew to find Mullins standing across from him. Even as he found himself in the upstairs hallways yet again, he knew that he had never felt so foolish as he had in that moment, at least not since he had been a child, in the days when the other children would ridicule him for saying just the wrong thing at just the wrong time. Those days so far behind him now that he never thought of them at all and yet with Mullins standing there it had been much the same sensation, the weird wave of panic and the realization that there was no taking back what had already happened, time ever corkscrewing out into the curvature of space.

He had been thinking he should call, that he should simply call Mullins's office and ask him directly what his status was, even flipped open his phone once on the way up the stairs, the second beer of the evening clutched in the opposite hand, and then closed the phone as he yet again entered the hallway that led to Quinn's room, telling himself that he had nothing to say to Mullins whatsoever, and then turning back before he reached that still-open doorway, wandering into his own bedroom where he spent the next hour flipping absently through the television stations. At some point he had removed the phone from his pocket and had been clicking it open and closed without conscious thought. And that was when he finally dialed the number.

It was well past eight o'clock and he had not anticipated an answer, expecting—perhaps even hoping—to make some kind of statement to Mullins's voice mail, but then there was a click and Mullins was there, saying his own name as a greeting and Keith actually stuttered and then said, "Jim, it's Keith Corcoran."

"Hello, Keith," he said. "How's the time off?"

"It's OK. Good, I mean." He had been sitting on the mattress but he stood now and then leaned back down for the remote and clicked the television off and then began pacing slowly through the room, setting the empty beer can on the dresser as he did so.

"Glad to hear it," Mullins said.

"I didn't think you'd answer."

A pause. "What can I do for you, Captain?" Mullins said. Monotone. Businesslike.

"Uh . . . look," he said. He paused again. Then: "So maybe we ended on a bad note last time?"

"No, it's fine," Mullins said. "Stressful situation for everyone."

"OK," he said.

"Don't worry about it," Mullins said but there was no change in his tone of voice. "What can I do for you, Keith?"

"Well, so I was just checking in on something," he began. He cleared his throat. "I spoke to Eriksson today. Anyway, I was looking for that box of files I asked the office to send."

"Yeah," Mullins said. "Hang on." There was a pause and Keith could hear muffled movement and the sound of a door closing. Then Mullins returned to the line. "I can't send anything like that out of the building. It's in the regulations. National Security. You understand."

"But we all work from home sometimes."

"Even when that happens no official materials are supposed to leave the building."

"But they do."

"That's not official policy," Mullins said.

"So where does that leave me?"

"I'm sorry, Keith. I just can't send you anything. I wish I could. Believe me." A lull and then Mullins added, "So is there anything else?"

Keith said nothing for a long moment. Then, simply: "I guess not."

"How's your time off?"

"It's fine," Keith said. "You know I have clearance."

"It's not the clearance. There's just no way I can do it."

"Maybe I could sign something."

"You're not hearing me on this."

"I'm hearing you but you don't understand."

"I do understand," Mullins said. "It's policy though so my hands are tied."

Keith had walked down the stairs during the conversation and had retrieved another beer from the refrigerator and was returning to the second floor now. He cracked open the can and paused on the landing and took a long drink.

"So you're doing OK?" Mullins said.

"Fine."

"Mind if I ask what you've been up to?"

"Do I mind? I don't know. I guess not." He was irritated but his tone was flat and even and Mullins did not respond. "I've been trying to get my house ready to sell. That's what I've been doing."

"That's working for you?"

"It's working fine." Keith said. "So how long am I out?"

"What do you mean?"

"On vacation. Or leave. Or whatever it is."

"I guess that's something you should decide."

"So I can come back to the office anytime?"

"I wouldn't say that exactly."

"What would you say then?"

Mullins exhaled. "You need to take a little time and take care of yourself," he said.

"I've taken a week."

"Look, Corcoran, I'm just not sure you're ready to come back yet. The thing that happened . . . I just . . ." He trailed off, then added: "Look, a week doesn't seem like very long."

"Why not?"

"We've been through this already, haven't we?"

"I don't think so," Keith said.

"Well," Mullins said, "I don't know what you want me to say here." He sighed audibly. "I checked the logs, Keith. You did eighty-four hours the last week you were here. Seventy-nine the week before. Almost ninety the week before that. Do you want me to go on here?"

"Yes, I want you to go on."

Keith could hear Mullins's breath through the phone. The rhythm of it was like a circle.

"Look," Mullins said at last, "when one of my astronauts is working himself to death that's a problem I need to deal with."

"I'm not working myself to death."

"Look, Keith, you've gone through a significant trauma and I'd be lying if I told you I was following some kind of protocol here. There's no protocol for this. The loss of a child—that alone is significant—but with you up on the ISS . . ." Again his voice trailed off. Then he said, "Look, I'm trying to help."

"Crap," Keith said. There were more words he wanted to say but he would not say them. Instead he said, "This is . . . ," and then paused and then said, finally, "This is a crappy deal."

"I'm sorry you feel that way, Captain," Mullins said.

"So am I."

"What does the flight surgeon say?"

"Don't you know?"

"Why would I know?"

"She doesn't say anything other than that she doesn't know what's wrong with me."

Silence on the line.

"What if she gives me a clean bill of health?" Keith said.

"We'll cross that bridge when we get to it. The first step is you take some time off. That's true of any mission, not just this one. After that we'll talk about your flight status."

"My flight status?"

"Well, yeah, of course."

He said nothing. He had been walking through the upstairs slowly during the conversation, looking at the walls he had yet to paint, looping into and out of the various rooms, sipping at the beer as he did so, and now found himself in the bedroom that had been Quinn's, in that room at last, and he stood and stared out the window to the street below. He could see to the end of the cul-de-sac but no farther. Nothing past the chain that divided the sidewalk from the vacant lot.

"You know you're important around here," Mullins said. "You must know that."

Again, Keith did not respond.

"Take some time to take care of yourself," Mullins said. "Go see a national park or something."

"Yeah," he said, "I'll do that." He breathed. No movement out there in the night. He was angry and he knew that his tone likely reflected that anger but he could not change that now.

"Call me when you know what you're doing," Mullins said.

"I don't even know what you're asking me."

"I'm asking you to keep me informed."

"OK," Keith said.

"Take care."

He did not answer, instead clicking the phone closed and standing in the empty room for a long moment. After a time he leaned his back against the wall and let gravity pull him to the floor. His eyes closed. He pressed his fingertips against them.

The room around him was a gray and silent cube. He had not entered it a single time since he had returned from the mission. Not once. And now that he was within its walls, he realized that it was likely he had never actually stood in the room at all, instead hovering in the doorway during their conversations, Quinn herself answering from within. This room, he reminded himself. This room: the same space in which she had spent some small portion of her life and which was now an empty gray cube of intersecting planes. What significance could such a location have if only to symbolize the absence of those who had departed? He could recall the words he had said and the way she had peered up at him. But how could that matter now?

The sum total felt as if some part of him had crumbled or rather had simply ceased to be, the indomitable engine of his ever-forward motion blinking out all at once and his longing for that box of files from his office in Houston appeared to him now exactly as it actually was: an absurd and pointless clinging to an image of himself that already did not exist. They thought of him as damaged, had ordered him out of Houston, out of his office. He had lost his flight status and might never regain it. But then perhaps he still did not fully accept it for what it was, sitting with his back against a gray wall in a room that he knew had been Quinn's room but which was also not Quinn's room, which was no one's room and thinking, of all things, not of Quinn but of his job. My god.

He was an engineer and a mathematician and he had done everything they had asked of him and more because that was who he was and he knew that his experiences during the mission had been unique and so he would be studied and tested and tabulated and recorded. He understood that and had expected it to be so and so it was. He had endured. And when he returned to Earth he had continued to endure the only way he had ever known, which was to work because work was how he had accomplished everything and after the mission that work had come to feel like the only tether still capable of tying him to some semblance of normalcy and was therefore the only tangible method of continuing his ever-forward motion.

Hoffmann had asked him repeatedly about Quinn and about his disintegrated marriage, but he had little to say about these subjects. It was as if he had remained in space or rather that Quinn and, to a lesser extent, Barb were separated from him by the atmosphere itself and he could not reach them and therefore he need not think of them in any way that breached the miles between orbit and Earth. Something had changed during those last months in space after Eriksson had told him of Quinn's death; between the migraines and the medication, whatever idea of grief there had been congealed into a glaucous and impenetrable distance, his mind turning or trying to turn back toward the ratiocinative, the discursive, the direction from which he had always found his way forward.

At first it must have been the pain that had caused them to question his ongoing ability to function as an astronaut. The migraines had certainly affected him during the mission; there was no denying that fact. But when the crew returned to Earth, the pain did not come with him. At least that was what he had thought. Then, during the fourth week in gravity, he had had his first earthbound episode. It had begun in the late morning during his physical therapy session in the pool. He had just completed a fifty-yard lap, clocking in just at the minute mark, and the trainer was congratulating him on his progress. But he was not listening. Instead, he could hear the whining sound deep in his skull and then the dull thrumming in the center of his brain. Dr. Yasbek had told him to immediately notify her if another migraine was coming on and so he clambered out of the pool and told their trainer that the flight surgeon needed him. He could sense the rest of them watching from the water as he grabbed his towel and his robe and walked back to the locker room and changed, his heart beating in his chest, on the verge of panic. He slipped into his shoes and returned to his room and dialed Dr. Yasbek's office. There was no answer. He left a stammering message and lay back on the bed and then rose again and closed the blinds. And so it began.

He knew at least that the pain would be extraordinary but that it would end. The previous episodes had taught him that much. And here he would be able to vomit into a toilet that actually flushed, an improvement over vomiting in the microgravity where escaped droplets would float trembling in the air before him like tiny burnt-orange planets both pearlescent and grotesque. After three hours in his room, trembling and sweating and yes even weeping under the blankets in the darkness, he did indeed vomit into the toilet in his quarters and, as was always the case, the pain began to dissipate soon afterward. He thought Eriksson might have visited him at some point but then those hours had been reduced to a kind of weird blur of ghosts and motion and the zigzagging lines that obscured and overlaid everything with an erratic violence that could not be avoided no matter how tightly he closed his eyes. He thought too that he had spoken to Quinn in that bloodred agony, as if she had somehow reached him through the conduit of his pain.

The feeling that she had sat at his bedside during the night was slow to dissipate and the following day he was in his office again with that feeling still clinging to him, as if her ghost was seated across from him, staring at him bleakly throughout the day and in response he did the only thing he could think to do, which was to pour himself into his work like a man jumping into a dark sea.

Mullins visited him in the early afternoon: an official or unofficial check-in, he did not know which. Yes, he was feeling much better. Thank you. Yes, he would talk to Yasbek later in the day. Yes, he would be able to complete his physical rehabilitation appointment. Everything was fine. No need to worry. Everything was fine.

There were still two weeks of physical therapy as their trainer and NASA medical personnel worked to bring their gravity-weak bodies back to their pre-mission selves. Most of his fellow crew members came in for the appointments and then went home to be with their families. Occasionally he would see Tim Fisher or Petra staying an hour or two to look at the medical data but that was all. But Keith was different. He would return to his office after showering and would sit at his desk and work and rework his equations. Hours would pass without notice. And he hardly thought of Quinn, her face swimming out of the darkness only in those last few minutes before he drifted off to sleep. Barb's nightly phone calls upon his return to Houston had not served to alter the anesthetized quality of his days and nights. She had even asked him to put the house on the market when and if he returned, as if her request served to underscore the finality of their dissolved marriage, and he had agreed. And of the conversation he had had with Quinn, the final argument: he had managed to will himself into a steady forgetfulness that was akin to ignorance. It had never happened so there could be no guilt and so he did not think of it at all.

The night they were released from the physical rehabilitation program, the crew went to a local bar to celebrate. All of them were taking brief vacations with their families, all returning home. There had been a time when Keith too might have voiced similar anticipation but that time now felt distant and alien to him. They all knew that his wife had left him, that she had told him she was not returning to the house, that her own "vacation" to her mother's home in Georgia was not a vacation but something else entirely.

At the celebratory beer-drinking, Eriksson took him aside and invited him to stay with him and his family near Houston, told Keith that they had room and would be glad to have him. The offer was so unexpected that Keith was rendered silent. But then he told Eriksson that he would be fine, that he appreciated it but he would be fine. Eriksson slapped him on the back and told him that he thought he would say that but that he was serious and the offer was there.

It occurred to him now that some part of him must have already known, that Eriksson's words must have resonated in him somewhere so that he could feel the ending of it, the crew in its last moments of being a crew, an understanding that this might be the only crew he would ever be a part of.

They returned to their corner table and toasted everything they could think of: the ISS itself, the shuttle, the ground crew in general, the ground crew by name, their replacement crew, the CAPCOM, NASA, their waitress, the bartender, the bar itself, the city, the country. The beer became tequila and whiskey and the evening blurred and blurred and blurred.

When they left the bar, he embraced each of them in turn and they disappeared into their separate worlds and he drove his weaving car back to JSC, returning to his office and sitting again at his desk. If he was aware at all that his crew members had come to feel responsible for him, it was not a conscious awareness, although now, sitting on the floor of Quinn's empty room in the cul-de-sac, the fact seemed obvious. They thought he was coming off the rails. Perhaps they were correct.

But there was no such self-awareness then, only the desire to return to his office and continue the work he had already started, if only for an hour or two as a way to clear his head before returning to the crew quarters and sleep. The multiple pitchers of beer and various shots of tequila and whiskey had thinned him at the edges and there was a sense of confusion in his thoughts, a shaking or trembling amidst the field of logic he had constructed or reconstructed. He thought again of being at the end of the robotic arm and what he felt was a strange and inexplicable feeling of panic, as if his boots had broken loose of the foot restraint and his body was adrift in the infinite reaches of space. The panic was the same when he recalled the vague half memory of Quinn somehow visiting him during his migraine weeks before. The whole of his thoughts had come to reflect a reality he did not want to acknowledge, a reality wherein he might shatter all at once into the brittle unannealed shards of a grief he had managed so effectively to avoid.

And so he had returned to his office. He had discovered a problem in the calculation of the orbit paths, a problem in the system itself, and had set himself to repairing that problem, to writing a better equation and a better program and he sat down at his desk again to continue that work and thought momentarily of the offer Eriksson had made, and then realized he was weeping, alone in his office, his crew members all around him fading like nebulae, their various colors offgassing into the darkness. The chair across from his desk remained empty.

When he woke in the morning it was to a voice: "Captain Corcoran. Hey, Keith, time to wake up." It was Jim Mullins. Of course it was. Mullins who closed the door and then sat across from him, the desk between them with its scattered papers and wet patch of drool. Mullins who explained to him that the office was concerned about his behavior, that he was working too much, that it was time to take some days off.

"It's not appropriate," Mullins had told him and when Keith had asked what that meant Mullins had said, "Appropriate for the grieving process." He called it PTSD, actually used that term, as if he was a war veteran of some kind, although even Keith knew that the operative initial was for trauma, that they saw him as being a victim of a trauma. What he could not understand was how they failed to see how much work he was getting done. Why did they not see that? Why had they decided that they would be better off without him?

And he had told Mullins, point-blank, that he did not want to leave and what had Mullins said in return? That he would be willing to make it official by putting Keith on some kind of medical leave. That Keith needed time to grieve. As if Mullins somehow knew what he needed.

So it had gone. He had packed up his personal items from the crew quarters the next day and NASA arranged a flight to take him home.

No voice-mail messages and like a fool he had continued to dial in every day, as if someone would call him with a question or a project. Some equation that could not be solved. Some engineering issue that needed his particular expertise. Eriksson had only called twice and his offer to let Keith stay with him and his family seemed a weird joke now. What could he hope to accomplish by offering such a thing?

He rose from his seat on the floor then, the beer can empty, and stood at the window. His headache was becoming increasingly impossible to ignore and his body felt heavy, so very heavy, the emptiness around him palpable, as if the air had solidified and he had become locked within it like an insect caught forever in a droplet of amber, the empty house a vacuum sucking everything he ever thought he knew into the black of space. Dark matter. The curvature of light. His empty house. His daughter gone and never to return. His absent wife. And his apparently failed career. How does one work for so many years to become an astronaut and have it be like this?

He walked back down the hall to the master bathroom and opened the medicine cabinet there and retrieved the little bottle of pain pills and the blister packs of Imitrex and swallowed the tablets with a handful of water. Then he showered and put on his bathrobe, returning to the bed and propping the single pillow against the headboard and reclining there with his finger on the remote control. The images on the television were of faces and bodies in motion, their expressions like false mirrors. They thought he had lost it somehow. He could not imagine how any of this could be true and yet his phone had been silent. Voice mail empty. E-mail in-box empty save for human resources circulars regarding open enrollment for health insurance.

After a few moments he rose and retrieved another beer from the refrigerator downstairs even though he knew he was already well on his way to being drunk, and opened it as he returned to the bedroom, stepping past the dropcloth he had left in the stairwell. Then a heavy slump onto the bed. He clicked the television remote again. Talking faces and gesturing bodies and occasional cartoon figures and commercials. How many times had he flashed through the stations in their endless loop already? Twice? Three times?

Drive-by shootings in towns he had never heard of. The usual economic terror. Foreclosures everywhere. Apparently the entire country was suddenly unemployed. A small plane crashing into the freeway. There were forests somewhere according to the news, but they were all aflame. Where were these places? And floods somewhere else. A kind of biblical mayhem then. The earthbound comet again.

Inexplicably, he thought of his neighbor, Jennifer, who was probably across the street even now, and actually felt himself rise to the thought of her. He went through the channels once more, hoping in some distant part of himself that there might be some adult channel somewhere that he had missed but he found nothing and after an additional trip through the stations he dropped the remote to the bed again and then tried to adjust the pillow behind him but nothing he could do was particularly comfortable. The giant sofa remained downstairs, a piece of furniture he hated and had not wanted to buy but which now felt like a beacon. There had been a huge flat-screen television in the corner across from it at one point, another purchase Barb had made, but of course that was gone with everything else. It occurred to him that he could certainly move this television downstairs, a prospect that immediately seemed a logical solution to the current problem of his aching body and mind and his general state of anger and boredom and frustration.

In some other moment than this he might have thought the action through, or least might have considered it more carefully than he did now but this was not such a moment. Instead he downed the remainder of the beer and rose from the bed, his head fuzzy from the mixture of painkillers and alcohol, and shifted the armoire away from the wall with some effort and unplugged the television and the cable jack and then stepped back and wrapped his arms around the television itself and lifted it. Like the armoire itself, the television was much heavier than it looked and the smooth angles made for tentative purchase. He jogged it in his hands for a better grip, his mind aching from the effort, and then started for the doorway leading to the hall and then the stairs, his bathrobe flapping at his calves as he moved. Who did they think he was? Who the hell did they think he was? He banged the corner of the television against the wall, staggered back a step and shifted his hands for a better grip. "Crap," he said aloud.

He managed the first run of stairs to the landing and momentarily leaned the corner of the television against the wall, using the angle to reposition his hands again, the box square but with smoothed angles and rounded corners so there was little to hold with any confidence. Then he leaned away from the wall and turned and began to step forward again, his back aching and his arms already like rubber.

Had he been less exhausted or more sober he might have remembered the dropcloth that remained in the stairwell. But of course that was not the case. When his feet went out from under him he reacted with self-preservation, pushing the heavy object in his hands away from him with explosive force as his body dropped all at once to a sitting position, the impact driving sharp needles of pain through the back of his skull. And there he sat, watching, as if in slow motion, as the television rocketed end-over-end down the remainder of the stairs, his arms remaining outstretched in front of him as if he could somehow will the flying plastic and glass box back into his grip. But then it was already over, the television slamming into the far wall between the entryway and the living room and knocking a triangular hole through the freshly painted drywall with a resounding crack.

He sat midway down the stairs as if that had been his intent all along, his vision already clear and the shock of pain subsiding into the fuzz that was his drunken mind. Crap. Crap crap crap. He closed his eyes and took one long breath. Then he opened them again and rose to his feet and kicked the dropcloth out of the way, descending to the television and shifting it out of the hole it had made in the wall. Tufts of pink insulation. Something else to repair and repaint. Fantastic. But surprisingly the television itself looked intact. He twisted it slightly so that it was propped up on one corner, shifting it into his grip and closing his eyes for a moment before rising to his feet with a loud grunt, the television cradled awkwardly in his arms. Every thought he had left was focused on lying down on the sofa and closing his eyes.

He entered the living room and managed to set the television in the empty space once occupied by the big flat-screen. There was no stand of any kind in the corner and the small television looked pathetic there on the carpet, the enormous gray leather sofa facing it as if the black box was something of grand importance.

At first nothing happened when he plugged it in and pressed the power button. Then, from somewhere far inside, a hissing and popping followed by the faint smell of burning plastic. He jerked the power cable out of the wall and sat there in front of the television on the floor as the whole house rocked woozily around him. The gray sofa lay in silence in the center of the room, a sofa he had told Barb he disliked when they first saw it at the furniture store but which she had purchased anyway after he had returned to Houston for more training. Now it was one of the few items she had left behind, a lumbering whale that had beached there in a room lined with blue masking tape and stinking of paint. The scene was enough to make him wonder why he had chosen to bring the television downstairs at all.

"Goddammit," he said aloud. Then he said it again, loudly and drawn into a kind of angry howl, "Goddammit!"

He returned to the front door and opened it and stepped outside into the night, wheeling the big garbage bin from the side of the house to the front door and returning to retrieve the television. The pain in his mind was constant now despite the Vicodin and beer, as if his slip on the stairs had broken a glass jar inside his skull and the pieces were now free to rattle and scrape the raw red tissue there. He staggered outside with the set, attempting first to heave it into the open garbage container, but the television was simply too large to do much more than sit on the top and so he lifted it again and shuffled out toward the curb, the whole box slipping repeatedly in his grasp.

He might have thrown it against the concrete. There was certainly that urge. The screen would shatter. The sound of it would reverberate through the streets and houses and the vacant lot. But someone was moving down the street toward him and so he knelt and awkwardly lowered the box to the sidewalk, panting, his arms weak and his hands numb from the effort. For a brief moment he tried to stand but instead sat on the television itself, trying to catch his breath, his bathrobe slumping over him like a burial shroud.

The figure had been walking toward the end of the cul-de-sac and it stopped now. "That work?" A man's voice.

Keith looked up. The face was mostly obscured in shadow. "No," he said. Then he added, "I just dropped it down the stairs."

"Maybe they can fix?" the man said.

There was a trace of an accent and the man's face looked vaguely familiar, although Keith could not place it. "I doubt it," Keith said. Then he added, "Have we met?"

The man looked at him and his white teeth shone in a broad grin. "You are famous astronaut Keith Corcoran," he said. "I meet you at Starbucks."

"Starbucks?" Keith said. There was a moment of silence and then he realized that it was the loud Ukrainian man. Fantastic.

"Peter Kovalenko," the man said. He extended his hand and Keith took it and said his own name but did not rise, noticing for the first time what the man was carrying. It was a white telescope, a relatively large one with its tripod gripped under the man's left arm and the telescope itself riding up across his shoulder and pointing skyward above his head.

"Yes, I know this," Peter said, still smiling. "You live here?"

He thought briefly of telling a lie or at least a half-truth but instead he merely gestured vaguely behind him toward the empty house. "Yeah, here," he said. He tried to relax his wrinkled brow and his tight, squinting eyes in the cool night air but it was difficult to do so.

"Amazing. We are neighbors, then," Peter said. "My wife and the children are there." He gestured similarly over his shoulder toward the main road that led, eventually, out of the cul-de-sac maze. "Very exciting. My neighbor is famous astronaut."

Keith nodded. "Very exciting," he said. It was quiet then but for the crickets and the constant hiss of distant freeway traffic. The sidewalk seemed to drift beneath him. So slowly.

"You are between space missions maybe?" Peter said.

"I don't know."

"You don't know? What is meaning?"

Keith looked up at him. "It means I don't know," he said.

Peter looked back but said nothing. The smile did not falter. After a moment he said, "Less light here." He gestured down the street to the end of the cul-de-sac and the empty lot that lay now in blue-black darkness. Keith did not answer. "For telescope," Peter said after a time.

Keith nodded. He had caught his breath but still did not stand. Gravity seemed tilted slightly. How many beers had he consumed? He could not recall. Everything felt distant. The feeling was exactly the opposite of being in the microgravity orbit of the space station and he wished more than ever before that he was back there, right now. In the illogic of his current state he imagined pushing himself through the air and back inside, back into his bed.

"Maybe they can fix," Peter said, gesturing at the television.

"No," Keith said. "I dropped it down the stairs. It's history."

"Too bad."

Again, a pause in the conversation, this one long enough to feel awkward and Keith was just ready to stand and return to the house when Peter said, "I'm pleased to meet famous astronaut."

"Thanks," Keith said, and there was bitterness in his voice that he could not disguise. "Good to meet you too."

Peter smiled broadly. "Famous astronaut is my neighbor. I am lucky man," he said.

"Look, I'm sorry," Keith said abruptly. "I'm beat."

"Of course," Peter said. He extended his hand and Keith shook it again as he tried to stand. He stumbled a bit and Peter put a hand on his upper arm to steady him as he rose to his feet.

"OK," Keith said. "I'm OK."

"Yes, yes," Peter said.

"I'm going in," Keith said but he made no move toward his door.

After a long moment Peter said, "I am glad to meet you." There was a quizzical, puzzled look on his face. "Good night," he said. "Sorry about this television."

"Yeah, thanks," Keith said. He thought he should have probably taken the opportunity to tell him then that he was not an astronaut, that he had only been joking, but he would not do so, not even now. It was true and that meant it was true for everyone and that included this man and Jim Mullins and Eriksson and everyone. He was an astronaut. Fact.

"Good night to you," Peter said. He did a little bow and Keith nodded and then Peter swiveled slightly on his heel and moved past him and into the darkness of the field beyond. There was a chain across the entrance—assumedly to keep people from driving into the field—

and Keith watched Peter step over it and stump off into the night darkness. Keith found himself wondering if whatever that great dark bird had been feeding on was still present in the field. Some desiccated tangle of bone and sinew.

For a long time he was still and alone. Again he felt like lifting the television and smashing it to the concrete. But instead he turned woozily toward the empty house and opened the door and stepped into the dull flat light of the drifting entryway.

Interval: Time

$$(c\Delta t)^2 > (\Delta r)^2$$
$$(\Delta s)^2 < 0$$

SHE WAS ATOP the slide, smiling, the other children swarming the playground equipment around her, periodically peeling away to charge across the grass and asphalt to their waiting parents. Keith stood amongst them but he did not call out her name, not yet, instead standing and watching her as she shot down the polished metal slide and turned, trailed by two or three other children, apparently her friends, and clambered to the top once again, sliding down, then giving up on the slide altogether to begin running around the playground equipment. The children were playing tag or something like it, and he could hear the high-pitched screeches and laughter even from across the grass and asphalt, all the way to the edge of the parking lot. His daughter's laughter. The laughter of her second-grade friends. And yet each time she moved too far away from them or they from her he could feel his heart seize in his chest, the moment in which she was alone there on the playground stretching out before him, time no arrow but a wobbling series of loops like yarn sprung loose of its bundle. But the children she was playing with returned to her again and again, and even as one and then two of them were called away by their parents, they would be replaced by others and he came to realize that she was not joining their game, that they were joining hers, that she was the center of their play, an idea that he found so surprising and which he embraced with a sense of relief that very nearly brought him to tears.

She did not see him until there were no longer enough children remaining for the game to keep going. It was only then that she glanced toward the parking lot and saw him there, the other parents mostly gone now, a few continuing to arrive.

She waved toward the playground, one or two children return-ing the gesture, and then sprinted up the hill toward him, her face a bright smile and her tiny backpack flapping behind her like a weird single wing.

"Hi, Daddy," she said when she had arrived at his side.

"Quinny Quinn Quinn," he said.

"Where's Mom?"

"She had to go out so I told her I'd pick you up."

"Where'd she go?"

"Grandpa's sick so she went to see him."

"Sick how?"

"He has cancer."

"What's that mean?"

"It means he's really sick," he said. He was looking at her, at her tiny self, her tiny being. "Do you have all your stuff?"

"Yeah, let's go," she said.

"OK, bossy pants," he said.

In the car, she asked him again how sick her grandfather was and he told her, bluntly and without preamble, that it was likely he would die. He had not even speculated what her response would be because he had not thought his way through the conversation they would

have. Barb's father had already gone through a full cycle of chemo-
therapy treatments the previous year, but two months ago it had
been revealed that the cancer had returned and had spread throughout his body. He had deteriorated rapidly, and when Barb's mother
had called to tell her daughter that her father was in hospice she had
booked the first available flight and called Keith at work to tell him
that it was time. He bundled a thick sheaf of papers into his bookbag
and returned home in time to drive her to the airport. She had not
spoken in the car, clutching his hand and staring forward out the
windshield, and when they arrived at the airport she did not release
her grip for some minutes, continuing to stare straight ahead as
various travelers crossed and recrossed the walkway before them.
He did not say anything to her then, turning from her face to the
windshield and there they remained until at last she broke the silence by telling him that she had left a list with Quinn's schedule
and that there were some things in the freezer he could reheat for
dinners. He told her he would be fine. She would call him from
Atlanta when she knew more. He told her he loved her and she did
the same.

"So Mommy's with Grandma and Grandpa?" Quinn asked him.

"Yes," he said. He looked at her in the backseat. He could not read
any emotional response there at all.

"Is Grandma OK?" she said.

"Yeah, Grandma's fine."

"OK," Quinn said. "When's Mommy coming home?"

"I don't know. It might be a couple of days. Might be longer than
that. She's making sure Grandpa's OK."

"But Grandpa's going to die?"

"Yes, he's going to die."

"Then how is she going to make him OK?"

"She just wants to be there with him. To make him feel better."

"But he's still going to die," Quinn said. It was not a question.

"Yes," he said. "He's still going to die."

She did not speak for a few moments. Then she said, "Could you turn the radio on?"

"Sure can," he said.

He did so. When he looked at her again, at that part of her he could see in the rearview mirror, she displayed no emotion whatsoever. He knew already that Barb would likely be irritated with him for telling Quinn the truth of what was happening or at least for telling her on his own without Barb at his side, but Quinn had asked him and he had answered and as far as he could tell she was handling it well enough.

"When's Mommy coming home?" she said again.

"I don't know exactly," he said, turning the radio down. "Maybe a couple of days. Maybe a little longer than that."

"I want her to come home."

"She will."

"I want her to come home now," she said.

He looked at her in the rearview mirror. She continued to stare out the window. "We can call her tonight," he said.

"OK," she said. She did not look at him.

Her face held in profile within the rectangle of the mirror. Around that reflection unscrolled the world: an endless flow of cars on the southbound interstate, full neighborhoods lined with trees, distant farm fields just rolling into spring.

The night went better than he thought it would. He knew Barb had been called in to the elementary school on several occasions over the previous year for what Quinn's teachers had come to call their daughter's "strong will," a behavior that amounted to an ongoing problem according to the school but which Keith had seen little of during his time at home. Nonetheless, he knew it was not something Barb or Quinn's teachers had invented. His daughter was, if nothing else, a little girl who expected to be treated like an adult, a facet of her personality that Keith was actually quite proud of but which Barb found annoying. And indeed he had to admit that, when Quinn asserted herself, her personality—her strong will—was more than either of them knew what to do with. If she decided she did not want to do what she had been told to do, she simply would not do it. She would throw no tantrums; she would simply refuse to do what was asked unless it was her will to comply.

So he had been concerned that Quinn might be difficult that first evening but in actual fact she gave him no trouble, perhaps because he did not ask her to do anything she did not want to do. He was aware that he was not really parenting her but he simply did not see the need to adhere to the house rules Barb had set down for their daughter. Not now. He bathed her later than she was usually bathed and dressed her in pajamas and they sat on the couch for half an hour—this already an hour past her bedtime—and watched a cartoon about an animal Keith could not identify.

"That's dumb," Quinn said at some point during the program.

"What is?" he asked. He was not even really looking at the screen at all, instead was thinking of the project he had been working on the day before in his office, wondering how much of it he could complete tonight given the materials he had returned home with. Had he remembered the last set of drawings from drafting? He was not sure.

"Four isn't even that color really. It's kinda more like red."

He felt his chest tighten. He had not been paying attention to the screen but he certainly was now. Had there been a number? He thought so. The number four. An orange number four. "What do you mean?" he said.

"They didn't do the colors right," she said. "Four is red. Everybody knows that. Now it's gonna be mad."

"Because it's the wrong color?"

"Yeah," she said.

He might have scolded her for her tone but he was not attentive to such things now. Instead he felt a turning inside of him, a kind of excitement.

"The four was orange but it's not really orange. It's supposed to be red. It would be really mad if it was orange."

"It's irritated because it's the wrong color?"

"Yeah, because it's supposed to be more like red."

He paused and then said, "Red or more like brownish red?"

"Yeah, a little like brownish red."

"But not orange."

"No way José, not orange."

The television continued its sounds. He was staring at the screen now, not looking at her, the sense of what she had said flooding through him all at once.

"What about nine?" he asked.

"Yellow."

"Two?"

"Blue two. It rhymes."

"Three?"

"Kind like blue and green together. Like water."

"Four?"

"Jeez, are you gonna ask me all of them?"

He was quiet for a long moment. Then he said, "Probably." But he already knew all the answers she could possibly give. The colors all the same. The colors exactly the same as his own.

This was how it would start. He knew that now, in the house in the cul-de-sac, his hands ever-flecked with paint. He knew that this had been the moment to dictate everything to come after. But he also knew—had already known—that Quinn was similar to him in some essential way, Barb even making that a household joke, laughing when their daughter's responses were so blunt and direct, without preamble or thought or concern. "She's just like you," Barb would say to him.

"Exactly." He would merely shrug in response and Quinn would peer back at them both, exasperated, as if she knew there was some kind of joke between her parents but she would not deign to acknowledge it. But he knew it was true. Even as a very young child she had displayed a sense of logic and analytic skill. It was the same language Keith spoke, not the language of numbers—that would come later—but rather a language of simplicity and directness. Perhaps it would have been the same with any child, that his own tendency to speak with blunt efficiency, to cut right to the point, mirrored the way children communicated. But then this was not any child; this was his own and she was so much like him that it sometimes felt as if, finally, he had found someone he could communicate with who gave no quarter to pretense or confusion.

She shared, as well, his ability to focus on whatever task was at hand, silently and efficiently. When she had been four or five it had been building elaborate structures with Lego blocks. Much later, it would be her homework. Sometimes, in the years to follow, he would stand in the doorway to her room and watch her at work, her back to the door, and if he was quiet enough he could watch her there for a long time, her silence, the intensity of her progress. It reminded him of being alone in his office with his pencil and calculator and his numbers and with no one to disturb him. He could think of no place on Earth, no situation he enjoyed more. The only questions that existed in that room were ones he directed himself and all such questions, no matter how complicated, could be answered and in this too, he imagined, she was like him.

In the weeks following Barb's father's death, he had already decided that the numbers would provide a trajectory for her, a way for her to move forward, not just ahead of her peers but away from them because she had the gift. She shared the same secret and inviolable sense of numbers that he did, their personalities and their colors immutable. At first he had been too surprised—shocked, even—to think of anything beyond the moment they were in because what she had said in passing, casually, in front of the television, was something he had thought private: that the numbers themselves held within them a sense of relationship. He had known this as early as the second grade, when he had told the class that three did not like seven and that seven and eight only got along when they were seventy-eight and otherwise did not want to be neighbors at all, that this was clear from their colors alone. The other students had laughed at him and the teacher praised him faintly for his overactive imagination and Keith stared back at them, dumbfounded, his eyes not tearing up but rather only opening wide to mark his sense of incredulous confusion. What he had told them was fact, something he understood as intimately as he knew his own mother and father, perhaps even more so. He did not understand the reaction the other students had toward him. He did not understand it at all.

By the time he reached junior high school, he had learned that he had an ability that his peers lacked, for the numeric relationships he intuitively understood had made the numbers akin to friends. But perhaps even more than that, in the burning and disconsolate sexuality of his young self the numbers provided a sense of intimacy. He would not have identified it as sexual—in fact would have denied this with a vehemence fraught with embarrassment—but there was no other word to describe the clear and secret detail in which he knew and understood them. The numbers and symbols and functions were beings unto themselves and while they were often represented as stark and concrete and unchangeable forms in textbooks and on chalkboards, he never saw them that way. Even as a child, he could see them the way he believed they actually were: as part of the three-dimensional space in which they existed as genuine and independent objects that were not alive and yet were possessed of all the manifest and unmistakable indicators of that state of being, of life itself. He could see the relationships between them and could hold those individual relationships in his mind, as if they had become physical structures which floated within an infinite empty container, and he could zoom into or out of those structures as if possessed of some enormous and all-encompassing lens. Entire equations could be worked out that way: solved a piece at a time by developing the relationships between sections, for in the end they were not even equations but rather collections of personalities that could be classified and understood the way one might understand the structure of a family: in conflict or harmony or some state between and their solutions the logical endpoint of those relationships.

The strength of that feeling faded with time, replaced later with a simpler and no less profound sense of familiarity. He did not think of them as having personalities now, although he could still see their colors. Instead, what he had felt about them as a child had given way to the sense that they were actively functional and representational. And yet even now he could feel them slotting into their locations with grace, perhaps even with longing, because they needed to complete their tasks. He had learned that much from them. He owed them that much. That was why he had chosen to become an astronaut, had worked toward that singular goal for so many years, because he owed the numbers for everything he was and anything less than pushing the practical limits of human knowledge would have been a betrayal of that trust. He never could have put this obligation into words and, if pressed, likely would have denied that any obligation existed at all and yet it was there nonetheless, a kind of counterweight to balance those things he would never understand. That was his gift and it was his obligation.

Even so many years later when he was alone in the empty house in the weeks and months after Barb had left him and Quinn had gone into the ground, after everything he had come to think of as having permanence had disappeared from his grasp, did the numbers not remain? In the chaos of everything that had come, did they not remain his constant companions even in the endless gloaming of his days in the cul-de-sac? The numbers were clear and precise and when he aligned them they told the truth, always, without question or innuendo and that truth had provided a path for him to follow. He had thought that

Quinn could follow much the same path. That she could be like he was. That she could be just like he was.

He called Barb right before Quinn went to bed and they spoke briefly and then he handed the phone to Quinn and said, "Tell Mommy good night," and instead Quinn said, "Daddy says Grandpa is going to die." Again he told her to say good night and this time she did so. He took the phone back without comment and said, "We miss you."

"What in god's name did you tell her?" she said.

"I told her the truth," he said, and when she did not respond he said, "I thought she needed to know what was going on. She misses you."

"I miss her too," she said. "I miss you both."

"We can come out there," he said. "If you need us to."

"There's no reason to do that. It'll just upset Quinn."

"She can handle it," he said.

She did not respond. In the silence, he wanted to somehow tell her that he had learned something about their daughter, that she had a gift, but he could think no way to express that now. He could find no words.

They talked for a few minutes longer and then he said good-bye and hung up the phone and looked to Quinn. "You know, that's not a nice thing to say," he said to her.

Quinn was seated on the bed in her pajamas. "What isn't?" she said.

"Telling Mommy that I said Grandpa's going to die."

"But he is going to die."

"She already knows that."

"But she didn't know that I know that."

"That's true," he said. Then: "It's time for bed."

"Can we watch another show?"

"No."

She was looking at him as if getting ready to make another request but instead she simply said, "OK," and let him tuck her into bed and kiss her good night and when she lay there, at last under the covers, he said, "How long have you known that four was red?"

"Brownish red," she said.

"OK, brownish red, then. How long have you known?"

"It's always brownish red."

"Did you know that almost nobody can see that?"

"What do you mean?"

"Only special people can see the colors."

"Well, that doesn't seem fair," she said.

He smiled. "No, I guess not but it's true."

"If they don't have colors then what color are they?"

"Just black. Like words in a book."

"Oh," she said. "That seems dumb."

"Yes," he said, "yes, it does." He continued to look at her. "I can see the colors too," he said. "And I know they have feelings."

"Good," she said.

"I don't know anyone else who can," he said. "Just you and me."

"Really?"

"Really."

"Cool."

"Yeah, cool. You're going to do great things, Quinny."

"So are you, Dad," she said.

He smiled again. "Yes, I am," he said, still smiling. "You and me." He paused a moment and then said, "Good night."

"Good night, Daddy," she said.

He rose and turned the light off and closed the door halfway but he did not get much farther than the hallway because she immediately called him back with a loud, "Daddy!" and he turned and reopened the door and found her sitting up in bed with tears streaming down her cheeks.

"What's wrong?" he said. He had already crossed the room to take her in his arms and crush her body against his own. She said something

111

in response to his question, something choked through tears that he could not understand, so he asked her again and this time she said, more clearly, "I don't want Grandpa to die."

"Oh," he said, "I don't either."

"I can't stop thinking about it."

"I know."

"Can we go see him?"

"We can't do that now."

"Why not?"

"Because we can't."

She continued to weep against his chest and he held her until she grew quiet in that dark room. Until everything grew so very quiet. Until she had fallen asleep at last.

The following day was Friday and he thought he might need to keep her home from school but when he offered this as an option she looked at him quizzically and told him that she was not sick. When he told her that sometimes people just needed to stay home and rest even if they felt fine she told him that was a silly thing to say and that she needed to go to school. He thought that he should probably keep her home anyway, that Barb would have kept her home, but he had no real plan of what he would do with her for those hours of the day and so he helped her get ready and made her lunch based on Barb's care-fully worded instructions ("Mayo: Not too much!").

When they reached school she burst out of the car, very nearly be-fore it had altogether stopped. "Hey you," he called. "No kiss?"

She shook her head, exasperated, but came around to where he stood beside the driver's door and kissed him quickly and then yelled, "Bye, Dad!" over her shoulder and was gone down the sloping asphalt to the morning-wet grass and then to the playground. He returned to the driver's seat and sat watching the children through the window. Barb was the one who both delivered and picked up their daughter each day and as he sat there he felt a strange grip of terror in his chest that rendered him immobile even as other vehicles began to nose their way around his car. It did not seem possible to just leave her here, in the company of children he did not know and adults he could not even see except for one or two wandering the playground. Who were these people to care for his daughter?

And yet she seemed quite comfortable with the entire situation. Of course she would be. It was only her school, after all: the place she went each weekday from eight in the morning until half past one. Even now she was in such frenetic motion that it was difficult to follow her amid the forms of the other children. She had not hesitated at all. In fact she had spent most of the morning pushing him to hurry up.

"We have to go, Dad," she had told him.

"Mommy said you didn't have to be there until eight."

"That's when the bell rings," she had answered. "But I need to get there earlier."

"Why?"

"To play."

"Oh," he had said. "Then we'd better get going."

He could not remember when he had really set upon math the way he eventually did, as a serious academic subject, although he knew that by junior high school he was spending far more time on homework and studying than his peers and the proof was in his grades and the praise his teachers gave him. He knew that the other students looked at him as some kind of weird brainiac, a definition that he did not much mind and even took some pride in even if they used or tried to use it as a kind of taunt. When he was, on rare occasion, invited to some social event—a birthday party or a get-together at the local skating rink—he would most often turn them down. He did not tell his parents about these events. When his mother once found an invitation crumpled in the trash, he told her that going to the skating rink did not interest him. His response apparently did little to assuage her concern as she continued to believe his apparent lack of friends was something akin to a dysfunction. It might well have been one. "Where were you, Corcoran?" they would sometimes ask and he would have some excuse ready. He had a sick aunt he had to visit. He was out of town. He was too busy. Of course the question itself was a taunt, meant to underscore the simple fact that he was not and never would be one of them.

He told himself the same lie that he told his mother: that he was somehow beyond such childish gatherings, adding—this only to himself and not to her—that he did not want to be one of them, that they were crass and stupid and brutal. It was true that he preferred to remain home, working on engineering ideas, thinking about becoming an astronaut, already this a goal although not yet as concrete a goal as it would one day become. There were moments of loneliness, of course, at times so sharp and profound that he found it difficult to focus on anything else and even the numbers became a tedium, but the numbers always felt more comfortable than the roller-skating rink. The numbers were clear and beautiful and he understood them; the skating rink was endless circular motion with people he ultimately did not even like. It felt like an easy choice even though it was, at times, hardly as easy as he made it out to be.

"Sometimes you just have to put yourself out there, Keith," his mother told him. "I know it can be scary but it's good to be with people."

He would answer her only in clipped, short sentences, careful even then not to reveal too much, wanting only for her to exit his room so that he could return to whatever book or article he had been reading, his columns of figures, the angles and materials of imagined machines he fantasized about one day building. He knew that she was right, or at least partially right, and he might have studied it as if it were a mathematics problem of some kind, searching for a solution. But he did not do so. Instead he poured himself into the numbers. This was what he had always done and this was what he continued to do on into high school and through college.

And then he met Barb.

He had acquired a job in a mid-level engineering firm, his first real job, which would have been utterly forgettable had he not met his future wife there. She had been wrestling with the soda machine and he had offered some replacement change for that which the machine had just taken and then fished into his pocket to find he had no coins to give. In his experience, that alone might have been the end of the conversation but Barbara Anderson had found his monotone response to the crisis—"I don't have any change"—to be so funny that tears came to her eyes.

He did not understand her reaction but something about her stuck with him the rest of the day, and apparently stuck with her too because she found his desk at five o'clock and asked him to dinner. She was so beautiful; he could hardly believe his luck, but then there was also the sinking feeling that he had come to associate with virtually any experience that was not directly related to his work as an engineer. He would say the wrong thing or have the wrong response to something she said and that would be the awkward end to the evening.

But it had not turned out that way. "Sweetheart," she told him many years later, "you tried so hard to be charming and failed so miserably that it couldn't help but be charming. It's just simple mathematics. Two negatives make a positive, right?"

His response had been to launch into a discussion of signs and sign functions, for while her statement was in essence true there were, of course, exceptions and complications. She had stopped him before he was through with the first sentence. "This is exactly what I mean," she said, a thin smile on her face. "Best quit while you're ahead. I love you but you can be overcharming sometimes."

She asked him on the second or third date what his goals were and he told her, point-blank and without preamble. He planned on going to graduate school at MIT or perhaps Caltech or Stanford. He would earn his Ph.D. and then would take a commission in the Air Force, where he would do research and advance through the ranks. After four years or so he would take a position with NASA at Johnson Space Center with the ultimate goal of becoming an astronaut.

"You really have it all worked out," she had said in response.

"Yes, I do," he said.

"You think you can really do all that?"

"Yes."

"Really?"

"Really."

She was smiling but he was not and she held his gaze as her own smile faded. "Well, all right then," she said at last. He thought that he might have lost her at last, that the bluntness of his answer had finally been too much for her and that he had crossed over some invisible line. But then she nodded and said simply, "That's quite a plan," and leaned across the table to kiss him.

He wondered for a long time if she really understood that he was serious, that the plan was solid and that he could accomplish his goals because Barb seemed almost too good to be true. While they were dating she would sometimes bring him dinner when he worked late at the office and more than once they made love there on the desk or on the floor. In that way she seemed to understand that the goals he had set for himself took commitment and discipline. She was smart, too; not like he was but certainly capable enough to help him with the graduate school application process, his application for financial aid, and then, later, to take care of the day-to-day work of running the household, all of which freed him to focus on the larger goal of one day becoming an astronaut. And if she did not truly understand what numbers meant to him, that could be forgiven, for how could she possibly understand that?

.   .   .

There were so many tiny moments during those four days. He bought ice cream cones and they sat on a stone bench at the edge of the town's main square and ate them. He had hardly known that the town even had a main square but she seemed quite familiar with it, even directing him to the location of the ice cream parlor. They went to the park then and he pushed her on the swing for a long time in silence and when she was done they walked back to the car and she reached up and put her tiny hand into his and he held that small thing, warm and soft, and they said nothing. A flock of birds drifted out of a tree as if a single cloud—sparrows or starlings or something else—and she pointed to them, saying nothing. He likely could have calculated the individual points they made in the sky, their flight in elliptic curves as they spun and wobbled and then returned, for reasons known only to birds, to the same tree from which they had, only moments before, taken flight. He could have calculated all of it, but the thought did not even come to him then. As if some moments were beyond such a reckoning. As if some moments were beyond any reckoning at all.

In the evenings they ate reheated frozen dinners from their plastic compartmentalized trays and watched cartoons and silly comedies and movies featuring horses as prominent characters. Some of the horses talked. Some did not. He tried to talk to her further about the way she saw numbers but she was distracted by the television so her responses were all in fragments or she would forget to answer him entirely. What he learned was that she already could solve simple equations, even understood the function of a variable so that he could ask her to solve x plus four equals nine and she could answer five without apparent thought or effort.

"That was fast," he said.

"Easy."

"What do see when you're thinking of the answer?" he asked her.

"What do you mean?" she said. The purple horses on the television

117

screen were trailing rainbows now. Some of them were apparently singing.

"I mean, what do you see in your head?"

"Just numbers and stuff."

"Where? Like in space or in a room or on a sheet of paper?"

"Like in space," she said.

"Yeah, that's how I see math too. Like it's floating in space. Do the colors help?"

"Help what?"

"Help you solve the problem?"

"That's silly," she said. "The numbers all know where to go. It's easy-peasy."

"What do you mean? What do you mean they know where to go?"

"They just do. They just go where they're supposed to go. I can't make them go somewhere they don't want to go."

He stood behind her in the kitchen, watching the back of her head. It all sounded like something he had thought long ago but would never have said aloud. Even now he would never say such a thing although it was true; he knew it was true. She saw numbers exactly as he did. Exactly. My god. And without effort. Like a natural process of her own mind. He wondered if he had possessed so much confidence at her age and then decided that he had not.

Barb's father died on Monday. She called him in the late morning after he had dropped Quinn off at school and told him simply, "He's gone." He could hear the emotion in her voice, how close she was to weeping.

"I'm so sorry, Barb," he said.

"Yeah, well," she said. "At least he can breathe now."

She asked about Quinn and he told her what they had done together but she did not seem to be listening to his response and after a few minutes she said she had to go and help her mother with something. She told him she would call back when she had information about the service. Then the conversation was over.

It was quiet in the house. He could not think of a time when it had seemed so profoundly silent.

He had been in his final year at Princeton when his own father had passed. He had worked for an insurance agency as a middle manager and had suffered a heart attack at home while dozing on the couch in front of the television. That was what his mother had told him. "Honey, I'm afraid I have some bad news," she had said. "Your father had a heart attack. He's dead, honey. I'm sorry." The shock of the announcement sent him staggering backwards to his dorm room bed where he sat upon its edge trying to figure out a way not to believe the news. It was not that he had been particularly close to his father but still the man had been a constant presence in his life and now he was gone. Keith returned home for the funeral, standing by his mother at the gravesite and staring bleakly at the empty hole and the polished box that would ferry his father into the dirt. That night he sat in the room he had vacated for college and wept, not for the loss but because he realized that he was sitting in the room of a child and it was a room to which he could never return.

Six months after the funeral, he graduated with his bachelor's degree in applied mathematics. Later that afternoon, he walked with his mother through the tree-lined neighborhoods and she told him how proud his father would have been. She did not tell him how proud she was or at least did not tell him then. Instead, she asked him if there were any parties he was going to later. He told her that there were a few he would probably attend and in fact this was true. At Princeton there had been many more bright students than he had encountered in high school and he had formed a handful of friendships based on a shared interest in math and difficult engineering questions. "You know I can't help but worry about you," his mother told him.

"I know," he said, "but I'm OK."

"You always say that," she said.

"Because I always am." He looked at her carefully. "I'm fine, Mom. I am."

"I know you are, honey," she said. She patted him on the arm. "You've done a good job."

"Thanks," he said. "One step closer to becoming an astronaut."

"One step closer," she said.

Three months later she told him she had breast cancer and three months after that she followed his father into the grave, her own plot of soil directly next to his. If there had been any question before about where he stood in relation to the world it had been clarified. He sold the house he had grown up in without any clear feeling of sadness, not because he lacked a sense of grief but because he was, even then, pragmatic. He did not want to live in the town he had grown up in, and now that he had the opportunity to stay he realized just how strongly he had come to hate it. There was not a single person there that he cared for now that his parents were gone, and when he thought of the people he had gone to school with for twelve years he could recall only generalized isolation and occasional embarrassment.

He only regretted that his parents would never see him fulfill the goals he had made for himself, that they would not see him become an astronaut. He did not even really know if his mother had truly understood that his goals were real and tangible and achievable. Certainly his father had not. Keith had shared the man's pragmatism but his father lacked ambition, settling into what was a mediocre career and riding it all the way to his grave. His mother had no concrete career of her own and whether she was satisfied with his father's choices was something he would never know. At least she seemed to understand that college was useful and that grades had value; whenever he had talked to his father, the question was always where he would work, what kind of job he could get with this degree or that degree, or if it would be more useful to get working right away and eschew the degree altogether. "You could get pretty far in a company in four years. You'd be four years ahead of all those college kids just getting their first real job."

"That's not what I want to do," Keith had said in response.

"Well, it's your choice," his father had answered. "Just my two cents."

Now they were both gone. In the years that followed he would miss them, especially his mother, who had been one of the only demonstrably affectionate people he had known in his childhood, although he certainly bonded with many of his teachers and managed, despite everything, to have a few brief relationships with girls. His mother had been concerned about his approach to the world, though, and after she passed there had been no one to dissuade him of the notion that his fulfillment would come from work and numbers and not from human interaction. Had it not been for Barb he might have simply drifted away into that world; he certainly had the capacity to do so.

He thought that he should pick Quinn up at school, that the news of her grandfather's death was something he should tell her straightaway, although when he actually arrived there and asked to take her out of class early he was less sure of his decision and when she arrived in the school office he lost his resolve to tell her anything at all.

"I thought we could go out and do something fun," he said. It was the only explanation he could think of and he was relieved that she agreed to go with him for somehow he thought she might refuse and return to her classroom.

"Mommy's coming home soon," he said when they were in the car.

"Why?" she said. "Is Grandpa dead now?" She looked so small in the rearview mirror, staring out the passenger-side window at the street.

"Do you want me to tell you right now?" he said.

"Yes," she said.

He did not answer for a long while. Then he said, "Yes, honey. Grandpa died yesterday."

"Crap," she said.

He nodded, although she was not looking at him. "Crap," he said in agreement.

"Did it hurt?"

"No, it didn't hurt. Mommy said he couldn't breathe very well so she said now that he's gone he can breathe better."

"Because he's in heaven."

"That's right."

I-675 turned toward the east in a long, lazy curve. He could see horses in a distant pasture. Tract homes here and there amongst the fields. She continued to stare out the window. "You want to go to a movie or something?" he said at last.

She did not answer for a long time. Then, finally, she said, "I just want to go home."

Again he looked at her, at the road scrolling out before him, back to her again. "Me too," he said. "Let's go home."

"Tell Mommy to come home too."

"I will," he said. In that moment he could think of nothing he wanted more. The interstate beyond the windshield: signs passing, cars moving all around him.

"This isn't the right way," she said at last.

"I know," he said.

She was silent again, this time for a long, long while. Then she said, simply, "OK."

They continued to drive like that, not speaking. He could see the twinned vectors of their forward motion where they pushed toward the horizon, curving not along the interstate upon which they rode but up and out and away. He might have believed that the lines calculated a single path for them both, father and daughter. Would we not all believe such a thing about our families, our children, ourselves? Even as the perfect lines continued: not parallel or convergent but rather diverging so subtly their distance would be impossible to mark or measure, the lines moving away, moving away from each other. A few zeroes past the decimal and everything is changed. A ten thousandth. A hundred thousandth. A repetition. A vinculum. And you would not find their intersection even were you to plot those thin vectors for all your days to come.

Part II

Six

DURING DINNER, NICOLE continually peppered him with questions, all of which he answered between mouthfuls of food. Occasionally Jennifer would say something, asking her daughter to let him eat or insisting that some questions were not to be asked in polite company. He said he did not mind, although some questions—questions about his separation from Barb—he answered vaguely enough so that his words amounted to no answer at all. He assumed that Nicole's parents had divorced, took this to be the reason why she asked so many questions about the topic, but he did not ask Jennifer if this was the case. Perhaps later she would tell him what had happened. Or perhaps it was irrelevant.

The interior of Jennifer's house was shockingly similar to the way his own wife had decorated their home, the way it had looked before he had left for the mission, and the similarities made him uneasy. The blinds were down and curtains covered the windows. Dried flower arrangements here and there. A giant wreath over the fireplace. Photographs of Nicole at various ages. Impersonal knick-knacks. It was as if she had found a page in a magazine and had taken that page to one of the megastores and had bought everything pictured: particleboard angles and curves, gauzy window dressings.

He had been anticipating the dinner for most of the day, mostly because he did not really understand what would be expected of him. The anxiety he felt and the similarities in decor had very nearly turned him away at the front door but Jennifer had touched his arm just at that moment and led him farther into the house, toward the dining room and its table of food. But even when he was seated, something about the whole situation felt wrong to him: this woman and her daughter seeming so similar to everything he had lost and yet here they were, as if surrogates or doppelgängers that had appeared in a house nearly identical to his own.

And there was Nicole, a little girl asking him questions about his mission when his own daughter never again would do so. He had agreed to field the questions but now that he was here he had no desire to talk about what he had done, at least not in the beginning, when he found himself wishing he were back in the empty house across the street, back in the cocoon of his solitude and his loneliness. But he did not rise from the table. Not during the first five minutes, nor the next five. Each time he looked up, the little girl was waiting for another answer and each time he glanced across to Jennifer he found her staring at him, her eyes wide and her body inclining toward him as if hanging on his every word, and such attention drove all other thoughts from his mind. He would catch her eyes momentarily and she would not break the contact and each time he felt a flutter of warmth run through him and the feeling that he was an impostor in a house of ghosts began to fade. There was a simple logic to the questions, requiring of him only a basic rendering of the story of his mission and of his experience, the questions specific and blunt: "How did you go to the bathroom?" and "What was the best thing to eat?" and "Did you get to watch TV?"

He told her about the installation of the robotic arm and subsequent
"windshield wiper maneuver" by using his fork, a piece of French bread
stuck to the tines, and his lasagna-smeared dinner plate as the surface
of the space station, his fork swinging across the plate in a long smooth
motion. There and back again.

When he had finished she said, "That doesn't seem like much."

"I guess not," he said. "But no one had ever done it before."

"Was it dangerous?"

"Probably."

"Why?"

"I don't know. Maybe it wasn't."

"Well, which was it?"

He looked up at Jennifer for a moment and she winked at him, a gesture that made him shiver. "It's always dangerous doing a space walk,"
he said. "Things can go wrong."

"So it *was* dangerous."

"I guess so."

"Then why did you say it wasn't?"

"Because it didn't seem any more dangerous than anything else
we do."

"Why not?"

"There are lots of things that help an astronaut stay safe in space."

"Like what?"

"How long does this report have to be?" he said.

"Five paragraphs," she said.

"She wants to be a reporter," Jennifer said.

"She'll be good at it," he said. He turned back to Nicole. "Do you
want to know what the windshield wiper maneuver was for?"

"I already know. I looked it up online."

"Oh."

"It's where you had to have the robot arm carry you over the whole
space station and drop you off on the other side to fix some thingie. It
said you were really high up and it was great."

"That's right," he said. He realized that his fork, bread, and plate explanation likely seemed silly and foolish.

"So what's the dangerous part then?"

"Well, you're only separated from space by the suit you're in," he said. "If something went wrong you'd lose your air and that would be that."

"You mean you'd die," she responded.

"Yes, I mean I'd die."

"But that doesn't happen very often really."

"No, I guess not," he said. "Not ever actually."

"But people die sometimes when they take off."

Jennifer's voice came from the end of the table, "Sweetheart, maybe Captain Keith doesn't want to talk about that."

"It's OK," he said. "I don't mind. Yes, once the shuttle exploded during takeoff and once it broke up when it was coming back to Earth."

"Did you know those people who died?"

"Some of them."

"Were they your friends?"

"No, but I knew some of them in the second one. They were already astronauts, so they were a bit further along than I was."

"What do you mean?"

He was silent, thinking. Then he said, "What grade are you in?"

"Fourth."

"They were like sixth-graders."

"You mean they picked on you all the time?"

He smiled. "No, I mean they were people you could look up to. They were already doing what I wanted to do. They had experience and were going into space already. I wasn't even training for a mission yet."

"Were you sad when they died?"

"Would you be?"

"Yes."

"That's my answer then."

The evening had gone like that, or at least the question-and-answer-session portion of it had gone that way and he did not know if it was Jennifer's presence, her tangible sexuality, that had calmed him or Nicole's direct and logical questions but he had ceased thinking of Quinn and of Barb. In the light of the dining room, the sense of physical similarity he thought he had recognized when she had been at his sliding glass door dissipated and as the evening continued his comparisons of them stopped altogether.

Jennifer said very little during dinner, instead only staring at him and occasionally commenting on her daughter's precocious behavior. "She's like that," Jennifer would say. She had taken a microscopic slice of lasagna and did not eat the bread at all, and Keith realized only later that he had eaten half of the lasagna tray on his own and most of the bread as well and was uncomfortably full. Since returning to the cul-de-sac he had subsisted primarily on fast food and TV dinners. It was taking its toll on him and he knew it; the lethargy he felt could no longer be attributed strictly to his postflight fatigue. He had not done any serious exercise since he had returned to the cul-de-sac and had not even given it much thought until now, seated across the table from Jennifer and catching her unmoving eyes. He should join a gym. He wondered what gym Jennifer went to. He could feel himself stir when she looked at him, when she did not break eye contact, a fact that was itself surprising.

When dinner was over, Jennifer announced it was Nicole's bedtime and Keith had expected the stubborn obstinacy that had sometimes accompanied his own daughter's bedtime at this age, but Nicole merely stood and thanked Keith and walked up the stairs. The room was immediately quiet. Keith looked down at the tabletop, then at Jennifer, who was staring at him yet again, then back to the tabletop. His plate was gone and there were no more questions. A wave of fluttering in his chest like the scrape of wings. He tried to think of something clever to say but no words would come to him.

"Thank you for doing that for Nicole," Jennifer said.

He looked up at her, relieved that she had said something and that it was no longer up to him to begin. "It's no problem," he said. "She's a surprising little girl."

"I sure think so."

"It's true."

"I hope she wasn't too much."

"No, it was fine." He waited for her to say something more and when she did not he rose to his feet. "Thanks for dinner," he said.

"Oh, stay a little while longer," she said. "We grown-ups haven't had the chance to talk. At least stay long enough to have a glass of wine."

He glanced around the room, knowing that he wanted to stay but then again that he did not want to stay. Perhaps he had misread the entire evening. Still her eyes were on him, but what kind of sign was that?

"Look, I'm not very good at this," he said at last.

"Good at what?"

He paused before answering. Then he said, "If you tell me to stay I'm going to think that's what you want me to do."

She smiled. "I'd like you to stay. What do you want to do, Astronaut?"

"I want to stay," he said. There was no hesitation in his answer.

"That doesn't sound very complicated," she said.

"It's not," he said.

"Good. So you sit and I'll uncork the wine."

He nodded and sank down again, folding his hands before him on the tabletop as she rose to her feet.

"So there was some talk about you at the homeowners association last night," she said. "Everyone's really interested in the return of the astronaut. They all want to meet you."

"Who does?"

"Everybody. They also complained about your car."

"They complained about my car?"

"Yeah, they want it washed. I told them to leave you alone. Nicely, of course. You don't want to make enemies of your neighbors."

"They want to meet me *and* they want me to wash my car?"

"That pretty much sums it up."

"Glad I wasn't there," he said.

She laughed. "They're just busybodies. They want the gate put in but there's just no money for that right now so there's nothing else to talk about. They complain about the foreclosures and the fact that half the development is still just dirt after three years."

"It'll get done, I'm sure," he said.

"Oh, I know it will get done. Just doesn't leave much for the busybodies to talk about except who needs a car wash."

"I guess so," he said. He could think of nothing more to say and certainly did not want to continue a discussion that involved the admittedly filthy rental car in his driveway. These were the moments he dreaded in any conversation. The lulls. The spaces he was supposed to fill in. He tried to smile. Then he said, "You know my wife and I are split."

"I know," she said. Her back was to him and, as she reached up to an upper cabinet to pull down a wine bottle, her top slid along the curves of her body. "Barb and I talked a few times," she said. She pulled two bottles down and turned toward him again. "We went to the same gym."

"I need to join a gym," he said. "My trainer in Houston would be disappointed if he knew I wasn't working out."

"You should come with me to mine sometime."

He rose suddenly. "I'm sorry," he said. "Let me help you with that."

"No, no," she said. "You're my guest. When I'm your guest you can wait on me, OK?"

"You know, she took everything," he said abruptly.

"What's that?" she said. She had opened a drawer and had been fishing through it but now she stopped and looked at him, the neck of the wine bottle held in her grip.

"Sorry," he said. "That's probably too much information. It's just . . . your house is really similar to mine inside, but Barb took all the furniture. So my house is empty. I mean completely empty."

"Completely empty?"

"There's a sofa and the bed."

"That's it?"

"Yes."

"That's awful," she said. She actually reached out toward him, not quite touching him, her hand just inches from his on the tiles. He wondered momentarily if he should slide his own across that gap but then she returned her free hand to its hunt for a bottle opener. "I guess you have some shopping to do," she said.

"I guess so," he said. "I can't decide if I'm staying or going. Or where I'd go if I'm going."

"You're trying to sell it, though."

"Well, it's on the market."

"Any interest?"

"I don't know. The realtor showed it to some people or said she was going to but I don't know if anything came of it."

"Fingers crossed," she said. "Sounds like you have a lot of decisions to make." She uncorked the wine bottle with a loud pop. "We'll let that breathe a bit."

"OK."

Nicole's voice came from upstairs, a thin piercing sound calling, "Mom!"

"Hold that thought," Jennifer said. She smiled at him briefly and he nodded and then she disappeared out of the room and up the stairs.

He had never been nervous during the mission, not even during the launch, and yet now, here, in this woman's house, a thin stream of adrenaline ran through him from the pit of his stomach to his fingertips. The room was very quiet. He thought that he should have already left her house, but then wondered why he had such thoughts at all. There was nothing for him in the empty house across the street. Indeed, over the preceding two days since he had dropped the television down the stairs he had even stopped painting, instead sitting at the Starbucks in the dark corner and flipping through the newspaper without any real interest, feeling his anger and frustration at Jim Mullins and the others at NASA fade into a dull sense of irritation and then disappointment. He might simply have left the house in the cul-de-sac, might have actually gone away for some kind of vacation as both Mullins and Eriksson had told him to do, but he had remained for no reason he could define and now sat in a house across the street from his own and waited for the woman who lived there to return from upstairs, his fingers drumming anxiously on the tabletop. He looked around the room without purpose or direction. The decor and furnishings did not seem as similar to those of his house as he had first thought. A vague similarity in style, perhaps, but nothing specific.

He poured wine into the two glasses and looked at the label but he knew little of wine and noted only that the name was French and that the bottle was three years old. He sniffed at it and started to take a sip but then thought that it would be more polite to wait for her and so he did.

After a moment he could hear her on the stairs and then she reappeared in the room again. She was barefoot. He did not recall if she had been barefoot before or if she had taken off her shoes when she was upstairs.

"I poured the wine," he said.

"Good thinking."

He handed her one of the glasses and she took it.

"To new friends," she said.

"To new friends," he repeated. They clinked the two glasses together.

Keith sipped his wine. It was fruity and slightly bitter and left his tongue dry.

"When do you go back to being an astronaut?" she said.

"I'm not sure yet."

"Taking some time?"

"Maybe. A little break, I guess."

"That's a good idea. You need time."

"Yeah," he said. "I'm just trying to get the house sold now. Then we'll see what happens next."

"No big plans?"

"I guess not."

"Oh," she said. There was a silence in the room, a softness that descended over them. Then she said quietly: "So how are you doing?"

"Fine," he said.

"Really?"

"Really."

She actually reached out and placed her hand on his arm. It was a warm thing there, and soft. Then she pulled it away again. "I'm sorry. You probably think I'm being really forward."

"It's OK," he said.

"I'm a really physical person," she said. "I can't help it. You looked sad."

"Did I?"

She blushed. Had he said something to make her blush? "Yes," she said.

"I'm not sad right now," he said.

"Well, good then." She seemed to shake off whatever had entered her thoughts because she was smiling again. "Like I said, if you need anything just let me know. Even if it's just a good home-cooked meal."

"I'll do that. I can always eat."

"I can see that." She smiled at him. "Stop me if I'm being too personal," she said. "I like to know what's going on."

"It's fine," he said.

"We looked you up on the Internet today. For Nicole's report. That's all I really know about you."

He said nothing. Her eyes locked to his. "My daughter's name was Quinn," he said at last.

"Quinn," Jennifer said. "I remember seeing her a few times. Coming and going."

"They went off to my mother-in-law's. She was driving back from some teen party out there. And she apparently went off the road on her way home. They think she was going eighty miles an hour. Hit a tree in someone's yard in the middle of the night. Coming back from the party."

"That's terrible," she said. There were actual tears in her eyes.

The information felt abstract to him, even now, as if he was relating the plot of a film he had seen and had there been any instinct in him to acknowledge the folly of this abstraction it was quelled in the moment he looked at her. Her hand had left his arm and had not returned but he could feel a sense of the warmth it left behind. He knew he should say something, should try to steer the conversation away from his sense of tragedy, but his mind was empty.

She suggested they move to the couch and they did so and she curled her legs under her body and sipped at the wine and at some point he rose and retrieved the bottle—the second bottle—and refilled the glasses. He was not sure how many glasses of wine he had drained, but he had taken a painkiller earlier that day and the combination had set the room to tilting slowly as if the house had become awash on a gently rocking sea.

She asked him about his work for NASA and when he asked if she was not already tired of hearing about that subject, she told him that she wanted to hear about it for herself and he tried to tell her what it had been like at the end of the robotic arm looking down at the space station, but his memory of it could not be put into words. He told her it had been beautiful, so very beautiful. What could he say? He had opened upon an infinity and it had become an infinity of loss.

When she leaned forward to kiss him his mouth was closed and she slid her tongue between his lips and he thought, in actual words: Well, OK then. It was in a voice that was his own sober voice still in

137

his head and it did not tell him to stop and so he kissed her back and she pressed her hand against his chest and his arms went around her.

"I'm pretty drunk," he said.

"Shhh," she said. "No more talking."

Her force was something to be reckoned with almost immediately, as if he had uncorked a bottle that had been no bottle at all but was a dam that uncorking had pressed to bursting and she climbed astride him, her face somewhere between anger and joy, determined and feral. A wild creature.

It felt as if it had been an eternity since he had touched a woman and he thought of nothing else, his hands on her beautiful tan breasts, encircling them and feeling her breath suck in just as he had imagined it would. When she lifted her arms so that the tight fabric slid up over her and away and he looked at her and leaned in and took one of her pink nipples in his mouth, his own breath was pulled away with hers, his heart thumping in his chest like an ancient, enormous machine that had been resurrected after so many years of forgetting.

They stumbled to the bed, practically at a dead run, his drunken feet staggering up the stairs and then their twin bodies crashing sideways onto the mattress, clothes awkwardly strewn about them, she much more adept than he at undressing under alcohol although who could say how drunk she was in comparison. How many times had he refilled his glass? He could not recall and indeed it mattered little. All that mattered was the thought that there are moments like this in real life, and he was amazed by the realization, as if there was another world inside of this one that was hidden in plain view and then her mouth was on his belly and then his chest and then finding his mouth at last and clamping onto it. Her body was something amazing to him: a hard and muscled creature that for reasons he could not even begin to understand had allowed him to take possession of it even as he grasped her around the waist and threw her over to her back and she moaned, her teeth clamped together in a kind of sneer surrounded by full red lips.

When he entered her it was like falling into a memory: like a body flashing through the surface of a lake and disappearing under the surface, the surface itself remaining silent only for that final instant and then, almost imperceptibly, the slow undulation of ripples rolling out from that central point, the body itself already disappeared in some otherworld of muffled and dimly lit fishes and reeds. Then he was above her and her entire body tightened and loosened, her hips and her waist curving around him, her eyes half closed and then closed tight as she made her sounds and he above her looking down at her face, her shoulders, her breasts, the way her legs were wrapped around his hips, this woman who was not his wife, who was a woman he did not even really know.

And when he came he actually shouted and she clamped her hand over his mouth and her voice too was a kind of cry that twisted up and out of her body. Her hand slipped from his mouth then and their breathing was heavy and whipped past their ears and slowed and quieted as he rolled to the side. She made no motion to cover herself and after a moment she said, "Fuck, I needed that."

"Yeah," he said.

"Shower?" she asked at last.

"OK," he said.

She rose and stood for a moment at the side of the bed, completely naked and looking more like a goddess than any mortal woman, her body a perfect thing that he had held in his hands. "Come on, then," she said.

"OK," he said again.

She stepped to the other side of the room and he heard the shower in the darkness. He could see the edge of the glass door from the bed and he closed his eyes and felt his own breath and after a moment he opened his eyes again and rose and walked through that tilting darkness. When he reached the shower door she emerged from the doorway of the bathroom and smiled at him. "Hello, neighbor," she said.

He smiled and said, "Hello." She smiled at him again and he thought that she might kiss him or that he might kiss her. Perhaps he should kiss her. Perhaps that was what he should do. Instead he said, "I'm not sure what I should be doing now."

"In there," she said, and she pulled the shower door open behind him and her hand was warm on his hip as she steered him through the door. She stood there, not speaking at first. Then she said, "Mind if I join you?"

"I don't mind at all."

She shook her head but said nothing as she came through the door.

The shower was not quite big enough for two so their bodies continued to bump against each other and he surprised himself by thinking that he would be able to make love to her yet again but then she stepped out of the shower and dried herself and returned from the closet wearing a terrycloth bathrobe. She handed him a towel and he dried himself. He found himself looking at her with a kind of longing that was already something like nostalgia. The room continued to slosh around him in its slow, drunken rhythm.

He dressed in the clothes that were in the bedroom, his shirt and shoes downstairs somewhere, strewn about the house like a crumbtrail to the exit. "I didn't expect this," he said suddenly, more to himself than to her.

"Neither did I," she said.

"Fun," he said.

"It was that," she said.

"I'm pretty drunk."

"So what?"

"OK. So what," he said. Then: "Let's do this again sometime." She laughed.

"I didn't just mean that. I meant having dinner. All of it."

She smiled. "Oh, you didn't mean that? Not interested?"

"No, I meant that too."

"You know where I live."

"Maybe you can come over to my place next time."

"You'd need furniture."

"Yeah," he said. Then: "Well, I have all the furniture we used."

She leaned in and kissed him on the cheek. "Probably time for you to go now, Astronaut," she said.

He did not want to leave her bedroom but even through the increasing winedrunk drift he knew that he had arrived as a dinner guest and had shared her bed and her body and that now it was over. She led him downstairs and he stumbled much of the way and leaned heavily on the banister and then found his shirt and his socks and shoes and ran his hands through his wet hair. "You want a glass of water?" she said.

"Sure," he said, and then: "Wait, no, I think I'd better head out."

He half hoped that she might invite him to stay longer. Maybe the glass of water was just this invitation and he had missed it. The clock on the wall read ten: still early. "Well then, neighbor, it was nice to get to meet you," she said. Her body was covered by the robe, but he could still make out the shape of her, a rare and wondrous thing that even now he could not believe he had held naked in his arms, a vision already fading from him as if a dream he had awakened from.

"Thanks for dinner," he said. He was not sure if he should kiss her.

"My pleasure."

"Good night," he said. He felt warm and wide awake and stared into her eyes for a moment longer and then he turned without touching her and moved in a slightly tilting path into the cul-de-sac and toward his own empty house. He wondered if Jennifer was still watching him from her door but when he turned and glanced back he saw that the door was already closed. The house so similar to his own and yet containing within it a woman, a girl, and furniture.

He paused there in the darkness of the street, still facing her house, the street tilting beneath his feet. Above, the dim stars cast upward from the horizon of rooflines and into their dome of pinpointed light and he staggered below them in the center of the street. Up there somewhere was the ISS with the retinue of astronauts who had replaced him: Yoshida and Eichhorn, both of whom had been part of his ASCAN group. Who else? Jones. Collins too. Someone else, but he had forgotten. Why have a daughter only to be told of her death two hundred and seventeen miles above the surface of Earth? Why have a wife at all if the end result is a house without furniture? Why become an astronaut only to end standing in a cul-de-sac in the darkness?

A black ocean above him. Stars cut into that false firmament. And Keith Corcoran standing there, drunk, maybe even smiling, the ring of the cul-de-sac and the lit orbit of streetlamps circling him, and when he stumbled forward toward the dark edge of the sidewalk he did so without conscious thought, only with a drunken sense of curiosity or perhaps not even that. Perhaps instead only the drift, the alternating sense of heavy stumble and high floating that drew him back and forth across the concrete. He nearly lost his balance stepping over the chain that blocked the empty lot from the sidewalk but did not fall, moving forward into the shadows, his feet crunching the thistle and stumbling some on the uneven ground. "Shit," he said as he regained his footing, his voice a hollow in the slow flat darkness of the field.

When he was a few dozen feet beyond the chain he stopped and stood. It was as if he was in a pool of black emptiness. A vacuum. In the distance he could see the angular shapes of the houses where they stood against the thick depths of the low dark sky, their windows cutting squares of soft sharp brightness into those silhouettes and the streetlight near the end of the cul-de-sac illuminating that bight of sidewalk where it circled a patch of round colorless asphalt like a lopsided equator circling a globe, the world it depicted one devoid of all possible physical features: bleak and empty and meaningless. Even the intersecting lines and angles and rays of that landscape described only themselves.

If there had been a reason he had wandered out into the field he had already forgotten it. "Shit," he said, his breath exhaling into the night. Then more quietly: "Shit." His body drifted in the ebb and flow of the tides, the million billion stars wheeling above him in their abstruse and recondite darkness.

Shit.

Seven

He awoke with his ears ringing and a sickening feeling in his gut that he feared might resolve itself into vomiting and when he opened his eyes into the harsh angular light of early morning his head was pounding. For a long while he simply lay in bed, the blankets and sheets awash around him like flotsam cast upon some geographically improbable shoreline. It was not yet seven o'clock and he hoped that sleep would return and that the pain in his head would dissolve but after a time he reconciled himself to the knowledge that sleep would not return and so he rose groggily and struggled into his bathrobe and descended to the kitchen. He did not think he could keep any real food down but he poured himself a bowl of cereal anyway and stood at the plastic-wrapped island and ate, the sound of crunching in his ears alarmingly abrasive. To his surprise he found that the breakfast helped settle his stomach some, although his head continued to pound in rhythm with his pulse. It was a different sensation entirely from the migraines and yet it served to remind him of their ongoing threat and so when he shook the Vicodin into his palm he included a second tablet.

Through the dirty upstairs window he could see the closed blinds of Jennifer's bedroom windows across the street. He thought she was likely still asleep although he could not recall how much wine she had actually drunk. He had certainly had too much but perhaps she was not hung over. Looking at those twin covered rectangles, he could hardly believe any of it had happened. He had stumbled into a moment that sounded like the setup for an adult film. The sexy neighbor lady across the street. The astronaut, recently single and lonely. Incredible. And now he stood in the same empty room he had occupied the morning before, as if it had been some dream from which he had awakened, finding himself once again in the container he had occupied since awakening from that other dream of being in space and of his wife and of his daughter. Dreams within dreams, although of course in reality there was nothing from which to awaken, all objects unrelenting in their harshly lit yellow lucidity.

In the three days between dropping the television and his evening with Jennifer he had not resumed painting at all, his carefully planned daily schedule slipping away as if stolen from him in plain sight over and over again. Each day began with the thought that he would continue painting the house and each day he had instead returned to Starbucks and checked his e-mail and voice mail and surfed engineering websites and did little else, the hours washing away from him like a sand castle dissolving with the incoming tide.

He had been home for less than two weeks but already the still emptiness had become an expectation to him, as if this was what his life was to become, his life without wife or daughter, without furniture, perhaps without even a job, for indeed the forced vacation had begun to feel like a kind of exile. Each morning he would wake to the silence of the house, some mornings shaking off whatever memory of Quinn had visited him in the half-light of dawn, and he would shower and dress and swallow his painkillers and step into the equally numbed silence outside. Each morning the same. Each identical to the one that had come before.

Such were his thoughts as he drove out of that same silent cul-de-sac yet again, scowling into the early-morning traffic and even cursing periodically under his breath, thinking of Jennifer and wondering why he was somehow unable to simply enjoy what had happened, why there was, instead, a strong and unshakable sense of unease and disappointment, the equation continuing to roll out in front of him in a faded ghost scrawl impossible to read. His work, the only part of his life that had always maintained within it a sense of clarity, had faded into that equation as well. He was a mathematician, an engineer, an astronaut, but whatever meaning or significance these terms had once held had become as obscure as everything else.

The two parking spaces directly in front of Starbucks were taken up by a light brown sedan that slung across both spaces diagonally so he pulled the rental car into a space slightly farther away and parked. He grabbed his laptop bag from the passenger seat and stepped out into a morning already unbearably hot and humid despite the relatively early hour, the sun a flat white disc above him, his head no longer throbbing but tender and fuzzy. It occurred to him that he did not even know what day it was.

He was just stepping past the sedan when he saw the blonde barista, Audrey. She stood by the door of the coffeeshop and another young woman, also in the green apron of her employment, stood at her side. Both stared at him intently as he rounded the hood of the car. "Oh thank god!" Audrey said. Her eyes did not leave him.

Before them, in a wire chair next to the door, slumped a man who Keith at first did not recognize, the table before him tilted to lean against a jumbled collection of chairs as if to match the position of the sedan parked just in front of it.

The barista Keith did not know had been holding a phone to her ear and snapped it shut as he stepped onto the sidewalk. "He still won't pick up," she said.

"Thank god you're here," Audrey said, apparently to Keith. "This is the astronaut guy I was telling you about," she told the other girl.

The response: "Cool."

"He passed out," Audrey said.

"Yeah, we can't wake him up," the other girl said.

"We don't know what to do," Audrey said.

"I called my boyfriend but he's not answering," the other girl said.

They had spoken in a nearly unceasing outrush of words and now they both paused as if waiting for him to say something in response. He glanced down at the man in the chair, at the top of his close-cropped scalp. The man snored loudly.

"It's Peter," Audrey said.

"Who?" He looked more closely at the man now—a thick wrecked frame in the wire chair like some rare breed of ox that had passed into unconsciousness—and with a shock he realized that it was, once again, the loud Ukrainian man. Fantastic. "Hey," he said. He leaned in and tapped him on the shoulder. "Hey, Peter." He tried to remember his last name but it would not come to him. "Hey," he said again. He leaned closer: Peter's breath so awful smelling that he actually jolted back from it as from a snake or a spider, the stench making his own stomach churn. "He's passed out drunk," Keith said.

"Wow," Audrey said.

"What should we do?" the other girl said.

"I don't know," he said. After a moment he looked up and saw that both of them were staring at him. "What?"

"He was really weird," Audrey said.

"What do you mean?"

"He was stumbling around telling Auds how much he loved her," the other said.

Audrey did not respond.

"You OK?" Keith said.

"Yeah," Audrey said.

"Then he went outside and sat down and fell asleep or passed out or whatever," the other girl said.

Keith stood there looking at them both. A woman crossed in front of him, dragging two children by their hands and eyeing him with suspicion. She reached the door and released one of the children's hands long enough to open it and then disappeared inside the coffeeshop.

"What are you gonna do?" Audrey said.

Keith looked at her and then looked back at Peter again. "What am *I* going to do?"

"You know what to do, right?" the other said. "I mean, you're an astronaut and everything."

He looked at her, at the confused sense of fear in her eyes and at the man slumped in the wire chair. Then he said, "Do you know his phone number or anything?"

The other barista was smiling, likely excited that something separate from her regular work routine was happening. "No number," she said.

"He lives near me somewhere," Keith said.

"Maybe I should call the police? That seems like a good idea," the other girl said.

"No," Audrey said. "Don't do that."

"Why not?" the other said. "We can't just leave him here. This is a place of business."

Audrey took a step toward Keith, her hands gently wringing her apron strings. "David's not answering either," she said. "He's the manager. He's supposed to deal with this kind of thing. What am I supposed to do?"

"Everything will be fine," Keith said. "Calm down." He knew that he should tell her to call the police and have them pick Peter up and take him home, but he did not. Instead he looked at the man asleep in the wire chair. He thought momentarily of his migraines: those he had suffered on the space station during the mission and those after his return to Earth. Then he leaned in and placed his hand on Peter's shoulder and shook him gently. "Hey, Peter," he said. "Wake up, Peter. Wake up."

"Wow, he's really out," Audrey said. She leaned forward to look at him. She might have appeared older when she was behind the counter in her apron and was responding to orders and firing up the espresso machine—perhaps that was what Peter saw—but now she looked like what she was: maybe eighteen or nineteen years old. Only a girl. Beautiful, but only a girl.

"Yeah, he's out all right," Keith said.

"Wow," she said.

"He's, like, superloaded," the other girl said.

Peter had gestured in the general direction of his home when Keith had seen him in the cul-de-sac the night he dropped the television, but there was no way to know which house was his. He thought it must have been on Riverside, the street that Keith's cul-de-sac emptied onto, but beyond that all the houses were the same.

"OK," Keith said. "We need to get his address from his driver's license. I'm going to try to roll him forward and you're going to see if you can get his wallet."

"I'm not touching him," the other girl said.

Audrey did not look at him, keeping her eyes focused on Peter's lumbering shape in the chair, his mouth open and a few gray teeth visible. "All right," she said.

Keith leaned in and slipped his arms under Peter's and shifted him forward. Peter's head lay gently on his shoulder. Apart from a slight shift in his breathing, Peter made no sound. It was as if they were involved in some lovers' embrace, these two men, so tender that one had fallen asleep in the arms of the other.

"What if he throws up on you?" the other girl said.

"That's not going to happen."

"How do you know?"

"I need you to step back and be quiet," Keith said.

Then Audrey: "A little more. I can't quite get it."

He shifted Peter's body forward as far as he could, cradling most of the man's weight against his chest and shoulder.

"Got it!" Audrey said, her voice an excited giggle.

Keith grunted and shifted Peter's bulk into the chair again, his own stomach lurching from the effort, the hangover a rotten tumbling inside of him. He knew at some point he would need to get the man into his car. Unless he could get him at least partially awake he did not think he and these tiny girls could manage it.

He held Peter's sweating head in his hands for a moment and let it drop slowly back to a resting position. Audrey was smiling and handed him the wallet. It was nearly empty—no credit cards or business cards or much of anything else—but his driver's license was there. Petruso Kovalenko, 3444 Riverside Street.

"Hi, George," Audrey said.

One of the regulars had come in from the parking lot: a gray man with a blue "U.S. Navy Retired" cap perched upon his head and a bent wooden cane gripped in one gnarled fist. "Young lady," the man said. "What's the situation?"

"Ask him," Audrey said.

The man had extended his hand. "George Campbell, U.S. Navy retired," he said.

"Keith Corcoran." He took the man's hand and they shook.

"You're the astronaut," Campbell said, his eyes flicking to Keith's polo and back to his face again.

"Yes," he said.

"USAF?"

"Yes, sir."

"What's this guy's story?"

"Long night."

"I can see that. What's the plan then?"

"Plan is to get him home."

"How are we gonna do that?"

"Still working on it." He looked up at Campbell. The old man's eyes were wide, his cane held in his grip more like a weapon than a walking aid.

The woman who had entered Starbucks earlier with her children now poked her head out of the door. "Excuse me," she said.

"Just one moment," the second barista said.

"How much longer?" the woman said.

"One moment, ma'am," Audrey said.

The other barista rolled her eyes and the woman disappeared back through the door.

"Go inside," Keith said.

The second barista looked at him as if to confirm the order was meant for her and then exhaled loudly. "I don't see why *I* have to," she said.

Keith continued to look at her and a moment later she turned and did as he had asked.

It was quiet then, the three of them surrounding Peter on the sidewalk in the ever-increasing heat of the morning. "I'm going to need to bring my car closer," Keith said and both Audrey and George Campbell nodded in unison.

He stepped out to the parking lot and slid behind the wheel of the rental car. Through the windshield the three of them were a comical group: George Campbell and Audrey looking expectant under the green awning and flanking the slumbering Ukrainian as if unlikely bodyguards. He put the car in reverse and backed up to the sidewalk so that the passenger door opened directly in front of Peter's slumbering form. Then he exited the car again and returned to stand beside the inert body.

"Think you can give me a hand with this?" Keith said.

"I may be old but I'm not crippled," Campbell said. "What say I lift some and you pull?"

"He's heavy," Keith said.

"I have no doubt of that," Campbell said. He moved behind Peter's chair and hooked the cane handle around an adjacent chair and slung his hands under Peter's arms. "It didn't occur to me this morning that by oh-eight-hundred I'd have my hands shoved into another man's armpits," Campbell said.

Audrey giggled. More customers had begun to arrive, each eyeing them as they passed, but Audrey remained where she was on the sidewalk in front of the store.

Campbell strained briefly against Peter's armpits and then quit. "OK, so that didn't work so well."

"Grab an arm," Keith said. "We'll pull him up." Then, more loudly: "Peter, we're going to put you in the car." Then, quietly again: "Give him a push, Audrey," and Audrey put her hands on Peter's shoulders and the three of them managed to push and pull him at least partially to his feet, a tottering configuration of muscle and bone, his head lolling about in a kind of bewilderment, eyes half open and then drifting closed again. He mumbled something that might have been a question, his voice a slur of vowels and elongated consonants: English or Ukrainian or some other language entirely.

A short journey punctuated by a dozen declarations of shit and whoa and hold on and finally they tipped him into the small passenger seat of the rental car. Not a car made for such a situation as this but they managed to fold and press him into it as if stuffing a series of springs into a box slightly too small to hold them all.

"Now how are you gonna get him out of there?" Campbell said.

"I'm not sure. He lives over by me. Maybe some of the neighbors will help."

"I'd better follow you in my truck," Campbell said.

Keith nearly told him that this further act of kindness was not necessary, but then he also knew that he could not get Peter to his front door in this state, not by himself. "OK," he said. "That's very kind of you."

"Damn right it is. I'm a busy man. I have the whole day scheduled to sit here on my bony ass and listen to Frank Poole bullshit about the good old days. Let's get out of here before that old windbag shows up."

"I thought you two were best friends," Audrey said.

"Friends of necessity, sweetheart. We're the two oldest people alive. We're like ancient moths both trying to fly toward the light at the same time and we got tangled up in each other's bullshit on the way."

"You're so funny," Audrey said.

"Don't I know it. I'm a regular comedian," Campbell said. "Let's get out of here, Corcoran."

Keith closed the passenger door and swung around to the driver's seat and they pulled out of the parking lot. Peter snored loudly from the passenger seat, his knee partially blocking the gearshift so that Keith had to push it out of the way every time a gear change was necessary. He realized that he had not even managed to get a cup of coffee. Nonetheless, the activity had cleared his head and the sense of immediate purpose had driven away the brooding guilt of his morning. In the rearview mirror was Campbell's blue pickup truck, the U.S. Navy Retired cap upon the old man's head and a look of purpose and determination on his face.

They turned into the housing development and Keith pulled the driver's license out of his shirt pocket and looked at it and then compared it to the nearest home that passed. Kovalenko. He looked at the card again. Kovalenko. There were no trees or shrubs tall enough to obscure the home numbers, each one a black sign moving by in even increments on nearly identical earth-toned homes: 3438, 3440, 3442, and finally 3444. He pulled his car to a stop at the curb and then changed his mind and backed up a few feet and pulled into the driveway. Campbell's truck stopped in front of the house, the door swinging open and Campbell himself emerging, the cane clicking on the concrete, his movements as quick and fluid as a teenager's.

"Let's see if anyone's home," Keith said.

Campbell nodded and Keith approached the front door. It opened before he was able to knock. "Mrs. Kovalenko?" he said.

She was about his age, perhaps slightly younger, with skin the color of paper and black hair curling in at her shoulders as if to frame her pale shining face and dark almond-shaped eyes. "Yes?" she said.

"I have Peter in the car," he said.

She looked at him, confused.

"He's pretty drunk. He was passed out and I brought him back here." His own head remained fuzzy and in this moment between exertions he felt weak and exhausted.

"Oh," she said. It was more an involuntary sound than a statement or question. She looked confused and for a moment Keith wondered if she understood English. Then she stepped outside. Behind her, a child's voice said, "Mama?" and she said something in Ukrainian in the tone of a mother trying to quiet a worried child.

She moved past him to the car, her eyes on the window. When she passed Campbell he said, "Good morning, ma'am," and she looked at him briefly and without expression and then went to the passenger door and opened it carefully. Peter lolled back against the seat. "Petruso," she said. She leaned in close to him and touched his face. "Petruso," she said again. Peter mumbled something incomprehensible in response, his head rolling back and forth until she lay her hand upon his sweating brow and stilled it and then stood there for a long while, staring at him, and even from where he stood Keith could hear her softly whispering: "Shhh."

When her husband had calmed she stepped back from the car to where Keith stood at the edge of the concrete walkway. "Thank you from bringing him home," she said. As soon as the last syllable had been spoken she turned toward her husband again.

"It's not a problem," he said. He waited for her to say something else but there were tears in her dark-lashed eyes and no further words came. "We should bring him in," he said at last.

She leaned toward her husband. "Petruso," she said again. She paused and then said something in Ukrainian, a whisper.

Peter did not move at all. The only sign that he was alive was the sound of breath rushing into and out of his body.

"We'll get him," Keith said.

"Best clear a path for us," Campbell said from his station by the truck. "He's as heavy as a load of bricks."

Peter's wife stepped away from them. She had closed the front door to the house when she had stepped outside but now it was open again and two children peered out from the shadows. She said something that Keith could not understand and both children disappeared into the house and she walked to the doorway and then turned toward Keith again. She looked like a war bride awaiting news of her returning husband, something from an old black-and-white film, beautiful and fragile and somehow resigned to the situation, a thin, elegant woman who stared out at them with her eyes curved slightly into a kind of desperate sadness. Keith wondered if Petruso Kovalenko often appeared in this condition and if she had grown accustomed to her husband's wrecked body being dumped back into her home.

"Let's do this," he said.

He grasped Peter by the arms and together he and Campbell heaved the man onto his feet. Peter seemed somewhat more awake, for when they tipped him forward his legs actually took some of the weight, feet moving in jerking, stumbling steps even though his eyes remained closed and his head rolled back and forth against his chest.

They managed to get him through the doorway and into the house as far as the sofa, where they lowered him as gently as his weight would allow. All the while, Peter's wife stood nearby with her fingers against trembling lips. Peter himself did not stir. Keith stood over the body. "Well, that's it then," Campbell said. "Safely home."

"I am sorry," Mrs. Kovalenko said. It was the voice not of an angry wife but of a frightened child. "He does not . . . he has never . . ."

"It's no problem," Keith said.

"Where you found him?" she said. She moved to the sofa and sat on the arm and leaned over to stroke her husband's forehead with her fingertips.

Keith paused before answering. "He was at the coffeeshop up the street. His car is still there."

"You are his friend?" she said.

"Neighbor," he said. "I live right over there." He gestured over his shoulder in the general direction of the cul-de-sac.

"Oh!" Her hand went to her mouth. "You are astronaut."

Keith smiled uneasily and waited for her to continue and when she did not he said, simply: "Yes."

There was a moment of silence between them. Then she said, "Thank you both from bringing him home."

"For, you mean," Campbell said. "*For* bringing him home."

"Yes, *for* bringing him home. Thank you," she said. "My English is not so good as Peter's."

"It's fine," Keith said. "Let me know if you need anything."

"You are good friend to him," she said.

Keith did not say anything in response to this, instead looking up at Campbell and nodding. The two of them turned toward the door in unison. On the stairs, the children peered at them as they passed, their eyes wide and emotionless. When he and Campbell reached the door, Keith could hear them scurry into the living room, their mother's voice attempting to quiet their questions in hushed syllables. Then the door closed.

Audrey confirmed what they already knew: that Peter's car was the filthy sedan parked at a diagonal in front of Starbucks. They found the keys in the ignition and took a second trip to the house, an activity that was at the behest of Campbell, who considered the job incomplete without the delivery of the car. Keith was not opposed to the "mission," as Campbell had deemed it, but he wondered how far they would go to help this man that Keith knew only in passing and

Campbell knew not at all. Still, it appeared that neither he nor the old man had any other more pressing plans and the task gave them both a sense of purpose and accomplishment. The world had been askew and so they had endeavored to set it aright once more.

Keith drove Peter's car, a vehicle incongruously clean and tidy in its interior and which knocked and banged when the engine was running and emitted clouds of black smoke whenever he pressed the gas pedal. Peter's telescope was on the floor of the passenger side, leaning up against the edge of the seat pad and extending almost to the backrest. He had only seen it slung over Peter's shoulder in the darkness but now he saw that it was a scuffed and dented white tube with silver duct tape wrapped around its midsection as if it had split open at some point and no better solution could be found for its repair.

Campbell drove him back to the coffeeshop in the blue pickup truck and talked incessantly about his time in the U.S. Navy, a topic that Campbell seemed to feel was something they shared even though Keith's time in the service was forgettable. It had been a stepping-stone to NASA and he had spent his time there in an engineering office working on projects involving weapons systems and power usage and he could think of no way to make this a topic of conversation Campbell would understand or be interested in and so he said nothing. His daughter had been a beautiful little girl there. Once they had gone for ice cream together. Her tiny hand enveloped in his own. That was what Ohio was for him now.

When they reached the Starbucks parking lot again he thanked the old man, half expecting him to salute in response, and then entered and asked Audrey for a cup of water and a coffee. He drank the water greedily. The activity of returning Peter to his home had dissipated much of his nausea and indeed his head had begun to feel clear and awake again, although he was incredibly thirsty. Audrey asked him various questions about their delivery of Peter and he answered them but there was not much to say. Yes, he had gotten home safely. Yes, all would be well again. The excitement was over.

He thought about driving home but then wondered what he would do in that empty shell and so he drove across the parking lot to the first of many megastores and there selected a small dining room table that came in a cardboard box, and a chair, similarly in pieces, managing to fit both boxes in the trunk. When he arrived home he brought them into the silent, plastic-wrapped kitchen and sat on the floor and assembled the parts with the disposable tools that came packaged within. It was likely that his own tools were outside in the garage but he still had not crossed into that space. Maybe he would sell the house without ever having opened that door. A collection of screws and bolts on the kitchen floor, the shapes vicious and curved like miniature weapons.

He managed to complete the table and the chair and sat looking at this makeshift furniture. Then he kicked the detritus of cardboard sheets and nuggets of broken Styrofoam out of the way and poured himself a bowl of cereal and sat at the table to eat it, the bowl resting on its laminated wood surface. When he had finished he set his spoon in the bowl and sat back in the chair and surveyed his work: a particleboard table and chair amidst the dusty plastic wrap and blue masking tape of the kitchen. He had begun painting nearly two weeks ago. At what point would he actually admit that he would never paint the second coat or complete any of the upstairs?

It took two armloads to get all of the cardboard packaging to the garbage can outside and it was during the second armload that he saw Peter's wife on the sidewalk, her two children clutching her legs.

"Hello," he said, his surprise evident in his voice. He dumped the cardboard scraps into the plastic bin and then rearranged them in an attempt to close the lid.

"Luda," she said. "My name. Luda Kovalenko." She was carrying something in front of her, a glass dish like a casserole.

"Luna?"

"Luda," she said again. "Short for Ludmila."

"Luda."

"Yes."

Nothing for a moment. Then: "Keith Corcoran."

"Yes, Astronaut Keith Corcoran."

He gave up on the rearranging and tipped the garbage can lid so that it rested on the protruding bits of cardboard and Styrofoam and brushed his hands on his pants and walked down to the edge of the sidewalk, glancing up at Jennifer's house as he did so. All the blinds were closed.

"I wanted to thank you," Luda said. "So I made you this for dinner. For you." She held the dish out toward him and he took it.

"Oh," he said. "Really?" It was covered in foil and he could feel the warmth of the oven still radiating from it.

"I hope you like." She had a few sheets of paper that had been tucked under her arm as she walked and now she transferred them to her hand and smoothed them.

"Uh . . . I . . . ," he began, then stopped, then said, "Thank you." The gesture was unexpected and he actually found himself emotional, standing before this woman and holding a casserole dish of food she had cooked with her own hands while her two children swarmed around her legs and her husband slept off a bender on the sofa.

"Peter. He is not like this," she said.

"No?"

"Not ever. Not like this. It is hard for him here." She paused a moment, looked away from him. Then she said, "He was assistant to scientists in Ukraine. Here he works for Target. It is . . ." She paused for a long moment and then said, "humiliating."

Keith did not know if the pause was because she could not find the word or because she did not know if she should say it. But there it was. Humiliating, indeed. He said nothing, continuing to look at her, her eyes casting up and down the cul-de-sac as if avoiding his gaze and his silence, the children still clutching at her legs. Embarrassed perhaps. It was later in the day now and the sun was beginning to creep toward the roofs of the houses, toward the distant trees on the opposite side of the field where Peter sometimes sought the darkness with his battered telescope.

"He has no respect in this country," she said.

"How long have you been here?"

"Three years. I thought he would learn to be here but he has not. He is still in Ukraine in his heart." Now she did look at him, perhaps wondering if she was being understood properly, perhaps to gauge his reaction.

"I don't know what to say," he said.

"You are his friend?"

He looked at her, saying nothing for a long moment: the wife of a man he did not know in any substantive way at all. He wondered what Peter Kovalenko had told his wife. Had he told her that he had become friends with an astronaut? If so, it was not true. They had exchanged a few words, but that did not make them friends. Indeed, the last time he had spoken with Peter Kovalenko, Keith had brushed him off in irritation. But that had been right after dropping the television, right after that frustrating conversation with Jim Mullins and whatever kindness he had possessed had been freshly bled out of him.

He might have tried to avoid this whole situation but people had looked to him for leadership and so he had embraced that role because he was an astronaut and Jim Mullins could not take that away from him.

And so he stood in front of Luda Kovalenko, a woman who had made him a casserole, and she was waiting for an answer and so he gave her one: "Yes," he said, "I am."

"You help him then," she said. She handed him the papers and Keith took them awkwardly with two fingers, still holding the glass dish. "You help him," she said again.

He tried to look at the pages caught between his fingers but it was difficult to do so with the casserole dish in his hands. It appeared to be a résumé of some kind. Yes. Peter Kovalenko's résumé. "Oh," he said. He looked up at her, her eyes wide and darkly luminous before him, and he waited for her to say something more but she did not. "I guess I'll see what I can do," he said.

She reached for him then, so quickly that he had to shift the dish away to avoid a collision as she embraced him. She did so totally, as if he was someone she had known for a long time—a family member, a brother, maybe even a lover—her body against his for that brief moment, there on the sidewalk in that cul-de-sac as he held the casserole dish awkwardly to the side. "Thank you," she said. "Thank you, Astronaut Keith Corcoran. Thank you."

"OK," he said. He nodded, unable to even pat her on the back lest he send the dish to the concrete. Her entire body pressed against his own. "It's OK," he said again, but he was not sure that was true.

Eight

HE HAD GONE out for a run, an activity he had come to enjoy while
training for the mission and which he had attempted earlier that
week, the result of which had been an immediate and brutal calf
cramp that left him staggering in his driveway, his face racked into
the pained visage of a Greek tragedy mask. This time, though, there
was no cramping. He rounded the cul-de-sacs, concentrating on the
steady pounding of his feet and the undulating curvature of the sidewalk before him, this cul-de-sac drawing into the next and the next
after that and each containing earth-toned houses of four or five de-
signs, his own house amongst them, repeated and repeated and repeated again, a landscape he had initially tried to think of as some
scientific design that had been rendered incomplete but now which
seemed only an unsettling and cruel fractal geography, the entrance
of which was marked by two stone pillars and an empty gatehouse.
The Estates. What did that even mean? He turned onto Riverside
again, a street so-named for reasons even more obscure. If there had

been a river it had been diverted somewhere else to make room for this warren of cul-de-sacs. Underground into some subterranean pipe-works perhaps. The only water apparent was sprayed into the air to moisten the scattering of perfectly green lawns or appeared briefly and then descended back to the earth via sidewalk gutters, the black holes of flushed toilets, the metal grid of shower drains.

He still had not seen Peter since returning him home from Starbucks, a fact that was surprising only because he was certain that Peter would come to him the following day or the day after as if they were now the best of friends. He distinctly sensed that Peter Kovalenko would feel that he owed him something—maybe even his very life—but it was just not so. He dreaded the conversation that would follow and for several days afterwards had expected a knock on the door, imag-ining that when the knock occurred, probably late in the evening, he would open it to find his Ukrainian neighbor, smiling and then mag-nanimously clapping him on the shoulder and fishing for an invite in-side so that he could apologize for his behavior. That would be Peter's entrée into Keith's life: a loud, boisterous drunk who made a daily fool of himself by flirting with the teenage girl who made his coffee, who had even bought the girl a present, and now had made an even bigger fool of himself by showing up at that girl's workplace and pro-fessing his love before passing out in a chair outside.

Such were his thoughts as he passed Peter's silent home and slowed his pace, turning from Riverside onto his own cul-de-sac, slowing further until he was walking, hands on hips, breathing the already warm morning air. His head felt clear. He had realized a few days be-fore that he had been migraine-free for over a month and wondered if the shrill whining he sometimes heard in the morning was only his memory replaying some dark and uneasy fear. Maybe he was cured, although at this point he was not even sure if that would change any-thing for him at all.

The sun bright and warm and the sky a deep and luminous blue. He was still standing in front of the house finishing his quad stretches when the garage door across the street hummed open and Nicole ducked under it and came bounding outside, waving to him. "I got an A on my report!" she yelled.

"What report?"

"The report about you!"

"Ah! Good job!" he said.

A moment later, Jennifer emerged from the interior of the garage in her characteristic, skintight workout uniform. "Hi neighbor," she yelled across to him.

He waved at her, but said nothing. Just looking at her there made his stomach tighten at the memory of her naked body. He had waved to her departing car earlier that week but apart from that he had not seen her a single time since their one night of drunken sex, the blinds always closed, the house always quiet.

He expected her to step into her car and drive away but she did not do so, instead ushering Nicole into the car and then stepping toward him. She looked miraculous even when simply walking across the street. "Going out for a run?" she said. She stood next to him by the rental car now, one hand on a spandex-clad hip.

"Just finished," he said.

"You ought to come to the gym with me sometime. You'll have a lot more fun."

"I'm sure I would." He looked at her, her smiling face and the swell of her suede breasts.

"Something on your mind?" she said.

"Oh," he said. Just that. He glanced down to the sidewalk, then returned to her face. "Maybe dinner tonight?" he said.

"Your place?"

"Could be." His mind ranged over the fact that the downstairs was still mostly covered in plastic, that there was essentially no furniture, and that he had done no cleaning whatsoever since returning to the house.

"I'm kidding," she said. "Anyway, no dinner, but if you want to come by at, say, eight thirty or nine we can have dessert. How does that work for you?"

"Dessert?"

"Don't you eat dessert?"

"I do," he said and he smiled.

"Don't get any ideas."

"Oh, I won't," he said. "Dessert works just fine."

Nicole's voice came from across the street: "Mom, we're going to be late!"

"See you tonight, then." Then she turned and her thin, muscled frame moved back across the street. In a moment, her red sports car passed and Nicole's hand waved at him as the car roared around the corner and out of sight.

It occurred to him that he should be running more often.

He was just out of the shower when his phone began to vibrate. He lifted it from the dresser, the heat of his hand steaming the surface in a brief disappearing arc. The tiny screen read "Barb". Seeing her name there made him think of Jennifer and a sharp lurch of guilt ran through him yet again. Shit. He let it ring through to voice mail and then finished drying himself. A moment later there was the chime tone indicating a new message and when he had finished dressing he dialed into his voice mail and listened.

"Hi, it's me," she said. Then a pause. "Listen, I wanted to tell you this in person. I mean not on a voice mail. But you're not there." Another pause, a longer one this time. He thought that she might have hung up the phone but then her voice came again, with a sense of resolve and finality that he had not anticipated: "I wanted to tell you that I filed divorce papers," she said. "So someone will come to serve you papers. Officially, I mean. OK? All right. Bye then."

The background hiss of the message ended and the computer voice indicated that there were no additional messages. And so there went his marriage, with a voice mail not even a full minute in length. Over and gone. A zero sum. He looked at the phone as if it were some inexplicable life form he had never encountered before and then slowly lowered himself to the edge of the bed. He had known she was not going to return. She had told him as much. And yet it now felt as if some equation of finality had scrolled out before him and had been solved in the only way it could ever have been solved. He had simply failed to reach that solution.

He did not know how long he sat there but he did not move until he had reached the next part of the same equation. He had been staring through the window into the neighboring yard where a patch of yellowed, dead grass was boxed in by a fence only a few years old, and when he came to the next variable his solution was not meant to be vindictive or malicious, or at least he did not think of his actions in those terms, but rather was a simple act of logic. She did not live with him anymore. She had made the decision to have an affair and to move out and to leave him in this empty house and he was simply following out the logical endpoint of the equation she had formed. She had called to tell him she had filed for divorce. She had solved for one variable; he would solve for another.

So he dialed the payroll office at JSC and asked what he would need to do to change the direct deposit of his salary to a new bank account and found it was as easy as filing a sheet of paperwork that the payroll office would be glad to mail him.

When the call was over he set the phone on the table and sat looking at it. Once again there was a silence in the room, in the house, perhaps in the whole cul-de-sac. He had seldom thought about himself as making decisions that were right or wrong—his work had not allowed for the attachment of such a moral compass—but now that was exactly where his mind went, into that gray tenuous area between one variable and the next. He did not know what Barb's financial situation was in Atlanta. He had assumed she was living with her mother at her parents' house but it was clear to him that there was no reason she should have access to his paycheck. Not anymore. She had left him; he had not left her, perhaps would never have left her even had he known about her affair. But was that even true? Once again he wondered if she had brought him into his house. Into the bed that was, even now, upstairs. Once again he wondered if Quinn had known this man. My god.

In the late morning he dialed information and was given the address of a local branch of his bank and then slipped on his shoes and drove there. When he arrived he told the teller that he wanted to withdraw half of his savings and then changed his mind and withdrew all of it and closed what had been their joint account entirely, both checking and savings accounts. Then he took the bank's cashier's check and drove down the street until he saw a different bank and parked and entered and opened an account there and then deposited the check. Done. He did not want to feel guilty about the act, not this too, but the feeling was present nonetheless even though it was too late now to go back, this thought too filling him momentarily with self-loathing. What kind of weak man had he become? He wondered then how long it would be until she discovered the bank accounts had been closed, until she called him to complain. Hours? Days? Weeks? He had completely stopped thinking about painting the second coat of eggshell downstairs, let alone starting the upstairs, but he had managed to move his bank accounts. That was something people did when they divorced. It was something he needed to do and it was done and he had done it.

The remainder of the day was spent making phone calls, none of which served to continue the promise of forward motion that the change of banks had engendered. He spoke with Jim Mullins but the conversation was circular and pointless. Mullins had told him to check in and he had done so but what more was there to say? When he told Mullins he was ready to return to work, Mullins's only response was to ask if he had been keeping any regular phone appointments with his psychiatrist and if he was making any progress in that arena. Keith did not know how to answer such a question, could not even begin to imagine how an answer could exist at all. He had a phone appointment scheduled with Dr. Hoffmann within the hour but beyond that he had nothing to say and Mullins's repeated urging to take care of himself only frustrated him further.

He spent the time between the call with Mullins and the scheduled appointment with Hoffmann drinking beer and looking at engineering documents on his laptop, all of which he had already read. He could think of little else to do to fill the time. The truth was that he had been dreading the phone call with Hoffmann for most of the week and now that it was nearly upon him he had resigned himself to its inevitability the way one might be resigned to a tooth extraction. It would be unpleasant—he knew that much—but it was expected of him, apparently as part of what Hoffmann had called his "grieving process," although it was also clear that any grieving process he was to have would be determined by others. Even this had been removed from his control as if he was a child or an imbecile.

When the appointed hour arrived at last he dialed the number and Hoffmann's secretary answered and then Hoffmann himself came onto the line. He started right in with the same huge and unanswerable questions he always asked: How have you been doing? What challenges have you had this week? What progress do you think you have made? And Keith answered the same way he always had, with the same short, clipped responses he always gave, not because he intended to be abrupt or obfuscating but rather because these were the only answers he could think of. Fairly soon after Keith had returned from the mission, the psychiatrist had told him that he was free to share anything with him and that the more information he shared the better equipped he would be to offer insight into his experience, and Keith had listened to him and had thought that he would try, that he would try to find better answers, and to offer more detail about what he had done and what he was doing, but then he had found there were no words for how he felt. There was an emptiness within him. It was not unlike space itself. Like one infinity containing another. What words could there be to express such an absence?

Hoffmann asked him if there had been much contact with Barb and so Keith told him that she had filed for divorce and that he had gone to the bank soon after to change his accounts, effectively removing her access to his paycheck.

"That must have been difficult," Hoffmann said in response.

"Difficult? Not really."

"No? How would you describe it then?"

"Well, not difficult," Keith said.

"You're going to have to give me more than that."

"It's a logical outcome."

"Divorce?"

"Yes, divorce."

"I'm not sure I understand."

"I'm not sure what you're asking me."

"I'm asking you how you feel about your wife filing for divorce."

"Confused."

Hoffmann was quiet on the other end of the phone, across those hundreds of miles of landscape. Then he said, "How so?"

"I don't know." He paused. Then said, "I don't know what else to say."

"That's all right. I'll wait," Hoffmann said.

Keith stared into the vacant space before him. The eggshell paint on the walls. The kitchen island with its clear plastic wrapper. "OK, well, I felt good about changing the bank account because it seemed like something I could do without her. But also I felt, I don't know, a little guilty about it. Like I shouldn't have done it."

"Why not?"

"Because she's my wife. Was my wife, anyway."

"The term you're looking for is ex-wife," Hoffmann said.

"Ex-wife," Keith said. The words sounded strange to him. "OK."

"She *is* your ex-wife now," Hoffmann said. "Or she will be soon enough. Legally, I mean. She's filed to legally dissolve your marriage. Is that confusing?"

"No."

"But that's the term you used."

"It just feels weird. Her moving on. But it makes sense."

"Moving *through*."

"What does that mean?"

"It means it might be more helpful if you thought of moving *through* your experiences rather than moving on. It's not like you're going to forget the time you spent with her or the experiences you shared with her or with your daughter. Those will always be a part of who you are."

Keith did not respond.

"Anyway, congratulations," Hoffmann said.

"For what?"

"For taking charge of your situation and doing something about it. It's a good step forward."

"A step forward toward what?"

"Toward moving through this experience."

He did not respond for a long moment. Then he said, "This is the kind of thing you say that I never understand."

"Oh?" Hoffmann said. He sounded genuinely surprised and concerned. "I didn't know you were having trouble understanding. What part of it are you having trouble with?"

"The whole thing. Moving through my experience? What does that mean?"

"Well, it's going to mean different things to different people. To me it might mean figuring out what's going to be next and taking some positive steps toward it. Or developing some new goals and working toward them. That sort of thing."

"My goal is going back to work."

"That's a professional goal, yes, but there are personal goals as well."

Keith did not answer for a moment. Already he had said more than he was comfortable with, the conversation wobbling out onto some uncharted plane the structure of which he could not determine. "I know that," he said at last. "I guess I just don't think in terms of personal goals."

"Why not?"

"Because my professional goals have been the ones that I've needed to work on. The personal stuff just happens. It's not something that you work toward. There's not even an endpoint."

"I disagree."

"I'm not surprised."

"What about your grieving process?"

He could not help but sigh audibly into the phone. "What about it?" he said.

"That could be a goal."

"That doesn't make sense."

"That's an example of an experience you're moving through."

"You mean with the steps or stages or whatever they are?"

"That's one way, yes. Do you think that would be useful?"

"No," he said flatly.

"Can I ask why?"

"Because I don't need someone else's steps to work through. I'm sad that she's gone. I wish she was still here but she's not. She's never going to be. I don't need a twelve-step program to help me realize that."

"That might be true," Hoffmann said. "People deal with grief differently. There's no right way. Some studies suggest that many people are resilient and come through loss on their own and are fine. Others need a more structured approach to it."

"That's what I mean," Keith said. He was irritated now, bordering on real anger, and even as he spoke he could feel part of him quietly urging himself to calm down, knowing that losing his temper would not help anything. But it was too late for that. "You think you have it all programmed but it's not like that. There's no sequence to it so there can't be any goddamn steps. So we talk and you act like you're reminding me that my daughter's dead and my marriage is over and then you ask me how I feel. I feel sad. All the goddamned time. So why do you keep asking me?"

"Because you don't sound sad to me," Hoffmann said. "You sound angry." In contrast to Keith's elevating volume, his voice displayed the same calm composure it always had.

"I *am* angry. What's the goddamned point of this? What's the point of dragging up everything again and again and again?"

"The point is not being angry anymore," Hoffmann said.

Keith was silent, silent for a long time. He could feel gravity pulling him toward the center, toward the iron center of the planet. One hand held the telephone to his face; the other trembled against his chest.

"I can hear that you're upset," Hoffmann said, "and I know this is difficult. But there's a concrete goal here. There really is."

When Keith spoke again his voice was quiet, nearly a whisper: "All I want to do is get back to work," he said. "That's what I miss. If you want to help me then help me do that."

"That's what I'm doing," Hoffmann said.

Keith said nothing. He wanted to simply hang up the phone but did not do so. The conversation had turned in on itself like an endless loop and he knew that no matter what he said it would simply swing back around to him again. It was maddening and reminded him of just how much he disliked these kinds of interactions. Personal conversations of any kind were like numeric fields that appeared to be equations but which were impossible to solve and were therefore no equations at all, the algorithm looping back upon itself once more. "OK," he said, "then what do I have do for you to give Mullins a clean bill of health?"

"That's not something I do."

"Then you're not helping me."

"You misunderstand," Hoffmann said. "It's literally not something I do. That's not part of why we're talking and I wouldn't give Jim Mullins that kind of information even if he asked. I'm just here to help you through your daughter's death, your divorce, and yes some stuff related to work if that's what we need to talk about. I'm trying to help you work through your experiences and I hope that will result in easing your migraines. That's all I'm here for." There was a pause and Keith wondered if Hoffmann was waiting for him to respond but before he could say anything the psychiatrist's voice continued: "Look, Keith, I get a sense that you don't want to do this anymore. You certainly have that right. But I want you to think about why you don't want to do it. Is it just because it's hard to talk about these things? Because avoiding talking about them isn't going to make it any easier for you. So what do you really want to do?"

Keith did not respond. He wondered what Mullins would say if he simply stopped making appointments with Dr. Hoffmann. He had dreaded the approach of each and every appointment and yet now that the specter of canceling his appointments permanently had been raised he found himself hesitating. It was as if he was on an EVA, stiffly moving in his space suit, and it had been suggested that he remove the tether that connected him to the body of the ISS and even though he knew he would not need to rely on it, the fact that it was present meant that he did not have to think about it at all. The tether was there so that it did not need to be considered. But then he did not know why he thought of this comparison now, for Hoffmann's appointments were only a source of dread and irritation, a time each week when he knew Quinn would be discussed in the most stark and terrifying ways, with a bluntness that Keith still found jarring and troubling. And this time he himself had said the words: "My daughter's dead." He could not recall ever saying it before. Not like that. Not with that level of blunt clarity. He never wanted to hear such a thing. Not from himself. Not from Hoffmann. Not from anyone.

"I don't know," he said at last.

"Good. So let's talk about that next week."

"You want to have a counseling appointment about whether or not to have more counseling appointments?"

"That's exactly what I want to do," Hoffmann said.

Keith sat there for a moment with the phone to his ear. Then he said, "OK, then."

The phone call lasted a few more minutes and when it was done he clicked the phone closed and sat for a long stretch in the silence of the house. Maybe during the next conversation he would tell Hoffmann that he was through with the appointments but then he worried about the effect the cancellation would have on Mullins and the Astronaut Office and his ability to return to Houston and he was not sure he wanted to run that risk.

The house a vacancy and his footfalls wearing a path through its carpeted spaces. He drank a beer from the refrigerator. Then another. He was going to see Jennifer that evening and he hoped more than ever that she would have sex with him again. But the clock moved so very slowly. His own motion a curved and distended zigzag drifting ever away. My daughter's dead. Quinn. My god.

Nine

THE SUN HAD disappeared behind the houses on the hill beyond the vacant lot and the sky glowed with a furious spectral blue that cut all the corporeal things of the earth into individual black darknesses. Keith Corcoran too, stepping into that blue night of silhouettes. Whatever feeling of confusion or defeat or rage or frustration he felt or might have felt after the conversation with Hoffmann had faded into the anticipation of seeing Jennifer again, a feeling not unlike that of a child on Christmas Eve waiting for the multicolored promise of the dawn. This time, though, it had been dusk he had been awaiting and the present he hoped to open was not for any child. Now at last the time had arrived and there was Jennifer's house across the street, the porch light glowing a pale yellow the color of the moon. His stomach felt light and the night air was still warm but moved against his face softly like a dark and gentle hand.

And that was precisely the moment when Peter Kovalenko's voice came booming out of the darkness at last: "Astronaut Keith Corcoran!"

The voice was sudden enough to make Keith jolt in surprise. "Christ," he said. His own voice sounded loud and flat in the open air of the night. He had stopped walking and peered in the direction of the voice, into the black emptiness that was the vacant lot.

"Come, let me show you something," the voice called to him.

"I'm just heading out," he called. He paused then, waiting, but there was no response. Had he been heard? He looked at Jennifer's house again, then up the street. The streetlamps not yet activated and the field beyond the end of the cul-de-sac was a black pool. He had been expecting Peter to want to talk with him about what had happened and he knew there was little use in avoiding the interaction but how he wanted to. At least now it would be a short exchange. It would have to be. He would listen to the apology of Peter Kovalenko the Ukrainian. Then he would tell him, as graciously as possible, that he was glad to help and would do it again if such a situation were to arise. Is that not what an astronaut would do? Then the conversation would be over and he would continue on to Jennifer's.

He stood in the dusk-colored darkness, unmoving for a long moment, and then at last said, "Hang on," and turned and moved up the cul-de-sac to where the concrete ended and he stepped over the chain there and into the dirt and the weeds. The field was a black emptiness of unresolved obstacles. "Christ, I can't see anything," he said.

"There is path on left," Peter's voice came. "Watch out for thistles."

He stepped to the left, objects shifting in his view so that it appeared as if everything at his feet was in motion all at once and in all directions. His shoes crunched into what sounded like dead leaves but which felt hard and stiff, like a bundle of small sticks gathered together underfoot.

"Little further, I think," Peter said.

He took a few more hesitant steps in that direction and then could just make out a pale path threading through waist-high thistle.

Twice he stumbled but at last he arrived at Peter's side and Keith extended his hand, his eyes still not quite adjusted to the night, and

Peter took it and they shook and Peter said, "You did me great service."

"Not a problem," Keith said.

"I'm embarrassed," Peter said.

"No need."

"I don't want to talk more with this. Only with thanks."

"OK, then," Keith said. There was a brief pause and he expected Peter to continue his apology despite his statement to the contrary but he did not do so, instead standing in the dark silence, his shape emerging out of it as Keith's eyes adjusted to the twilight. The telescope reflected a stripe of radiance, the last of the sunset.

"Let me show you something," Peter said.

"It's all right," Keith said. "I'm just on my way out."

"Bah," Peter said. "I'm happy to do this." He leaned into the eyepiece and then stepped back and motioned Keith toward it. "Hard to see now because we are too early, but still there."

Keith leaned in and looked through the telescope, the circle of light shifting as he tried to align his vision with it. There might have been something there, a kind of blur, but all he could really make out was the luminescent blue field of the eyepiece. "I can't really see anything," he said at last.

"Yes, too light up there maybe," Peter said. "M57. Ring Nebula. Better to see later."

"I've heard of it," Keith said.

"Yes, is famous nebula," Peter said. "In constellation Lyra. Between stars."

Keith took his eye from the telescope and looked into the low eastern sky toward which it pointed, out past where the cul-de-sac emptied onto Riverside, the houses there quiet and still and the streetlights yet dark and above them a scattering of dim stars.

"You see?" Peter said.

"I've never been good at finding that stuff."

"And yet you go up there."

"Yes, I do." He returned his eye to the telescope. It was a static thing: like looking at a slightly blurry photograph in the far corner of an empty room. "I'm not an astronomer," he said.

"I know," Peter said. "I know this." It was almost an apology, as if he had said something wrong and then had said something wrong again in covering for it.

Keith took his eye from the eyepiece and again looked up at the sky. The moon a faint arc and the deep blue awash with tiny points of light that hung motionless. The idea of what he had seen from the end of the robotic arm returned to him now, but only as something not to be believed, as if a dream he had recalled briefly only to have it sift again into vacancy. The stars themselves had held within them a brilliance he had not expected or understood, their colors so bright and vibrant that they seemed all at once to clear away all possible methods of describing them.

He continued to stare up in the direction of whatever constellation Peter had said the nebula was in, the remembrance of the starfield during his mission already gone, the stars before him dimmed by the atmosphere. It was difficult to believe that these were the same stars at all.

He wanted to walk back to the concrete and asphalt of the cul-de-sac and on to Jennifer's door but instead of excusing himself and leaving the field he said, "You must have been really hung over."

"So much sick I could not walk," Peter said, "but wife takes care of me."

"I wish I could say the same."

"Yes, yes, she is thinking she's like mother to me." There was a sense of irritation in Peter's voice and he actually waved his hands in the air as if brushing away a fly.

Keith did not say anything in response, only standing and looking from Peter to the stars and back to Peter again.

"Only my wife she does not complain. She is happy here."

"Well, that's important."

"Yes, yes, she is happy and I complain."

He stared into the sky at the few stars visible above them and then around the ever-increasing darkness of the field. He could make out the slightly luminescent forms of the thistle in the night now, their twisting, ragged feather shapes stretching into invisibility.

"She is a good person, I think," Peter said. Then he added, "My wife."

"Seems that way to me."

"It is true. Her brother and her mother all complain and complain."

"Why did you come here?" Keith said. He did not know why he asked it and yet he had, and now he stood and listened as Peter exhaled noisily, something between a breath and a sigh.

"Luda," he said. "She wanted to and so we did."

"You don't like it here, though?"

"It's not same. I mean I know it's not same, but I was not this stupid in Ukraine." He paused and then said, "I mean job. This job I have here is stupid. Not good."

"What did you do in Ukraine?"

"I worked at National Academy of Sciences. At observatory."

"Oh," Keith said. He realized that he had not so much as glanced at Peter's résumé since the day Luda placed it into his hand. "Sounds like a good job."

"Yes, yes. Good for me. I was not astronomer but I knew them all. Some cosmonauts too. I did university but with Luda and the kids then I did not finish. But I have brain. I do have brain. Here in America, I put stock on shelves. Unload trucks. And then I make a fool of myself for pretty girl. Here I am not so smart as I was."

"You mean the girl at Starbucks."

"Audrey. I do not know why. Too young for me, maybe. I don't even know. It is embarrassing."

"I wouldn't worry about it too much."

"I have Luda," Peter said.

"Yes," Keith said. "Lesson learned, then."

"I think you are right. But I'm thinking about her still. That has not stopped."

"She's pretty young."

"I know that. She is . . . American. Beautiful like flower. Like yellow flower. And nice too. A nice girl."

Keith said nothing, once again staring up into the night sky.

"Ah," Peter said suddenly. It was an exclamation, a sound of disgust. "This place has made me stupid." Then he paused as if considering his choice of words. "No, not stupid. Foolish."

Again, silence.

"I make you uncomfortable with this talk," Peter said.

Keith looked at him, his own expression of surprise probably concealed by the lack of light. "I guess so," he said.

"Yes," Peter said, "and I have already delayed you from plans. I apologize again."

"No need," Keith said. He did not know what else to say and so he said nothing. He wondered then if this was what his wife had been talking about, his reluctance to discuss the emotional quality of human life, to share his feelings, but what was he supposed to say?

"You are successful man," Peter said. "Famous astronaut. This is not something they can take away from you. If you moved to Ukraine right now people would know and you would still be you. Here I move to America and I am nothing all over again. It is like I was again born like new baby and have to start over with job any teenager could get." He paused and then added: "I don't think you will understand."

"It's a problem," Keith said. "What are you going to do about it?"

"I don't know this," Peter said.

Keith said nothing for a moment. Then: "Look, all problems are the same. You figure out what the problem is, then you quantify it, then you work on solving it."

"It is maybe not same," Peter said.

"Everything's the same," Keith said. "You have a wife and children. You have a house. These are not problems. The problem is that you have a job you don't like and you got drunk and made a mistake. Figure it out." He was surprised at his own tumble of words. It was as if he had been waiting for the right words to come and when they did at last he could not stop them or even temper their tone or direction.

Peter's response was to say nothing for a long time. The stars in their ever-increasing luminosity above them. The moon a sliver at the edge of a dark bowl lined with the squared outlines of silhouetted houses.

"I think you are right, Astronaut Keith Corcoran," Peter said at last.

"I don't know."

"I think you do. You are astronaut."

"That doesn't much matter right now."

"This always matters."

"I wish that was true," Keith said.

Another pause and then Peter said, "You mean because your wife is not here?"

Keith was surprised, surprised by the question and surprised that Peter knew anything about his marriage at all. "I don't know if that has anything to do with it," he said. It was silent again and he knew that Peter was waiting for him to volunteer more information but what more could he have said? That his wife had had an affair? That his daughter was dead? That he was fucking the woman across the street to fill the time? That he did not know if he would ever get a clean bill of health even though he had not had a real migraine since he was back in Houston? That the biggest thing he could accomplish on any given day was making a phone call and changing a bank account?

"Maybe things are better for you now when she is gone," Peter said, slowly.

"Not really," Keith said. He paused and then, for reasons he did not even understand, said, "She took all the furniture."

"All?"

"All except the bed and the couch."

"She took television too?" There was real concern in his voice.

"She left the little one but then I dropped it walking down the stairs. That's the one you saw me set on the curb."

"Shit," Peter said.

Keith actually laughed now. "Yeah, that was a shit kind of day," he said.

"I believe you," Peter said. Then he added: "Bad, bad, bad, bad." His breath whistled slightly through his teeth.

"Yeah," Keith said. "Bad is what it is."

"But you are free to do whatever," Peter said.

"Yeah, I'm free to do whatever. But I don't do anything."

"You're going to do something now, yes?"

"Yeah, I'm going to visit the lady across the street."

"Oh, you have date with pretty lady. That's something."

Keith laughed. "Funny," he said.

"Why funny?"

Keith shook his head. "It doesn't feel like much."

"It is something, though, that I cannot do. You can go into space. You can date pretty lady. I stock shelves. I have wife. There are things I will never do."

Keith was smiling in the darkness but he knew it was unlikely that Peter could see him there. "I'm not the guy to admire," he said.

"If we could trade lives maybe everything different," Peter said.

"Yeah," Keith said. A pause. Then he said, "I have to get going."

"Thank you for your time," Peter said.

"Not necessary."

They shook hands in the darkness. "You are welcome to be here," Peter said.

It was an awkward statement and it took Keith a moment to understand what he meant but when he did he said, "Thank you."

"I look at Messier objects mostly," Peter said abruptly.

"I don't know what that means."

"Does not matter. Is just something to look at. Like Ring Nebula."

"OK then."

"Next time I show you more of them."

"Sure, next time," Keith said.

The sky had darkened and his eyes had adjusted to the shadows, the path a silver line snaking through the spindly, skeletal arms of thistle. Beyond them, the cul-de-sac absurdly bright, the edges of the field silhouetted against it: tiny black knives arrayed as a kind of barricade against an unseen foe. Neighbors and suburbanites. The whole world out there lit like a film set: all the actors retired to their homes, the neighborhood scene frozen in stasis. A photograph. A still life. A museum piece.

Nicole was still awake and so he sat on the sofa downstairs and waited for Jennifer to return and when she did so they sat at the dining room table and ate cheese and crackers and drank a bottle of wine. When the wine was gone she asked him if he would like to follow her upstairs. Of course they made love. Of course they did: on the bed at first and then again in the shower. He may have enjoyed it even more than he had the first time, as now there was a sense of familiarity and possession that he did not have before. He knew he would have her and he did and that sense of ownership was something that both startled him and heightened his sense of pleasure, her body a thing that he craved like food. It seemed the same for her. She had pulled off his clothes as if some emergency necessitated the act, clawing at his shirt and his pants and taking him first in her mouth as if the need was too great to wait for her own nakedness to reveal itself.

The second time it had begun in the shower and ended with them both returning to the bed and when it was done he lay back, his legs extended over the edge of the mattress, her body poised over his, her breasts still touching his chest. She kissed him on the neck and breathed out, long and beautiful, a kind of sigh mingled with a moan of release. "You just keep on coming by, neighbor," she said.

She was beautiful there, perched above him, his body still penetrating hers even as he softened. There were tiny freckles on her shoulder and he stared at them, so close to his face. "That sounds like something I'd like to do," he said.

"I'll bet you would." She lifted herself up, sliding him more deeply into her for a moment and he tightened under her and sucked in his breath and then she lifted herself off. "I think I was showering before I was so rudely interrupted," she said, smiling.

"Rudely?"

"You coming?"

"Yes." He propped himself up on his elbows and looked at her as she stood there, the curves of her body, the hardness of muscle.

She turned and walked to the far side of the bedroom and he heard the shower start up again and the click of the door and she stepped out of sight.

His own body looked pathetic, his penis a weird pale worm that had wriggled up from some dark underground. Yes, he was free to date the pretty woman across the street, as Peter had said, and indeed here he was and Peter was probably still out there in the field with his telescope looking up at some nebula or another. Here he was, reclining on her bed, a fine slick of sweat cooling under the overhead fan, his member shriveling.

He rose and stumbled forward to the shower and she stood there under the spray, a bar of soap in her hand. "Don't get any ideas," she said.

He opened the glass door. A blast of hot steam. "Hmm," he said. "You take a lot of showers."

"Twice a day at least," she said. "Sometimes more if there's time."

"Really clean," he said. The water was the temperature of fire. "Damn," he said.

"Too hot?"

"No," he said. "Christ, yes."

She reached out and turned the knob, just barely. He could not perceive a change in the temperature. "Sissy," she said.

She finished with the soap and handed it to him and again it was too small a space for the two of them and their soapy bodies were slick against each other and when he tried to kiss her again she held him off with a gentle hand to his chest and said softly, "I think we're done for tonight," and he looked at her and she said, "Don't be disappointed. It was fun."

"I'm not," he said, but he was.

She stepped out of the shower and into the closet and put on her white robe again and he showered quickly, turning the water temperature down until it was no longer scalding. When he was finished she handed him a towel and he dried himself and she moved past him back into the bedroom as he dressed. A moment later he heard the voices of the television in the room: a talk show with its occasional wave of laughter and applause.

She was seated on the bed against the headboard and glanced over at him as he entered the bedroom again.

"What are you watching?" he said.

"Oh, I don't know. Letterman."

He sat on the edge of the bed. "Who's the guest?" he said.

"I don't know." She paused and then she said, "I'm just going to go to bed now, Keith."

He did not understand what the statement meant at first and then he spluttered, "Oh, OK, yeah," and stopped again and looked around the room, at the television, then back at her.

"Right," he said. He stood. "I'll see you later, then."

"All right," she said. She rose from the bed and embraced him briefly and then separated from him again. "See you later in the week, I'm sure."

"Maybe next time you can enjoy my lack of furniture," he said.

She smiled as if patronizing a small child. "Maybe," she said. "You can let yourself out, right?" She turned, climbed back onto the bed, settling once again into her TV-watching position but continuing to look at him.

"Yeah, OK." He was quiet for a moment and then said, "Bye then."

"Turn the lock on the doorknob, would you?" she said. She smiled at him once more.

He looked at her but her attention had already returned to the television. He turned and paused and then turned the rest of the way and walked out of the room. Behind him the applause rose up momentarily as if in response to his departure and then muffled back into the voice of the host. Words he could not make out.

At the end of the hall, Nicole stood in the open doorway of her bedroom in her nightgown, rubbing one of her eyes absently. "Where's my mom?" she said.

"In there," he said, pointing behind him. She did not move and after a moment he said, "Are you OK?"

"Why are you here?"

"Just visiting."

"Mr. Corcoran was just leaving," Jennifer's voice came from behind him, the words clipped and quiet. She moved past him and picked up Nicole in her arms and the bedroom door closed abruptly behind them.

Keith stood alone in the hall, the muffled sounds of television and mother and daughter murmuring around him. Then he turned and walked down the stairs in the darkness. The lower floor quiet. He stood at the foot of the stairs, the silence complete, and then stepped forward through the plaster arch and into the living room. The sofa and the television like giant creatures that had fallen into a deep slumber. Knickknacks on the mantel cast into a collection of angles and shadows. Everything in the house had a place and each place had been chosen not for utility but for display: towels in the bathroom that could not be used, floral soaps that would never be unwrapped from their unbleached paper wrappers, pillows on the bed that could

not be slept on. An entire life organized based upon the notion of being watched, of being monitored and judged by neighbors, by friends,
perhaps even by himself, and here he stood in the quiet, shadowed and
frozen as if part of it somehow: a man from one house in the darkness
of another.

"What are you doing?"

The voice startled him and he spun around abruptly. She was standing behind him on the last stair, holding the neck of her bathrobe in
one hand, the other still gripping the banister.

"Oh," he said. He looked into the darker shadows of the living
room. "I was . . . I'm not doing anything."

"And?" she said. There was an edge to her voice.

"And I'll see you later," he said.

"Yeah," she said.

He turned toward her, toward the door, and she stared at him as he
passed. There was no pleasure or joy in her eyes. He opened the door
and turned the lock on the handle as he had been told and stepped
outside. He thought she would say something to him before the door
closed, a simple parting word or words, but she did not and he pulled
the door closed.

There was a brightness to the sounds outside. The humming streets
beyond the roofline of darkened houses. From the field: crickets. The
brush of the air against his face was just barely cool and he looked
across the street at his own bleak house. Nothing there. No one home.
Never anyone home. It occurred to him that he had been summarily
dismissed from Jennifer's house but he found himself more surprised
than irritated or angered. Maybe it was the second time, when they
had sex in the shower; maybe he had been too insistent. But then he
knew he had not been too insistent, that it had actually been Jennifer
who had instigated that second time and indeed had instigated the
first. What was it then?

He stepped across the street toward his house but then swiveled
and moved instead toward the dark streetlamp at the farthest edge of

187

the cul-de-sac. It was akin to the end of the world, the light fading out. He looked into that emptiness for Peter and it was not until he took his first tentative step past the sidewalk and into the thistle-lined path that he realized he was disappointed that he could neither see nor hear him. No one in the field but himself and no telescope to justify the night.

Interval: Light

$$(c\Delta t)^2 = (\Delta r)^2$$
$$(\Delta s)^2 = 0$$

IT HAD ALWAYS been part of his plan to make captain before resigning for a position with NASA and it worked out as he knew it would, although that first position would not be at Johnson Space Center as he had hoped. The head researchers there told him they were very interested in his skills and qualifications but that there were few positions open and none that he was particularly suited for. It was disappointing, but he knew there were advantages to coming into the astronaut program from some other NASA facility. And so he settled on Dreyfuss Research Center, a smaller facility but an important one. The position there was a perfect match for his mathematics and engineering skills and would extend the kind of work he had been doing at Wright-Patterson during his time in the air force: low-energy / high-power propulsion and guidance systems. There was the further incentive that the research at Dreyfuss fed exclusively into various ongoing missions and this meant, at long last, that his work would be going directly into space.

A month before his start date at Dreyfuss he flew out to look at neighborhoods in the vicinity of his new employment, touring the endlessly sprawling metropolitan area on the arm of a realtor. Barb's opinions had always been strong in regards to house styles, floor plans, shopping proximity, school districts, and the like and now those opinions saw the three of them—he and Barb and Quinn, the latter sullen and quiet in the backseat, angry at having to move away from her friends in Ohio—driving in seemingly endless circles, farther and farther from the research center until they finally happened upon a suburb that met her standards. It was a relatively new neighborhood across from a small park but what made this area different from any of the other twenty or so neighborhoods they had already driven through he could not begin to understand and he argued against the location with some vigor even though he knew that he would ultimately lose. With traffic, the commute to Dreyfuss would be a full hour and a half in each direction on four lanes of freeway blacktop through an endless maze of chain stores and parking lots, and through five apparently separate but identical communities. He told himself he was unconcerned with the tedium of the drive, but each evening on his way home he would pass a freeway sign that read: "If you lived here you would be home by now." It was savage irony that the community the sign advertised appeared to be exactly like the one in which they had settled.

The lone upside was that they were close to a high school for gifted students, the Academy of Arts and Sciences. At least Quinn would have some place to study, a school that might match her talents and which would push her forward on her own unbound vector, the magnitude of which had yet to be measured. She had been examined for the gifted program at the end of her fourth-grade year—the earliest she could at the grammar school she had attended in Ohio—and had tested at the tenth-grade level in math.

"Don't get any ideas," Barb had told him then.

"Ideas about what?" he answered

"You're going to try to turn her into a math geek or something. I just know it." Her tone was playful and she was smiling, proud of her daughter, of their daughter.

"I think she's already a math geek," he said.

She looked at him. "Well, don't make it worse."

"Don't worry," he told her. "I won't."

Of course she excelled in her math classes. It was what he expected of her. And she had a gift for it so how could it be any different? Was she not her father's daughter? Sometimes, when he arrived home early enough in the evening for her to still be awake, he would watch her do her homework, watch the numbers she wrote down and the numbers she did not, the gaps in the process that nonetheless led to accurate answers: her tiny girl's hands skipping along the page, answering another problem, moving on to the next. Her pencil like a butterfly alighting here and there: a symbol, a number, a variable, and then, finally, the answer. He had not been so adept at her age. She was better than he was and she would go further. This was what he had decided, but there had been few classes at her school to develop her gift. Her last teacher had given up entirely on having her follow the curriculum, instead bringing a college algebra textbook from home and having her work through those problems during class time.

And yet when he brought up the academy to Quinn her immediate response was to call it "nerd school."

"Oh come on," he said. "What does that even mean?"

They were at the dinner table now and Quinn did not even look up from her plate, stirring green mushy peas around the outer edge, slowly, as if working out a problem or a design of some kind. "It means it's nerd school."

"Honey, don't call people names," Barb said. "I'm sure they're very smart."

"That's what *nerd* means, Mom. Smart."

"That can't be a bad thing, then, can it?" Barb said.

"No, it's not *bad*," Quinn said. "It just *is.*"

"I don't like your tone," Barb said.

Quinn said nothing for a long moment and in the silence Keith speared a cube of pork chop with the end of his fork. "I think it would be really good for you," he said. "Going to a school like that."

"Sounds like it's for super-smart kids."

"You don't think you're smart enough?" he said.

"I don't know," she said.

He looked up at her now. His daughter. "Then what is it?" he said.

"Because it's nerd school."

"You mean the reputation of the school?"

"Yeah, it's for nerds."

"Who cares?"

"I do," she said.

And then Barb, from across the table: "Really, Keith?"

"She's smart," he said.

"I know she's smart," Barb said, "but *private* school? Do you know how much something like that costs? Maybe we should talk about this later."

"It's probably expensive," he said. "But that's not a good reason not to do it."

"It's not?"

"We'd have to make some sacrifices."

"Hello, parents. I'm still here," Quinn said.

"Quinn, listen," he said.

"I *am* listening. You guys are freaking me out."

"Don't freak out," he said. "There's no reason to freak out."

"Well, then don't make me freak out," she said. "We just moved and now you want to put me in some weird school."

He sat there at the table, not speaking now. He had not even brought up any of the aspects of the school he found particularly interesting or useful, had not even brought up how it might help her embrace the gift he now knew she possessed and which public school had not accessed at all. Already he felt defeated.

"Christ, you two," he said. "I'm trying to help here."

Quinn was quiet. Then she said, "I know, Dad. I know you are."

"Can we at least not call it 'nerd school'?" he said.

"What should we call it then?"

"The academy."

"The Academy of Nerds?"

"Quinn, that's enough," Barb said.

"OK, OK," she said. She was smiling though, seemingly on the verge of laughter.

"It's a good school," he said.

"It's for smart people."

"You are smart people."

"Yeah, but not like that."

"Yes, like that."

"No, I mean, not like they are. They're . . . like you."

"Like me? What do you mean?"

She was silent now, staring at her plate.

"Seriously, Quinn, what do you mean?"

"Can you just drop it?" Barb said.

"No," he said. There was no anger or irritation in his voice, perhaps because it did not occur to him what she meant. So he said it again, "What, Quinn? What?"

"Dad, it's just . . . you know . . ."

"No, I don't know."

She still would not look at him, her eyes focused on her plate. Her peas. Her pork chop. "You're not, like, normal."

"I'm not normal?"

"Don't be mad."

"I'm not mad."

"I don't mean it like it's bad."

"How do you mean it then?"

"You know . . . you're, like . . . different."

"Different how?"

"Can we talk about something else?" Barb said.

He did not respond or even look at his wife until he felt her hand on his arm. Then he turned. Her eyes were wide and the look on her face was one of concern.

"We'll talk about this later," Barb said. "Can't we? Can't we talk about this later?"

He was quiet for a moment. Then he said, "OK. Later then."

"Thank you," Barb said. "Now let's talk about something else." She exhaled audibly and turned back to her dinner plate. "How was work?" she said.

"Fine," he said. "Work was fine."

Then it was quiet at the table, each of them chewing, focused on their dinner plates. On pork chops. On rolling green peas.

In the months that followed, he might have continued to press her on the issue of the school, or at least might have focused on her progress. Later he would pick apart his inability to do so but at the time his own life had become a frantic push. Missions were constantly in development and his engineering work was regularly going up with those missions. He was in ongoing communication with astronauts and like-minded research scientists and while there was, of course, some level of bureaucracy to deal with, the work itself was everything he had ever wanted. For the first time he could see himself actually becoming an astronaut, that ideal goal solidifying out of the dream or fantasy it had been in New Jersey so many years ago and achieving an incandescence fueled not only by his own desire and ambition but also by many of the high-level personnel at the research center, several of whom told him point-blank that they would love to see him apply for the astronaut training program in Houston and that they would be willing to help him get there.

For the first time, too, he was encountering physicists who worked with mathematical ideas he was utterly unfamiliar with, material that seemed in many ways to be completely impractical and yet was apparently providing at least partial answers to huge questions about how the universe itself functioned: its size, its shape, its speed, its lifespan. The mathematics here were staggering and he found himself drawn to the ideas even as they unsettled him. All his life he had focused on the tangible, the physical, the direct application, and some of the abstraction necessary for the enormous questions being asked was beyond his ability to embrace, if not understand.

It reminded him of his first encounter with fractals and chaos theory, and indeed more than one of the scientists at Dreyfuss had images of fractals pinned to the walls of their offices and labs: filigreed and ornamented shapes like flaming dragons comprised of delicate ferns, fire, soap bubbles, and snowflakes—all of which was, in actuality, the graphed results of subtly changing algorithms repeated thousands, hundreds of thousands, of times. He had been a junior in high school when he had first encountered similar images, these from a library book that he had checked out among several others. He had long since forgotten the other books but he had not forgotten the book on fractals. At the time he had heard of the subject but knew very little about it. And so he lay upon his bed after dinner and read captions about the Mandelbrot set and the dragon sweep and the Peano-Gosper curve and the Koch snowflake: all images presented in the text and all of which he viewed as mere mathematical curiosities or games, diversions that a mathematician might perform to pass the time. There were algorithms in the book and he punched one into his home computer—a rare gift from his parents upon the start of high school, rare because they could not afford such extravagances—and then turned to the other books, and later his homework, and then to the shower and his bed.

The next day he returned home from school and did not even think of the computer, had completely forgotten about what he had typed into it the previous evening, so that when he went to the screen long after dinner and saw the blocky bitmapped image there he did not at first know what it could be: a series of circles within circles, all of them arrayed in a kind of arc not unlike an oversize necklace. Then he remembered the algorithm, the math he had asked the computer to work on and realized that it had been working on that algorithm ever since, for over twenty-four hours, and what he was viewing now was the result of that period of time, the extent of what the computer could calculate. He changed the scale on the graph to highlight one of the smaller circles and realized then what he might have already known had he read the text more carefully: that each of the circles was comprised of yet smaller circles and these too were comprised of even smaller circles. The image might have gone on like that forever had he a computer capable of the calculation.

It was interesting but nothing more than that because he still viewed it as a kind of game or diversion. He sat with the book again and worked out a few rows of numbers with his calculator and by hand, plotting them on a sheet of graph paper, moving on to another sheet when that first was full and continuing to graph. At some point he started the computer working on another algorithm, returning then to the pad of paper. The calculations were easy enough but the numbers that stacked themselves in their columns on the page made little sense to him and so he continued to work, to calculate. Iterated numbers of no central relation and a graph that appeared as if peppered with random points of no particular order. He could see no shape there, no sense of direction or method by which a curve or parabola or some other line could cut through the points.

He continued to work, absorbed now, not understanding, still feeling like he was missing some essential step or that he was performing the task somehow incorrectly because he had seen the image on the screen and knew there was order, that somehow the rows and rows of numbers would repeat to continue the motion of a particular shape, that such a repetition must be periodic, predictable, because the algorithm was folding back on itself to create the image. But the numbers did not seem to repeat, even though he already had a list of at least a hundred calculations. He returned to the book several times to make sure he was working through the process correctly, confirming that indeed he was, and during one of these confirmations he paged through to the center of the volume, there finding a small collection of color plates, not only of fractals—the shapes were called fractals, he had already learned—but of art as well: the beautifully painted waves of Hokusai, a pencil sketch of roiling clouds and water by Leonardo da Vinci, a series of photographs of clouds in a yellow sky, of moss on a gray stone. Self-similar shapes. Snowflakes that appeared finite to the human eye and yet were infinite in circumference. Not the numbers and yet indeed the numbers.

Of course he knew that numbers—all numbers—were meant to represent the physical world. That was their point and their purpose. But these numbers, these rows upon rows of numbers, described nothing he could point to and yet, eventually, when they reached the tens of thousands, they would apparently build into images of intricate and indeed infinite beauty: shapes nesting in secret within other shapes, order from what, to his eye, continued to look like chaos, the numbers drained even of the colors he had always seen them in, their forms now gray and lifeless.

He was so absorbed that when his mother knocked on his door he did not at first understand what the sound could be. Then she said, the door still closed, "Honey, it's about time to come down for breakfast."

"Breakfast?" he said. "OK."

He looked up from the books and papers, looked to the window where the first gray light of dawn was filtering through the ash trees, and then to the pages around him, sheet upon sheet filled, each and every one, with row upon row of numbers. He had stopped trying to graph the information at some point during the night, letting the computer's concurrent tabulations do that work for him, and now he went to the screen. Upon its lit rectangular surface was displayed a filigreed shape not unlike a beetle, a shape generated by the same numbers he had been working with on the bed, numbers he returned to and looked at in confusion for they held within them no sense of order. No sense of order at all.

He went to school that day and when he returned home he immediately went back to work on the same problems, once again neglecting to sleep, eating only because his mother called him down to the kitchen and then bolting his food, claiming he had homework to complete, that he was working on a project. He could see the numbers upon the page, hundreds of them, and they all seemed to have deserted him, as if they had gone inexplicably silent all at once. Mute. At yet he could see them, could move them and could reorder them and so he tried to make sense of whatever system they represented, for there was always the fact of the image itself, the graphed results of the algorithm, but the individual numbers did not seem to hold any relation. What he saw on the page was stochastic, chaotic. What he saw in the image, in the graphed results, was intricately organized and staggeringly beautiful.

By morning he was so utterly exhausted that his mother took his temperature and told him that he needed to remain home from school, a decision he protested feebly and then returned to his room only to awake in the late afternoon with papers and pencils and calculator strewn around him and the colorless home computer still chattering upon his desk: the beetled screen more detailed now, lightning extending from the edges of the shell as if reaching out into the white space beyond the limits of the graph, perhaps reaching into the room itself.

He returned the books to the library a few days later but the aftereffects remained with him for months and even years to come. In some ways he could trace his desire to become an astronaut to those two days where he seemed to fall down some mathematical wormhole, or rather not the desire to become an astronaut—he had been calling that his goal since he was in grade school—but the development of that goal as his singular focus. He could still feel the taste of those days upon his lips, the flavor of metal, the hint of rust on his tongue. He might have turned directly toward the abstract, might have pushed himself to better understand what was, in essence, the first and only mathematical encounter he had failed to understand. It was certainly his immediate thought to do so, because every problem had a solution. That was the fundamental rule of the numbers, the only rule that actually mattered. Everything could be solved. Everything. Why develop an unsolvable mathematics to describe something as intangible as beauty itself? What purpose could it serve?

The truth was that even though he was inexplicably drawn to that beauty, the very idea of it terrified him because it confused what he had always understood as the purpose of the numbers themselves: fixedness, location, direction, force, mass. His ideas were of sharp angles, clear divisions, straight lines, elegant clean pistons, gears that flowed into each other without effort, jet propulsion, heat diffusion, power, energy. Perfect machines. Perfect, perfect machines. That was math. That was what the numbers had always been for and any other purpose or function they might have served was irrelevant. The numbers resolved into an answer, even if that answer was complex, and therefore a problem that could not be solved was not a problem at all. It was something else. A distraction. A mistake. An error.

He would tell himself over and over that he wanted to become an astronaut because of the challenge and the pinnacle that this achievement would represent but he knew that there was a component of his desire that this explanation did not reach, for of course he could just as actively work on mathematics without becoming an astronaut. But after the fractals there remained within him a source of gravity he had never conceived of or comprehended, a force that seemed to pull at him from space, from the chaos itself, from the fractal and crystalline darkness that existed everywhere beyond him, as inexplicable and indomitable and infinitely beautiful as the pull of life and death itself. And yet he remained as practical as he ever had been, perhaps even more so, and he would take that practicality with him to spin at the fringe of whatever mankind did not know, would probably never know, about the whole of the universe outside Earth's orbit, as if the abyss itself could be placed in a frame and as if such a framing would make it easier to understand. These thoughts not even conscious and yet present nonetheless.

He was only a few steps away from his goal. This was what he had been focused on when Quinn's school year started and it was what he was still focused on when that school year ended and another began. He was so close to becoming an astronaut that it was all he could think of. Perhaps he had assumed that the vector upon which he had imagined his daughter to move continued to guide her progress. Or perhaps he had simply lost track of her. By then he might have lost track of both of them. He had worked so hard, so very hard, every day, for so many hours, and then the phone call from the Astronaut Office came, telling him that he had been accepted into the training program at long last. He was almost there. He went home and told Barb the news and she squealed in delight and leapt into his arms.

She seemed excited but later that same day, before Quinn came home from school, she told him that she did not think it was necessary that they all move to Houston with him, that he should go ahead and start the training and they would talk about moving her and Quinn later, after he had finished the training and was working regular hours at Johnson Space Center. "You're going to be busy all the time, Keith," she had said. "And we'll just be a distraction anyway. You can come home when you can. On weekends or whenever you have a break. And Quinn's just settled into her new school. Remember what happened when we moved last time? That's hard on a kid like her."

He tried to raise counterarguments but she shot them down one after another and there was that central important fact: that he was going to be busy, very busy, all the time. Still, he could not understand why she would want him to start his training without them. But maybe that was not it at all. Maybe she was only stepping aside so he could embrace his training more fully, so that he could charge, unencumbered, toward his destiny, toward their destiny, for they had chosen it together and now it was almost upon them. Maybe she was right and it was premature to move the entire family to accommodate the training period. They could be a family again in Houston when he was done with training. They had their entire lives, after all, and the best part had nearly arrived at last.

"OK," he said, simply and definitively. "OK, we won't move."

Of course he had thought then that Quinn would be relieved for the same reasons that Barb had raised, for indeed he did remember her dramatic reaction to their last move: the weeks of sulking, the angry slamming of doors. Quinn was thirteen years old now and she was already doing the kind of work he had not even known was possible until he was eighteen or nineteen. They had a gifted program at the junior high, one significantly more advanced than the program at her previous school, and the level of mathematics to which she was being introduced was staggering and exciting. He still brought up the academy sometimes, continuing to hope that she might enroll there for high school, but she did not seem any more enthusiastic about the idea. And yet he could not help but think how much greater her experience at the academy would be nor could he understand why anyone would choose something lesser whan a greater solution presented itself, especially because her enthusiasm for mathematics had only grown in intensity. Sometimes she would call him to the kitchen table—still where she did most of her homework—and would ask him to double-check her numbers or would tell him about some project she was doing about black holes or perpetual motion machines or something else and he could feel her excitement, her discovery, the path of her forward motion.

203

The evening he was to tell her his good news, she was working on a math paradox called Hilbert's Hotel, a puzzle he had forgotten about entirely concerning a hotel with an infinite number of rooms, all of which were full, and the various guests that arrive looking for a vacancy. She told him this with a smile on her face, as if imparting some impossible wisdom to her father, as if finally she had something to tell him that he did not know and he played along with that notion.

"So what happens then when an infinity of guests arrive and all of them are looking for a room?"

"I don't know," he said. "They tell them the hotel is full?"

"No, Dad, it's an infinite hotel. Remember?"

"Right," he said.

"Pay attention."

"I am."

"Infinite hotel. Infinitely full. Infinite people arrive and they all want rooms. What do they do?"

"I don't know."

She paused as if for dramatic effect. Then she said, "They ask every other guest to move down one room." She was really smiling now. Beaming. In his memory it was like there was light shining from her. From her face. From all parts of her at once.

"How so?" he said.

"Look," she said. She took a scrap of paper, already mostly covered with numbers, and wrote n on it and then said, "If n is a room with a guest then n moves to n plus one and then—" her pencil moving as she spoke, finishing the line and then sliding the paper around so it faced him. "There," she said.

He looked at it, at the scribbles of numbers and lines and equations rambling across the page. "Nice," he said. "That's interesting."

"That's awesome."

"That's what I meant. Awesome. What's that called again?"

"Hilbert's Hotel. I can't believe you haven't heard of that. It's kinda famous."

"Yeah, maybe I have. Seems familiar. I probably forgot."

"Oh yeah, you forgot. I doubt it."

He smiled at her. "So do I," he said. He leaned over the paper and took the pencil from her and wrote two symbols:

$$\aleph_a$$

"What's that?" she asked.

"Aleph," he said. "It's the symbol for the cardinality of infinite sets."

"The whatsit?"

"The cardinality of infinite sets."

She stared at him.

"The aleph symbol is the cardinality. It just means infinity here."

"Infinity like the hotel?"

"Exactly like the hotel."

"So then the little a is the set?"

"Correct."

"Cool."

"So how would you apply that to the hotel?"

She sat for a moment. Then she said, "Well, the hotel at start would be aleph-a."

"Maybe," he said. "Most mathematicians would probably call it aleph-null."

"Null why?"

"Because that's the smallest possible set."

"OK, so the empty hotel would be aleph-null."

"Yeah, OK," he said.

"Then the infinitely full hotel would be aleph-a."

"Aleph-one. Remember, the sets would be numbered. The a is just the variable."

"Right right," she said. "So aleph-one."

"OK," he said. "Then one more guest arrives and that would be what?"

"Aleph-two, I guess," she said.

"I guess so," he said. "So what does that mean?"

"I don't know."

"Think about it."

She did and then said, tentatively, quietly: "Some infinities are smaller than other infinities?"

"Or larger," he said.

"Or larger," she said. And then, after a moment, she said, "Holy crap!"

He smiled at her. "Yeah, holy crap," he said.

"That's awesome."

"Well, yeah, kind of." He wondered if he could get the same response if he taught her the mathematics of building something, how the numbers could predict the size or density or dimensions a piece of metal would need to be, how the numbers could be made into something solid and useful and tangible. Maybe he would try that next time. "You can't do anything with it but it's fun to think about," he said.

"Yeah, awesome." She sat looking at the paper, at the pencil marks they had both made upon it.

"Glad you're having fun."

"Yeah," she said. "This is heavy stuff."

He smiled again. "Wait until something you do is in space," he said. "That's the heavy stuff."

"Yeah." She looked up at him now. Perhaps she saw him then differently than she had before or perhaps she was just looking at her father. He did not know and would never know. But she looked at him for a long time and said nothing and then her eyes returned to the paper again.

"So about that," he said. "I have some news."

"You heard?"

"I heard."

"Tell me tell me tell me."

He paused and then he said, "I'm in."

"Oh!" she screamed and she threw her arms around him. "I knew it. I knew you'd get in. I knew it."

"Well, so did I," he said, smiling. "I'm glad you're excited."

"Yeah, I'm excited. Of course I'm excited. It's awesome news." She released him and sat staring up at his face.

"So here's the thing. Your mom and I have talked about it. You know the training is all in Houston?"

"Yeah, we're moving. I get it. Bummer but OK."

"No, wait, the idea your mom and I talked about is that I would fly back and forth. At least for a while."

"What do you mean?"

"It would just be for a while. You know. Until we figured out how well it was working."

"How often?"

"I'll be home most weekends, I think."

She looked away and then turned toward him again, her eyes luminous. She looked like a woman then, or like the woman she might become. "But you'll hardly ever be here," she said to him.

"I'll be here every weekend."

"Most weekends, you said."

"Yeah, most weekends."

"Then what about the rest of the week?"

"During the week I'll be in Houston," he said, "and some weekends I probably won't be able to come home either."

"Shit," she said.

"Quinn."

"Shit, shit, shit," she said. Her eyes were already bright with tears.

"We think it's the best idea."

"How is that the best idea?"

"I'd be away those weekends even if you and your mother moved to Houston with me," he said. The first tear slid down her cheek. "Look," he said, "Your mom and I talked about it and we thought it would be better if you didn't have to move again. I mean the school here seems really good and you're learning all kinds of stuff I didn't even know about until I was in college."

"I don't care about that," she said.

"I know," he said, "but it's important."

"No, it's not."

"Yes, it is. You're gifted, Quinn."

"It's not my fault," she said, and now the tears really started to come, pouring down her face, and he knelt next to her on the kitchen floor and pulled her toward him, her head tilting to his shoulder, her arms wrapping around him as she wept.

"Don't say that," he said. "It's not anyone's fault. It's great. I'm proud of you."

"I don't want you to go."

"I have to."

"Why?"

"Because I'm going to be an astronaut."

"Then let me come with you," she said.

He tilted her away from him, his heart a hard burning knot in his chest. "You and I are different from normal people," he said. "We have a gift. That's why I have to be an astronaut and that's why you have to stay here and learn, because that's your gift." The words came slow and halting, perhaps because he had never spoken of her ability in these terms. Or perhaps because he knew there were schools in Houston that could teach her, schools probably even better than the academy. But Barb had made her case and that discussion was over. And it would be easier for everyone this way: less turbulent, less confusing. This was what he told himself.

"I don't care," she said. Her tears had wet his shirt through at the shoulder but she had stopped crying.

"Yes you do," he said. "It'll be OK. You'll see."

And he believed it too, believed, in that moment, that the arrow he had made for himself would continue its long upward motion. As if there was no possibility of return, no aphelion or perihelion to chart the long spiral of his orbit around whatever false burning center he had made.

Know this. That the things that go into the fire are forever changed. That all you have ever done can be measured not by distance but by circumference. That these twin spirals of smoke: they are your life, rising in curls.

Part III

Ten

THE SCREEN READ "Barb—mobile." He tilted forward, the chair legs all returning to the floor with a single loud clack. He had been reading an article off his laptop screen and now he held the phone in his hand while it continued to buzz and vibrate, thinking that he would let the call go to voice mail, but then also knowing that if he did so she would only call him again. Like Peter's apology, it was not something he could avoid and so he answered—"Hello"—and the voice at the other end was shrill and loud: "What the hell do you think you're doing?" she said.

"About what?"

"That's not your bank account; that's *our* bank account!"

"What?"

"You know what I'm talking about," she said. "How am I going to pay my bills?"

"What bills are those?" he said.

"Credit cards. Food. Gas. It's not like life got free."

He did not answer, looked instead at the blank wall before him, the strip of blue masking tape there. "I don't know," he said at last. "What was your plan?"

"What do you mean 'plan'?"

"I mean plan. What are you asking me here, Barb?"

"I'm not calling to play games. That's our shared bank account and you can't just close it. I write checks from there."

"Why don't you open a new account in Atlanta?"

"That's not the point."

"Your point is . . . what then?" he asked.

"My point is that it's a shared account."

"How do you figure?"

"How do I figure? It's a shared account. It's our money not your money."

"Did you put that money there?"

"Don't play that game."

"I'm not playing any game," he said. He rubbed his forehead with his fingertips and stood.

"Yes, you are. Don't play stupid. You know what I'm talking about."

"Do I?" He moved to the sink and then to the cabinet. The tape there had been pulled off and reattached so many times that it no longer stuck at all, the blue strip dangling limply from the darkly stained wood. He opened the cabinet door and retrieved one of the chipped glasses.

"Yes, you do. I was raising our daughter. That's how it works. You can't just close the bank accounts."

He filled the glass with tap water and then sat back down. "Why not?" he said.

"Why are you playing this game?"

"I'm not playing any kind of game," he said. "I don't understand what you're saying."

"Really? You don't understand what I'm saying? It's a shared account."

"It *was* a shared account."

"It's still a shared account."

"I don't see how it could be," he said.

"What are you talking about?" she said.

"You said you filed for divorce."

"So?"

"So why would we share a bank account if we're getting a divorce?"

"It's called alimony, Keith."

"Alimony?" he said.

"Yes, alimony. I spent the last seventeen years raising Quinn while you were trying to become an astronaut. I have no job skills. We get divorced and you pay alimony. That's how it works."

"You had an affair. You filed for divorce. That's what happened."

"That doesn't matter."

"Yes, it does."

She began to yell now and he held the phone away from his face and looked at it. Her voice a shrill, tiny chirping through the miles of line. Like an insect. Then he simply closed the phone and set it on the counter where it almost immediately began to vibrate again—four, five times—and when it stopped he flipped it open quickly and pressed the power button until it cycled into darkness.

The room suddenly seemed very quiet. Before him rested his laptop and the newspaper. He knew he had been dreading the guilt but he did not feel guilty now, in fact felt nothing at all, just a sense of quiet and calm that relieved him. At some point he would likely need to turn his phone back on but then again why should he? Who would need to call him? His work? His ex-wife? Who else? His parents long since dead and his daughter gone into the ground and what friends he had were work friends and hence not people he saw or associated much with outside of the office and now that he was in a kind of exile they were even less likely to call. Jennifer did not have his phone number, not that she would have called. She had not so much as looked at him since she had kicked him out of her home three days ago, her postcoital eviction still a source of irritating confusion. He had waved to her the previous morning as he came in from his morning run and Nicole had waved back but Jennifer simply stepped into her car and closed the door. Things end as soon as they begin.

Who else would call him? The real estate agent. There were people he might have wanted to talk to from NASA—Eriksson, Mort Stevens, Petra Gutierrez—but only Eriksson had ever called him. A short list consisting of a null set, then. Simple math, indeed.

There was a stack of unpaid bills on the kitchen counter—an unwanted surprise when he finally had decided to check the mailbox— and he flipped through them until he found the phone bill and he turned on his mobile again and dialed, paying them with his credit card and then requesting his mobile number be changed. The task was complete in ten minutes. Then he closed the phone and powered it down and returned to the silence of the house. He knew Barb would get his new number eventually but at least there would be some respite.

The local newspaper had begun arriving on his doorstep a week before, apparently part of some kind of subscription promotion, and he had gathered the five or six editions that had appeared next to the rental car. Now he searched for today's paper and when he located it amidst the others on the counter he unrolled it and rested his hands on the newsprint. The headlines always the same. The entire country falling into some kind of economic disaster he did not even understand or care about and yet which was in evidence all around him every day. Even the news a kind of algorithmic loop. He tried to focus on the lead story but the conversation with Barb had rattled him more than he would admit and the words drifted across the page so that he eventually found himself staring not at the newsprint but at the leather sofa that rested between himself and the empty corner of the room like some aquatic beast that had wriggled huge and needy from the ocean and then had expired at long last in the center of the living room. The goddamn sofa. Maybe he could sell it. Or maybe he should push it out to the curved end of the cul-de-sac and light the whole thing on fire. This idea had the most appeal. The fire department would likely come and perhaps the police would fine him but at least the sofa would be gone.

After a time he rose and walked outside without any clear idea of his intent, although he hoped to see Peter standing with the telescope in the field. The sun had long since dropped below the horizon and the night was cool and already there were the first tentative sounds of crickets. What time was it? He did not even know, his entire day a periodic and ever-repeating motion between sofa and chair. Two points and the line that connected them.

He walked to the edge of the cul-de-sac and stepped off into the dirt and into the field, following the path a bit awkwardly at first, the thistle brushing against his thighs and producing thin, scraping sounds as he moved. When he reached the cleared area he stopped. The crickets directly around him had ceased their chirping but far away, across the field, a tiny army of them emitted their overlapping collection of sounds like a long, grainy single note that would continue until morning. The thistle glowed softly and there, far above, the stripe of the Milky Way and stars arrayed in all directions.

He did not know how long he stood there. Perhaps a long while. Perhaps only a moment. At the edges of the lot he could still hear the wide band of yellow sound that was the endless night's call of the crickets. Beyond that, on a slight rise, a series of identical glowing cubes that he knew were windows from the next subdivision. From the field he could see a faint glow from the upstairs windows of Jennifer's house, as if lit from some interior room deep within. The rest of the house remained a black shape.

Farther down the street, a short, squat figure appeared from Riverside and moved into the cul-de-sac with an outsize bundle strung up over his shoulder. It could only be Peter with his telescope and Keith found himself wondering if he wanted to be caught there in the field as if waiting for him. Indeed it might have been that he was waiting, not for any reason other than the desire to have a simple conversation with someone, itself a surprising idea since even before the emptiness of the house he had long enjoyed the silence of being alone.

Peter crossed under the last streetlamp and stepped over the chain. Keith could hear the crunch of dry thistle. "Peter," he said.

Peter froze. "Who is it?" he said.

"Keith Corcoran."

"Ah!" Peter said. "Astronaut Keith Corcoran. You surprise me." He stepped forward again and Keith waited as the crunching footsteps continued and then they were shaking hands in the darkness. "You are outside enjoying night air, yes?"

"I am," Keith said.

"Not with pretty neighbor?"

"No."

"These things happen."

"Seems so."

"Good then." They were silent and then Peter dropped the telescope from his shoulder. "You hold this and I set up tripod," he said, and he handed Keith the telescope itself, a metal cylinder that was cold and smooth in his hands. "You have maybe something else to do?"

"Well," Keith began, paused, and then stopped altogether. "No," he said at last. "Not really."

"Good," Peter said.

Keith stood holding the telescope dumbly as Peter flipped levers and turned knobs and the tripod unreeled itself from its more compact form and then Peter took the telescope from him and set it upon the tripod, the whole of it like an insect perched there in the darkness.

Peter unfolded a sheet of paper from his pocket and then produced a small flashlight that cast a red glow upon the sheet. He stood smoothing and looking at it for a long moment.

Keith stood in the silence, trying not to watch him but wondering what else to look at. The stars. The luminous night. His eyes had adjusted and now he could see shapes in the faint moonglow. Beyond the edge of the cul-de-sac, four streetlights traced where the court formed a T against Riverside. That short distance seemed to mark another world entirely.

"I have this list," Peter said at last. "It is nothing. A list that someone made. Things to see."

"OK," Keith said. It was silent again and then he said, "Things like what?"

"Not stars. Well, yes, some stars also. Mostly odd things. Things that they did not really know about then. When list was made."

Keith stood looking at the telescope. "I don't really know what you're talking about," he said.

"A man, Messier, made this list long ago of things he thought were not stars, so I go through this list and find them."

"OK," Keith said. "Sounds good."

"No, this is stupid thing."

"Oh," Keith said. "Well, OK."

"There is nothing of challenge. Like swimming laps in pool. Like exercise. But what else to do here?"

"I don't know," Keith said. "Can't see the comet?"

"Funny," Peter said. "Comet is on other side."

"Too bad."

"In Kiev maybe but not here."

"That might have been interesting," Keith said.

"Yes, I think so. You want to look?"

"At what?"

"I don't know yet. I can find something."

"OK."

Peter looked up at the sky. "Sometimes I just feel like nothing," he said. "I just stand and smoke and try not to think."

Keith followed his gaze. Then he said, "I guess that's the same thing I'm doing out here."

"Yes. You too, then."

Keith was silent. He kicked absently at the dirt with the toe of his shoe. Then he said, "I saw a big bird come up out of this field the first day I was here."

"Is that so?"

"Yeah, maybe an eagle or something. It was huge."

"How much huge?"

"I don't know. Big. I don't know what it was. I wondered if there was something out here it was eating."

"Eating?"

"You know. Like a dead cat or something."

"Oh," Peter said. "No, I do not think anything was here. I would have smelled some dead cat, maybe."

Keith was silent again. Then he said, "We could use some chairs."

"Ah yes. I bring chair most times. Not this time, though."

Peter went to the telescope and adjusted and readjusted it. He was silent as he did so, his hands deftly working the various dials and knobs, a few times making brief groans and sounds to indicate that the telescope was not quite working as he expected or wanted it to. When Keith had seen it on the passenger seat of Peter's car, it looked like something destined for the trash heap: a battered white tube pieced together with duct tape. Now, though, it was an instrument being utilized by someone who clearly knew how to wield it. After a few minutes, Peter stepped back as if surveying his work. "This telescope is hard to keep steady," he said. For a long while he did not say anything more. Then his voice returned: "I thought about what you said last time," he said. "About my work that is problem to be solved."

Keith had mostly forgotten the conversation but he nodded anyway.

"I think maybe you are right about this," Peter said.

"Maybe."

"I will be trying to find better job, I think. Something that's more what I want to do. Maybe Luda does not want to move."

"You'd have to find that out."

"I think so." He adjusted the telescope again. "It's a big good house for us. We have some money saved from Luda's family and then this house is foreclosure so we have money for it. How you say . . . timing is everything."

"I guess that's true," Keith said. "I'll probably never get my money back on mine. We bought at the height of the market or something."

Peter did not speak for a long moment. Then he said, "You tell me good thing to do, I think."

"Well, if it helped I'm glad. I'm not really someone who gives advice."

"It did help. Very much." A pause. Then he said, "I'm glad you're here."

"Thanks," Keith said. He was mildly embarrassed by Peter's honesty but then there was a sense of gratitude as well. At least someone was glad he was somewhere.

"Maybe you tell me something of space mission?" Peter said then.

"Oh, I don't know. I'm trying not to think about that stuff so much."

"But this I would like to hear."

Keith looked at the ground. In the darkness the dry thistle seemed to glow, spindly and white, like a field of tiny bones. "Well," he said. Just that.

"Maybe you tell me about first walk into space?"

Silence for a long moment. Crickets continuing their endless sine wave.

"OK," Keith said at last. "The first one was to install the new robotic arm. It was to replace the previous model, but the other arm was already removed and had been taken back to Earth on one of the shuttle missions before us."

"Yes, but when you go outside what is this like?"

"Like?" He thought for a moment, his mind stammering. He might have stopped then but instead he said, "It's like falling without moving."

Peter was quiet. Keith expected him to ask for elaboration but he did not do so and after a few seconds Keith said, "I don't know if that's right."

"No, I think that is right," Peter said.

Keith looked at him, his dark form there in the night. "In math it's the normal vector, the line from your position to Earth. But it's like there is no normal vector when you're actually there. So you're moving forward, falling forward, along the path of the ISS, but it doesn't feel like you're moving except that Earth is spinning below you. So you're falling but it's not like you're afraid because it's also like you're not really falling."

"Yes," Peter said. "Like falling without falling. And you are in suit with falling."

"Yeah, falling without falling. In the space suit. EMU, we call it. It weighs close to two hundred pounds in Earth's gravity."

"Heavy."

"Very heavy."

It was silent for a long moment, neither of them speaking, Keith wondering what he could say that would somehow describe the sensation of being in orbit. The depth of stars. The depth of the universe itself.

"And Earth you see below?" Peter said.

"Yes, down the normal vector. That's down there and it looks like it's moving fast and you're still because there's nothing that feels like forward motion. So it's like there's a tangent vector but it's an illusion. There is no tangent vector. Earth is down there and it's moving and you can see everything there is to see. It's all super clear even through the atmosphere. The clouds and the continents. You can see everything."

"Cities?"

"Yes, cities too. Especially at night when you can see the lights."

"That is interesting to me," Peter said, pausing, and then adding: "You are lucky man to do this work."

"I don't know about that."

"Not lucky maybe," Peter said, pausing, and then adding: "Good enough. Good enough to do that work."

Keith said nothing now.

Peter rummaged in a pocket and brought out something that Keith could not see in the darkness. "Do you mind?" he said.

"Do I mind what?"

"I have something to smoke."

"That's fine," Keith said.

Peter worked at something small and after a minute there was the light of a flame and Keith could see Peter's face illuminated, a small pipe in his hand. A moment later, the sweet scent of marijuana smoke filtered through the air to him. Keith smiled. "You're out here smoking pot?" he said.

"Yes, do you want?"

"No, not for me." The idea seemed absurd and he actually laughed at the thought. "Does your wife know that's what you're doing out here?"

"Not really," Peter said. "Maybe. She knows more than she tells me sometimes, I think. You do not approve?"

"No, I don't care. It's just funny, that's all."

"Funny how?"

"I don't know. Just funny." There was a pause and then he added: "I could use a beer. And I need to sit down. Seeing you smoke makes me want to sit down and have a beer." He was silent again and then he had the solution: "Wait. Wait a minute," he said. "I have an idea. Will you help me with something?"

"Of course," Peter said.

"Good, let's do it before you get too stoned. Come with me." He stepped back toward the light now, back to the cul-de-sac and its ring of concrete, his feet crunching the dry thistle and dead grass and chunks of dirt and gravel and he could hear Peter's footsteps behind him. "What is this?" Peter said.

"I need you to help me move something," Keith said.

"Right now?"

"Right now."

"OK," Peter said. "Wait, I will go put down pipe." He disappeared into the darkness for a moment, his footfalls at a slow jog, and then returned and they walked in silence for a few moments, the houses in the cul-de-sac silent and watchful, the vacant lots still vacant, the only difference a black sedan parked in front of Jennifer's house. Had the car been there before? Would he have noticed? He was not sure. Perhaps she had another date tonight. Perhaps that's who she was.

He had left the door unlocked and opened it now and they both passed through.

"She took everything," Peter said.

"I told you she did," Keith said.

"You said furniture. There's more to home than furniture. She took everything. She left nothing at all."

"True," Keith said.

"I cannot believe," Peter said. "I cannot believe she would take all this away from you."

"Well," Keith said. He moved to the far side of the couch, next to its overstuffed leather arm. Then he said, "Let's take this outside."

"This?" Peter said, his voice incredulous. "This is nice sofa. Leather too, yes?"

"Yes, it's leather."

"It is all furniture you have, though," Peter said. "What she left."

"I hate this sofa," Keith said. "She left it because I hate it. It's like a bad joke that it's still here."

Peter looked at him. "Too good to be outside maybe."

"No, it's perfect. It's the perfect sofa to be outside."

Peter looked simultaneously sad and excited. "OK," he said at last. "It's heavy."

"I am sure."

"No," Keith said. "It's heavy like you wouldn't believe."

"You are a man who brings good times."

"Tell me that when we're done with this," Keith said. "If we can't get it out the door we'll saw it in half and take it out in sections."

"Too nice for that. We will get sofa outside."

"Let's do this." He counted to three and a moment later they held the sofa aloft and were moving toward the entryway.

They managed to get the sofa partially through the door with a fair amount of grunting and groaning, the living room and entryway behind them littered with the fallen cushions that marked their path. The process was not unlike turning an overstuffed key in a huge, oddly shaped lock and there was a moment where Keith thought it might be impossible to go farther, the sofa wedged at some odd angle where he could not move it forward or back, but then Peter rotated his end slightly, saying nothing, neither of them saying a single word, and the whole thing slid through the aperture at last, Keith stumbling forward as Peter pulled both him and the sofa through the doorway.

They tried to set it down in the driveway and ended up dropping it with an awkward clunk and both leaned against the arms and panted wordlessly for a long moment in the yellow glow of the streetlights. The front door to the house was open and one cushion had been kicked through the doorway and now lay like some odd welcome mat placed upon the threshold. Keith was exhausted by the effort but he was also smiling, and when he looked over at Peter he saw that the Ukrainian was grinning as well.

They lifted the sofa again and moved down the sidewalk and were once again panting heavily as they stepped, one leg at a time, over the chain and began to crunch through the thistle, the path irrelevant to their aching arms and slowly slipping grip. "Watch out for telescope," Peter said, the only words spoken during their walk from the house to the field until at last they crashed the sofa to the ground in the thistle and dirt and once again stood out of breath, leaning on the gray stuffed arms.

"Heavy," Peter said.

"I told you it was."

"It is maybe too nice to be left out in field."

"You want to pick it up and take it back into the house?"

"Not so much."

"It's better out here. Let it rot."

"You have very sharp tongue tonight."

"I've had a weird day."

"Weird day made you angry."

"I guess so."

They walked back to the house and collected the cushions and Keith pulled a six-pack of beer out from the refrigerator and tucked it under his arm. Then they moved wordlessly out into the field again.

They returned the cushions to their proper places and then both sat and Keith cracked open a can of beer and handed it over to Peter, who nodded and mumbled a brief thanks, and then opened another and sipped it, settling into the cushions and closing his eyes for a long moment in the darkness.

The flick of a lighter. A moment later the scent of smoke drifted over from Peter's side of the couch, and then his voice came: "It is good to sit."

"Yes," Keith said. "Yes, it is." He sipped at his beer.

"Sometimes I bring folding chair here. This is much better than folding chair."

"True," Keith said. It was silent for a long moment. Then Keith said, "I've been having headaches. Migraines."

"Migraines? How bad?"

"Pretty bad."

Silence for a moment. Then Peter: "You have headaches but no smoking?"

"No," Keith said. "I probably should, though. I've heard it works for some people."

"You want?"

He thought about it. "I think I should stick with the beer," he said. "I have painkillers for the headaches."

"This is probably better," Peter said.

"Probably true."

Peter offered him the pipe and Keith looked at it for a long moment, held in the Ukrainian's outstretched hand. Then he took it and put it to his lips and sucked in the smoke. The feeling of burning was immediate and he exploded into a series of choking coughs.

"Easy there," Peter said.

"Whoa," Keith said, still choking. He handed the pipe back. "Maybe I'll stick with the beer."

They sat in silence for a long time, Keith sipping on his beer, finishing it, opening another. The stars luminous above the giant leather sofa, the two men slumped upon it like discarded manikins. Like crash test dummies.

Then Peter's voice: "Hey, your girlfriend over there is looking for you, I think."

Keith opened his eyes and looked up toward Jennifer's house. Indeed the window curtains were pulled open and Jennifer's body was framed within its rectangle. Whether she was looking out into the field or not he could not tell and indeed he knew that she could not have seen him in the darkness; the vacant lot would be, from her perspective, simply an empty place beyond the ring of concrete and streetlights. Her silhouette was an apparition in the window, as if floating above Earth in a coffin of light. A moment later another silhouette appeared behind her and then the curtains closed, the only remainder a thin thread of light that wavered and then disappeared entirely.

He downed the beer in just a few swallows. Peter smoked quietly beside him. "This is a comfortable sofa," Peter said.

Keith said nothing. After a time, he let his head loll back onto the cushions, his face pointing straight up into space. There were so many stars and to him they remained entirely nameless, a fact that, at least for the moment, did not seem to matter at all.

Eleven

HE HAD JUST returned from his morning run when he heard Walter Jensen's voice for the first time, a calm, friendly sound that called to him from the opposite side of the street: "Hey there, neighbor."

Keith glanced toward the sound in confusion, hands on hips, still sweating and breathing hard as he walked back and forth on the sidewalk. The speaker was a man in a gray suit who stood in front of Jennifer's house by the open door of the black sedan. Neighbor? Had he called him his neighbor?

He nodded in the man's direction, saying nothing, still recovering his breath, still feeling the weight of the run upon him. When he turned back toward his house he was surprised to see the man walking briskly across the street toward him, his charcoal tie wagging like an oddly placed tail. For a brief moment, Keith wondered if he could act as if he had not seen the man, could simply return to the house as if oblivious but instead he stood there in his worn nylon running shorts and tennis shoes and waited, squinting in the white blaze of morning light. The man was smiling.

"Walter Jensen," the man said when he reached the sidewalk, his hand extended.

Keith stepped toward him and extended his own hand and they shook. The man might have been in his mid-fifties, although his unnaturally tight face suggested some amount of money spent on plastic surgery of various sorts. Everything about him was immaculately groomed: hair dyed a somewhat unnatural light brown with a few strategic lines of gray at the temples, gray suit pressed to perfection as if constructed of metal, black shoes polished into dark mirrors. Shaking his hand was like shaking a bucket of Cool Whip, so smooth and devoid of texture was the sensation. He smiled. His teeth were a perfect white line.

"I don't think we've yet met," Walter Jensen said. Across the street, Nicole appeared from the house and waved.

"No, I guess not," Keith said. He waved to the little girl.

Walter Jensen glanced over his shoulder. "Go ahead and get in the car, sweetie," he called. She smiled, waved again, and then climbed into the black sedan. "I guess you know my daughter."

"Sure," Keith said, his sudden confusion mixed now with something else, a feeling of nausea.

"She's a pistol, isn't she? Just like her mom."

"Sure is."

"Well, I've been away on business and then you've been away on your business." Walter Jensen offered a faint, ambiguous laugh. "Anyway, it's good to run into you."

"OK," Keith said. "Likewise."

"Listen, I don't . . . uh . . ." He paused a moment as if at a loss for words and then said, "Well, let me just come out and say it. I'm awful sorry to hear about your daughter. If there's anything we can do over here just let us know, all right?"

Keith stood in silence, soaked through with sweat, squinting and blinking in the early-morning sunlight. The entire situation seemed unreal to him, impossible. And yet here was his neighbor, apparently Jennifer's husband, certainly Nicole's father, Walter Jensen, with a false look of concern clouding his face. "Uh . . . yeah, thanks," Keith said and when his neighbor did not immediately respond he added, "I think I have it under control."

"Sorry to bring that up," Walter Jensen said.

"That's OK."

"So the house is up for sale?"

Keith nodded.

"But you're staying here right now?"

"For now."

"That's good. Save the money while you can. I get that."

Keith looked at him.

"You know," Walter Jensen said, "my wife Jennifer said you were lacking in the furniture department."

"Lacking?"

Walter Jensen waved his hands in the air, an action that reminded Keith of Peter. "Look, I know you're selling and all but you still have to live, right? Jennifer and I have some extra stuff we've just been hanging on to. A dresser and a pullout sofa and some tables and chairs. You're welcome to it. That's what neighbors should do for each other."

Keith did not know what to say in response. He stood there, staring at this man. Jesus Christ. Really? Really? He stood there on the concrete next to the steaming grass and blinked silently at Walter Jensen before stammering, "That's really not necessary," and then backing away slowly as if from an angry dog.

"Ah, you'll see," the man said. "It'll work out fine."

"Well, then," Keith said, still retreating.

"Anyway, I have a meeting to get to so I'll see you around."

Walter Jensen half waved at him and then trotted back across the street, into the black sedan, and was gone around the corner in seconds.

Keith stood in silence next to the rental car, watching the empty street where the man had been, the house across the street that he had appeared from.

My wife Jennifer? Really?

Around him, faint curls of steam extended upward from every visible surface: the closely shorn lawns, the asphalt and concrete, the streetlamp post at the end of the cul-de-sac. In the near distance, past the houses, the visible horizon was ringed with a faint blaze of dark green trees and the rooflines of an older and more distant subdivision, all of which had been cast flat and shadowless by the slantlight of early morning.

He knew that the information about Jennifer should not have surprised him but it had nonetheless. He was having an affair with a married woman. Someone with a daughter no less. The irony was not lost on him. How could it be? Nor was the sense that he had been, and continued to be, a fool, although how the vector upon which he had always envisioned himself had become so entangled remained impossible for him to understand.

Sally Erler called soon after he returned to the cool interior of the house to tell him that she had lined up a potential buyer for the late morning. He nodded, although she obviously could not see him, and repeated "That's fine, that's fine," not even hearing her now, not even really understanding that the call had ended, instead thinking of the last time he had shared Jennifer's bed—a bed she shared with her husband, as it turned out—and the abruptness with which he had been asked to leave. She was married. He was not. He tried to make this into a kind of justification but he could trace no such argument.

On the counter before him rested the paperwork the process server had delivered to him the previous day. A quick knock on the door just after noon and he had been handed a few sheets of paper and had signed his name in receipt and the man told him to have a good day and was gone. The paperwork that facilitated his divorce. It had been as simple as that. A voice-mail message and a few sheets of paper that denoted the end. Now he did not know who she was to him. His wife? Hoffmann had called her his ex-wife, although that still did not feel true. Someone between states of being, in some interstitial zone. Perhaps that.

He ate his breakfast cereal and when he was finished he pulled the sheet of plastic clear of the sink, tearing it free of its blue-taped edges, and wadded it up and then stood looking at the gap it had made. Then he reached up and began pulling the plastic from the nearest cabinets in a kind of frustration, throwing each scrap into the living room where the sofa's footprints were still apparent on the carpet. When the cabinets were clear he removed the plastic from the kitchen island and then knelt and peeled back the masking tape that ringed the linoleum and the various strips that still clung to wall, window, and cabinet edge, moving without any clear thought or purpose other than his own anger and frustration.

The stepladder had been folded against the far wall of the living room and he retrieved it to pull the loose strips of masking tape from the tops of the cabinetry and the edge of the ceiling, wadding it into a series of sticky balls and tossing them in the general direction of the increasingly large pile of refuse. How carefully he had placed each line of tape, following the bound coordinates of clear precise points he had charted to keep his mind occupied with something tangible. How futile that project seemed to him now. He had not even completed the job. There was a single coat of paint here and if he looked carefully he could see the blotchy yellow of the original color where it soaked through the eggshell like fresh yolk but he just did not care now, nor could he imagine caring in the future.

It took him an hour to remove all the tape and plastic sheeting and when he was finished the loose pile of trash in the living room seemed much larger than was possible, given the compact stack of supplies it had been generated from. He thought for a moment that he might simply leave it there, a strange replacement for the sofa he and Peter had moved out to the field, but the thought was just as soon gone and he scooped up an armload of plastic and tape and walked to the door, opening it awkwardly and then stepping outside into the sunlight, his eyes clamping shut against the blazing light of the morning and the sudden onslaught of heat.

By the time he was in the shower the whining sound had come again and this time it was more present than it had been in all the weeks he had spent in the cul-de-sac, a long and endless and shrill sine wave moving toward him from some distant place. He had hoped that the migraines were gone altogether, that he had been miraculously cured of whatever medical mystery had beset him, and yet here again was the sound of his mind in its tinny unraveling. He would take another pill, thinking—praying even—that if he took one quickly enough it might be sufficient to stop what already felt like an inevitability, the whine, the sine wave, already bearing down on him from some initial point he was ever unable to locate.

The shower had been hot and he turned the water off in a fog of steam that had covered every surface of the bathroom and when her voice came out of that fog—"Hey there, neighbor!"—he turned abruptly enough to bang the shower door closed with a crash.

"Shit," he said. He grabbed a towel and wrapped it around himself quickly. "What are you doing in here?"

"The door was unlocked," Jennifer said. "Hope you don't mind."

He looked at her. She was once again dressed in her workout clothes: skintight purple this time. Black shorts over tan thighs. "What's going on?" he said.

"What's going on?" she repeated.

He was silent, staring at her. "You're in my bedroom," he said at last.

"You're right."

"Is there a reason?"

"Not really. Just thought I'd come by to say hello."

"OK," he said.

"I saw you talking to Walt," she said.

"Yeah, Walt," he said. "You might have mentioned him."

"I might have mentioned Walt?"

"Yeah, it would have been good to know."

"Why?"

"Because I didn't know you were married."

She laughed. "Oh don't be so dramatic. It's not like you're divorced."

"You knew exactly what was happening," he said. "And you lied to me."

"I did not," she said. Her hands were on her hips.

"You did, Jennifer. It's not right," he said. He realized just how absurd he probably looked, standing there in the steaming bathroom, gesturing with one hand while his other gripped the hem of the towel he had wrapped around his waist.

"You didn't seem to mind," she said.

"That's not the point," he said.

"Really? I thought that was exactly the point."

"I'm going to get dressed now."

"Don't let me stop you, Astronaut," she said.

He shook his head and as he did so a lump of pain rolled back and forth, sloshing against the sides of his skull. What was he doing? What was happening? Who was this woman and why did he know her at all?

"Look, I'm sorry you found out about Walt so . . . abruptly," she said. "But, hey, it's fun, right? It's not like we have something serious."

"It seems more serious now," he said. He opened the chest of drawers and pulled out a T-shirt and underwear and then pulled the underwear on under his towel.

If Jennifer had some response to his statement she did not

acknowledge it. Instead she looked around the room and clicked her tongue against her teeth. "She really did clean you out," she said. "The furniture, I mean."

"That's not what we're talking about." He let the towel drop and pulled the T-shirt on over his head.

"I don't know why you're so mad," she said. "It's just for fun, you know?"

"I'm not mad. But you're acting like this isn't something important and you're wrong. It is important. My wife had an affair. I know what that feels like."

"So do I," Jennifer said.

He was quiet for a moment, standing there in his T-shirt and underwear, staring at her. Then he said, "I don't understand why you'd want to do that to someone else, then."

"Yeah? How do you think I know what that feels like?"

He did not respond.

"And guess who he was having an affair with?"

"I have no idea," he said.

"Your fucking wife."

He looked at her, frozen now, his slack-jawed disbelief replaced by belief and then disbelief and belief again and then finally an exhaling of breath as if the wind had been knocked out of him and the same question that seemed to ride with him always in the empty house in the cul-de-sac under the pressure of a gravity that would not release him: Why? Why marry someone if this was what it would be? Walter Jensen. And right across the street. He wondered if Quinn had known about it. The thought made him feel sick, the whining buzzsaw of his impending migraine rising all at once. He needed to get to his medication. He needed to get to it without delay.

"Christ," he said. Just that one word. He did not move.

"Yeah," she said. "And then she moves out and a couple of weeks later he's out on business for a month? Am I stupid? Does he think I'm an idiot? I know what's going on. He's off with that whore in Atlanta.

He's not even good at hiding it either. He'll just pay for hotel rooms and dinners on the same credit card bill that comes right to the house. Get a post office box at least." Her eyes glassy with tears, her voice a thin monotone that rose in volume and intensity at random moments, as if she was very nearly unable to keep control at all.

There was silence in the room. He wondered if he should step into the closet and get a shirt and his jeans and then thought better of it. He wanted to pull the blinds and get into bed and hide. His mind and its thin wire of buzzing, the painkillers doing nothing to stop the onslaught now, the tide of his pain lapping up the beach. What time was it? Wasn't there something happening today? "I don't know what to say, Jennifer," he said at last. "I'm sorry that happened."

"No shit," she said. "Walt never did anything like that. He's not that kind of guy. He wouldn't do that unless she just shook it in his face, you know?"

"OK," he said.

"OK? What's that supposed to mean?"

"It's not supposed to mean anything," he said and when she said nothing in response he said, "I'm getting a shirt."

He stepped backwards into the closet and pulled a short-sleeved button shirt from the rack and a pair of khaki pants and then stepped back into the room and put on the shirt and then stood buttoning it slowly, the pants draped over his arm. He looked at her, this beautiful woman whose husband had betrayed her. Indeed, they were more similar than he thought, not Jennifer and Barb but Jennifer and him.

"Look at me," she said abruptly. "I'm actually tearing up over that asshole." She closed the gap between them and embraced him and set her head lightly on his chest and was quiet. He put his arms around her, just as lightly, out of a fundamental instinct that was humanity itself.

"It's OK," he said.

She did not speak for a long time. Then she lifted her head from his chest.

"It's fun, you and me, isn't it?" she said.

It was an odd question but he answered it: "Yes."

"We can keep it going," she said. She kissed his neck. "Not at my house but maybe we can find a nice place to go to. A nice hotel or something." She slid her hands up his shirt so that her warm palms moved lightly against his stomach. "Maybe not even in this town but somewhere else. We can go away for weekends sometimes."

"I don't think I'm up for that, Jennifer."

"Really? Feels like you're up for it," she said.

"It's complicated," he said.

"Complicated?" she said. "How complicated is it, really? I like you. You like me. We get together. We have some fun. Then we go home. That doesn't sound very complicated." As she said this she dropped to her knees. In one fluid motion she pulled down his underwear and took him into her mouth. It was so fast that he barely had time to mutter a faint, weak, "Wait," an utterance that was more abstract sound than word. He wanted to say, "I have a headache," but the sentence sounded so absurd that he managed to hold his tongue and besides, with her own tongue on him all possible sentences faded quickly from his mind.

She paused only for a moment, to look up at him from where she knelt and to say: "Does it still seem that complicated?" Then she was at it again.

Keith closed his eyes. He knew that he should be telling her to stop but his mind was already blank and empty of anything—even his pain—and he looked down at her, the top of her head, her lips where they covered him, where they pulled him into and out of her mouth. Then he closed his eyes again. His migraine was a dull rumble somewhere far away.

And it was exactly at this moment that Sally Erler entered the room, the young couple to which she was showing the house just behind her. Keith heard her voice just a moment before she appeared in the doorway, heard it as part of the sharp and distant buzzing of his oncoming migraine, as an annoyance. She was saying something about "potential" as she turned into the opening and Keith looked over at her, without speed, without concern, and she took three clear steps into the room before she stopped and at last understood that there were already people in the room and what they were doing.

Then she screamed.

Twelve

"LET'S NOT TALK about what happened," Sally Erler said over the phone. "Let's just say I happened in on something. In the real estate business you hear stories about things like that. I've never . . . it's never happened to me before . . . but let's just say I happened in on something and we'll leave it at that."

"OK," he said. "Let's leave it at that."

"I just don't know what happened. I wasn't early was I? Was I early? Maybe I was early."

"I don't know," Keith said. "Does it matter?"

"No, I guess not," she said. "Maybe it does. I don't know. No, I guess not."

It was later in the day now, cresting toward evening. He had not been surprised when his mobile phone rang and it was Sally Erler on the line. He assumed that she was calling to remove her name from the house but she had been talking for some time and no such stoppage of services had occurred; instead, a constant affirmation that she would not talk about what she had stumbled in on and then talking incessantly around the occurrence despite her various statements to the contrary.

It might have seemed comical had he not been so terribly embarrassed. Sally Erler had screamed and then had turned immediately and had herded her two clients out the door, down the stairs, and out of the house like some crazed farmer frantically trying to direct a flock of chickens away from a predator. Jennifer had only laughed—indeed it was as if she had wanted to be caught in the act—and, before he could even so much as say her name, had returned to him with a gusto that had finished him off inside of a minute, leaning away from him in the moment of release so that his seed spilled onto the carpeted bedroom floor. Then she leaned in, took him in her mouth one last time and returned his now red and pulsing member to his underwear, snapping his waistband as she did so.

"That doesn't really seem all that complicated. Does it, Astronaut?" she said, rising to her feet.

"Christ, Jennifer," he said.

"You're welcome," she said. "I'll call you and let you know where we can meet."

He retrieved his pants from where he had dropped them onto the floor and slid them over his legs awkwardly, tottering, and then he sat on the edge of the bed. "You're really something," he said. He could think of nothing else to say.

"You're right about that, Astronaut," she said.

He sat looking at her. Then he said, "We can't keep doing this."

"Oh really?" she said. Her voice was quiet but there was instantly an edge to it, the edge that had been present when she had dismissed him from her home earlier in the week, and Keith knew that this could easily devolve into an argument, which he simply did not have the strength for. The distant whining was well established now and already in the deep core of his mind there was a singular white arc of pain.

He wanted to ask her if she was embarrassed at being walked in on

241

but it was obvious that this was not the case. He felt ashamed somehow but could think of no words to articulate that condition either and so he said the only thing he could think of: "You're married, Jennifer."

"So what? I'm married. You're married. Who cares?"

"I'm not willing to do that. It doesn't make sense."

"You're overthinking the whole thing," she said.

"I'm not overthinking anything," he said. "I'm just not doing it."

She stood and looked at him, hands on hips. "You've just been using me," she said at last.

"I've been using you?"

"Yes, you've been using me."

"I didn't ask you to come over here."

"Is it a game to you? Do you think I'm stupid?"

"No, I don't think you're stupid."

"That's how you're acting. Like you have all the answers and I don't know what I'm talking about. But I know exactly what I'm talking about."

"OK," he said.

"You don't think so?"

"I don't know," he said.

It was silent and she shook her head. Her face was flushed. "All you men are exactly the same," she said at last. "You're all a bunch of . . . fucking faggots." She stood there for a moment longer, her face moving from carefully controlled rage to disgust to simple disappointment and at last she said, "Fuck you," and then turned on her heel and walked out of the room.

"Jennifer," he said, but the room was empty. He could briefly hear her on the stairs and then the opening and closing of the front door signaled her exit.

That was it, then. He sat on the bed, looking at the white pearls of fluid on the carpet, thinking that he should probably get a towel and clean them up but making no move to do so. He listened for further movement in the house but all was silent and after a time he stood and buttoned his pants and finally took the Imitrex tablet and then walked downstairs, hoping more than anything that the silence was real and that Sally Erler had left the house and had driven away and that he would not have to speak to her about what she had seen.

Indeed the downstairs was as empty as it had been when he had first returned to the cul-de-sac those weeks ago, or even emptier now that the sofa was gone.

"She made it worse when she came outside," Sally Erler said now over the phone. When he asked her what she meant, she told him that Jennifer appeared on the sidewalk when the realtor was trying to placate the young couple and that she had said "some very negative things" about him, said them directly to the potential buyers and then had stormed off across the street and back into her own house, a house that Sally Erler had acted as selling agent on three years before, a point she made with no small sense of irony.

"I'm sorry to hear that," he said.

"Let's just call it water under the bridge," she said. "So there's good news. That's why I'm calling. It's a good-news call."

"Good news?"

"Yep, yep, good news," she said. "You're not going to believe this. It's unbelievable but it's true. They made an offer anyway."

"Those same people who were here in the morning?"

"Those same people. They made an offer and it's right in line with what we talked about so it looks like it's a go."

He was at the little kitchen table. They discussed the dollar figures and it turned out he would break even on the sale, an almost astounding concept as he was certain that, given the crashing of the economy, he would lose money. He was smiling now despite the whining and the distant pain. Every day the newspaper had more statistics on local foreclosures and yet someone wanted to buy the house. It was possible that happening in on the blow job had been a good selling point after all. Perhaps realtors should hire prostitutes and porn stars and astronauts to perform sex acts for viewing by potential buyers as an industry-wide standard. Once again, he had beaten the odds. And the painting had never been completed. Nor the cleaning. The place was a pigsty; there was no denying it. Fresh stains on the bedroom carpet and yet there had been an offer. Incredible. There was still magic, even if small and inconsequential.

He verbally accepted. There would be paperwork to sign, after which the house would be in escrow for sixty days. Two months to figure out what to do and where to go. There would be time enough for that. Right now he could not even begin to work on such an equation. Instead he closed his eyes and rubbed absently at his temples. He had managed to get through the blazing sun of midday by closing all the blinds in the house and was relieved that if the migraine was going to hit him, it would do so in the relative cool and dark of the evening. If he could just get through the next hour or so of daylight he could cocoon himself in his bed, turn the air conditioner temperature down and hide in the darkness. He knew it would still be a terrible ordeal but there was some relief in a quiet room, in his bed, in the cool of the humming air conditioner.

He managed to take a short nap. When he woke he padded immediately to the bathroom and swallowed yet another painkiller, the fat white tablet resting in the palm of his hand for a brief interval before he popped it into his mouth, took a brief swig of water, and swallowed. How many had that been? Four? Five? An Imitrex in the morning and another a few hours ago. A man whose life was numbers and he could not recall the count. He thought of calling the flight surgeon but he did not do so. What would it matter now?

When the doorbell rang, he was still standing at the sink, leaning against it, and he continued to stand there for a long time, hoping that whoever was ringing would give up and go away but as the bell rang a third and then a fourth time he opened his eyes and moved out to the entryway and looked through the peephole. He could see no one and then a moment later Nicole appeared in the window to the side of the door, peering through the glass, her face cupped in her hands. She was in much the same position as when he had first seen her at the sliding door and as she saw him she pulled one hand away from her face and waved. The motion reminded him again of Quinn but there was no longer any sense of shock or surprise; instead, that reaction had been replaced by a sense of vague and nostalgic beauty that floated just out of reach and would ever continue to do so.

He pulled the door open slowly and stood there, his eyes squinting, head whining steadily and with increasing violence. "Hey," he said.

"Hi, Captain Keith," she said, looking up at him. Her body had a faint glowing halo around it, an effect of the oncoming migraine and certainly not a positive indicator of his immediate future. "What are you doing?"

"What am I doing? Nothing," he said.

"You look sick. Are you sick?"

"I have a migraine."

"Oh, a migraine. My mom has migraines when she's having her period."

"Is that right?"

"Yes," she said. "She gets grumpy too. We just have to leave her alone."

"OK."

"My dad's home."

"Yeah, I met him today."

"His name is Walter but people call him Walt. They had a fight but he's home now."

He leaned against the doorframe and covered his eyes with his hand.

"You probably want me to leave you alone just like my mom," she said.

"Yeah, I think so." There was another pause. Keith's eyes were clamped closed. The rectangle of the open door he stood in was like an airlock opening directly onto the changeless and agonizing surface of the sun.

"I just wanted to say hi," Nicole said at last.

"OK," he said. He looked down at her to say good-bye and in doing so saw that Walter Jensen was walking toward them both from across the street, his face in an easy smile, his hand already half outstretched to shake his hand again. Fantastic.

"Hey neighbor," Walter Jensen said.

They shook, Walter Jensen wrenching his palm into a series of shock waves that ran up his arm and into his head like a small jackhammer ramming at the meat behind his eyes. Everything red and blurred. He thought he might be sick. If he did he hoped he would have the strength to vomit into Walter Jensen's face.

"Listen, did you give any more thought to that extra furniture we have?" Walter Jensen said. "We can get it over here right away if you want it."

"Oh, I think . . . ," Keith said. He paused. "Can we talk about this tomorrow?"

"Jesus, are you OK, buddy? You look pale. Are you feeling all right?"

"I think I'm coming down with something."

"Oh, I'm real sorry to hear that. Listen, if there's anything you need from us just ask. Really, I mean that. We neighbors have to stick together. Hell, there aren't that many of us that speak English if you know what I mean."

Keith looked at him blankly.

"Listen, I'll let you get some rest but really let us know if you need anything."

Again, he said nothing, only staring. He wondered how it would feel to punch Walter Jensen in his perfect white teeth. But even the thought of it made the pain wobble in his skull.

Nicole peered up at him from the doormat with a look of concern that was touching and comical at the same time.

"Come on, Nicole," her father said.

"Thanks," Keith said.

"Don't mention it, neighbor," he said. He took Nicole by the hand and they both turned together.

"Can Captain Keith have dinner with us again?" Nicole said to her father as they moved away.

"Again?" Walter Jensen said.

Then the door swung closed and the outside world was silent.

He stumbled upstairs. Already the zigzagging lines had begun to blur across his vision and his head thrummed with the rhythm of his blood. He stopped at the thermostat, knowing he intended to do something there—adjust the temperature up or down or something else—but he could not focus and instead moved past it into the bedroom and pulled his shirt over his head and then fumbled with his pants and removed them as well and fell sideways onto the bed. There were still bright slashes of light burning through the blinds and after a moment he pulled the blankets back and slid under them and pressed his head into the pillow as he slid the darkness up and over until it enveloped him.

He reached for the numbers in their empty spaces but they were difficult to find now, seeming to jerk and twitch, to scatter like frightened birds at his approach. A few fives and sevens, a flock of threes and nines, a pair of ones and a similar pair of twos, and then the symbol of the aleph he had once spoken with Quinn about, naming the idea she had been fascinated by, that symbol eclipsing all others as he relaxed into the cool of the bed, the temperature already shifting upward until he began to sweat and even then he did not move but lay there, one arm over his face, the other still clutching the edge of the blanket where he had lifted it nearly to the headboard. The zigzags appeared even with his eyes closed, his mind a collection of glass shards that turned and ran their jagged edges against each other in a constant and terrifying shifting and the aleph floating in the midst of that chaos of dark motion like a beacon or a sentinel.

.   .   .

Within an hour the full agony had come upon him and he dissolved into a pain both shattering and inexplicable, his body already a wreck of exhaustion and the pain continuing to crest toward its magnificent and destructive apex. He felt as if he was caught in some eventide between sleeping and waking, and in this gray semidarkness his mind seemed to fall toward the memory of Quinn, gravitating toward her as if her memory held within it a specific density greater than all others, the pull so strong and real that he felt an immediate impulse to rush into her room, as if now in the pain that was his crushed mind there was a chance that he could reach her. But Quinn was dead and nothing would change that. His eyes locked closed in the black heat under the sweat-soaked sheet and blanket and in the red darkness that was his pain.

During the long, impossible night even the undulating wave of chirping crickets had entered his mind and he closed the window and folded the pillow over his ears to muffle that sound but even then he was still able to feel it, a physical pressure just behind his eyes as if the sound was a grinding stone that had entered him and spun there against the front of his brain as he drifted into and out of consciousness, never sleeping but passing through a kind of gloaming that was memory and hallucination all at once, his vision, even with eyes closed, a collection of black and white zigzagging lines that covered everything, that covered even his thoughts until the final aleph of his pain was the form of a single question that repeated endlessly: Where was she now? Where was she now?

And as if in answer he could hear Barb's voice somewhere in the room: "Can you hear me?" she said.

And his own voice responding as if it came from some other place entirely, as if he was someone else: "I can hear you," he said.

"Oh, I can see you."

He could feel himself floating, as if the bed and the room had dissolved around him. "I can see you too," his voice said, somewhere. A pause. Then: "How . . . how are you?"

"I'm OK," she said. Tears were already streaming down her face.

"It'll be OK, Barb. We'll be OK," he heard himself say, his voice in the darkness speaking into his memories as if she could hear him. And so she could.

"I wish you were here," she said.

"I know."

"When can you come back?"

"I don't know. They're trying to get me down."

"But when?"

"I don't know yet. They're trying. It's hard to get back."

There was the laptop with her face, the screen tilted at a slight angle. "I wish you weren't there at all," she said, sobbing. "None of this would have happened if you were here."

There was a hollow space inside him, a vacancy, an abyss that was not filled with stars or with dark matter or with anything at all but was more like a black hole that had already drawn into itself the accumulated mass of whatever he was or had been or would be. Pain everywhere. He did not even know where he was anymore. In the empty bedroom? In his sleeping quarters on the ISS? His location shattered to the staggering electric wire of his pain.

"I want you to come home," she said.

"I know you do," he said. Silence from the screen. "Do you know any more about what happened?"

"I don't know," she said, her voice a high-pitched keening. "She was going too fast. She went to a party and she was going too fast on the way home."

"Was she . . . had she been drinking or . . . anything?"

"No. They said no. Do you think she would do that?"

"I don't know what she would do."

"No, I guess you wouldn't," she said.

He said nothing. Floating but not floating. He could see her face on the laptop and the walls of his sleeping quarters and yet he could also see himself in the bed, a shattered agony drenched in sweat, stationary below him at the base of the room as if his form huddled in silence at the bottom of a cardboard box.

"Was it raining?" he said at last.

"Was it raining? I don't know. No, it wasn't raining. Why do you want to know if it was raining? What's wrong with you?"

"Nothing," he said. "I don't know. You were there. I wasn't there." He breathed out, his carbon dioxide flowing into the tiny space of his sleeping quarters and into the vents and then being scrubbed back into oxygen again via the nitrogen tank he had installed. Recycling their breath again and again, forever. "She was my daughter too," he said. The empty room in the house in the cul-de-sac was drifting through the microgravity now, was not drifting, was anchored to Earth, was loose of it again. My god.

"I know that," she said.

"I want to know what happened."

"I told you what I know."

"What car was she driving?"

"Yours," she said.

"Mine," he said. It was not a question.

"Yeah," she said.

"Oh." The station's dull and constant hum around him. Then: "She hit a tree?"

"A big tree in someone's yard."

"What kind of tree?"

"What? I don't know what kind of tree."

A long pause as he listened to the constant erratic engine of her breath. "What happened, Barb?"

"What do you want me to say, Keith?"

"I want you to tell me what happened."

"I am telling you what happened," she said. "The car hit the tree. She went through the windshield. She's dead. She's dead, Keith. Our baby's dead. Oh Jesus. Oh Jesus," her voice devolving into an inarticulate moan.

He floated in front of the laptop in silence. There were no tears. There was no feeling, only that sense of hollowed-out emptiness. The woman on the screen might have been anyone: a stranger, a distant relative, someone he had known long ago but had since forgotten.

"It's OK," he said. "Everything's going to be OK."

"How can you say that?" she said.

"I'll be there as soon as I can," he said. "They're working on it. I'll be there soon."

"Please get here," she said. "I need you here."

"They're trying."

Her face silent on the screen, her eyes staring at him, mascara smeared into a gray blur. She started to speak again, her mouth moving, but the sound came in jagged bursts, cutting in and out so that he could hear only bits and pieces, single syllables, the image on the screen freezing and then moving and then freezing again, like a collection of still images strung together. "Barb, I can't hear you," he said. "Can you still hear me?"

There was no answer from her save the syllabic bursts of sound. Her face continued its broken, jerking motion and he floated in the room before it, watching her face as it spluttered into digital chaos and then froze altogether.

"We'll try to reconnect," Mission Control said from the intercom.

"No need," he said.

"Are you sure?"

"I'm sure. We're done."

A few more words and then silence and he drew the curtain closed across the narrow doorway to his compartment and thought that he should probably weep, that this would be the time to do so, but no such tears would come to him and so he floated in the quiet half darkness of the sleeping compartment, staring at the blank screen of the laptop and then at the blank emptiness of the fabric wall.

. . .

His first migraine had occurred three days after that call with Barb, three days after he had learned of Quinn's death. Apart from the silence that seemed to cling to him, the intervening days were as regular and normal as any other. His fellow crew members said almost nothing to him that was not directly related to the various experiments and projects they were working on, but he busied himself with his work, with the specific manipulation of numbers and metal and electricity, turning objects over in the microgravity and recording the data in the journal on his laptop and sending that information down to the ground, no one interrupting him, no one talking to him at all.

When the pain came it was Eriksson who suggested that he was having a migraine and it was Eriksson who helped him to his quarters and into his sleeping bag. He clicked off the blinding bar of light and pulled the curtains closed and there Keith floated, in and out of consciousness, trying to sleep, feeling like he was asleep but also in an agony he could hardly believe. Various members of the crew checked in on him during the first hour and at some point Keith discussed the matter with the flight surgeon on the ground in pained, broken phrases and there was an agreement amongst them that he was experiencing some combination of panic attack and migraine and Eriksson retrieved some additional medication and returned again and took a blood sample and then returned yet again and injected him with something. He was told later that it had been a combination of sedative and pain-killer.

He could hear everything: the humming and buzzing of the whole craft where it spun in its seventeen-thousand-miles-per-hour orbit path, two hundred miles above the surface, his vision warped with white and black zigzagging lines that drifted and shook and in the midst of that shaking he pulled himself once again into that otherworld of numbers, trying now to invent mathematical situations that might serve to bring him back from whatever edge he had come to but each time he was dragged right over that edge again, back into the pain. He concentrated, tried to concentrate, his heart's thudding rhythm in his ears. Where was Eriksson? His eyes clenched like fists and somehow he managed to grasp hold of a single number—the light blue of number one—and then of one again and he placed a plus between them and then an equal sign and the zigzagging lines were everywhere now, even here, and he no longer understood what those symbols meant in his mind or what they were doing there or why he should be thinking about them at all. He could see Quinn then, her face before him in the darkness and her eyes shining out at him, her face as if caught in some eternal eventide, staring back at him as if waiting for him to speak and he opened his eyes. He thought he might have been speaking to her but his voice was a terrible silence that fell out of him into the capsule, was recycled, was breathed in once again.

And now the tiny stars had returned, moving away from him as if in response to the whole of the universe, all points moving away from all other points and these too, these glowing stars in the darkness, reflecting the slit of light filtering in through the curtained opening. Once again he was weeping. He was weeping tiny diamond stars into the recycled atmosphere.

He said her name but then he remembered once again that she was dead and would ever be so and it was not Quinn who was there but Eriksson and he was talking to him: "How are you doing?"

"My head hurts so much," Keith said.

"Where?"

He tried to look past him. Someone was just outside his quarters. Fisher? Someone else. "Everywhere," Keith said.

"I need you to be specific," Eriksson said.

"My head mostly but it radiates out."

"OK. They're afraid you have a bleeder in your brain."

"An aneurism?"

"Could be. Could be something else too."

"I'm sorry," Keith said. "I don't know what's happening."

"You'll be fine. Rest up. Plus, you're giving our doctors something to do."

"That's good."

"I'm serious. It's the most excitement I've ever seen from those two. They're in hog heaven. It's like you with a crazy math problem."

Keith said nothing in response and the two of them fell into silence.

"You'll have to call CAPCOM," Keith said.

"I already did."

"About the schedule. You're going to have to clear my schedule."

"Don't worry about that. It's done."

"Goddammit," Keith said.

"I'm sorry, buddy."

"So am I."

Eriksson said nothing more for a long while. Then: "I'm going to take all your stats again. And I'll need to do another blood draw."

"OK," he said. But he did not move and after another moment of silence Eriksson unzipped the bag and freed his arm and he did not look, could not even feel the needle and a moment later Eriksson had finished, Keith's blood floating somewhere in a vial in the micrograv-ity and he was zipped back into the bag and his blood was off to the experiment racks in the Destiny Module.

That had been the first but it was not the last. When the pain finally departed, he slept for ten hours and then woke and tried to resume some truncated version of his schedule but after three hours he could hear the sine wave again and Eriksson told him to go back to his quarters. The experience was much the same as the previous evening, this time with the anticipation of what was coming like being drawn slowly into a saw blade, unable to move, unable to even avert his eyes, but watching the blade come closer and closer until it tore into his flesh at last. And like the previous night—and this would be one of the aspects of his experience that would be consistent—he vomited and that seemed to indicate the end of the episode, his body relaxing and the pain subsiding again and he drifted into exhausted sleep at last. Each time Quinn came through the zigzagging darkness like the ghost she already was. He reached for her face, for the crushed remains of her broken body, but his fingers passed through that image as if moving through a cloud of steam. A vapor. Where are you now? Where have you gone now? And no answer from that darkness. He had missed the funeral, missed even listening to the audio feed. It had been recorded and they could play it for him later but what kind of answer could that possibly be?

So it had been and so it would continue: migraine after migraine, sometimes with four or five days or even a full week between them. He knew Houston was trying to get him back to Earth but it was not to be. There were problems with weather and with logistics and technical problems and then problems with the mission itself so he did not take one of the emergency Soyuz capsules down—would not have taken one by himself anyway—and ground control attempted to get a shuttle up earlier and then later a relief crew on another Soyuz capsule but both were delayed and delayed until just a week before he and his crew members would have returned to Earth anyway.

Then another episode during the six weeks of physical therapy at JSC and then nothing, a kind of respite from the pain long enough that he had begun to think the condition had disappeared altogether. But now here it was again and the tears that streamed from his eyes were not the diamonds of his orbit but rather the slick heavy liquid of gravity. How many episodes did that make? He had lost count, or rather had never actually counted, and although it was true that his mind worked in numbers, there were some things that were uncountable, or that equated, in the end, only to a single symbol which was prime and central and represented the start and end of everything that was or could ever be: inescapable and impossible to manipulate and glowing with a radiance that only served to underscore its position, the aleph-null of his consciousness indeed eclipsed by the ever-unfolding infinities to follow.

There had been a life he had led before and a life he would lead after and those two states had been broken along a line stretched between two points on a single plane. What remained was something hollow and ancient and vacant and he realized then that it was simply loneliness and it was everywhere around him and inside of him and there was no one he could call to his side, not on Earth and not in space. He was alone. He would never go into space again. He would never again be an astronaut. His eyes closed to the zigzagged darkness and the blanket over his head, the room itself dark and the early evening shading into night as the whole of Earth spun into its own shadow and Keith Corcoran, former astronaut, lay shivering in that multilayered black night darkness, weeping now, the pain not even reaching its apex yet, that still two hours away at least. Time itself slowing and slowing and slowing in his agony until it seemed as if it had stopped altogether and he was held there as if within a sphere. All things silent for an instant: the empty house, the cul-de-sac, Jennifer and her husband and Nicole as well, even the crickets pausing in their vigil in the vacant lot, Peter and his wife and his children all pausing, perhaps the whole endless interlocking subdivision complex and parking lots and businesses, all traffic lights blinking to red for a single moment and all conversations falling to silence. Can you feel now how memory itself would well up in such a moment? How it would be like a tide that had flowed out long ago and now rushed down into the pools, cupping the rocks and sand and circling the dunes and the waving razor grass? And how we would be alighted upon by a memory, you and I, to fill that silence, to rush into those empty pools? That memory was of her tiny hand curling into his own. Her tiny little girl's hand on the day of ice cream when Barb's father was dying or already dead. Ohio glowing everywhere with red and yellow and orange light. How could such a thing be gone and gone forever? How could the universe he had seen give him such a memory only to take her away from him?

When at last he opened his eyes into the empty room, the sense of drifting, of being back in the microgravity orbit, disappeared all at once, replaced with a sense that he had just tumbled back into his own body once again, the delirium of his pain rising to a sharp jagged point. He was sitting up now, although he had no recollection of doing so, his heart hammering in his chest and the jumbled collection of metal and glass tumbling in the dry socket of his skull. He knew he was going to vomit and managed to stumble across the room, the zigzags of his vision overlaying everything in his path, and crashed to the floor of the bathroom and heaved the contents of his stomach into the toilet in a weak stream like water from a burbling garden hose. His stomach turned again and again until he was coughing and choking on emptiness, a thin stream of drool extending from his mouth to the swirling waters of the bowl.

Then he stumbled back to the mattress, the shape of his body outlined in the pool of sweat he had left behind, and tumbled to its surface, trembling for a long, quiet moment before falling, at last, into sleep.

Thirteen

THE STARS AS impossible and quixotic as they had ever been. For three days he felt as if his mind had become an empty box containing nothing but his fatigue and the day that followed was slow and quiet as he staggered through the exhaustion of his recovery. Then another night. He had come to expect the recovery period, the two or sometimes three days of weakness afterwards, but his weakness had stretched into five days now, continuing to feel as if he had just returned to Earth's gravity, the specific and precise and quantifiable density of his body as it dragged from the kitchen to the bedroom, from downstairs to upstairs. He wished to god that he had a television so he could at least watch the mindless moving images of cooking shows and nature documentaries but alas there was no god who would deliver a television to him, regardless of his weakness or his pain.

During these slow days he found himself thinking often of Quinn and now, sprawling upon the sofa under those dark and meaningless and cruel stars, he continued to think of her. NASA had sent a camera crew to the funeral and the DVD of that footage had been in his mailbox when he arrived in Houston and he had watched it even though he did not want to do so. Barb and her mother and a group of anonymous figures Keith did not know or did not remember ever meeting all in a row as if croaked down from the boughs of huge and leafless trees. A priest or pastor he did not know talking endlessly about things that did not matter. No one he knew or cared about. A woman who had betrayed him. A polished box holding the crushed body of his daughter. A poem he could not understand read by someone he had never seen. Then that same box being lowered into the ground. Christ. Why would any father want to see such a thing? And yet he had watched it, mostly because Dr. Hoffmann had insisted it would be good for him to do so. Even now he did not know how any funeral could be good for anyone and yet the memory of it returned to him in his quiet exhausted solitude, not the memory of watching the recorded images but rather the memory of the funeral itself as if images recorded by the camera were the sight of his own eyes, as if he had felt the faint cool breeze as it filtered through the pale green leaves, as if he himself had cast the first shovelful of dirt down onto the box that cradled his daughter into the earth. My god. Tell me about your cheerleading competitions now and I promise I will listen like no other father has ever listened to a daughter. Not now nor ever to be. All promises falling to the bleak law of gravity, like a skein of gray smoke pulling backwards into the fire from which it came.

He sat there for an hour, alone on the sofa, and by the time Peter appeared he had downed two beers in quick succession and was sipping the third. He said very little as Peter set up the telescope and focused on various stars, the blur of a galaxy, a sliver of moon, the smeared color of a nebula, and when Peter told him to look he rose from the sofa to do so, not because he was particularly interested but because he did not know what else to do. He had been waiting for Peter to arrive and now he had and Keith did not know what he had been waiting for.

"Here is something beautiful to see. Come and look," Peter said and he did so once and again and then a third time, each time looking at—what exactly?—a smudge, a star that looked like a star and hence was little different from what he could see when looking straight up into the night sky from his position on the surface of Earth, a scant blaze of color.

The fourth time he refused to rise: "Thanks, but I don't want to see anything else," he said. "Not tonight. Just let me sit here."

"You are frustrated," Peter said. "I know. It will make you feel better, maybe, to look."

"No more."

"Yes, no more." Peter leaned to the telescope and turned it on its tripod and then looked through the lens and then with his bare eye and then to the lens again, adjusting and readjusting. He looked and moved, looked and moved again. Occasionally he would say something to himself or to the telescope or to the stars themselves: "Oh" or "There you are" or "Beautiful" or "Where are you?"

After a time Peter too had seen enough and he sat back on the sofa and pulled a small black bag from the larger bookbag at his feet and unzipped it and removed his small glass pipe and a Ziploc and filled the bowl of the pipe and then clicked his lighter into flame and applied it to the bowl. The red glow rose and fell in light as he inhaled. Then the long, slow exhale. He leaned back against the sofa.

"This is Cassiopeia," he said. "This *W* shape there. See?"

"You just don't know when to quit," Keith said.

"Yes, true," Peter said. "My apologies."

For a moment, Keith did not respond. Then he said, "OK, fine. Where's the *W*?"

Peter's finger in the darkness. "Just above houses there," he said, tracing a shape in the air directly in front of them, as if that shape was hovering close enough to touch in the night.

"It's all stars."

"Look for this. Like a wide *W*, stretched out some. You see? Just above houses. Almost on top of them."

A blur of stars everywhere and then yes he saw it: a jagged *W* as if scrawled by a child, the bottom points of which were nearly resting on the distant rooftops. "Shit," he said, nodding. "I see it." He sipped at his beer.

"Yes, good then," Peter said. "That is called Cassiopeia."

"I think I remember that from Boy Scouts."

"Good. If you know nothing else about sky, you know that at least."

"Cassiopeia the *W*," Keith said. Then he added: "Shit."

"Yes," Peter said. "Shit." A pause. Then: "You know Big Dipper?"

"Yes."

"Show me."

"I'm tired out, Peter."

"Come now," Peter said. "Show me. If you know what it looks like, find it. Show to me this."

He sipped his beer, his eyes casting around the sky, the pinpoints of ever-twinkling stars like a veil. Where? He breathed out with a loud hiss and then rotated his head slowly, tracking from one side of the sky to the other, then again mumbling, "Shit," and leaning back and there it was: the Big Dipper, tilted up on one end with the Little Dipper pouring into it. "There," he said.

"Yes, good. Pretty high up right now."

"I guess so."

"Yes, because all your life you have seen Big Dipper and you know where to look. Yes?"

"I don't know."

"Yes," Peter said. "You do know. You know more than you think."

Keith silent now.

"And then bottom of cup of Dipper points up to handle of Little Dipper. That handle is Polaris."

"OK."

"It is star that never moves and it is north."

"The North Star."

"Yes. You already know this."

"Not really."

"You can see it?"

"Yes."

"Then you can always find north."

"I guess that's good."

"It is always good to know where you are."

"Is it?"

"Yes," Peter said.

He said nothing in response. Is it? Really? Another swallow of beer. He wished suddenly that he had something stronger, that he had a bottle of vodka or whiskey or something he could drink that would obliterate him, send him crawling home through a world spinning without control. But there was nothing like that in his house. Only beer. And he was already beyond driving.

To their left, the cul-de-sac glowed yellow and quiet in the night like a movie set. Walter Jensen's black sedan was gone. Jennifer's car likely inside the garage. His own rental car across the street: an increasingly filthy sedan. Perhaps it was finally time to open his garage and start the process of sorting through whatever boxes of personal effects Barb had deposited there. The sofa like a boat on slowly moving waves, a quiet rolling beneath him.

"I had a migraine a few days ago," he said suddenly.

"You keep having these migraine headaches?"

"Yes."

"You should come and ask me and I will give you some of this and you will feel better," Peter said. He tapped at the pipe.

"You're probably right," Keith said. "They drug-test, though. I mean, not regularly but they could and that would be the end of that."

Peter made a sound, something like "Ach!" and waved his hands around in the air in front of him. "Fools, I think," he said.

"Maybe," Keith said. "Shit. Maybe it doesn't matter anymore."

"You have angry tongue tonight."

"Yeah, I guess so."

"Not at me, I hope."

"No, not at you."

Silent for a moment. Then Peter: "Who then? The pretty lady across street maybe?"

"I don't know."

"Things not going so well with her?"

"It's not that," he said. Peter was silent, perhaps waiting for him to continue, but he could find no words for the simple desperation that had settled into him. After the migraine he had come to feel like he was at the end somehow, that he had come to the end of some equation the answer of which he already knew he would never find for indeed there was no answer possible and yet he had continued to move through it as if there would be a solution, that the numbers would do what they had always done for him: they would provide a way forward. He had known that this idea was a fiction or a fantasy and yet somehow it had remained with him for those weeks since returning to Earth but now even that fiction had departed him. He could not fathom what was left. Perhaps nothing at all.

They said nothing and after a time Peter set the pipe down and stood and began making adjustments to the telescope's position. Night sounds around them. Occasionally the crunching or shuffling of an animal somewhere amidst the thistle. The crickets in their chirping. The more distant sounds of freeways and parking lots.

"What are you looking for?" Keith said.

"I do not know," Peter said. "I was looking for Messier objects. But that is work for students. I do not know what to look for now."

"Can you find that comet yet?"

"Not in this hemisphere."

"I saw it in the paper again this week."

"Bah," Peter said. "Comet is not hitting Earth I think."

"Too bad," Keith said.

Peter stopped now, looked back at him. Keith could see only his silhouette. "Do not say this," Peter said.

"I'm kidding."

"It is not something to make jokes for."

"You keep saying it's not going to hit Earth."

"How do I know that?"

"I figure you know these things."

"Why? Because I have cheap telescope? I do not know anything. I work at Target. It's not something to make jokes for."

"Christ, OK."

Peter said nothing, returning to the telescope, adjusting it, shifting the whole tripod slightly and then readjusting the base, leveling it. After a moment, he said, "I am sorry to speak to you like this. I apologize."

"Don't apologize. Shit."

"I respect you too much to talk to you like this."

Keith shrugged. His eyes were increasingly bleary as he finished his fourth beer in quick succession and opened another, leaning back on the sofa, watching Peter move and manipulate the telescope and then drifting back to the stars again.

Peter's voice casting over those pinpoints of starlight: "Maybe I would have known something before, if I was still in Kiev at Golosiiv. I could not see this probably, but they would know about this. Not here."

"Who would?" Keith said, his voice moving out into those same stars. At drift. Drifting.

"The astronomers at Golosiiv observatory. They would know."

"Are you still in touch with them?"

"No." There was a pause and then he added, "Not so much anymore. When I first was here in America, yes, but then not anymore."

"Lost touch?"

"No reason to bother them. I was not help to anyone by calling. They are busy people. And I have nothing to add here."

"The telescope you worked with in Kiev was a big one?"

"You do not know Golosiiv?" Peter said, a hint of incredulity in his voice.

"No," he said. "Should I?"

"I do not know." He paused, then said, "Maybe not. It is famous for me, but I forget you are no astronomer but engineer."

"True," Keith said.

"Astronomy is important to me," Peter said. "It's most important thing that I can do. More important than stacking boxes at Target."

"Most things are."

"This is right, Astronaut Keith Corcoran." Peter paused for a long time now, then looked through the eyepiece, then stepped back and looked up at the stars. "I went to university in Ukraine. I mean I have education."

"I figured as much."

"Education but not degree. Luda came along and then Marko and then Nadia later. Hard then to keep going when there is feeding family."

"I'm sure," Keith said. He sipped at his beer. The crickets chirped somewhere in the field. Everywhere.

"There is famous observatory south of Kiev in Golosiiv Forest. Famous in Ukraine. Very beautiful forest with paths and trees. Most beautiful when night is coming and shadows are in trees. Everything so green and beautiful. And in winter when snow comes. Every-thing quiet then. Like bird comes and is over everything. Like white bird. Like whole forest is nest for white bird."

Keith was smiling in the darkness, his head back on the sofa, eyes straight up and staring into the stars, Peter continuing to talk some-where as if the voice was being narrated by someone who was no longer there, as if on the soundtrack of a film about this moment with two men in the darkness staring up into space, each in their own world and that world the same.

"And there is Main Astronomical Observatory there. Right there in forest." Peter paused, lifted his pipe again and Keith could see his face lit by the orange glow of his lighter and could hear him breathe in the smoke and hold it as the glow disappeared, once again a silhouette as if made of some darker matter than that of the universe around him, around them both. "I wish you could see this as I did. It is magnificent. Not like this little thing but beautiful thing with forest all around. You see what I am saying?" He paused and once again the orange glow of the lighter, the inhaling of smoke and holding, then the exhale. "A place you could dream about if you are like me and you spend your nights looking at books about stars and you read about stars and planets and you go to university to study. And then they give you job as assistant. And it barely pays but maybe you are not caring because you love."

There was a long pause now, long enough that Keith lifted his head from the back of the sofa and looked over at Peter there, at his silhouette in the darkness. He wanted Peter to keep speaking if only because there was a story being told that was not his story and so did not involve the tiny cul-de-sac of his own life. There were other lives and other stories and he had forgotten this simple fact until this moment, in this night. "Must have been incredible," he said and he hoped it would be enough because he did not want to speak; he only wanted to loll his head back on the sofa and drink his beer and feel the aftereffects of the painkillers as they mixed with the alcohol and drifted through him as he floated on the surface of Peter's story like a man in a moonlit boat on a flat and silent sea.

"Yes, incredible," Peter said. "The work was, but nothing else. We lived in apartment in Teremky, west of city. I took municipal bus to Golosiiv and sometimes this bus would not be there and I would have to walk mile to train. And pay is terrible. Luda was home whole time in apartment and she did not know what to do. Her family was across city. There was no car for us, so hard to get anywhere. Sometimes buses regular like clocks and other times they do not come, sometimes for days. You could walk under road in tunnel and you could even take baby carriage up and down stairs but maybe not two of them. Not by yourself. So you cannot get anywhere then. Not by yourself with children."

And Keith could see it: the tunnel under the road, graffiti covering the walls. The concrete stairs. The rush of people coming and going.

"I would go to university in day and then Golosiiv and would work there in night with astronomers and in beginning I'm helping only with putting data in computer. There is little office there with very old computer and some equipment. No windows even, but I do not care. Dr. Federov there was in charge of data and I work for him for year and they think I'm doing good job and I keep asking questions and learning always and taking classes in daytime. Dr. Vanekov sees and recommends me to Dr. Kuzmenko and so I am work then for him and it is with telescope then. That is what I wanted. Dr. Kuzmenko even publish paper and thank me by name in this paper."

"That's great," Keith said.

"Yes, I was very proud. That was later, after I was there for long time already." Peter puffed at his pipe again and then stood in the cricket-filled silence that was no silence at all. The stars spinning around them. "It is difficult thing to keep going to school and to work when you have two small children."

"I can understand that."

"Yes, very difficult. Impossible for me, I think." Quiet then. Peter returned to the sofa and sat.

"You want a beer?" Keith said.

"Yes, I will have beer."

Keith reached down and pulled a bottle from its cardboard container and handed it across to Peter and then sipped at his again and leaned his head back.

The sounds of Peter opening his own beer and drinking. Then: "They made some discoveries too when I was there. Things I helped with. Dr. Kuzmenko worked on very new galaxies and he found blue dwarf galaxies, not very far away, and I helped him on finding that. Markarian 59 and 71. That is what they are called."

He rested his head on the sofa again. The North Star high and Cassiopeia below its point but his eyes gazing straight up at the blaze of stars directly above. Peter's life in the forest with the telescopes and dwarf galaxies that even now glow faintly somewhere in the night sky all around them. "So why did you leave?" he said at last.

"Ah, because of Luda and children."

"She asked you to?"

"No, she would not do this. But I knew this is better. First university I had to stop because it took all daytime and then job at Golosiiv was not really job. It was like . . . how do you say . . . like assistant or something."

"An internship?"

"Yes, like internship. But I knew I was good at this and I knew more than most who might have been hired there, but still they could not really hire me and then when they found out that I had quit university they could not keep me there anymore. So that was end of Golosiiv as well."

"Shit," Keith said.

"Yes, shit," Peter said. "That is what this was. Fucking shit."

"Fucking shit," Keith repeated.

"Yes," Peter said, as if considering. "They liked me there, I think. Dr. Kuzmenko tried to keep me on but this needed to be official. He could not change rules for me. I had no diploma for working. So someone else came in and works there for me."

"That hurts," Keith said.

"This is fucking shit."

Keith laughed.

"Funny maybe," Peter said.

"Fucking shit," Keith said.

"Yes," Peter said. A pause. Then: "Luda has brother with idea to come to America. Then her mother. Then finally Luda. And it seemed like maybe it would be better idea than whatever was in Ukraine. America is dream place for us. Like this. In my dream, things could happen like in Golosiiv. The scientists there wrote me letter of introduction to astronomers at American university so I thought there would be job waiting for me here. They told me that there was."

"Who told you?"

"University here. Better pay than at Golosiiv and same kind of work. Laboratory assistant position and I can take classes for free. So I tell Luda that we will move to United States and she and her mother and her brother all are very happy to hear this. I am happy too because this looks like I have job at university." His voice trailed off. Stopped. Silence now. Keith in his drunken, painkiller haze, head drifting against the sofa. Peter silent somewhere. The stars in their places. The stars everywhere.

"No job?" Keith said at last.

"What?"

"No job at the university?"

Peter quiet for a moment. Then: "No job." A pause. "It is not so good here as we thought maybe. The economy like Ukraine. Lots of people losing jobs. Some of it good for us. We got here and we think it is very good because houses are cheap and they are everywhere for sale. Very good. But it is not good. It is same as Ukraine maybe. So many people with no jobs. The university does not hire me. University does not hire anyone."

"Shit."

"Yes, shit. That is right. Shit for me. So Luda's brother gets job and so we do not even live by university anyway. We live here because Luda's brother is dishwasher in restaurant and he has work here but he cannot even get me job washing dishes because there are no jobs now for anyone. Miracle maybe he has any job."

"You wouldn't want a job washing dishes anyway."

"Maybe not but more money than Target."

"I guess."

"This is true. And he cleans up tables too and gets money for this."

"Tips."

"Yes, tips. That is money right into your pocket."

Keith sipping at his beer. How many? He had lost count. "What about the college?"

"What about it?"

"You take classes there?"

"I take English there and I take all astronomy classes, but they do not have much."

"No, I imagine it's not like the telescope in Kiev."

"They do not have telescope. Just this." He pointed to the telescope: a collection of sharp angles against the deep blue sky. "They let me take this home because I take so many classes. But it is like toy really. Not real telescope. But I should not complain. At least I have this."

"I guess so."

"How do they say it? Beggars can't be choosers? You have heard this?"

"Yes."

"That is my life story. Beggars can't be choosers."

"Maybe that's not true," Keith said, his eyes closed now, so drunk that his voice came as a slurring, blurred mess of syllables, the consonants with their long flattened-out shapes, the vowels like the moaning of ghosts.

"Oh, this is true," Peter said. The telescope somewhere behind them. Then: "Your girlfriend is watching us, I think," he said.

"Who?"

"Your pretty neighbor."

Keith looked at the house. Again he could see her figure in the window: the cut of her shape in a nightgown against the lit interior of the house. "Her daughter thinks it's weird that we're out here," he said.

"It is weird," Peter said.

"You're probably right."

"I am right. Before it was just me with telescope. Now we have Astronaut Keith Corcoran. And sofa. That is weird part."

"Me or the furniture?"

"Both I think, but mostly sofa."

"Well, it's a comfortable sofa."

"It is," Peter said, falling then into a long silence. Then, loud enough to make Keith's eyes jerk open with a start: "Fucking shit!"

And Keith actually chuckling and then laughing and Peter: "What? Laughing at me? What?" and then starting to chuckle himself, both of them in their various states: stoned and drunk and laughing in that bleak darkness under a million wheeling stars.

Fourteen

DAYS AND NIGHTS, not of eclipse but akin to a perpetual twilight that seemed to bathe everything in a thin and insubstantial dimness as if his eyesight had shifted so subtly that he did not even know he was squinting, not only the far distance blurred but the whole of his experience covered in a wispy film of half-light so that clarity itself became a kind of abstraction. He knew that some of the medications he had been taking were meant to treat depression and he had continued to take them not because he thought they had any real effect on his body or his mind but rather because he did what the doctor told him to do as if it were a military order, which indeed it somewhat resembled, but his mind continued to cast itself against the rocks over and over again despite the constant flow of pills. If he was being treated for depression it had become clear that such treatment was no longer working if it had ever worked at all.

And so the same sense of quiet that had settled over him upon first returning to the cul-de-sac had now been met with a kind of gloaming.

He had updated his phone number at JSC and with Sally Erler and the latter's call represented the only time his phone actually rang, the realtor calling with a further confirmation of the young couple buying the house. There was paperwork to be signed and he suggested they meet at Starbucks rather than at the house and she breathed a long sigh of relief and agreed. When they met, she ran through the offer in detail and he signed and signed and signed the various lengthy and incomprehensible pages. He was surprised to see that Barb's signatures were already in place, a feat accomplished via overnight mail, and so with his last signature all required parties had signed. Two months. Slightly less than that now. Then he would need to be gone.

She had arranged a variety of inspections and he had a duplicate key made and then purchased a welcome mat so that he could leave the key beneath it at the front door, thereby ensuring that he need not be home for the inspections to continue. A business card on the kitchen island from Buddy's Termite Service was the only evidence he saw that any inspections had occurred. If there were other inspections besides this one, he was unaware.

He still had not spoken to Barb since changing his mobile number but her e-mails were frequent, waffling between angry diatribes and calm pleas for some access to Keith's paycheck. He did not respond. The only reason to be in any contact whatsoever was related to the impending house sale and he had decided that Sally Erler could handle that herself and obviously she already had.

Peter was not always in the field after dark but he had taken to stopping by Keith's door and knocking gently when he was passing and Keith would be inside waiting for the knock, listening for it, had even begun to be disappointed when it did not come. Of course there were nights when Peter was busy inside his own furnished home with his two children and his wife but most evenings Peter would knock and Keith would step outside with him, a six-pack of beer under his arm. Together they would trudge out into the field, Keith collapsing into the sofa as Peter set up the telescope. They would look at a few stars. Nebulae. Clusters. Planets. Sometimes they would talk about their lives. Other times they would sit in silence, each to his own quiet thoughts.

Keith realized that he could actually identify a handful of constellations now and, even in his state of increasingly perpetual self-pity, the fact filled him with some sense of pride. He had added the rest of Ursa Major to the less-distinguished pot of the Big Dipper and could find Cepheus between Polaris and Cassiopeia, all the while Peter patiently spooning him information. Names of stars that, when repeated the following night, had begun to achieve a sense of familiarity in Keith's mind so that he had just begun to understand that the mass of stars and nebulae and galaxies and perhaps universes, all of which spun above him on the axis of Polaris which was the axis of Earth itself, could be comprehended, that the whole of it had order even if it did not have rationale, even though he knew that he was not looking at a flat plane of stars but rather a three- and even four-dimensional space that moved far beyond them all and into the ever-retreating and isotropic distances that far outstripped the mechanical eyes of any telescope. Whole universes out there in the deeper luminous black beyond. And he had seen them. At the end of the robotic arm he had seen into that distance and it had gone on forever and would never stop. Everything out there fractal, infinite, beautiful.

Sometimes he thought of Peter's résumé, but only when he was out on the sofa in the dark, listening to Peter explain the story behind the discovery of some feature of the night sky. He had long since come to the conclusion that Peter was indeed an intelligent man, too intelligent to be working at Target, and he knew he could at least send the résumé to someone who might read it, someone at NASA or at one of the many independent scientific organizations he had worked with. But when he was inside during the day he did not think about the résumé at all. The pages remained on the kitchen island, buried now amidst the pile of bills and a variety of unopened mail. Looking at it would mean he would need to call NASA and he did not want to do so. Not yet in any case. Perhaps he was afraid of what they would tell him about his own future. Perhaps he was afraid that what he had already decided about that future was true. That it was over.

His phone rang when it was still early, a JSC number. He flipped the phone open and said, "Hello," and as he did so the sound of a truck came from the front of the house, a loud, rumbling that shook the windows and sent a huge, low-frequency sound wave through the room so that even the milk in his cereal bowl burst into concentric rings. Whatever voice came from the other end of the line he could not hear apart from a sharp tinny sound. "Hang on," he yelled into the tiny grill. He could hear the sound of air brakes, the squeak and hiss, the windows actually shaking as the engine outside sputtered for a moment and then roared again and moved past the front of his house at last, the rumble fading then to a hum that continued but was at least quiet enough for him to hear the voice on the phone now.

"Hello? Hello?"

"What's going on over there?"

"No idea," he said. "Who's calling?"

"Forgot the sound of my voice already?"

"Eriksson," Keith said.

"Your friendly mission commander."

"I didn't recognize the number."

"Yeah, I'm in a different office."

"You're at JSC?"

"Yeah, the paperwork never stops. Just wait until you're a mission commander. The paperwork will kill you."

"I'm sure," he said. The rumble faded to a dull hum that continued somewhere out toward the end of the cul-de-sac near the empty lot.

"So how are you doing?"

"OK."

"Getting through it?" Eriksson said.

"Yeah, I'm getting through it," Keith said. He stood from the increasingly rickety kitchen table and set his cereal bowl in the sink. He could still hear the hum of the truck down at the end of the cul-de-sac. A delivery truck perhaps. Dropping off a package for someone. Not for him.

"Barb?"

"Long gone."

"Damn. Sorry to hear that, buddy."

"Yeah, well. She's filling my in-box with angry e-mails. That's something to look forward to."

"I'm sure."

"How's the family?"

"All good. Little guy is in swimming lessons. Boring to watch but fun anyway."

"That's good then."

"So you're doing OK?"

"Yeah, fine."

"Seeing the doctor and all that?"

"Yeah I'm seeing the doctor and all that."

"Psych doing anything for you?"

"Not really," he said. "So this is a checkup call?"

"Come on, Chip. We've logged a lot of time together. Can't I call to find out how you're doing?"

"You can," he said, "but that's not what this is."

"That *is* what this is."

"OK."

"You can really be a pain in the ass," Eriksson said.

"What do you want me to say?" Keith said.

"I don't want you to say anything. I'm just asking how you're doing."

"I don't know how I'm doing. I wake up, get a cup of coffee, wander around town. At night I sit around with my Ukrainian neighbor and drink beer. That's all."

"All right," Eriksson said. "Look, buddy, I'm worried about you. That's all."

"Yeah, I appreciate that."

They were both silent then and in the gap Keith thought that, if he could find the words to do so, he would tell Eriksson exactly how he was actually doing because Eriksson was perhaps the only substantial friend he had. They had spent so much time together, training and working and then the mission itself. After Quinn was dead and Barb was gone, it had been Eriksson who had kept him working when he could work and had cleared the schedule when he could not. That had meant everything. Without it he did not know what he would have done. And so he thought that he would tell him that there was no end to the equation in which he now found himself and that he did not know what he should be doing anymore or what velocity he would need to reach to escape whatever orbit he was in.

But then Eriksson said, "Look, let's switch gears on this," and Keith said nothing, only listening as Eriksson continued and the moment was gone: "There are some people here with me and we're trying to figure something out and you're the only guy I know who might know the answer."

"OK."

"You're gonna laugh," Eriksson said. "We can't figure out the code for the MSS arm files."

"The access code?"

"Yeah. We should have it on file here somewhere but we can't find it."

"Oh," he said. "That's what you need to know?"

"That's it."

"What do you need those for?"

"We don't really. But IT is doing an audit here and it came up as something that needs to be in the backups."

"I have it backed up and it's probably on the mainframe too."

A pause. "Yeah . . . well, look, we still have to have access to it."

"Sure, the backups don't have password protection so you can run them from there into the main server."

"I don't think you're quite hearing me, Chip."

"I don't think you're asking me the right question."

"You're going to make this hard."

"Am I?" A second low rumble. The windows shaking. "Christ," he said. "Hang on." The voice on the other end of the phone speaking but what words were being said lost in the volume outside on the street. "Hang on. Hang on," he repeated, the rumble fading to a hum that pulsed in heavy waves outside past the house. He could hear Eriksson's voice continuing somewhere in the din. "Hold on," Keith said. "There was a truck. What did you say?"

It was silent for a moment and then Eriksson said, "When are you coming back to Houston?"

"That's up to Mullins."

"How so?"

"He told me to take some time off so I'm doing what I'm told."

"All right, all right," Eriksson said. "I get it."

"You get what?"

"Well, we miss you here."

He did not know how to respond to this statement and so he said nothing for a long time, both of them silent now, their breathing reverberating down the phone lines. Then he said, "Can I ask you a question?"

"Sure, buddy."

"Am I still an astronaut?"

"What kind of question is that?" Erikkson said. There was the sound of laughter in his voice, as if Keith was making a joke of some kind.

"I'm either an astronaut or I'm not."

"Oh come on, Chip. You're a superstar around here and you know it."

Keith said nothing.

"You're ten times smarter than anyone else in the building."

"Quinn was smarter," Keith said. Just that.

There was no sound from the phone now. Outside, the roar of big engines continued beyond the window. Muffled.

"Christ, buddy," Eriksson said.

"She was."

"OK." Eriksson's voice was quiet. Almost a whisper. Then he said, "I don't know what to say. I'm sorry about your daughter. We all are. And we could use you back here. That's for sure."

"I don't know if I can come back there right now."

"You want me to talk to Mullins?"

He paused for a long moment. Then he said, "I don't know." He sat down again, the little chair squealing under the weight of his body. All he could think of was the desire to be back in micrograv-ity again, in that low orbit aboard the space station where there was no perceptible weight, where everything in his life—the physical objects—would suspend indefinitely in midair until he retrieved them, where he would sleep attached to the wall of his closetlike living quarters. That was what he wanted, not to be back in Houston but to be up in space. And then he realized something he had never thought of before, that his desire to return to the ISS had less to do with working with the numbers and more to do with the feeling of being there, of seeing Earth unscroll beneath him, the tan mass of Africa and the blue ocean and the white swirl of clouds moving across the sphere of Earth as the day flashed to night and the universe itself was unveiled all around him. He wanted to see that again, to experience that again. Even if there were no numbers with which to make sense of it. More than anything, that was what he wanted.

"Look, I'm sorry but we're going to need that access code," Eriks-son said.

In the low-frequency hum of the trucks outside he thought he could hear the thin whine of his migraine but he could not be sure. He could hear their engines where they revved and roared. Not delivery trucks. Something else.

"Yeah," he said. There was a long pause but he could think of nothing that would convince Eriksson to include him in whatever work was ongoing and so he spoke the access code slowly into the phone, a long string of letters and numbers, and Eriksson read it back to him and he confirmed it and then Eriksson said, "Hold on," and he could hear the sound of typing and then Eriksson said, "OK, that worked."

"That's my project," he said.

"I know that." Eriksson said nothing for a moment. Then he said, "Hang on a minute," and there was the shuffling of motion from the other end of the phone. Then his voice again, quieter, closer than before: "Listen, between you and me, there're some big rumors coming down the pipe. Stuff you'll want to be in on and stuff that doesn't have anything to do with being active flight or not."

"I'll bet."

"I'm not kidding, buddy. Get well and get back here."

"Yeah, OK," Keith said. "I'll do that."

The conversation ended and Keith sat there in the empty house at the kitchen table, looking at the phone where it lay before him on the laminated wood-grain surface. The trucks continued to hum and rumble outside and after a long moment there at the table he rose and rummaged through the stack of bills and unopened mail and papers until he found the résumé that Peter's wife had given him and then he sat again at the table and read through it carefully. It was a generic résumé that listed every possible facet of Petruso Kovalenko's education and work experience, from menial jobs to the highly skilled work he had done at the Golosiiv observatory. There were references listed, good ones by the look of it, the scientists and engineers that Peter had mentioned during their conversations in the vacant lot: Federov and Kuzmenko and even Vanekov, the man who apparently ran the entire observatory compound. The last two sheets in the packet were photocopied letters from Kuzmenko and Federov, letters written in English on official letterhead festooned with Ukrainian characters.

He removed his laptop from its bag and opened it and looked through his address book and sent out two e-mails, the first to the head of Dreyfuss Research Center and the second to the head of personnel at Johnson Space Center. Apart from the greeting, the two e-mails were identical in content, each asking if the recipient would be willing to look at a résumé if he sent one over, that he knew a man who was an amateur astronomer who had worked with some of the big names in Ukraine and was looking for employment in the United States, that the man was intelligent and well qualified but had no official degree. He listed Peter's name and the names of the references he listed at Golosiiv and a few points about the résumé. He knew it was likely that nothing would come of the e-mails but he had at least tried. Perhaps he would never hear anything. Perhaps his own name was such that an unsolicited e-mail from him would curse Petruso Kovalenko's employment possibilities forever.

"A little early isn't it?" Keith said.

"Have you seen what has happened?" Peter said.

"To what?"

"Come and see. It is terrible, I think." Peter's eyes were glassy with tears.

"Christ, are you OK?"

"Come and see," he said again.

Keith's first thought was that Peter was drunk and that they would have some replay of the scene in front of Starbucks. The telescope was nowhere to be seen and the sun low but still present in the sky.

Keith checked that his keys were in his pocket and stepped outside. Peter led him toward the street to the sidewalk and started to point but his eyes were already there. He had not been out of the house since his conversation with Eriksson and had ceased to notice the rumble of what he had assumed to be trucks in the cul-de-sac; those sounds had faded into the background and with them had faded the threat of a migraine. But now he found himself wishing he had listened more closely, for it had not been trucks he had ignored for most of the day; it had been tractors.

The vacant lot at the end of the cul-de-sac had been crisscrossed repeatedly, the thistle and debris cleared so that most of the lot was flat and bare. In the distant corner, a mountain of fresh dirt rose up in a huge brown cone and closer, flanking the leather sofa as if guarding it, two huge yellow machines: one with a thick, heavy scoop in the front, the other a backhoe equipped with a curved bucket lined with square teeth.

"Terrible thing," Peter said.

"Shit," Keith said.

"They do not touch sofa."

"Not yet."

"What are they doing?"

"I don't know," Keith said. "Building."

"Building what?"

"Another house, I guess."

He stepped toward the end of the cul-de-sac and Peter followed almost as a child might follow a parent, always keeping one step behind as if Keith could somehow shield him from whatever evil lay before them.

"It does not even look like same place," Peter said. "Just terrible. Catastrophe."

"I wouldn't go that far," Keith said.

Peter did not answer. They stopped at the end of the sidewalk. The thistle was flattened there and a few feet farther in it was gone altogether, only dirt remaining. The thistle and weeds had partially obscured the sofa from the street but now in the bare field it seemed alien

and incongruous, tufts of dry undergrowth surrounding the lumpy
shape like the frayed edges of some weird throw rug.

"We should take sofa back into your house," Peter said. "Yes?"

Keith shook his head. "I don't want that thing."

"No?"

"No."

"They will take sofa, though."

"They will," he said. "Do you want it?"

Peter did not answer and Keith thought he was likely thinking it
over but when he glanced over at him there were fat tears sliding down
his face. "Fucking shit," Peter said. "I am embarrassed." He wiped at
his tears, tried for a moment to control himself and then sobbed vio-
lently.

Keith looked back at the vacant lot again. The tractors like awkward insects that had descended there from some planet of yellow
metal. "You can find somewhere else," he said. "There are still vacant
lots around somewhere."

"This one was mine," Peter said. "I am sorry to be like a girl with
crying. I am stupid man."

"It's OK."

"Fucking shit. I hate this country."

Keith said nothing now, the words meaningless, the sun continuing its descent toward the houses to the west of them, the cul-de-sac
already in shadow. Both of them quiet and the distant and constant hiss
of the freeway and the million parking spaces being filled and unfilled
by a million shoppers the only sound until Peter spoke again. "Look,"
he said.

"At what?"

"There." He pointed a finger above them at the sky and Keith followed the line and there it was. Far up above them, above the tractors and the sofa and the cul-de-sac and the endless sprawl, floating
there in the last light before the sun crested those endless houses to

the west and dipped out past the edge of the earth itself was the great dark bird.

"Oh," Keith said, not a word but an inrush of breath, his eyes wide.

"Your big bird, I think."

"Yes," Keith said. "Yes."

"Not eagle, I think," Peter said. "Vulture."

"Vulture?"

"What they call it. Um . . ." Peter paused and then said, "Buzzard."

"Buzzard?"

It was no eagle, no bird of prey at all but rather a scavenger. Shit. Fantastic. Even now it turned above them, perhaps peering down at the empty lot, the tractors and the sofa and the two men standing there looking back at it and perhaps it regarded them all as inconsequential to its welfare. There was nothing to eat and so there was no reason to descend. Perhaps it would never change its infinite circle. Perhaps now it would never come down.

"A vulture," Keith said. "That's just fantastic."

Peter said nothing. The two of them stood in much the same aspect as they had for those nights under the stars, side by side, heads tilted back, staring up into the dome of the atmosphere as if it might reveal something of itself that had been held in secret.

"Shit," Keith said after a moment.

"Shit," Peter said in response.

Then both of them were silent.

Interval: Space

$$(c\Delta t)^2 < (\Delta r)^2$$
$$(\Delta s)^2 > 0$$

HE HAD BEEN flying back and forth to Houston, staying during the week in a small apartment he had rented there and returning home for weekends when he was able. At times he was so busy with the training that even sleeping at the apartment became a rare event. There were weeks of flight training aboard a supersonic jet that mirrored the controls of the space shuttle and then a long period of survival training in Maine, in between which he flew home. At first he had attempted to do so each weekend. In the revisionism of his later days he told himself that he had done so in an attempt to maintain his connection with Quinn and to keep her, as gently as he could, on the right path to foster her gift and to continue the conversations they had been having about math and science, but the probable reality was that he simply felt obligated to return home when it was convenient to do so, at first every weekend, then three times per month, then every other week. Soon he was lucky to make it back once in three weeks. He tried not to think about it in too much detail. He was being trained as an astronaut, after all, and was that not the most important possible activity in his life?

By the time the summer returned, he had finished the flight training and had been strapped into his first space suit and had begun to familiarize himself with the full-scale ISS model submerged in the enormous neutral buoyancy pool at JSC. Maybe he should have recognized the signs that Quinn was already changing, for when he spoke with her on the phone or occasionally in person when he was home she told him she was spending most of her days at the city pool and, in her words, "hanging out." He talked to her about math from time to time as well but mostly she seemed to be in a great hurry to do something else, always on the way to the mall or the pool or the movie theater so that she was most often gone from the house during the daylight hours and sometimes well into the evenings, even though his own visits home were increasingly rare.

Of course when he did see her, when she was home for dinner or was lingering in the kitchen on some rare afternoon when she was not busy with her friends, she would ask him about his training, about what he was doing in Houston and what kinds of technology he had been able to work with. Had he any concern at all, these moments might have assuaged them. But there was no real concern, for he did not think about her changing, not in any specific or quantifiable way. Instead, he thought about his training and when he returned home he continued to think about his training. After all the long years of study and graduate school and the air force and the exhausting labor of his mind he was becoming an astronaut at last.

In any case, he felt she would soon enough be in good hands, for she had finally agreed to attend the Academy of Arts of Sciences, at least for a year, even though she continued to call it "Nerd School" and spoke of it with a kind of mirthful derision. He did not know if he had simply worn her down or if she now actually agreed with him that the school would provide the best place for her to continue her studies. The reason did not matter because he knew that she would blossom there and that the first year would turn into a second and a third.

If anything it was Barb who was more strongly opposed to the school. "She's not like you," she told him when he first brought up the idea, Quinn in seventh grade then.

"You've been telling me for years that she's *exactly* like me," he had answered.

"Not the way you think," she said. "You think you're going to turn her into an astronaut or something. She's not like that."

"OK," he said. "What's your point?"

"The point is that she's happy at the regular school."

"She's happiest when she has a challenge to work on," he said.

She just looked at him then, incredulous, saying nothing.

"Anyway, she wants to go."

"She wants to go because you want her to go," Barb said. "Jesus, Keith. Give her a break. She's just a little girl."

"This is important, Barb."

"To who?" She turned toward him, to where he stood unmoving in the center of the bedroom.

"To her," he said.

"To her?"

He said nothing in response. He knew what she meant. Of course he did. But it was not true that the school was important only to him or at least he believed it was not true and so he had not thought there had been any possibility that she would actually choose the public school over the academy. Such an outcome seemed impossible. Then he had started the training and Quinn was in eighth grade and then summer was upon them again and he had simply assumed that the plan they had discussed and decided upon remained in place, had believed it so strongly that when Barb told him that Quinn had decided not to go to the academy, that she wanted instead to attend the regular high school, the information made so little sense that he did not know how to respond and so responded in the only way that would come to him, that it was not her decision to make; it was his decision and, perhaps, Barb's, but if Barb was not going to support it then it would be his decision alone. Had he only been there every day, talking to her about math and science, pushing her along the path of her destiny, then perhaps she would not have drifted away from it the way she had and then he was angry at Barb for allowing her to deviate from that path or, short of this, for failing to keep him better informed. And then when he talked to Quinn he did not even understand what she was saying. She talked about her friends and the clubs and activities she was involved with at the junior high and how much better it would be in high school and he sat and looked at her and wondered where she had gone or how he had so totally failed to understand her or how she had so totally failed to understand herself.

"It's like you have a choice between Harvard and state college," he told her, "and you're choosing state college. I don't get it. If you can go to Harvard, you go to Harvard."

She was prone upon her bed, looking at a magazine of some kind—fashion or gossip or something similar—and she continued to stare down at its pages, not looking at him as he stood in the doorway, but not ignoring him either, hearing him even if she did not respond.

"I just want the best for you," he continued. "I didn't have this kind of opportunity when I was your age. I had to wait and wait and wait to learn the stuff I wanted to learn. I dreamed of a school like the academy. I really did. But there just wasn't anything like that then. At least not that I knew of or that we could afford. But you can do this."

"Maybe you should go to the academy then," she said. She still did not look at him and then he saw that tears had begun to streak down her face.

"Oh Quinny," he said.

He reached for her and she said, "Don't," her voice quiet even as she shrugged away from him. He was silent for a long time and then he said, just as quietly, "OK."

He turned out of the doorway now and moved in the direction of the living room. As he did so he could hear the sound of the door swinging shut behind him, not slammed in anger but closing gently as if in resignation or defeat.

It was well past eight in the evening but the midsummer days were long and yellow sunlight streamed through the kitchen windows and across the living room floor. Still at least a half hour until sunset. Barb out with her girlfriends. In the absence of the closing door there were no sounds anywhere except those he himself made.

He took a beer from the refrigerator and went to the slider and opened it, moving outside in his socks and brushing off one of the lawn chairs there and sitting down. He tried not to think of the conversation he had just had or had failed to have but of course it was impossible not to and he continued to feel irritated and, yes, disappointed, although this latter he still did not want to admit to himself. He opened his beer and took a long drink.

The coming evening surprisingly cool and the light filtering through the mulberry tree shuffled in the faint, thin breeze. A white glow, then green, then white again. The hum of a distant lawnmower. The voices of children somewhere.

The sun was lower in the sky when the slider shushed open behind him. He half turned to see Quinn in the doorway. "Can I sit out here with you?" she said.

"Of course," he said.

"Can we not talk about stuff?"

"We don't have to talk about anything."

Her face showed no expression. She moved forward onto the concrete and pulled a second lawnchair beside his, close enough that it was almost touching, and sat next to him and they watched as the day ended and the light paled to chartreuse and then shifted into a deep radiant blue and then began to yellow into sunset.

They remained together like that for a long while, unmoving, not speaking. At some point he reached out his hand for her in that silence and her fingers wrapped into his own. Her hand so much bigger than he remembered it. Not the hand of a little girl now but becoming a young woman. And yet the gesture was the same and the feeling of her skin was the same. The air had become the color of night, the sun dropping beyond the mulberry, the light of the town all around them rendering the sky a dusty emptiness devoid of stars, as if some quiet blanket had been pulled over them.

He would have held that moment forever. She would have done the same.

A month later Quinn began her freshman year of high school. He knew that he could not have changed her mind and anything he would now say would simply result in her pulling further away from him. But it felt like a reversal of roles somehow, not between he and his daughter but between he and Barb as her parents, for her willfulness had seldom been directed against him. He remembered that span of days—it had turned out to be nearly a week—in which Barb had flown to Atlanta to attend to the death of her father and how he had been concerned that Quinn might prove difficult to manage. But that had not been the case. It was Barb and Quinn's teachers who found her difficult to manage; he had always found her willing to accommodate most reasonable requests. He and Quinn had shared some kind of bond then, which he had thought to be permanent because it had been based upon their actual selves, their beings, the people they were, which had fit together with such fluidity that her talent, her gift of numbers, seemed like a natural progression. It was almost to be expected. And yet now she had made up her mind in a direction that made no sense to him, which indeed seemed counter to everything he cared about or desired or believed about her.

It was only her choice of schools and yet it was also much more than that. Indeed it seemed to him that the whole of her had changed while he was away at training and he hardly recognized the new tall brightly dressed teenager she had become. What bothered him even more was realizing that she had not signed up for any math classes whatsoever and hearing slightly later, from Barb, that Quinn had made the freshman cheerleading squad. He did not know that she had tried out or had even been interested in doing so. Barb had been a cheerleader but Quinn was not like her mother, although now he was not sure he knew his daughter very well at all. Indeed, it was as if the vacant rooms in that infinite hotel they had spoken about had somehow all been filled and no further expansion was possible, the sets of infinity eliminated, cardinality vaporizing all at once into a dull gray mist that drifted, became transparent, and was gone.

The plan had been that Keith would finish his training and when he was officially an active-duty astronaut Barb and Quinn would finally move to Houston and they would be a family again. He knew that Barb would not want to move, knew also that Quinn would be saddened by the decision but that she too would want to remain and continue her high school in the town where she had grown from a child into a young woman. Nonetheless when he was at last presented with the silver lapel pin indicating that the training period had ended and he had entered the roster of active-duty astronauts, he collected some information on relocating to Houston from the personnel office, a thick envelope of printed materials lauding the myriad cosmopolitan aspects of the city, and when he returned home he handed the entire packet to Barb and then watched, for a full week, as those pages remained on the kitchen counter, unread. He asked her if she had thought much about where she wanted to live or if she wanted him to poll those NASA employees he already knew who were living in Houston but her response was vague and he was left to wonder when the argument would come. When it finally did, it was exactly as he knew it would be. Barb maintained that he would be gone so often that it made little sense to move to Houston, particularly as Quinn was already established at her new high school.

"The only reason I was flying back and forth was because of the academy," he had argued. "If she doesn't want to go there I'm not going to make her, but there's nothing keeping us from Houston now."

"That's not the only reason why we didn't move," she said. "You're gone all the time. You're still going to be gone all the time."

He was silent. Incredulous.

"And Quinny has her friends," Barb continued, "and she's popular and she's so beautiful. The boys are falling all over themselves for her."

Silence, and then he said, "I can't believe you talked her into this."

"She talked *me* into this."

"I don't believe that for a minute," he said, but he did believe it, immediately and completely, and the sensation was like a vast star collapsing all at once in his chest. It had not been his idea to commute back and forth to Houston but he had agreed to do so and in making this agreement had set a precedent that could not be undone. Perhaps he had thought he could shift her into the faster current, the current that he could see flowing under her feet but which, for reasons he still could not understand, was somehow invisible to her. Had he pushed too hard or had he not pushed nearly hard enough? But these were not even the right questions to ask. He had simply done what he had always done; he had fallen into the numbers like a man falling into his dreams and thought that somehow the people he left behind were locked into the orbit paths he had calculated for them and would continue to turn in those perfect paths, a radial distance forever matching the most simplistic articulation and needing no further calculation or concern.

Of course Barb won the argument; he did not even know why he tried to talk her out of it to begin with.

And so they did not move to Houston but they did move one last time. She brought him the brochure soon after he had been assigned his first mission—the only mission he would ever undertake—amongst the first of his ASCAN group. The group had been told that the order in which they were chosen for the mission schedule was no reflection of their individual capabilities but he could not help feeling that he had been chosen for precisely such a reason. He had taken over a project to replace the current robotic arm on the ISS with a longer, more mobile version and rather than approaching it as if it would be a new model of the existing arm, he threw out the original schematics, the notes and ideas of other minds who had worked on the project, and thought instead about basic and fundamental notions of functionality— motion, power, strength, dexterity, control. He poured himself into the project, the numbers fluid and sleek and beautiful, and when he had a full draft of the whole project he showed it to the main office and within days was presenting it to various members of the NASA staff. They checked his calculations again and again but he already knew he was correct. Over the subsequent year he would work on making the numbers a reality.

Once the arm was complete he would bring it to the ISS. He would install it. He would test it in person aboard the station. That would be his mission. My god. He would at last be going into space. And Barb and Quinn both seemed excited for him this time, Barb even suggesting that they go out to dinner to celebrate and there were days when he felt as if some syzygial moment had come upon him: he was fulfilling his dream, his daughter was happy, his wife loved him. But it was only that span of days, for he was gone again for more work on the robotic arm and when he returned everything had regained its normal silence and distance. Barb wrapped up in her life, Quinn in her own, and these lives separate from his.

Soon after, Barb brought him the brochure featuring the image of a young couple with a blonde child and a red dog with long shining fur, all posed happily on an expanse of green lawn. "The Estates," the text read. "Your home. Your future. Your family." He did not know why Barb or anyone else would want to live in a neighborhood comprised entirely of cul-de-sacs, but when he raised this objection she reminded him that he was going to be gone on his mission for six months and he would be home so seldom between now and departure that his opinion was of little import. "Just let me do this," she told him, and his response was to nod and tell her, "OK, fine," and then, "Whatever you want."

She chose a floor plan and a color scheme and five months later they hired another moving company and everything was boxed up and loaded into a truck and delivered to the new house across town and then everything was unboxed and put away in bedrooms still smelling of plaster and fresh paint. One weekend when he was home Barb dragged him through six or seven different furniture stores, asking his opinions of various sofas and tables and chairs and finally purchasing the sofa he professed to like the least, the gray beast that she had subsequently left behind. There had been an argument, of course, but even then he did not know why he had bothered or why she brought him along to the stores if only to ignore every opinion he offered.

Despite this, he thought in the end that the new house might make Barb happy or if not happy then at least content and that it might even make Quinn happy, the two of them settling into a neighborhood so new that much of it remained empty, streets ending abruptly at dirt lots, sidewalks circling empty spaces where houses had yet to be built. She had wanted a new house and it certainly could not be any newer than this.

His last conversation with Quinn occurred the evening before he was to return to Houston for the launch procedure. He had been home for a few days. When Quinn was home she stayed mostly in her room or passed through the house talking on her mobile phone and so he hardly saw her at all even though she dwelled under the same roof. She had her own life of cheerleading, social gatherings, and high school dances and did not seem to notice him unless she wanted something from him. And he did not like to admit it but he was afraid too, afraid of her lack of interest in him, afraid of her silences, perhaps afraid of further pushing away whatever connection they had once shared, and it was this fear that continued to concern him even as the months and weeks and days passed and up until there was simply no time remaining. He had decided that he should talk to her about her future just once more before the mission and actually convinced himself that it was worth at least attempting, as if he might shake her resolve just enough for her to consider her future while he was away, and so, the night before he was to leave, when Barb was out at the supermarket, he walked up the stairs in the house that six months later would be empty of everything except for himself and knocked, waiting for her to say, "Come in," before opening the door.

"Hey," he said.

"Hey," she answered. "What's up?"

"Nothing. Just stopping by."

She was silent, looking at him. She was not a girl anymore but a young woman; the skinny gangly child she had once been had faded into some more distant memory and this daughter who looked up at him was a young adult. In his memory she was shining. In his memory she was alive.

He glanced around the room: a white box the walls of which were mostly covered over by music posters. "How's the new room working out?" he said.

"OK."

"Did you decide on a color?"

"Not yet."

"What's happening?"

"Nothing much." She waved her mobile phone at him. "Texting."

"Ah," he said. "Texting who?"

"Shawn."

"Boyfriend?"

"Yeah."

"He's the tall kid?"

"Yeah, he's the tall kid. I only have one boyfriend."

"Got it," he said.

"Don't be mean," she said.

"I'm not being mean. Why do you and your mother always think I'm being mean? I'm never being mean."

"Just don't be mean."

It was silent then but for the faint strains of music from the stereo behind her. After a moment he said, "How's cheerleading?"

"Good."

"Good game on Friday?"

"Yeah. We did our new pyramid at halftime. Mom said it looked great."

"I'll bet it did," he said. "Did she video it?"

"I think so."

"Good, I'll watch it later then." He stood looking at her and still she did not look back at him. "School?" he said at last.

"Fine," she said. A pause and then, "How's work?"

"Hard. We leave tomorrow."

"I know. Are you excited?"

"Of course."

"Cool." A long silence now.

"So," he said, "I wanted to talk to you about something before tomorrow."

"Uh-oh." She looked up at him and then sat up and leaned against the headboard.

"Well, I guess I wanted to know what you had planned. Or if you were thinking about that at all."

"What do you mean?"

"You're seventeen."

"Are you asking me what I want to be when I grow up?"

"Yeah," he said. "I guess."

"I don't know yet."

"Any idea what college you might want to go to?"

"Probably City. At least for a while."

He was silent, staring at her.

"What?" she said.

"You can do better than that."

She did not say anything in response.

"I just want to make sure you're thinking of your future. That's all I'm saying."

"I *am* thinking of the future," she said.

"City College is not your future."

"Says who?"

"Look, honey, I want you to do something. At least go to the university."

"And do what?"

"I don't know. I figured you'd be a math major or something."

"I probably will be a math major or something."

"I just want to make sure you have some kind of goal. That's all." She did not respond and after a moment he said, "This is important, Quinn."

"What's important?"

"This. All of it. The thing you can do."

"What thing?"

"You know what I'm talking about. You're gifted."

"God, when will you stop about that?"

"When you do something about it. Or if it's not that then something else."

"Something else like what?"

It was silent again. He could feel the blood pumping in his body, the thrumming rhythm of it. "I just don't understand," he said at last.

"What's to understand?"

"You," he said. "I don't understand you."

"That's because you don't talk to me anymore."

He stood there, surprised and confused, looking for some response but finding nothing.

"I know you're busy and I know your astronaut stuff is important," she said at last, "but you can't blame me for you not being around. It's not fair."

"OK," he said. "Then tell me what's going on."

"There's nothing going on."

He exhaled loudly, as if resigned. "That's my point, Quinn," he said. "You're not doing anything."

"I'm doing plenty," she said. "I have straight A's."

Even in that moment he knew he was telling a half-truth, the calculus of his argument reaching no clear conclusion except the conclusion that had been clear and true for him and which he had decided must also be true for his daughter. This, even though he knew that she was not like him, that she did not need the numbers in the way that he had, the way he still did. He knew that even then. And yet he continued pushing because he also believed that he was right. Her gift, her abilities, were stronger than his own. But she had chosen to be a cheerleader of all things, a cheerleader, a choice that made so little sense to him he could not even begin to work out a response. It was as if the girl he had known and loved—the girl who was not even a girl anymore but who was a young woman—had erased the equation he had made for her, leaving only the variables or not even that, leaving only the aleph and some range of infinities that could not be counted.

And so he said what he would regret for all his days to come: "I'm disappointed," he told her. "I'm disappointed in you." His daughter who was a straight-A student, who was brilliant, and popular, and beautiful. Even in that moment, standing in her doorway, he could feel his heart crumbling inside the cage of his chest. And yet he was angry and frustrated and somehow believed that if he said the right combination of words he might turn her back to the course he had envisioned, even though he knew that he could never find the right words, not in this situation nor in any other.

She was quiet for a long time after that and when she spoke again her voice cracked with tears. "You don't understand," she said at last.

"I guess I don't."

She stood from the bed quickly. "I'm going over to Shawn's," she said and when he did not move from the doorway she looked him in the eye and said, "Get out of my way," and of course he did so.

Those were the last words he would hear from her in person, the last not separated by atmosphere and electricity. She and Barb had come to the launch but he felt it was only because they were obligated to do so. He had seen Quinn one last time: from across a barricade since NASA rules dictated that any school-age children were potential carriers of illness and any kind of close proximity was therefore forbidden. He might have been relieved by this. If so, he now could not will himself to remember. It was late in the evening and she was standing next to her mother in the harsh artificial light. He walked along the road with the others in the crew, a line of men and women in orange launch suits, and she had waved to him and he had waved back. He could not even remember what she had been wearing. Had she called something to him? Had she yelled that she loved him? That she wished him good luck? If so, the words were lost to him. Instead, there was her wave. That was all.

When they talked later via the laptop while he was in orbit they did not mention the argument. Instead they both acted as if it had never occurred, their conversation a variety of pointless small talk. She and her mother were going on a vacation to Atlanta to visit Grandma. She had some cousins there that she was looking forward to seeing. Yes, she could take his car. Yes, cheer camp was going well. Nothing beyond such wandering and pointless topics but even these he now wished he could have recorded, wished he could play them back in the gray shadow of the days and weeks and indeed the years to come after, as if the whole of his memory had become a floating haze of detritus the outer reaches of which only tangentially obeyed him, circling, instead, some other false center, as if the brightness that had fallen from that distance would, at any moment, come rocketing in from the outer dark with its pale and luminescent shift dragging out behind it like a gown.

Part IV

Fifteen

OVER THE SUBSEQUENT days the field metamorphosed into something else entirely. He had only been visiting the vacant lot for four
weeks but even that short time had left him with a feeling of nostalgia. Now that time was over. It had become the standard endpoint of
his day and very nearly the only thing he had come to look forward
to, not only Peter's company but the ceremony of it: the telescope
providing the justification for being in the dark field and the drinking
and smoking providing the impetus to relax into that moment. Certainly there were other empty fields somewhere in the vicinity but it
would not be the same as simply walking out the front door to the end
of the cul-de-sac. The ease of it was gone and any other solution would
be complicated, not only by distance but by effort. He would walk
from his house to the empty lot and would sit on the sofa and would
drink and would talk to his neighbor idly about whatever came to
mind. But would he drive somewhere to do that? He thought it unlikely.

That evening, he stood at the edge of the cul-de-sac in the early hours of the night and stared into the darkness beyond the reach of the streetlamps. The lot was perfectly flat now and completely bare of any vegetation and it occurred to him that previous to the arrival of the tractors the field must have been leveled in preparation to build on and then the economy had crashed and all plans had been abandoned to grass and thistle and weeds. Weirdly, the sofa remained in the same location where he and Peter had first positioned it: in the relative center of the lot, the tractors flanking it like guards. Above flooded the black sky: Cassiopeia's flattened W tilting on end as Earth rotated around its axis and Polaris unmoving as if it were the pin upon which the planet was affixed to the universe itself.

So it had begun and so would it end. He could not fathom who would have the wherewithal to actually build a house now, given the economic situation that was, according to the newspaper he occasionally read at Starbucks, the worst since the Great Depression, but there was no other explanation for it: the two tractors were there and the plot had been scraped clean and soon there would be gravel and forms for concrete and then the concrete itself and the thing would start to take shape. It was engineering elemental and basic and he could see it all in his mind even in the dark. Perhaps the entire house would be built around the sofa and it would ever remain in its geographic center.

He might have imagined the telescope there between the giant machines but instead there was only a dark shadow between the hulking silhouettes, the tractor windows reflecting the streetlight that glowed just behind him, his own shadow stretching out over the bare moonscape like an arrow pointing toward the impenetrable darkness beyond.

Sally Erler called him late the following day while he was once again at Starbucks. He thought at first that the vibrating phone indicated that Barb had found his new phone number and he very nearly did not even look at the screen, doing so only after a long pause in which he hoped to silence it by sheer force of will, as if by ignoring the sound and concentrating instead on his coffee he might somehow erase the marriage. But of course such things do not happen at Starbucks. Indeed such things do not happen at all, and at last he glanced down at the screen and then flipped the phone open and answered.

"Hello, Sally," he said.

"Keith, it's Sally Erler," she said, her standard response to anything he could open with.

"Yes, I know." He was smiling. At least there was that.

"We have a little glitch. Maybe nothing but it's a glitch."

"OK."

"Well, it's about the termite inspection. Have you seen the results?"

"Oh," he said. Had he? "I don't think so."

"Well, they probably mailed you a copy so it will be there soon. It's not good news."

"No?"

"No, it's bad news," Sally said.

"Oh," he said, his syntax devolving to single words. "What? Termites?"

"Yes, the report says there might be significant damage."

"Significant damage?"

"Yes, significant damage."

"I'm sorry. That's surprising. It's a new house."

"Yes, it's surprising but it's on the report and that's a big problem. It needs to be addressed before we can move on with the sale."

"Addressed how?"

"Repaired."

"Really? Christ," he said. It was not the first expletive that came to mind. "How much does this kind of thing cost?"

"Well, I have to tell you that it can be quite expensive."

"Expensive like what?"

"I don't know. I've seen them tent houses though. Drill into foundations. That kind of thing. It can . . . kill a sale." These last words weak, as if she was on the verge of tears. And indeed it could be that she was.

"Kill the sale?" he repeated.

"Let's look on the bright side. We don't know much yet so call the termite inspection company and talk to them and we'll find out how extensive the damage is and they can come and give you a pest eradication bid and then you should call a contractor to come out to see what kind of repairs need to be done. Maybe it won't end up costing very much. I don't know."

"Come on, Sally," he said. "This is a deal breaker, right?"

"Well, I wouldn't say that." These were her words but her tone said otherwise. "I still want to sell the house for you."

"Don't they leave holes or sawdust or something? I haven't seen anything."

"They said it was in the garage. Maybe you didn't notice."

"The garage?"

"That's what it says."

They exchanged a few more sentences and then the conversation ended and he clicked the phone closed. His coffee cooling toward room temperature. The newspaper unfolded on the table. The cruelty of the joke was that he had finally accepted the notion that the house would be sold and that he would move somewhere else, would have a different life in some other place, and then this. There was no accounting for anything, as if all had become enslaved to a center of gravity around which he spun without cease. He found himself wondering what Hoffmann would say about this. He had told him that the goal was for him to move through his experiences and yet every experience continued to appear as another full and complete stop, a wall, an impasse.

He set the cup on the counter and Audrey said, "How's Peter?" and he mumbled something neutral in response. She might have said something else as he passed but if so he did not hear her.

. . .

When he arrived home he entered through the front door and set his keys on the counter and moved through the kitchen and into the laundry room. He had no explanation for why he had not yet opened the door there, the door that led into the garage, and now the fact that he had not done so struck him as feeble and strange.

And so standing before the thin white door that connected the garage to the house like a priest preparing to enter the vestibule of some spiritual mystery and even hesitating for a moment upon that glorious threshold before grasping the yellow faux-brass handle and, at long last, pulling open the door.

And of course the garage was empty. How else could it be?

He looked for a long time without entering, his eyes blinking in the blazing heat of the room, light leaking through the metal roll-up door, the air inside smelling of paint and sawdust and not unlike a tomb or an oven, the space a collection of hard angles and concrete and unfinished drywall with the tape and texture still visible. Not even a single cabinet to hide a box in. Not even that. Bare walls and concrete floor and a lightbulb screwed into the ceiling socket. The steel bar of the garage door opener across the ceiling. A few thin wires poorly plastered into a hole there.

He took a step inside and then moved to the center of the room and stood glancing around in silence. A window on one wall, the blinds closed and covered in cobwebs. Dead flies on the concrete.

An occasional insect fluttered past him lethargically. Along the wall that shared the door he had stepped through were a series of thin black lines a foot off the floor and running the length of that wall and when he stepped closer he realized that they were channels in the drywall, the concrete there a platform for tiny hills of white and tan sawdust. Termites. He reentered the house, returning to the air-conditioned rooms that were nearly as empty as the garage, and picked up his phone and dialed and when Barb answered he said: "Where's all my stuff?"

"What?"

"Where's my stuff, Barb? Where's all my stuff?"

"At the mini storage," she said.

"What mini storage?"

"The mini storage down the street."

"What's it doing there?"

"Wait, you're just now wondering where your stuff is?"

"What's their number?"

"I don't know. It's on the bill."

"What bill?"

"What do you mean 'what bill'? The bill. The bill. What do you want me to say? You change the bank account and I have no money and now you're calling to ask about the mini storage?"

"Yes, that's what I'm doing," he said. He had already gone to the pile of mail on the counter and was rifling through it now. He had paid the phone bill and the power and the gas and the mortgage. But there was a sizable stack of mail there, much of it three months old, that he had not even looked at.

"What's it called?" he said.

Perhaps she had been talking. "Are you even listening to me?" she said. "I don't remember what it's called. Something storage. It's right up the street. I don't get it. You're just now noticing that your stuff isn't there?"

"I haven't been in the garage," he said.

"Why not?"

"I just haven't."

"Are you serious?"

"How does it work? Is there a key here or something?"

"I left it on the counter along with the mailbox key and the extra house key."

He looked at his keys. There was the one key he had never used and now he knew what it was for. The mini storage padlock.

"Why did you move everything to the mini storage?"

"Because I thought you were going to sell the house. I didn't think you'd be hanging out there for months."

He did not say anything in response.

"I hope you've been paying the bill."

Again, his silence. Then he said, "I think I'd better call them."

"I'm not done talking," she said.

"I know," he said. "I'll call you back."

She started to say something but he mumbled a quick good-bye and clicked the phone shut. He had found a bill that read "EZ Storage" and then another and yet another, some with red letters under the address indicating "First Notice" and "Second Notice" and one marked in bold, triple-underlined and in all capital letters: "FINAL NOTICE." He opened that envelope and searched for the number and dialed. The bill was in his hand and he read through it as the phone began to ring. One hundred and twenty days overdue. There was a letter enclosed and he had just unfolded it when the line clicked and the call was answered.

He was asked his name and the account number and the storage unit number and because Barb had opened it they asked for her social security number, birth date, and home address for verification and he gave them that information from memory. The voice on the other line asked him to hold and then the line clicked and he sat and listened to Bob Marley being piped through the telephone speaker. He had spread the letter on the table, a document that described, in as precise terms as possible, the extent of the disaster were he to fail to pay the enclosed bill within thirty days. He slid the chair closer to the kitchen counter and retrieved the envelope and looked at its mailing date. Six weeks ago. Shit.

Bob Marley was singing forever and would never stop.

Then there was an abrupt click on the line and a voice returned. "Mr. Corcoran?" it said.

"Yes," he said.

"I'm sorry to inform you that your storage unit has been closed for lack of payment," the man said. There was a faint hint of a Middle Eastern accent, but it was so subtle as to sound more like cultural refinement than ethnicity, as if the careful pronunciation of English words was exacted to the standards of a private university education.

"I don't understand," Keith said.

"The account was not paid for one hundred and twenty days. Even then we waited another thirty days after we sent the final notice. It's not a free storage unit. It's a business."

"I understand that," Keith said. "I've been out of town. I'd like to go ahead and pay the full bill now."

"Sir, we appreciate that, but we have sent your account to the collection agency so you would need to speak with them about the eventuality of your payment."

"OK," he said. "Let me ask you this: How long before I can straighten this out and get my stuff out of the storage unit?"

"You misunderstand me, sir. There's nothing in the unit anymore. Your account is closed and that unit is now occupied by a new renter."

"Where's my stuff, then?"

"Sir, I'm sorry to have to inform you that the items in the storage were auctioned."

"Auctioned to who?"

"Sir, I cannot give you that information even if I had it, which I do not."

He sat in the kitchen, blinking slowly.

"Sir, when nonpayment occurs the contents of the storage are auctioned off."

"They got everything?"

"Sir, this is what I'm telling you. The whole unit is auctioned as a single item. What they do with the contents after that is up to them."

"Christ," he said.

"Sir, I'm sorry to have to give you this unsettling information."

"Unsettling? Shit."

"Sir, we made every attempt to contact you."

"I'm sure you did," he said. His voice was quiet now, slowing down. A weak thing. A dead bird. "When did the auction take place?" he said.

"Two weeks ago."

"Christ. Is the stuff still in it?"

"Sir, the items sold at auction are required to be immediately removed from the unit upon payment by the winning bidder."

"What does that mean?"

"It means they removed everything from the unit so it could be utilized by a new renter."

Keith was quiet.

"I'm sorry, sir," the man said. "Would you like the number of the collection agency?"

"Yeah, I guess so."

He was given the number and he wrote it down on an envelope and the call ended. The room reentered its silence. He sat there at the kitchen table. There were no thoughts now, only a deep well of regret as if the entirety of his life had slipped away from him and what remained was not even a shell or a husk but something akin to a spindrift of thin and insubstantial and sifted dust.

"Well, Quinn," he said to the empty room. "Here I am. What now?"

He stood again and returned to the stack of mail and looked for the termite inspection report but did not find it, instead bringing the mail to the table and proceeding to open each envelope and sorting the contents into piles. There were no bills he had not paid apart from the mini storage and a handful of magazine subscriptions that were Barb's and these he threw into the trash pile and finally he stood and gathered that pile and dumped the whole of it into one of the two identical plastic trash bins and then lifted both and carried them through the doorway into the garage, clicking the button that opened the big door there and then waiting as that blank white square rattled open at last.

He ducked underneath when it was high enough to do so and stepped around the rental car to the trash bin outside and opened it and dumped each of the smaller plastic bins into its mouth. The heat outside a respite to the temperature of the garage but still blazing. The sun moving into the west but what did that matter now?

His phone buzzed in his pocket and he looked at the screen. It was Barb and he realized that in calling her moments before he had given her his new phone number. Shit. He sighed audibly and flipped open the phone to answer the call.

"Did you get the storage unit squared away?" she said.

"No," he said. "You could have told me that's what you did. Christ, Barb."

"Don't get mad at me," she said.

"I'm not."

"Yes, you are."

He sighed again but said nothing.

"Where did you think everything went?" she said.

"The garage, Barb. I thought everything was in the garage."

"This whole time you never looked in the garage?"

He was silent. It sounded absurd and indeed it was.

"You need to call the storage," she said.

"I know that."

"And I left some of Quinn's stuff in there for you too. It's in a box by the door."

"What? What did you say?"

"I said that some of Quinn's stuff is in the storage by the door."

He was silent for a moment. Then he said, "What kind of stuff?"

"I don't know. Stuff I thought you'd want. Quinn's schoolwork that I was saving. And some photo albums."

"Her schoolwork was in the storage?"

"Yeah, it's in there in a box by the door. Don't you want it?"

He was silent now, breathing, trying to breathe, the sun blazing upon his head. The construction at the end of the cul-de-sac long since complete for the day. No sound from the vacant lot. Nicole

appeared from across the street, already jogging in his direction.
"Barb," he said into the phone.

"What?"

Then there was no air, only a terrible sense of void, of absence.

"What, Keith? What?" her voice came through the speaker, increasingly distant as he moved the phone away from his ear with a motion so slow it was almost imperceptible and then clicked it closed and stood there unmoving. A sense of sinking, of falling, flooded through him all at once.

"Captain Keith," Nicole said, arrived now, panting.

"Hey," he said.

"My dad's out on another trip," she said.

"OK."

"My mom said you'd want to know."

"Listen, I need to go in," he said.

"They had a big fight," she said, apparently ignoring him. "Your name was part of it."

He looked down at her. She was smiling, although he did not know why. "That's not good," he said.

"Anyway, I guess my dad was mad that you had dinner over here. He probably wanted to meet you because you're so famous. Anyway, he yelled a lot. Not as loud as my mom, though. She can yell *really* loud."

The tractors were silent in the field but at some point the workmen had moved the sofa to the edge of the space at last so that it rested very near the sidewalk, looking like a bloated park bench, and he stood watching it as if it might move back to its more familiar location of its own accord but it did not do so. What was happening now? How had his life come to such fragments?

After a moment, his phone began to vibrate in his pocket again and he did not look at it and after a time it too was quiet once again. He looked down at the little girl who stood at his feet, a girl who reminded him in odd moments of Quinn, and saw her mouth moving but could not hear her and he looked up then, at the flat blue of the sky as it fell slowly toward the darker gloaming of twilight and then across the street to Jennifer's house and again up to the end of the cul-de-sac and the field where the two tractors stood unmoving. My god. The world fading all around him or no not even that: the world steady and continuing ever and always and he the one dissolving into some endless and incomprehensible eventide.

"Anyway, my mom said you'd want to know that," Nicole was saying, her voice rising slowly from that mute and soundless eclipse.

"Christ," he said.

"You shouldn't say that."

"What?" he said suddenly, his eyes returning to her.

"You shouldn't say that."

He stood blinking, staring at her without comprehension.

"Were you even listening?" she asked him at last. "One-two-three, eyes on me."

"I was listening."

"What's the last thing you heard me say?"

"What?"

"The last thing you heard me say is 'what'? I didn't even say that."

"I'm going back inside now," he said, but when he turned back toward the house again he was met by the huge and staggeringly empty rectangle of the open garage door and he froze again there, unmoving. He did not want to reenter that terrible vacancy. That much was certain.

"Do you want me to tell my mom something?"

He turned to her once more. "What do you mean?"

"She'll ask me what you said."

He looked across the street at Jennifer's house again, realizing now that the little girl was asking him something and expected an answer and then wondering if he should answer her at all. Behind him the empty garage continued to loom out at him like some enormous well of gravity that had somehow managed to draw everything into a crushing void that was the cardinality of an empty set. How could he have been so stupid?

"So what do you want to tell her?" Nicole asked him.

He looked down at her and as he did so his phone once again began to buzz in his pocket. This time he looked at the screen. It was not Barb this time; instead, it was Jim Mullins calling from his JSC office. Christ. This too? He knew he should answer it but could not fathom talking to the office now so he waited for the call to ring through to voice mail as he watched the little screen that held his name.

"Anything?" Nicole said. She looked exasperated, hands on her hips and staring up at him.

"Tell her . . . ," he began, then stopped and looked at the two white plastic trash bins he had brought outside to dump, both of which flanked him now. Empty. Erased. "Tell her I'm sorry," he said at last.

Nicole cocked her head sideways. "Sorry for what?" she said.

"Just sorry."

"That's weird." She looked disappointed.

"Yes, it's weird," he said. Then he added, "Probably."

"Well, OK." She looked back at her house for a moment. If there was a signal from some quadrant there he did not see it. "I have to go," she said. "Bye."

She turned and ran to the sidewalk, looked up and down the cul-de-sac with ceremony lest some car come barreling down the asphalt, and then ran the rest of the way to her front door. He could hear her shout, "Mom!" as she opened the door and then it closed and what transpired therein he was not privy to and never would be.

He stood for a long time, staring off toward the street, the two white plastic trash bins on either side of him, as if waiting for something or someone to arrive but there was no traffic in the cul-de-sac. The twilight was approaching and he remained there until the sun reached the tops of the houses that stood on the ridge to the west and until the empty lot, now partially filled by the promise of construction, grew into a field of daggerlike shadows and then darkened and until the sky burned chrome and alizarin and then all at once flickered out and until all that remained were the uncountable pinpoints of light flickering against an atmosphere that ringed a further darkness that was the true color of the universe and ever would be. He did not know how long he stood there but he knew he was indeed waiting for someone, waiting with a gasping and terrible hope that verged on despair. He could not bring himself to reenter the empty house. Not now. Indeed in that moment he felt as if he would never be able to enter the empty house again, suspended between distal points so far away that their sources could no longer be ascertained. He stood there until at last the silhouette of the now-familiar figure rounded the corner of Riverside and entered the long bight of the cul-de-sac: the short, steady gait and the dark appendage of the telescope protruding up above him like a compass needle gone awry.

Sixteen

"WHAT IF THE comet is actually coming?" Keith said.

Peter did not stop looking through the telescope. One hand reached up to the fine-focus control, turning it carefully and then hovering there, frozen. "This is real question you ask?" Peter said.

"Well, yeah," Keith said.

"I do not know how to answer this question."

Keith remained sitting for a moment and then rose and stood near the telescope. "Let's have a look," he said.

Peter stepped back from the eyepiece and Keith leaned in and pressed his eye to it and reached up to the focus control and turned it carefully and then turned it back again. A blurry disc. "So what's this?" he said.

"M81," Peter said. "A galaxy. Simple to find. Simple to see."

"M81," he repeated. He waited for Peter to resume speaking and when he did not he said, "Aren't you going to tell me some story about it?"

"Why did you ask me about comet before?" Peter said.

"I don't know. I guess I was thinking about it."

"Yes," Peter said, "it is something to be thinking about."

The image in the circle of the telescope's lens was an insubstantial blur of color. "I don't know. What else is there to talk about?" he said.

"Yes, this is something," Peter said. "You know more about these things than I do, I think."

"I don't know anything about it at all."

"I mean about what might happen. They would send something into space to stop it maybe. Or missile. The technology parts of this you know about more than I do."

"Yeah, my knowledge of that stuff doesn't amount to much."

"You know though how this works. NASA and government. Space agencies and how they work together."

"Lots of meetings," he said. "That's how they work."

"Yes, I know something of meetings," Peter said. "This was so even at Golosiiv. Meetings and then meetings to make sure we have enough meetings. Never ending."

"That's how the world works."

"We had Dr. Vanekov at least. He was one to move things forward. Meeting too long. This is what I decide. Next item."

"That's good."

"Yes, good for meetings. Less good for those who are not agreeing with decisions. The scientists are angry sometimes. No, not angry. Wrong word."

"Frustrated?"

"Yes, that," Peter said. "Frustrated. Good word for this."

Peter's first words to him that evening had been to ask him for help moving the sofa back to its place in the center of the field and the simplicity of the request had done much to dispel his misery. They went immediately to the behemoth and hefted it across the bare dirt to the center between the two tractors and then dropped it roughly to the earth again, both of them collapsing into it simultaneously. Even the short walk had left them both winded and they sat there for a time in silence, having shared no words apart from the initial brief exchange. The two tractors flanked them on the north and south sides as if walls for some strange, open-air observatory, the big machines dim and blocky in the reflected light from the streetlamps at the end of the cul-de-sac. The simple act served to clear away the sickening feeling that had settled upon him and he realized that perhaps for the first time in his life he had grown to value human companionship and that the overarching feeling that had come to dominate his endless days and nights in the cul-de-sac was loneliness.

They had set the sofa facing west, directly away from the end of the cul-de-sac so that their backs were to the neighborhood. He wondered why they had not situated the sofa in that direction from the beginning as it created a sense of solitude simply by its geography: the flat open space before the more distant darkness of the oak trees, the cinderblock wall of the next neighborhood all cut into silhouette from glowing backyards and, above them, occasional squares of lit windows that hung suspended in the warm summer night. The stars spun over everything as they did forever and always, although the view above them was no longer familiar. Cassiopeia, the constellation that remained the most recognizable to him, was visible now only if he craned his neck to the right. Instead there was a large and mostly unintelligible sky before him.

He had not yet asked Peter what constellations and astronomical features lay in his new view but realized with some surprise that he was actually looking forward to doing so. He wondered if this was a mark of how far his mind had slipped, that he sat on a sofa in the dark and sought distraction in the names of the distant stars and did so with little care for the work he might have been doing. There was a time when he at least would have thought of angles and distances and energy and light. At least that. But now he felt content simply looking up into the sky and listening to Peter's discourse. The stars patterned in a way he would never truly understand but which was magnificent in its beauty. The distinction might have troubled him, but at the moment he did not feel troubled at all.

They talked at some length about Golosiiv again, about the kind of work Peter had done, about the landscape outside Kiev: horse-drawn carts and fields tilled by hand, lines of men and women bent over their work, each swinging the blade of a hoe and walking slowly backward in an ancient rhythm.

"Sounds brutal," Keith said.

"But so beautiful," Peter said. "Not like this." He pointed over Keith's shoulder at the cul-de-sac and then turned his hand and waved it generally around, encompassing everything around them. "So beautiful I cannot even describe. You would need being poet."

Keith said nothing. He opened another beer and then settled back into the sofa. Peter took a moment to relight his pipe and puffed at it, the coal glowing red as he sucked at the smoke and then fading as Peter held and then exhaled.

"Where do you buy that?" Keith said.

"The smoke? From my nephew. He is . . . how do I say . . . kind of bad."

"Kind of bad?"

"Mmm . . . I'm not clear. He does things that would be bad to talk about. Maybe not to talk about them, I think. That was not good English sentence. I apologize."

"OK," he said, chuckling. "Probably not a question I should ask anyway."

"No, this is fine to ask question. I am not clear." He paused a moment. "Some of my family, the young boys from my wife's brother, they are like Mafia. They buy and sell sometimes things that are not for buying and selling. It was this way in Ukraine so this is what they know to do here."

"At least they found a way to make money."

"Yes, maybe true. I worry police will take them away."

"What are we talking about here? Serious stuff?"

"I am not sure. They are seventeen and nineteen, the two of them.
They have money to buy cars and fancy clothes. Too much money for
little boys. I think this will not end well for them."

"Maybe they'll be fine."

"Maybe," Peter said. "They are stupid boys. They come to America and go back to what they are doing in Ukraine. This makes no
sense to me."

"Well, that's what you wanted to do."

"Do how?"

"You wanted to go back to what you were doing in Ukraine."

"Not same thing," Peter said. Then he said, "Well, maybe same
thing." He lifted his pipe to his mouth as if he was going to light it
but then he did not do so, instead holding it there poised before his
lips in the darkness. "Maybe I am too much like them I think," he
said.

"I doubt it," Keith said. "Wanting to go back to working in your
field is different than wanting to go back to a life of crime."

Peter did not answer. At last he lit the pipe and sucked at it for a
moment. A hush over everything. Keith found himself wondering if
all the crickets had been crushed into dust by the tractors, if their
desiccated husks were everywhere underfoot.

"If comet comes it will not matter who wants to go back and who
does not," Peter said.

"I suppose that's true."

"Yes, true. I do not think any comet is coming but still true."

"It's not front-page news yet."

"Maybe they keep this from front page so we are not afraid of
end."

"Maybe." He took another swallow of beer.

"The world is always coming to end," Peter said. "Comet is coming or is not coming. So this does not matter."

"Very philosophical," Keith said.

"Not philosophy. True. Stars and galaxies are being born and dying. This is what you see when you look through telescope. Things sometimes crash into other things. Galaxies absorb other galaxies. These things happen. The world is always coming to end."

Keith paused. Then he said, "Let's party like it's 1999."

Peter was quiet for a moment and then started to giggle. "I know this song," he said. He giggled again and then was caught up in the moment and laughed long and hard. Keith smiled, watching as Peter caught his breath and then exploded into laughter again. "You are funny man, Astronaut Keith Corcoran," Peter said at last.

"Apparently," he said.

Peter took another pull at the pipe and then came and sat next to Keith on the sofa. "I can't think of what to look at now," he said. "I have forgotten what I was doing."

"You've been smoking a lot."

"Is that so?"

"It is," Keith said. "I'm going to have to finish the whole six-pack to keep up with you."

"You should take up pipe. Not healthy for you to drink so much."

"Is that so?"

"Yes."

They were silent. Then Keith said, "Let me try that."

Peter handed him the pipe and the lighter and Keith lit the small bud in the bowl and sucked at the smoke and held his breath as he had seen Peter do many times. His throat burned and he wanted to cough but held back until he could no longer do so, erupting into a long dry series of choking, gasping coughs that doubled him over. "Christ," he said when it was over.

"You need practice."

"I need a beer." He handed the pipe back to Peter and then finished his beer and reached into the cardboard box for another. "You want?" he said.

"Not for me," Peter said. "When I drink and smoke at same time I end up at Starbucks making myself into fool."

"Yeah, we don't want that to happen again."

"No," Peter said. "I am being fool."

"Past history."

"Yes, but still true."

They did not speak for a time and Keith felt himself drifting, the alcohol and the single lungful of marijuana mixing with his daily painkillers, a sensation that had begun to feel familiar to him and one he relished during these nights on the sofa. He could feel gravity loosening its hold, the sofa dissolving into a weightless object beneath him so that his body seemed to pull away from its overstuffed cushions, a tiny gap, two small for measure, opening between his body and the sofa. As if he was escaping gravity by degrees. As if he had begun, just barely, to rise.

His head lolled against the back of the sofa, eyes staring into space, tracing fake constellations absently. A fish. A box, slightly askew and desperately empty. A series of triangles, the angles of which resolved into numbers. He superimposed Quinn's face amidst the stars and tried to resolve it into a constellation but the best he could do was a lopsided and dented oval. And yet he could still see her face in his mind. There was no conception of heaven that he could place her into. Lost, then.

Earlier that night he had told Peter about the mini storage, about how his failure to pay the bill had resulted in an auctioning off of its contents. He had managed to slough off the few consumer items he had retained: the television that he had dropped down the stairs, the sofa, and then, through simple inaction, everything else he owned all at once. It occurred to him during some point of the evening that he should have already made a series of frantic phone calls to the mini storage company. Perhaps he could coerce someone there into giving him the auction information. He had been told that the contents had been removed immediately and that they would be parceled out for resale, but perhaps the man on the phone had been wrong. If it was true, he knew that Quinn's schoolwork would simply be tossed into a dumpster somewhere. Very likely it already had been. How he wanted to crawl through the city landfill on his hands and knees to find each sheet of paper but he knew such a search would be futile. He had allowed the whole of her to slip through his fingers. Everything she had been or would ever be. What a fool he was.

"Hello?"

They both started simultaneously at the voice, half-sitting and then twisting around to look back toward the cul-de-sac. A woman was standing in the halo of the streetlight. She held something in her hands—a plate of some kind—and as they watched she stepped forward toward them and into the dirt of the vacant lot. Keith sat there, unmoving, too bewildered to do anything else. He thought for a moment that it could be Jennifer and wondered briefly what she could want but it was not Jennifer. He did not recognize her in the silhouetted light and sat confused and disoriented, his body and mind continuing to drift.

"Luda," Peter said. He stood and said something in Ukrainian and set his pipe on the sofa carefully.

"Oh," Keith said. He looked at Peter and then turned and looked over his shoulder again, over the back of the sofa and into the lit space beyond. Luda's shadow a strip of darkness bearing out toward the sofa and the twin slumbering beasts that were the tractors. He could not make out her face at all.

"Very hard to see," she said.

Peter stood and stepped around the sofa and took his wife's arm and Keith could hear a few muffled words he could not understand. They stopped for a long moment there beyond him and Keith wondered if he should say something and then did say, "Hi," loud enough for both of them to hear and Luda's voice came back, "Hello," and then he could hear Peter whispering to her again and could not make out the words be they Ukrainian or English or some other language entirely.

He turned back to the stars, returning his head to the sofa. Whatever Peter and his wife were discussing was no business of his and he would not have understood their words even if it had played out right in front of him, although he gathered from Peter's tone that he was irritated by his wife's arrival.

After a moment it was quiet again and then he could hear their soft footsteps in the dirt behind him. "My wife Luda is here," Peter said.

"Luda," Keith said. He smiled, his hand outstretched and she took it, a soft, insubstantial thing in his palm.

"Hello," she said. "I brought something to eat."

"Really?" Keith said.

Peter was holding a plate in his hand. "Please," he said. He held the plate out and Keith could make out triangular sandwiches lining it and he took one and bit into it and realized that he actually was hungry. Had he eaten? He could not even remember. "Thank you," he said, his mouth chewing. Peter pulled the plate away and Keith said, "Wait a minute," and Peter brought it back and Keith took another and set it on his knee. "It's good," he said.

"I am glad you are enjoying this," Luda said. "I apologize for coming here. I did not mean for intrusion."

"Oh, it's fine," Keith said. "Come and sit."

"I have to get back to children. They are asleep but who knows. They maybe wake up and I am not there."

"Yes," Peter said. "You should go back home."

"I'm sure they'll be fine for a minute or two," Keith said. "Come and sit. Have a beer."

Luda looked at him. "I should go."

"It's OK to stay," Keith said. He hardly knew what he was saying now and had he looked at Peter he might have seen a look of irritation on his face but he did not or could not and Luda stood in silence. "Have a beer," Keith said. "The sofa will be gone any day and there will be a house here and that'll be the end of it."

Luda looked at her husband and he smiled, perhaps resigned to the situation, and motioned to the sofa. She nodded and said, "OK, but not so long," and sat next to him. Peter stood by the telescope, watching them, still holding the sandwich plate in his hands like some errant waiter.

Keith reached down and pulled a beer out of the cardboard box and handed it to her and she took it and unscrewed the cap in one quick motion and, to Keith's surprise, flung it toward one of the tractors and actually hit it, the bottle cap ringing out against the metal machine like a silver coin and then zinging off into the darkness.

"Well done," Keith said, smiling.

"I am sorry for tractors," she said.

"She means she is sorry for me because of these tractors," Peter said.

"Yes, that is right," Luda said. "I am sorry for Peter that tractors come. And you also too."

"Well, thanks. Not much we can do."

"Yes, but bad news for you," she said.

"We're not very happy about it," Keith said.

"My Peter is very sad," Luda said.

"Luda," Peter said.

"You are very sad," she said, looking at him now.

Peter did not move from his station by the telescope, still holding the sandwich plate in his hands. "Our friend maybe does not want to hear this talk," he said.

Keith waved his free hand in the air. "It's fine," he said. "I'm pissed off about it too."

"Maybe you find some other place to set up telescope?" Luda said.

"Probably," Keith said.

"Not the same," Peter said.

"Not same but maybe even better," Luda said.

"You keep saying that to me but you don't know," Peter said.

"Maybe bigger field with no lights anywhere," Luda said. "Like Golosiiv."

"You know nothing about this," Peter said. He said something in Ukrainian under his breath and at the sound of it Luda sucked in her breath and muttered something in return.

It was quiet now, husband and wife there in the darkness, Keith looking back and forth between them as if trying to discover something otherwise unspoken, his mind already drifting from what had been said in whatever language it had been said, drifting from their silence. Had he been sober he likely would have excused himself from the field and would have returned to the quiet emptiness of his house. But he was not sober so instead he cleared his throat and said, "Give me another one of those little sandwiches."

Peter handed him the plate and then reached over next to Luda and retrieved his pipe and the little black bag and returned to his position by the telescope and lit it and smoked. Luda said nothing, watching him.

"These are good sandwiches," Keith said.

"Thank you," Luda said. She continued to stare at her husband.

"How are the kids?" he said.

"Good. Sleeping."

"Oh, that's right."

Peter's voice came abruptly: "You think you know what this is but you know nothing."

Keith looked up at him, still chewing. "What?" he said.

"I am trying to help you," Luda said.

"Yes, you try to help me but you do not know how to help me. Then you say 'like Golosiiv,' but you do not know what you say when you say this. There is no like Golosiiv. There is only Golosiiv and nothing else."

"Peter," Keith said.

"You hear her? Like Golosiiv? You know there is no Golosiiv here. Only this empty place. So we find another empty lot but this one is mine to come to. Fucking shit."

Keith could not understand Luda's subsequent response nor Peter's and in his inebriated state it took him several minutes to realize that the conversation had shifted to Ukrainian, their voices rising in intensity and volume and speed, and when he realized this he lifted his

head from the sofa and coughed. "Uh, hey," he said, the Earth drifting under him, "I can't understand Ukrainian."

They both fell silent instantly. There were cricket sounds but they
were distant. Peter was a dark shape by the telescope.

"We are being rude for your friend," Luda said. Peter answered in
Ukrainian and Luda shook her head. "I tell him come home to talk
but he will not do this," she said.

"I am not coming home," Peter said, in English now. His voice
was a sharp angle in the night air. "You go home to kids."

Luda stood abruptly and said something to him in Ukrainian and
Peter did not answer. "I try to help you but you do nothing," she said.
"Only complain."

"Because here is nothing."

"There is more here than Ukraine."

"No," he said. "That is not true." His voice cracked over these last
words and a long trembling hush descended upon the three of them,
Keith apparently forgotten on the sofa, his head resting in the crater
of padding.

"What do you want to do?" she said at last.

"I want to go home," Peter said. His voice shook. A faint glimmer
of tears streaked his face. "I only want to go home."

"Then we go home."

"I want to go home to Ukraine."

"Is that what you really want?" she said.

From far away, over the houses and roads came the constant shush of
cars from the interstate, shuffling over the endless courts and dead ends
that enmazed the landscape all around them. Keith quiet, the triangle
sandwich held in his frozen hand, not even breathing, the sofa rocking
slowly under him as if moving over a gentle sea.

"I do not know what I want," Peter said, his voice a hollowness
floating in that static.

"If you really want, then we go back," Luda said.

Peter did not answer.

"You are my husband," she said.

"You would do that?"

"Of course I would do that."

He said something in Ukrainian again.

"We do what is best for family."

"But you think America is best for this family."

"America *is* best for this family," she said. "But this family is you too."

Peter did not respond for so long that Keith had begun to wonder what had happened. Then he realized that Peter was crying, a quiet sound at first and then breaking in heavy waves through his frame and he covered his hands with his face in the darkness and Keith finally understood that he should not be there, that he should have left almost immediately and he shifted his weight to stand but then Luda rose from the sofa and went to her husband and embraced him. "Petruso," she said.

He whispered some tiny words in the darkness, words that might have been in any language and which Keith could not hear.

"Shhh," she said, her hand stroking his short-cropped hair, his arms coming around her body and holding her in that darkness.

Drunk, stoned, depressed, mildly confused, his mind sloshing from side to side, Keith Corcoran stumbled to his feet. He tried to lift the box of empty bottles but almost fell over in doing so and decided to leave them. "I'm going to go inside," he said, taking a step forward around the sofa and then letting the momentum continue to move him back toward the bright edge of the cul-de-sac.

Neither Peter nor Luda answered him, nor did they watch him half-stumble over the sidewalk and into the street and turn finally toward his house. In his drunkenness he grabbed the two white plastic trash bins as he passed, one in each hand, and entered the house through the empty garage, dropping the bins into the gap they had left at the end of the kitchen counter before stumbling up the stairs, leaning heavily on the rail all the while.

He undressed and lay back on the bed. Against his skin: the cool of the night air. The feeling of erasure that had come upon him earlier that evening had returned and the loneliness that fell upon his shirt-less chest was profound and biting.

Perhaps he might have wondered at the marriage of Petruso and Ludmila Kovalenko. Perhaps he might have wondered at the sense of hope and love and caring that he had witnessed. Perhaps it might have engendered within him a similar sense that all might be made right once again. But in the sheer descent of his drunken loneliness he had already forgotten about being outside at all. Instead, the bed spun slowly in the center of that empty house and he fell into that rhythm and faded at last into a dreamless oblivion that was not unlike the night he had just clambered out of: a darkness alone and so, so very silent.

Seventeen

HE WAS MILDLY hung over for much of the following day and, as every headache made him wonder if a migraine was approaching, he took two extra painkillers. The result was a drowsiness deep enough for him to sleep away most of the daylight hours. Over the days to follow he reentered the normalcy of his recent routine as best he could, returning to Starbucks each morning and reading the newspaper. He stopped by the warehouse-size bookstore midweek and, in the throes of what was an increasingly familiar sense of self-pity, found himself thumbing through the thick, heavy mathematics books there without much real interest or attention. He tried to imagine what kind of math Quinn might have been interested in had she continued with her studies, these thoughts like ghost images superimposed over the stark reality of thick paper and ink, all such ideas mere abstractions cast forward into a universe that seemed increasingly without meaning or purpose.

On his way out he glanced through the books on the sale table near the exit doors. There was a thick hardcover volume on astronomy amidst the various titles and he picked it up and paged through it. He had seen similar photographs before, Hubble telescope images of nebulae and star clusters and distant galaxies, but he had never really looked at them with any interest. Now, though, the pages brought to mind the stars he had seen in similar clarity from the end of the robotic arm, of the intensity of feeling that had struck him, that weird mixture of helplessness and awe and wonder and silence. The end of the numbers. Their immediate silence. Or no not their silence but something else. And then he knew that it had not been the numbers that had fallen silent in the moment; it had been himself, the sensation he had experienced at the end of the robotic arm he had designed and built had fallen into some kind of interval, a gap, and no matter what measurement applied—time or light or space or something else—there would be no concrete answer because the experience itself had no solution. There was no language to describe what he had felt. Not even the numbers.

He purchased the book and brought it with him to Starbucks and sat there sipping at his coffee, reading the first paragraph of text and then paging through the volume at random, looking at the photographs and reading an occasional caption as he did so. Hubble Deep Field a black rectangle populated by myriad efflorescent galaxies. Lupus with its scores of multicolored stars. The Tarantula Nebula a blur of blazing orange light. If he had seen these same objects through the lens of Peter's telescope he did not remember and he knew they certainly would not have appeared in such vivid detail. Perhaps they were invisible to all but the most sophisticated instruments. The Hubble. Golosiiv. Something else.

The phone rang when he was looking at an image labeled "Lagoon Nebula Detail," a luminescent turquoise field obscured by darkly glowing clouds. On the phone's tiny screen was a local number he did not recognize. "Keith Corcoran," he said.

"Captain Corcoran, it's Tom Chen at Dreyfuss."

"Tom," Keith said, surprised. "How are you?"

"I'm well. And you?"

"Good, good."

"Nice work on the last mission," Chen said.

"Oh," Keith said. "Thanks."

"I know you're busy so let me get right to the point. I got that e-mail about your friend from Ukraine."

"Oh, yeah." He sat up abruptly, knocking the table with his knee, coffee sloshing onto its surface.

"Well, listen, if you think this guy is for real I'd like to see his résumé if you can send it over."

"Really?"

"We might have something. It's not much but we have a kind of work overflow here and need someone to just kind of keep things moving. I called the NAS at Golosiiv and spoke with some people there just to find out who we were talking about and the people there think your friend walks on water."

"Is that right?"

"Yeah, he must really be something. Anyway, I don't know if this position will be too simple for him but it's a way to get him in here. But I need to see the résumé. Maybe you can give me his phone number and I can talk to him directly about it."

"I'll need to get the phone number off the résumé," Keith said, "but I will. I'll have him get in touch with you right away."

"That would be great. This position has been officially open for two weeks and it closes tomorrow. I would have contacted you earlier but things got backed up here. This isn't usually how we do things."

"I appreciate it."

"So I'd need the résumé and contact info today or tomorrow morning at the very latest. Actually today would be best because I'd likely have to do some kind of interview in the next day or so just to make sure we're on the official schedule. Anyway, I thought maybe I'd poke around about the guy a bit first before calling you. Just to make sure. I know you're busy."

"Yeah, well, that's good."

"I'm assuming you think he'd fit here."

"I think so. He's really dedicated to the kinds of things you're doing there. The astronomy side of it. That's where his head is."

"That's great. That's totally what we're looking for. And we're trying to avoid just getting someone right out of school. A couple of years on the job is better than the degree, at least for this. Cheaper too."

"Sure."

"Hey, listen, since I have you on the phone I wanted to say that I'm real sorry about your daughter."

"Thank you."

"Anyway, let us know if there's anything we can do. Of course, you know that."

"Sure," Keith said. "Will do."

They exchanged a few pleasantries and the conversation ended. Keith sat at the back of the coffeeshop smiling broadly. He finished his coffee and then returned the astronomy book to his bag and tossed the newspaper onto a nearby table. Audrey was at the counter and she waved to him as he passed. He was still smiling. "You look happy today," she said.

"I guess I am," he said, and he was.

When he passed Peter's house on his way home he stopped and walked to the door and knocked but there was no answer. He had been looking forward to telling Peter the news but now that he was unable to do so it occurred to him that he might just as well get Chen the résumé on his own.

He returned home with this in mind, retrieving the pages from the kitchen island and reading through them with careful attention. Perhaps he had underestimated Petruso Kovalenko's talents; were he a personnel officer at a research center, Peter's résumé might have appeared impressive indeed and while there was too much detail in the résumé—it seemed to list every job Peter had ever held—the relevant material, especially the work he had done at Golosiiv, was interesting.

He continued to ruminate on this as he once again entered his car and drove to an office supply store and asked them to scan and e-mail the document directly to Tom Chen. As he waited, his phone began to buzz, but it was Jim Mullins and he did not feel the need to speak to him now. The voice mail he left was curt: "Keith, please call me at your earliest convenience." He left the phone number, as if Keith might not have it. It was a call he would need to respond to at some point but it could wait.

When he returned home he sat in his car and watched as the big gray sofa was carefully loaded onto the back of a pickup truck by two men in powder blue denim shirts, men clearly on lunch break from their tractor work. The men eyed him with some level of suspicion but as he did nothing to stop them they continued without pause until the sofa was gently secured. The truck was dilapidated, the windows rolled down as the only defense against the summer heat and a moment later it drove away, the sofa longer than the bed of the truck so that it suspended a full foot over the moving asphalt. In the next instant it had rounded the corner and disappeared from view. The other workmen sat in the shadow of one of the tractors, eating their lunches, their conversation impossible to hear.

He was surprised when the doorbell rang a few hours later, the sound so foreign that it took him several moments to determine what it was, but he was even more surprised when he opened the door and Luda threw her arms around him and put her head on his shoulder, weeping. "Thank you. Thank you," she said between her sobs.

His own arms embraced her as reflex and then relaxed to patting her back softly. "Whoa," he said. "What's going on?" He looked past her at Peter, who stood smiling in a button shirt and tie, a wrinkled sport coat stretched over his broad shoulders.

"You are sweet, sweet man," Luda said. She leaned back from him and took his face in her hands and kissed his cheeks with a loud smacking sound. Her eyes continued to swim with tears.

"OK, OK," Keith said. He was smiling, more from the absurdity of the situation than anything else. As if Luda's behavior were not enough, Peter came forward, still smiling, still unspeaking, and grabbed Keith's face and again planted one wet, smacking kiss on each cheek, stepping back then and saying, "You are good friend to do this for me."

"OK," Keith said. "What are we talking about?"

"The NASA called," Luda said. "The NASA called for Petruso."

"Your friend, Mr. Chen, asked me for interview. It will be Monday at three and he will ask me about my experiences at Golosiiv."

"I'm so glad to hear that," Keith said. He let out a loud and involuntary laugh.

"You come to our home now and you have dinner with us. The children they are at brother's house so no bother," Luda said.

Before Keith could so much as nod, Peter said, "Yes, all true. You come. I know you have no plans tonight better than this and sofa is gone so nowhere to sit. You come and we eat *holubtsi* and you will never before taste *holubtsi* as my Luda will make for you."

Keith looked at them, all three of them smiling now. "It sounds like something I shouldn't pass up," he said.

He slipped into his shoes and they led him across the cul-de-sac and down the sidewalk and as they walked he thought he could see Jennifer peeking through the upstairs window of her house but he could not be sure and did not know if he even cared. The night air was cool but heat still radiated from the concrete and asphalt and above them the sky glowed with stars bright enough to be visible beyond the halo of the streetlamps and the houses that lined the streets and courts and ways around them, each holding a green square of lawn that sloped slowly and carefully to the sidewalk as they passed, the whole of it universal and orderly and silent, the unfinished lots and empty foreclosed homes presenting dark vacancies amidst the lit houses of the living.

Peter unlocked the door and swung it open grandly. "Enter, my friend," he said.

Keith nodded and waved Luda in first and then followed her. The smell of cooking food was everywhere. "My god that smells great," he said.

"Ah yes, you see," Peter said. "I tell you this is best food you will have ever."

Luda giggled and moved past them and into the interior of the house.

"I believe it," Keith said. Perhaps this was the way it worked: one man gets a job and another loses one, as an Olympian passes a baton. Perhaps this was an equation that would be solved by Keith taking Peter's vacant job at Target.

"Astronaut Keith Corcoran," Peter said. "This is honor to have you in our home. Please make yourself comfortable. I want to know everything about this Mr. Chen. I must know all. About research center too. I look up on Internet but you have inside story I think and this is not on Internet."

"Sure," Keith said.

"Petruso," Luda called from deeper inside the house.

"Yes, come, come," Peter said. "I apologize for excitement. I ask you here to enjoy yourself, not to get your information."

"I'm glad to help," Keith said.

Peter walked further into the house and Keith followed. He had seen it once before, when he had stumbled into this room to sling Peter's unconscious body onto the sofa, but he had paid little attention to it then. It was similar to Keith's house but not quite the same, the floor plan differing in ways that were subtle but noticeable. There was no kitchen island here; in its place was a broad, dark wood table with long benches on either side. The walls were decorated here and there with needlepoint tapestries that looked very old, each encased in an ornate wooden frame. A stag with a series of Cyrillic letters underneath. Another a series of small houses with curling smoke before them with a few sentences below the houses as if the letters sprouted out of the earth.

"Very beautiful," he said.

"Ah yes, from my great-grandmother, that one," Peter said. "And that one there from great aunt on father's side. They come from Ukraine. My family is from village and make these things for selling. Later cities come and life changes."

Keith nodded and stood looking at the hanging pieces.

"Many artists in family. My uncle carves whole scenes out of horns of oxen. So beautiful and detailed. Those are in Ukraine still. Too hard bringing here."

Luda moved around the kitchen with a kind of bustling energy that at first glance might have seemed foreign to her being. Keith was struck by how very lovely she was, her dark eyes shining from her pale face, black hair pulled back into a small bun. Her bearing was of class and grace but the fluidity of her motion was incongruous with its setting: like watching a queen bake a cake or hoe a field.

Peter was excited and did most of the talking and Keith did his best to educate him on the research center, explaining its structure and the kind of work that was developed there, all the while reminding him that even entry-level jobs like the one Peter would be applying for were highly competitive. Peter continued as if such information was irrelevant but Luda interjected from the kitchen.

"Please," she said. "Is this real interview?"

"Real? Yes," Keith said.

"They are serious about him?"

"Yes, they're serious. It's a real interview."

Luda had paused in the midst of her work preparing dinner and appeared to Keith now as if the center of a painting, the counter sloping toward her on one side and on the other the sink with leafy sprigs of wet vegetables fringing its polished steel surfaces, and then in the midst of that warmth stood Luda herself, not an image of a woman but rather an image of a human being in a location of weight or meaning, as if the locus of some physical space that he had forgotten about entirely but which was somehow present here, in this house, and the sight of which rendered him unable to speak.

They sat at the table, Luda and Peter on one side, Keith alone on the other, and Luda dished out a series of pillowlike cabbage leaves from a casserole dish, each stuffed with ground pork and beef and dripping with some kind of thin red sauce and topped with sour cream. The smell that emanated from it was wonderful indeed and upon the first bite the flavor of it flooded through him all at once. He simply could not remember the last time he had tasted anything so good and he said as much and Luda blushed.

"This is Ukrainian food?" Keith asked.

"The best Ukrainian food," Peter said.

"The only food I know from that part of the world is that beet soup."

"Borscht," Luda said.

"Bah," Peter said. "Beets are like terrible dirt. I hate them. Old grandmas make for children to eat for cruelty."

"Shush, Petruso," Luda said. "He might like borscht maybe."

"No one likes borscht except grandmas with no teeth. He has teeth," Peter said.

"I haven't eaten like this for so long I can't even remember," Keith said.

"Thank you."

"She is best cook," Peter said.

"I agree," Keith said. "And I don't think I've ever had borscht."

"I will cook you borscht then next time," Luda said.

"Not even you can make borscht good," Peter said.

Luda smiled and then said to Keith, "I am happy you have made my husband your friend."

"Luda, do not—," Peter began but Luda placed her hand on his and he quieted immediately.

"Petruso does not want me to say maybe but it is true. You are someone to look up to, I think. For Petruso and this family."

Keith searched for something to say in response. "I don't know," he said at last.

"Yes," she said simply.

Again the pause as he thought. Then he said, simply: "Thank you."

"He knows this," Peter said.

"Maybe true," Luda said, "but good to say."

Was he someone to look up to? Even now? He might have believed this to be possible once but that was so long ago now. "I'm glad to be here," he said.

The food warmed him to the core. He had been given a glass of fruit juice of some kind—peach, he thought—and a glass of wine and Peter kept both glasses full so that Keith had no idea how much wine he had drunk, knowing that given his medication only a few glasses were enough to bring on drunkenness, a state acceptable when sitting outside with Peter but less so when sitting in Peter's home as a guest. And yet he did not feel like a guest but rather was warm and comfortable and full as if he had become a member of the Kovalenko family somehow. It had been so long since he had felt such a sense of belonging. Not for many years with Barb. With Quinn, though, even during those last months when they were often at odds there had been brief moments of contact between them, silences in which they had simply been together, father and daughter.

And then he could feel her memory turning inside him and he looked up from his dinner plate. Her face floated in the room somewhere, watching him with vacant eyes.

"You are OK?" Luda said and he looked up at her abruptly.

"Oh," he said, "yeah." He looked from her to Peter. Both of them were staring back at him.

"You look maybe not well," Peter said.

"No, no, I'm fine." He paused and then said, "Maybe too much wine."

They both continued to stare at him and he took a quick drink of water and then looked back at Luda and said, "You know," and then paused again, cleared his throat. His heart thumped wildly in his chest. "I know a bit about Peter's life but I don't know anything about yours."

"This is nothing to talk about," Luda said.

"Please," Keith said. Just that. Quinn hovering against his chest. Then: "You grew up in Ukraine?"

"Yes," Luda said. Her eyes were downcast, not as if ashamed but as if embarrassed by Keith's attention.

"Not like me, though," Peter said. "In Pechersk. Very nice in Pechersk."

"Yes, it is nice there," Luda said.

"Very nice," Peter said.

"You were wealthy?" Keith said.

"It is long time ago," Luda said.

"Not so long," Peter said.

"My grandfather and father worked in Russian government. Many government workers lived in Pechersk. By river. It is very nice there."

The feeling of Quinn was fading now, the fear and terror of loss drifting out and away from him as Luda spoke, as if the story, someone else's story, was enough to press that secret gravity away from him.

"When Ukraine is independent we must leave. My father was good man and people like him and so we stay in Pechersk for years but then he has the cancer and is buried. Then not very good anymore."

"They kicked them out to street," Peter said with obvious disgust.

"Not so bad as that." She looked up at Keith, their eyes locking together.

"Bah." Peter waved his hands in the air.

"Where did you go?" Keith said.

"To university," Luda said. "For job, not for student."

"Is that where you met Peter?"

"Yes, that is where I met Peter." She did not break the eye contact, instead continuing to stare at Keith, her complete attention focused on him. "He is very different from those people I knew before."

"I was poor," Peter said.

And now Luda did look at her husband and when she spoke her tone was quiet and lilting, like a beautiful, sad bird: "Yes, but not like poor. Not . . . how do you say . . . not stupid."

Peter did not say anything, instead shaking his head, his eyes half closed in thought.

"He is very smart man," Luda said.

Keith nodded. "I know."

"Bah," Peter said again. "This talk is embarrassing to me. We talk more about job so I know what to do tomorrow for interview."

Keith looked over at him, and at Luda.

"We were married quickly," she said as he met her eyes once again. "Quickly?"

"Yes," she said. "Quickly."

"Ah," Peter said. "You embarrass me now even more." A hush fell and Keith sat and wondered what she meant and then Peter said, "You do not understand. She was to have baby Marko."

"Oh," Keith said. Nothing more. He glanced at Luda and her eyes were cast to the table again.

"It was very fast wedding," she said. "My mother was very embarrassing. There was no money left then."

"Yes, I know I dragged you down with me," Peter said.

"Petruso!" she said abruptly. Her voice was sharp and Peter actually cringed when she said his name. She cast out a quick sentence in Ukrainian with obvious anger and Peter was immediately silent.

The table awkward and quiet. Then Peter lifted his wineglass ostentatiously and said, "I apologize to my wife and to my guest, Astronaut Keith Corcoran. She is correct. I should not speak these things." He nodded and continued to hold his glass and Keith lifted his as well. "To our American friend, who is great man and famous astronaut."

"To new friends," Keith said.

Luda had lifted her own wineglass and she smiled at Keith's words, her irritation apparently over.

They continued eating. Peter asked questions about Dreyfuss and about Tom Chen and Keith answered as best he could, offering detail when it was possible to do so. Luda periodically cautioned her husband on his aggressive questioning but Keith did not mind, perhaps an effect of the wine or simply of the good spirits the dinner had put him in.

"This Mr. Tom Chen is good man, maybe?" Peter said.

"I don't know him well, but I think so."

"It will be fair," Luda said. It might have been a question.

"Yes. Don't forget, though, that it's still very competitive. I can't say that enough."

Peter waved his hands in the air, a gesture that had become familiar. "Yes, yes," he said.

"OK, but I'm just telling you, even with the interview you still might not get the job."

"I know," Peter said. "Difficult to get job."

There was a long silence. Luda began clearing the plates and then Peter rose and spoke in Ukrainian and Luda sat again and Peter took over the task. A moment later Keith moved to help and Peter told him to sit and continued to clear the table.

"Maybe you tell us story about being famous astronaut?" Luda said at last.

"I'm not too good at that."

"I would like to hear."

Keith thought for a moment. "I don't know what to say," he said. "There's a lot."

"Every day you must be pinching yourself," Luda said.

"What?"

"She means you are excited," Peter said. He had returned to the table with a teapot and cups and filled each of them as Luda continued to speak.

"No, not excited," she said, paused, and then said something to Peter that Keith could not understand and Peter answered her, nodding. Then she said, "Knowing you are there in space. Like you are finally there."

"Yeah, there was that. Especially in the beginning."

"You must have been feeling great then."

"Yes. I can't even describe it. Just . . . amazing."

"Like in a dream maybe."

"Yes, like in a dream. Better than a dream."

"You were waiting for that day."

"Yes."

"How much waiting?"

"How much? My whole life." He did not think before answering, his response automatic, and he almost immediately felt awkward about his words, even though he knew it to be true.

"Waiting to be astronaut a long time, then."

"As long as I can remember."

"For adventure maybe?"

"Not really," he said. "That might have been part of it but really it was . . . it's hard to explain. I wanted to do something real and useful. But also . . . I don't know . . . I wanted to see it, I guess."

"See what you made?"

"Yes, see it out there in space. And I wanted to be there to see it." He paused a moment and then added, "I guess that doesn't really make much sense."

"Yes, it makes sense," Luda said simply. "Very beautiful."

"So beautiful. Unbelievable."

"Like seeing God."

He did not know how to respond to this and so he merely smiled and nodded.

"Now we have dessert," Peter said. He was carrying something from the kitchen. A cheesecake of some kind.

"I don't know how much more good food I can take," Keith said.

Peter brought plates and forks and a knife and cut the cheesecake into slices and they ate and sipped at their tea for a time and when Luda's voice came from the opposite side of the table it was quiet: "Forgive," she said. "You must want to be in space again?"

"Oh, every day."

"Then you go back to astronaut soon?"

"It's complicated," Keith said.

"Complicated?"

"Yeah."

"How complicated?"

Then Peter: "This is not something our guest wants to speak of, I think."

"No, it's fine," Keith said. "Really. It's just that it's . . ." He paused and tried to find a better word but then said, again, "complicated." Luda did not respond and after a moment he said: "I got sick on the mission."

"Sick? How sick?"

"I started getting headaches. Really bad headaches."

"Now you are better?"

"Not really."

"What happens then for astronaut work?"

"I don't know. I don't think I can be an astronaut anymore."

"Because of headaches."

"Yes."

It was quiet then and he took a bite of the cheesecake. They all did.

He had never said such a thing, had hardly even thought it through, but it was the truth.

"More?" Peter said after a time.

"God, no," he said, smiling. "I'm going to explode."

"Maybe half piece only then."

"No, I can't. Thank you, but I can't."

"OK," Peter said.

After a moment Luda said, "I ask you about your daughter?"

Keith looked at her and nodded reluctantly.

"Petruso told me that you are not home when she goes to God?"

"I was still on the space station."

Peter said something to her in Ukrainian and she answered him. "I tell her you maybe do not want to talk about this," Peter said.

"It's fine," Keith said. "Really." But he did not know if it was.

"I apologize," Luda said.

"No, it's fine."

A moment of silence there in the dining room. Then Luda said, "If on space station then maybe you do not see funeral?"

"No, I didn't see it. But they made a film of it for me. On DVD. So I watched that when I was back in Houston."

"Because you are on space station for days?"

"Months."

"Months? How many these months?"

"Nearly three."

"After your daughter: three months?"

"Yes."

"In space?"

"Yes, in space."

It was quiet again and then she covered her face in her hands and Keith did not understand what she was doing at first but then her shoulders rocked and she began sobbing, the sound of it harsh and violent. "Oh," he said. "Oh, I'm sorry." He did not know what he was apologizing for, but he said it anyway.

"Shhh," Peter said. He stroked her back softly and whispered to her in Ukrainian.

After a few moments she quieted and raised a cloth napkin to her face and eyes and dried them. Keith sat uncomfortably, wondering if he should leave, if every meeting between the three of them would end with him wondering if he should leave.

"I am sorry," she said, her eyes smeared with black mascara like the eyes of a raccoon. "It is very sad to hear."

He stared at her in a kind of wonderment: her gaze dark, liquid, the outpouring of grief so sudden and unexpected that Keith found it incomprehensible. "It's OK," he said. "I'm fine. Really." He knew this was not true, not anymore, but what more could he say?

"No," she said. "No, no, no, no." Her voice fading out. A whisper.

The room descended into a soft, trembling quiet and held that way for so long that Keith again wondered if he should leave.

"It is very sad to hear this," Luda said at last, wiping at her running mascara with her napkin.

Keith nodded but did not answer.

"He is strong man," Peter said.

"No man is strong for this." Her eyes were trembling with tears and Keith could see that she struggled to regain her composure.

"I'm fine," he said

"Yes, yes, you are fine," Luda said. "Everyone is fine. You are strong man, like Peter says." She sounded bitter now, perhaps even angry, and Keith waited for whatever storm had descended upon the table to pass.

Peter said something to her in Ukrainian and Luda answered him with apparent irritation and after a moment Keith said, "So I think it's time for me to head home."

"No, you stay please," Luda said. Peter started to speak but she put a hand on his arm and he fell silent. "I am sorry for this making you uncomfortable."

"It's OK," Keith said, "but it's late."

Peter said something in Ukrainian again and this time Luda did not answer him. She continued to stare at Keith, fixing him with her dark eyes as if to hold him there. He knew that she did not believe him when he claimed that he was managing, that he was fine, but there was no other answer he was capable of giving for even though he knew that he was crumbling, there still remained no other answer he could fathom.

Eighteen

"Well, it's substantial."

Keith stood with his hands on his hips. "How substantial?"

"We won't quite know that until we really get in there but I can see where the little buggers have chewed up some of the support here. Usually when we see this kind of thing the damage goes down into the foundation supports. That's where it can really get pricey."

"Christ."

"Yes, indeed," the contractor said. "Sometimes it doesn't happen that way. I mean I've seen it where we pull off the drywall expecting to find a hell-on-earth scenario and it's just a little track like the termites got bored and went away to eat someone else's house. So we bang out a few boards and knock it back together and get the inspectors back out to make sure it's done right and presto we're done and out."

"How much work do you have to do just to figure out how much work you have to do?"

351

"That's a good question," the contractor said. "We'll need to pull all the drywall off this wall for sure to start with. Then we can try to see if there's anything else we need to follow. We'll probably need to pull some off the outside too and maybe on the inside of this wall where it comes up against the house. What's behind this wall?"

"The kitchen."

"Yeah, that's a problem. There's cabinetry and appliances so you might not even know they're munching away in there. You ever find sawdust in your cabinets? Like in a plate or a pot or pan or anything?"

"Not yet."

"Well, that might be a good sign. Or it might not. Termites are crafty and they're dumb at the same time. They don't know what the hell they're doing except eating. Sometimes they come right through the wall like they done here. Sometimes you don't never see them until you're leaning against something and it gives way and you fall right through it. Hell, I've even seen a whole big colony of them fall through the ceiling in a huge ball of sawdust and termite shit. Fell through right onto the dining room table of a house. All those little pincers every-where. Scared the hell out of the people who lived there. Little kids probably still have nightmares about it."

"I'm sure they do."

They had been in the blazing heat of the garage for the better part of an hour while the contractor and his assistant cut chunks of dry-wall and insulation and probed the interior structure with flash-lights. He had asked Keith to kneel on the concrete floor and peer into the dark recesses of his own empty house and Keith had done so as the contractor pointed out the channels in the framing where the termites had burrowed through the wood. At one point the con-tractor said, "Ah, shit. Shit. Well, shit, shit," and then shone his flash-light farther into the wall space. "See 'em?" he said, and Keith looked. "Mouse turds," the contractor said. "You've got yourself a regular pest infestation."

"Fantastic," Keith said

"Maybe for the pest control people, but probably not so much for you," the contractor said.

Through the open garage door, Keith watched Jennifer as she moved across his field of vision. She was dressed once again in her gym clothes and Keith wondered at the fact that he had experienced that body at all, the memory of it like some weird and distant dream he could hardly recall. She glanced in his direction but made no acknowledgment of him whatsoever and a moment later disappeared inside her house.

The contractor and his assistant moved through the house methodically. Keith did not understand how they managed to know where to look but when the contractor stopped near an interior wall and told him it was possible or even probable that the termites would have chewed the framing beyond, Keith insisted that they cut a hole to look. His assistant brought a saw and plugged it in and a moment later there was a two-foot aperture in the wall.

The contractor whistled through his teeth. "You have got yourself an infestation," he said. "Look here."

Keith did so and again saw the thin drilled lines that indicated termites. "Shit," he said.

"Yep. That's a good word to use now."

At Keith's insistence, the contractor cut three more holes in the walls of the downstairs and two of the three revealed additional damage. There was a secret disaster occurring just beyond the plaster and drywall, a disaster that Keith had known nothing about, had not even suspected, the engineering of the house itself weakened, the equations shifting in value and importance until he was left with a calculus of weakness and financial ruin that was so painful that it actually made him laugh.

"Doesn't seem so funny to me," the contractor said.

"Oh, it's not," Keith said, still chuckling. "It's definitely not funny."

"Listen, I'm going to let the pest inspectors cover the rest of it. They're probably gonna want to tent the whole house. Pump the whole thing full of poison. Kill every damn thing in here. Probably ought to have that done first and then we'll talk about what to do about the termites. Otherwise, I'm just cutting a bunch of holes in your house for no good reason."

"What about the mouse?"

"What about it?"

"The mouse probably did some damage too?"

"Hell, you've got bigger problems than that."

Indeed.

"This place isn't in escrow or anything, is it?"

"It is, actually," Keith said. "I mean it was before this. I don't know what the status is now."

"Damn, that Sally Erler is selling houses even in this economy? She's a spitfire. Anyway, if that's the case you're gonna want the pest company to get it tented up quick, like in the next week or two. Once that's done we can get working. Sally can crack the whip some but the stuff I'm gonna have to do to get it to pass code is still gonna take a while."

The contractor departed soon thereafter and Keith was left in a home cut with holes. The slash in the wall of the garage was ten feet long, as if some gargantuan termite had torn into that same space with wild, insatiable hunger, the contractor doing more visible damage than the termites ever had and so it would go. At least the contractor had moved on to chew on some other house. He wished he could say the same about the termites. Maybe they could be lured to Jennifer's house across the street. Some Pied Piper of termites. But he thought it unlikely.

So the house was secretly falling apart all around him. How he longed to be in orbit once more, to feel that sense of weightlessness, as if the dense matter of his body had become a gas, a vapor, the ether itself. But there was no return. And as if to underscore this simple fact, he looked up to find Jennifer walking across the street toward him. She was not in her workout clothes this time, instead in jeans and a tight white T-shirt, her hair pulled into a rough ponytail. He wondered if he should retreat into the house but then continued to stand there, framed by the open door of the empty garage. "Hey," he said.

"Hi."

He stood there in silence, looking at her. "What?" he said at last.

"I just wanted to know what you thought."

"Of?"

"Our construction project." She nodded in the direction of the vacant lot, of the tractors, the freshly cleared earth there.

He looked at the lot and then back at her again. "What I think?" he said.

"Walt and I decided to forge ahead," she said, as if not hearing him. "It's just been sitting there and we're getting a great deal on the contractor."

"You're telling me you own that lot?"

"We bought that lot with this one. And one other on Creekside but that one got built and rented out."

"OK."

She smiled. Her teeth a perfect white arc. "Anyway, sorry you won't be able to sit out there and do whatever it is you do with your friend. Don't ask; don't tell. That's my policy. Anyway, it's an investment and the time is now." Her eyes flicked from his face to the construction site and back again. Bright and wide as if crazed. No, not crazed. Not that. Triumphant. "Just wanted to let you know," she said.

"That you're building a house?"

"Yep."

"OK. You're building a house." He looked down the cul-de-sac to the field. The earth flat and dead and empty apart from the two tractors.

"This could have worked out differently, you know," she said.

"How so?"

"You know."

He looked at her again. "I don't know what you're saying."

355

"Really? You really can't figure this out?"

It was quiet. Then he said: "You're doing this as some kind of punishment?"

"Oh, come on, neighbor. You're not *that* important."

"The house is sold, Jennifer. I'm moving anyway."

"Good for you."

He threw up his hands. "Well, OK," he said. "Good for me. Good for you. Good for everyone."

She stared at him in silence, her eyes slowly brimming with tears. "Asshole," she said at last. She swiveled around and began to walk back across the street quickly. Halfway across she turned back toward him and shouted, "You're such an asshole," and then swiveled back again and continued until she reached the door of her house, wrenching the door handle, and then stepping back to pound that flat surface with her clenched fist. Even from across the street, he could hear her words clearly: "Nicole, you unlock this goddamned door right now, young lady. Unlock the door this instant or you will be grounded! Do you hear me? Grounded!" She continued to bang on the door, a dull thunking sound that reverberated and echoed through the subdivision, each report met and repeated by a second and third so that the sound of it seemed a poorly executed drum roll, Keith watching her all the while from the frame of the empty garage. Incredulous. Dumbfounded.

Work on the vacant lot continued all the next day and the day after, the earthmovers replaced with backhoes to dig out the foundation area. Gravel trucks arrived to dump their loads and workmen began putting together the forms for the foundation. The basic footprint of the house was already roughed out with stacks of boards ready to be propped and staked into the various shapes necessary for the pouring of concrete. After that, the solidity of the structure would begin to rise.

In the early evening he opened the garage door and stepped through it and looked out at that scene. The area where the sofa had once rested now carried the rudiments of a foundation and there was a layer of gravel extending across it. He supposed they could walk the telescope over the various impediments and could stand out there or could even bring some metal lawn chairs to sit upon but such an attempt would be a weak substitute. What once had been was already gone and it was likely best to accept that and move on, a lesson he knew to be one he was loath to learn but which kept arriving at his doorstep like a dead bird delivered by a pet cat. Here it was again. He found himself wondering if he could find information on the Internet on hot-wiring a tractor. Perhaps the termites had weakened the structure of his house enough that he could push the whole thing over. That would be something, indeed.

Sally Erler called him in the early afternoon, clearly relieved that he had agreed to the tenting of the house and telling him that the young couple who were buying the place remained interested, assuming the termite damage was dealt with. An hour later, Sally Erler herself arrived with some documents for him to sign, indicating that the sale would continue pending the repairs. The escrow closed in just over a month, which meant the contractor would have to work quickly to finish during that window. Keith knew he was agreeing to pour a substantial amount of money into the house and that it was money he would be essentially throwing away. He would have had to have split any profits with Barb, had there been any, but he had no doubt that the losses would be solely his to bear. Somehow he would have to pay.

Mullins called again soon after Sally Erler and again he let the call go to voice mail. He could not have explained why he did not want to take the call but knew he did not want to talk to Mullins or Eriksson or anyone from NASA, at least not until the house was tented and he knew what he was doing next. He imagined that they were dismantling his office, pulling out the furniture for the next astronaut to occupy, that they had already reclassified him into some other position that would require him to move to a different building entirely. Such were his nightmares. He wondered how far he had fallen and he did not want to know. Not yet. He would have to be out of the house starting tomorrow or the next day, depending on when they tented the house and filled it with poison. He knew he should call the home office but there was also a sense of irritation at the phone calls. They had ejected him from Houston; let them wait a few days for his return call. He had trained himself to think only of the future, had started that training on his own when he was in grade school and he thought he had actually reached the future he had been made for. And maybe he had, at least for that brief moment. The cold fact was that each time Mullins or Eriksson called he thought not of the future but of the past and there was nothing there but his failed marriage and Quinn's death.

He thought that he should just find some deep recess in the house somewhere—the attic or the crawl space under the stairs—and let them tent the house around him, an idea that left him with a sense of outrage that shivered through him like an electric knife, leaving him raging in silence at the kitchen table, the shadow of the idea remaining under his tongue like a sharp and terrible stone.

He stood and opened the sliding glass door and stepped out onto the concrete patio under the blazing late-afternoon sun and waited for the feeling of unease to pass. His heart beat heavy in his chest and indeed there was the faint whine of his migraine now, the first time he had heard that sound in several weeks, his eyes already clamping shut against the light of the sun as he scuttled back through the sliding glass door sideways like a crab.

At the sink he swallowed a pill and drank from one of the chipped mugs Barb had left behind, and after a time he leaned into the sink itself and splashed cold water against his face. His heart continued to thump in his chest but perhaps not as insistently as it had only a few minutes before. The whine more distant? He was not sure. He thought he should probably get out of the house for a few hours, if for no other reason than to stop staring at the same blank walls, but when he finally looked at the cover of the newspaper he immediately sat at the kitchen table and all thoughts of the house and the poison and the termites flooded out of him all at once.

There it was at last: the earthbound comet on the front page.

Shit.

He had watched its approach through the columns of newsprint, its great parabola of gravitational motion swinging it back and forth through the pages, sometimes disappearing altogether and then appearing in some back section, once even in the Sunday magazine that nestled amid the full-color advertisement inserts. And now here it was on the cover, with a photograph and a block headline at the top of its column reading: "Comet to Hit Earth?" It was a headline as if from a tabloid. He wondered where Peter was right now, if he yet knew that the comet had finally become real news. Surely he was well aware already.

He read the column and flipped to the next page where the story continued. A one-in-a-million chance of strike. A greater chance of winning a major metropolitan lottery jackpot. One scientist quoted as calling the whole thing a knee-jerk reaction to something astronomers see all the time: objects moving in various trajectories all over the solar system. Difficult to track them all. With the proper funding they could dedicate more time and effort to it, but the economy was terrible. A call for additional funding for tracking and various technologies. Peter had intimated that Keith might know more about the capabilities of NASA to ward off a comet strike but if there were missiles that could explode any object that came blasting through the outer planets on its trajectory toward Earth, he did not know about them. He could likely create the math for this kind of scenario but beyond that there was little he could do.

If the comet's impact had any sense of urgency beyond the talking of politicians and occasional scientists he also had no idea. He wondered if there was any talk of it at NASA, if the people he knew there were joking about it as they went about their daily work, the regular public being at some disconnect from the realm of scientists, physicists, mathematicians, and, yes, astronauts. The universe a mechanism with more moving parts than could ever be calculated but the chance of any given part colliding with any other given part infinitesimal. His greatest achievement had been the robotic arm. What good was that against the actual universe?

Nineteen

THE MORNING HAD returned to the firestorm of heat that he thought had ended a month previous, the air humid and stagnant and lying upon the cul-de-sac as if to press everything to a motionless stop. The whining sound of the previous day had ceased at some point during the night, apparently obliterated by slumber and painkillers. What remained was only exhaustion: his mouth a burning, cotton-filled hole and his body creaking in the late-morning sunlight.

He lifted the newspaper from the step and stood in the doorway, glancing at the headline and noting that there was no further mention of the comet, at least not on the front page. The lack of news was disappointing if only because the comet had become a momentary excitement, now apparently already over.

The two suitcases had been repacked with the same clothes he had taken on his mission and these sat at his side in the doorway. The remainder of his clothes had already been packed into two cardboard boxes and had been stowed in the trunk of the rental car. As for the rest of it: he did not know what he would do with the bed but he would likely leave the cheap table and chair behind or take them out to the curb for whoever might happen by. Perhaps they would travel to the location of the sofa and some family would eat their cereal at the table each morning. The thought gave him some sense of pleasure.

On the street before him, various workers from the pest company were busy removing equipment from the trucks and vans lined up along the cul-de-sac. He had been told that the tenting process would take three days, after which the contractor would return to give him a proper estimate for repairing the damage. For now, he would stop in at Starbucks with his newspaper and then would drive across the freeway to the long string of hotels. He would rent a room for three days; beyond that period stretched an infinite field of blank space. He could return to the house, of course, but it would be undergoing major reconstruction to repair the termite damage, and once that was complete the escrow would be over and the new owners would move in. It made more sense to simply remain in a hotel. Somewhere. Maybe it was time to fly out to Atlanta and look at his daughter's grave, but what purpose could that possibly serve? Her name engraved on a stone. An immaculate expanse of green lawn. What else? Silence everywhere on Earth.

He opened the trunk and dropped the black suitcase and its matching overnight bag into the vacancy beside the cardboard boxes of his clothes. There rested all the possessions he would retain. He might have needed a moving truck had he simply opened his mail and paid the storage unit bill but of course he had not done so. And there had been only one box in the storage he had any real desire to open or possess anyway and it was the only one he could never replace.

For the next hour he drifted through the house, each room just as empty as on the day he first returned from the mission, the only significant change being that blotchy single coat of eggshell, pale yellow leaking through, and the holes in the walls from the recent termite search. He wandered upstairs and stood for a moment in the doorway to Quinn's room and then entered that gray cube but he could not hear her voice or feel her hand or touch her face.

Nearly every time they spoke, Hoffmann had said he sounded angry and each time he had left their conversations perplexed. But he knew now that what he felt was indeed anger, or had been anger, and that there was a reason for it because what he had been ever orbiting in his thoughts had not been Quinn's death after all but rather his own utter and complete failure to be what she needed him to be, what he needed himself to be. Because the decisions he had made, again and again, had been wrong and now he could not go back and fix them. It was too late for that. It may have been too late from the moment he had decided to follow the absurd impossible equation of his life through to the absurd impossible place in which he had come to find himself: not as an astronaut or an engineer or a mathematician but as a man who had failed as a father, as a husband, perhaps even as a human being. Hoffmann had told him the goal was to move through his experiences. He did not know if this was what he meant, but he certainly did not feel angry now. Only disappointed, lonely, and sad.

He moved through the hall and down the stairs, shouldering the laptop bag and stepping outside at last. The foreman from the pest company stood by his company truck and Keith told him he was leaving and they shook hands.

"Maybe you won't even have to pay for this," the foreman said.

"How so?"

"Comet."

"Right," Keith said. "The comet."

"Maybe it'll just fall on the credit card company."

"Maybe."

His house was a flurry of activity now: the door wide open as workmen in blue jumpsuits carried their fans and equipment inside, the thick vinyl of the tent itself unrolled all around the perimeter. At the end of the cul-de-sac, construction workers in hard hats were starting their day of labor in the dirt. The cement truck had arrived and was backing into position to pour the foundation, the rest of the crew standing with their various implements at ready as if warriors preparing to fill in some mass grave, their faces masks of resignation.

He set the laptop bag in the trunk and when he turned back momentarily to look at the cul-de-sac he saw Jennifer in the upstairs window of her house across the street watching him, the blinds pulled open. She was framed in the bare window, the sunlight cresting across her face from the east so that she was half consumed in shadow. He expected her to turn away when he looked up but she did not do so and after a moment he raised his hand in a gesture that was somewhere between a wave and a salute. She did not move at first and then her hand rose and pressed against the glass and whether it was meant as a greeting or was simply an involuntary movement he did not know.

There was nothing holding him but for a long time he did not drive away from the empty house, remaining in the rental car and watching, through the greasy sunbaked film of the windshield, the scene before him. He had thought once that the landscape was some failed attempt at perfection, as if the manifestation of some Euclidian ideal, an equation that was both solvable and tangible with predictability built into it as a standard. Perhaps that was why Barb had chosen this place: because it promised to be eternally the same, never aging, always new, always clean, always perfect. But what they had come to was a landscape branching endlessly into a vinculum of zeros. The only visible differences between one point and the next being vacancy and absence: empty homes, empty lots. At some point even these would be filled in. Then every cul-de-sac the same. This house. Some other house. Every house a box containing a family dreaming their lives within a closed loop, always repeating. And yet Peter and Luda were here with their children, from halfway across the world. And Jennifer and Walt and Nicole, with their own lives and their own problems. Each cast into a landscape constructed of sameness and yet each dream unique unto itself.

And there stood his own. He had told himself—and kept telling himself—that the house had no meaning to him at all; he had barely lived there in the days before the mission and in fact had spent more time in its empty shell than he ever had when it had been occupied by his family. He knew he had exchanged more words during the past year with anonymous grade-school students on the station's shortwave radio than he had with his own daughter in this house. And yet he did not leave. It was as if the shape of the container held a resonance, the whole of the structure gently cradling the idea of what might have been despite the fact that he had not a single concrete memory of its contents except for the days of endless unpacking when they had first moved and that final conversation with Quinn. Even now what images he could form of her in the house were as spectral as the waking memories of his dreams and his ability to recall himself within those same walls, at least from the time before the mission, failed in equal measure. But despite this insubstantiality there remained a sense of attachment to the idea of the place, this box that should have been filled with memories but was filled instead with loss and guilt and emptiness.

He did not clearly know where he had been when she had careened into the oak tree in his car. In orbit, somewhere, above Earth. He had occupied some stretch of fluid miles, but what did such a location mean? He had been on the surface during most of her cheerleading activities and had failed to attend a single event. Perhaps this was the true calculus, here as everywhere: the calculus of location and the understanding that the numbers themselves were possessed of a fundamental gravity comprised not of fluid motion but of fixedness. He had simply not been here, even when he was. He had formed an equation that had shaped his life and that equation had offered a solution that seemed, at the time, as clear and precise as any he had ever worked to solve. And yet it had not been the right solution. It had been no solution at all. And when he had come home at last it had been to emptiness. His family had lived here, here in this house, and it was the final location where this statement would ever be true. And where had he been?

He was on the verge of tears when he put the car into drive at last and pulled into a wide U-turn and moved out to where the court connected to Riverside. He might have looked in the rearview mirror at the receding shape of the termite-ridden structure but he could not bear to do so, instead continuing straight ahead, staring at the road, then at Peter's house, where Luda and the two children were outside. He actually managed to smile and wave to her as the car rolled by and when Luda saw him she motioned frantically for him to stop and he pulled over to the left side of the street and his window hummed down. "Wait," she said. Her eyes were wide and her mouth curled up into a smile. "I will get Peter."

She said something to the two children in Ukrainian and they both stood there staring at Keith as she disappeared inside the house. He sat there behind the wheel, breathing in the air conditioner's cold exhalant. There was an immediate urge to swivel around and look once more at his own house but he did not do so. "Hello, kids," he said.

They both giggled, their hands up at their mouths as if to hide some secret joy.

The doors to Peter's car were all wide open and there was the top of a bag visible from the open trunk. A few pastel-colored towels. "You guys going somewhere?" he said.

Again, the children giggled. One of them yelled something back to him in Ukrainian that sounded like "please," but with such a thick accent that Keith was not sure if the boy was asking for something or answering his question.

A moment later, Peter came bursting from the inside of the house. "Astronaut Keith Corcoran, my friend," he bellowed.

"Peter." Again he mustered a smile.

"You are good friend to me, Astronaut Keith Corcoran." Peter reached through the open window and clapped him on the shoulder.

"Well, thanks."

"You got me interview with NASA."

"Oh yeah. I should have asked you how that went." He glanced over his shoulder at the house now, did so without thinking. It looked just as it always had. He wondered how long it would take before the tent obliterated it from view, and then how strange it would look to have that monstrous tent in the cul-de-sac. As if some evil circus had come to town.

"You could have asked but I did not know how well this goes until today. Just this morning. Today they call me and say they want second interview to meet director of research center. This is good news, I think."

Keith sat blinking, cool air roaring against his face. He reached out and turned the knob down and looked back at Peter. "Are you serious?" he said.

"I am so very serious. I am so very serious."

"My god, that's great news," he said and despite the darkness of his mood he found himself smiling broadly.

"This is true. Great, great news."

"Peter, they only do that when they're going to offer you the job."

"Yes, this is same Mr. Tom Chen tells me on telephone. He calls this formality."

Peter was leaning in the window of the car and after a moment Keith said, "Let me get out," and Peter stepped back and Keith opened the door and stood and extended his hand and Peter's smile was great and luminous and there were tears in his eyes. They shook hands and Peter drew Keith into a one-armed embrace and into Keith's ear he whispered, "Thank you. Thank you, my friend."

"Damn good news." He clapped Peter on the back and Peter followed suit and then the embrace ended and they both stood on the sidewalk between the two cars, the children standing off to one side watching them. The sound of high, rhythmic beeping came from the cul-de-sac. A truck backing into position.

"That's fantastic," Keith said.

"Yes, to hell with Target and its boxes."

"To hell with Target," Keith said. "When's the second interview?"

"Tomorrow."

"I gather the first interview went really well."

"They ask me technical questions. Many technical questions. But I know this even though I have not been working big telescope for some years. The same questions I would answer in Golosiiv. Nice to be asked about this again."

"Haven't lost your mind working for Target?"

"No, I still have my mind," Peter said, laughing.

"That must be a relief."

"Yes." There was a pause. "Today we go to beach to celebrate."

"Day off?"

"Yes. Never work on Thursday."

"How far away is that?"

"You have not been to beach?"

Keith shook his head.

"Not so far," Peter said. "Two hours maybe. A long day and we are slow to leave. So much stuff Luda takes with us. Like we go to live there forever."

"Yeah, it can be like that."

"You see our field?" Peter motioned toward the cul-de-sac. "Already looks totally different."

"I keep thinking we should hot-wire one of the tractors and push my house down."

"My nephew can probably do this. The one I tell you about."

"Maybe I'll have you call him."

"Maybe not."

"You're probably right." Keith said. "It's in bad shape though. They're putting a tent around it to fumigate for the next three days. Termite infestation."

"Shit," Peter said. "You will be out of house for three days then. Where to go?"

"Hotel. And maybe for longer than that. Once the fumigation is done they'll do the repairs."

"What then?"

"I don't know."

"Back to NASA maybe?"

"Maybe."

"Complicated still?"

"Yeah."

Peter stood looking at him. Then he glanced at the children. They had grown tired of watching the adults talk and were now chasing each other around Peter's car, bounding through the two open doors and across the backseat. Peter said nothing to stop them and after a brief moment he said, "Just one moment, please," as if he was talking on the phone and had put Keith on hold. Then he walked toward the house and disappeared inside.

Keith stood there and watched the children in their game, wondering if he should sit in the car where it was cool. Then Peter reappeared from inside, Luda just behind him. "Astronaut Keith Corcoran," Peter said as he approached, "we would like you to come with us to beach today."

Keith moved his eyes from Peter to Luda and back again. Both of them smiled at him. The children stopped their running and stood just behind their parents now, staring. "Oh," he said. "I don't know."

"We insist," Peter said. "Unless you are busy with some astronaut work. Then we do not insist. But this would be an honor for us including you in our family. You have three days to be out of house. You spend first day with our family, if this is good for you."

Luda said nothing but continued to smile and nod. She looked beautiful there, shining with a kind of radiance that he had not seen in her before. All the sadness that had been in her eyes when he had first seen her was gone, replaced now by a deep and expansive joy. It felt to Keith as if that first meeting, when he had appeared at her door with Peter passed out drunk in his car, had been years ago. How long had it been? Two months?

"Is there room for me?" Keith said.

"You sit up front with Peter and I will sit in back with children," Luda said.

"There you are," Peter said. "There is room."

Keith stood on the sidewalk by the rental car in silence. Again he felt as if he should look at his own house again, one final time, another final time, but instead he said, simply: "OK."

Peter clapped his hands. "Excellent! You will do this," he said. "I am very pleased."

Luda moved forward and touched Keith's arm and then leaned over and said nothing but kissed him on the cheek and Keith felt heat rise to his face and he wondered if he was blushing.

Peter laughed. "She is very happy for you."

"Yes," Luda said. Then again: "Very much, yes."

They were only able to exchange a few furtive words about the earthbound comet as they embarked, Peter asking him what he knew in a whisper, perhaps expecting some inside NASA information that, of course, Keith did not have. "This is one-in-a-million chance," Peter said to him, still whispering, "but still good to know."

"Sure," Keith said. "I was surprised it made the front page."

Peter put a finger to his lips and then pointed to the backseat. It was unclear if he meant to indicate the children or Luda or all of them. "Not much news, I think," Peter whispered. "Otherwise maybe not so important for front page."

"I hope so," Keith said.

"It is good to pray," Peter said.

"It is always good to pray," Luda said from the backseat.

Peter was quiet. Then he said, still in a whisper, "Maybe we talk about these things later."

"OK," Keith said.

"They put in gate," Luda said from the backseat.

He nearly asked her what she meant but then he saw them: a crew of construction workers at the entrance to the development, finally installing the promised gate that would separate the Estates from the rest of the earth. Sealing it off. That was what he imagined. As if an airlock was being closed.

The car pulled through the strip of giant parking lots and then the interstate scrolled out before them, uniformly gray and endless. As they drove his mind returned to the comet. He knew its orbit would likely be some huge ellipsis, eccentricity perhaps pushing toward the parabolic, this side of the vast curve hooking through the Hill sphere of the sun, the other flung into the far distance beyond the edge of the solar system, such an orbit turning again and again and again over millions of years, the radius of apoapsis and periapsis unwatched and unmonitored until this moment when the line of one orbit happened to intersect with the line of another. A one-in-a-million chance but still a chance, the mathematics of which could hardly be believed. Two heliocentric orbits, one of which spun, perhaps, on a temporal cycle counted in millions of years, and the two actually intersecting. Even now he could feel the numbers shifting about in the darkness inside of him, filling in along the imaginary lines, circles within circles, parabolas and ellipses hooking and looping as the numbers arrayed themselves dimly along their shadowed paths.

He wondered what the variables would look like. Would Eriksson know anything about it? Maybe he would call him once they reached the beach.

Peter related the interview with Tom Chen in painstaking detail, even going back over the individual sentences and filling in nuance and implication, so much so that a half hour of interview time was rendered into an hour-long description and despite the repetition and convolution of the story Keith found that he continued to be interested. The sound of Peter's voice made him feel calm and normal and the children in the backseat with their handheld games and occasional explosions of boredom and fatigue were welcome diversions from the long inward turn that had been most of Keith's time since returning from space, since Quinn's death, since returning to gravity. Five minutes into the drive the children had begun to ask when they would arrive but now were settled and quiet in the backseat and Luda would periodically bring out little toys from a bag at her feet to settle them during those moments when they became bored with whatever they had been doing.

"You're a good mother," Keith said at one point, half turning to look at her.

Luda smiled at him. "I am sorry if they are too loud," she said.

"They're not too loud."

She blushed and smiled, averting her eyes in embarrassment.

"You are right," Peter said. "She is very good mother. Best mother." He looked at his wife in the rearview mirror.

Keith told them about the termites and the construction that would need to happen and that he did not know where he was going next or what he was going to do. As if in response, his phone buzzed and he glanced at the screen. Jim Mullins again. He might have been interested in chatting with Eriksson about the rumored comet but he was not interested in being lectured to. He let the call ring through to voice mail and then returned the phone to his pocket.

"Tell us story about your being famous astronaut," Peter said when the conversation slowed.

"I don't know," Keith said hesitantly.

"This is what you say but good time for story."

"Didn't you get your fill of that yet?"

"Not so much," Peter said.

"Maybe he does not want to talk now," Luda said.

"No, it's not that," he said. He paused a moment and then said, "What kind of story exactly?" All around them, the gray wastes of neighborhoods and cul-de-sacs and stores and parking lots continued along the interstate.

"Something that everyone will enjoy," Peter said.

The kids stopped what they were doing and fell instantly silent. "Yes," the little boy, Marko, said, his voice high and heavily accented. "Yes, please."

"Hmm," Keith said. He thought for a long moment and although he knew they were asking him for something about space, the images that came to his mind were of Quinn's funeral. "Let me think about it for a bit," he said.

"OK, you think," Peter said.

After a time the children took up their game in the backseat again and this time Peter joined in and they picked out colors in the landscape and the others guessed which color he was thinking of and Keith was silent in the front seat as Peter drove.

The freeway had been hemmed by walls as if some ever-flowing concrete aqueduct but those walls fell away now, revealing endlessly sprawling neighborhoods and strip malls linked together by familiarly named giant storefronts in faux-Tuscan architecture with arches and olive branch motifs. Then gone again.

He could not imagine an ocean being at the nether end of this epic suburbia but the fact of it was apparently true: there was an edge to the continent where the landmass lapped up against the sea and the shallows broke into the deeper blue of the ocean and while he had known in some dim part of himself that the ocean was a drivable distance from the empty house, it had never occurred to him to actually go there, as if there was some shift in physical dimension or desire that needed to be satisfied in order for the act to be undertaken at all, not in terms of motion but in terms of the idea itself.

He had only been to the beach a half dozen times, all of these when he was doing his graduate work at Stanford and they would drive out Sand Hill Road and through Woodside to the cold Northern California ocean at Half Moon Bay and he and Barb would watch Quinn run back and forth across the surf and he would try to keep his daughter as dry as possible given the near-constant chill rolling in off the Pacific, an impossible goal set along that endless strip of gray sand.

Those were the short days when they were still clearly a family, the three of them, parents with a child, a toddler quickly growing out of those years and unsteadily careening up and down the surfline on sturdy bowlegs. If anything had ever been said between them, husband and wife, he could not recall, the memories mute and blissful and empty. All such memories now seemed spliced into the images of the funeral: the ocean lapping against the heels of the mourners, the tide spilling into the grave.

Now in the front seat of Peter's car with his wife and children in the backseat and Peter asking him to tell a story: What story was there to tell? Everything in his life had telescoped into guilt and bereavement and a kind of emptiness that he still did not entirely understand. What was there to understand in the end?

Everything you have ever known will one day rise like smoke. The dreams and desires you have had or will have. Even now. This was no different. Nor could it be.

"We want a story," Marko said from the backseat.

Keith could hear Luda's voice quieting her son and a moment later the entire car fell silent. He thought he should tell them about how his marriage had failed without his notice, about how the decisions he had made had been the wrong ones, about how his daughter had been killed while he was floating in an oxygen-filled chamber two hundred and seventeen miles above the surface of Earth. He thought he should tell them that the moment he had worked so hard to achieve had only taught him what he could not understand, that the universe was beyond anything he could ever articulate, and that the one person who might have understood that idea was already gone. He thought he should tell them that he had failed her, that he had failed himself, that he had failed his team and NASA and so had failed everyone and there was to be no answer, instead only the thin burning whine and agony of his migraines and the long and unanswerable questions that would extend on before him forever and would never find an end.

The children in the backseat silent and expectant and he could feel their eyes against the back of his head, waiting for him to begin even as his phone began to vibrate once more. He knew there was a story he could tell them—the same story he had told Nicole—but he knew it was not really the truth, at least not as he had experienced it.

The mission had been wrapped into everything to come after but this was only because that was how he had placed it in his memory. The trajectory was simple indeed. But it had not been that way when he was actually there in orbit, when he had had no thoughts of family or of the things of the earth. When even the numbers had fallen silent. And when he simply was—an existence, a being, a man—and there had been nothing else, the situation of gravity falling away as a kind of abstraction. And then he knew he had felt that same way when he had come through the airlock into the space station for the very first time, a feeling of panic that flooded through him and then was gone so quickly that he had forgotten it had even come, forgotten it until this moment. And it had not been fear. Instead it had been the realization that he was finally entering the destiny he had always imagined for himself and yet he already knew that none of it could be described in the language he had spent his life studying. He could have calculated everything there, every physical object he encountered, but what would that tell him? How would that explain the sensation of simply being weightless, with Earth spinning below him as he crested forever into that endless fractal universe? There was no equation. There was simply no equation for such a moment even though all his life he had worked with the numbers in an environment just like this one: in a kind of weightlessness that was his own mind. He might have been able to tell the truth of this to Quinn but he did not know if she would have listened and who else could have understood it? Who else had ever understood him at all? My god. There was no equation for any of it. Not for the universe, not for his loss, not for the decisions he had made or for the feeling of her hand curling into his own.

And when he closed his eyes he could see her in the darkness, her face suspended amongst those tiny diamond stars he held ever within his heart, even with the freeway sounds all around him, could feel her next to him in the car somehow and she was waiting for him to speak. He opened his eyes. Before him the signs of the megastores moved past the windows in the flat white heat of the midsummer sun. "OK," he said. He cleared his throat. She waited. He could feel her waiting for him. "It seems like a long time ago," he said to her at last, "but once upon a time I went to space."

Twenty

WHAT MORE IS there to tell?

It took them four trips from the car to the beach to unload the various toys, coolers, food, drinks, towels, umbrellas, and chairs. When they were done Keith sat in a beach chair and pulled off his shoes and socks and emptied them of sand and then stuffed the socks into the shoes and set them next to the chair. The two children were already down at the edge of the surf screeching with excitement and Luda called their names repeatedly as Keith and Peter straightened the beach blanket between the chairs and shade umbrellas. Keith's phone was vibrating again but he did not answer it and did not look to see who was calling him or why and when it stopped he turned it off entirely.

The amount of gear they had amassed seemed enough for an extended family of ten or twelve, an overspilling collection of reds and blues and yellows and greens smearing over plastic and metal and cloth.

"Hungry or later?" Peter said to him.

"Later, I think," Keith said.

Peter handed him some black-and-white swim trunks and Keith took them. "I don't know that I'll go in," he said.

"In case you want to, now you can."

"OK."

Peter wrapped a towel around his waist and exchanged his pants for a similar pair of swimming trunks and then returned the towel to its position across his shoulders. "I am going in," he said.

Luda had appeared with the children. "Wait for sunscreen," she said. She hunted through a giant yellow bag and then retrieved a white bottle and squirted the thick viscous fluid into her palm and began the process of applying it to the exposed skin of the children.

The beach was long and crescent shaped and on either side of them the land pressed out into twin and distant points peppered with luxury hotels and the blocky shapes of giant stores. But the beach itself was situated in the center of the crescent and the murmur of the ocean's quiet rolling all but obliterated any other sound so that the location held the illusion of being isolated. Even the parking lot where they had left the car was separated from the beach itself by a strip of dunes where tufts of grass waved in the breeze. A few small families on either side of them, each with its own separate mountain of multicolored beach gear. In the distance, a single man threw a Frisbee to a black dog. The sand clean and tan and hot in the noonday sun.

"How'd you find this place?" Keith said.

"You look around for a place and this will find you," Peter said. Then: "Also, it is in Triple-A guidebook."

Keith smiled but said nothing in response. He was still seated in the beach chair, his feet bare now and pressed to the warmth of the sand. He leaned forward and rolled his pant legs up past his calves.

The children were festooned with a variety of inflatable safety devices, all bright orange, and then Luda moved to Peter and rubbed the sunscreen over his body, his heavy torso and the curve of his belly and then his legs and then returning to his face, rubbing his cheeks and forehead and ears and leaving enough on his nose that it had become a triangular white monument. The children jumped up and down impatiently at his side.

"I will take Marko and Nadia," Peter said. "You come when you want to."

"OK," Keith said.

He watched as Peter said something to the children in Ukrainian and the sound of their glee was an impossibly high-pitched scream and then the three of them turned and jogged down to the surf, Peter dodging as they chased him then letting them catch up and once again spinning away.

"You will burn," Luda said.

He looked over at her. She stood with the sunlight directly overhead as if illuminated by some great and magnificent spotlight. He reached his hand out toward her and expected her to hand him the sunscreen but she took his hand in her own and held his arm out toward her for a moment and then turned the sunscreen bottle over and dabbed it across his forearm.

"It is good thing you do for Peter," she said to him. She set the bottle on his chair and continued to hold his hand and rubbed the sunscreen into the exposed part of his arm.

"I'm glad I could help," he said.

She did not answer him, releasing his hand and retrieving the sunscreen bottle and moving to the other side of his chair. She reached for his hand and once again daubed the white fluid on his arm and rubbed it into his skin.

"He is selfish man," she said. Her hands strong and smooth and warm. She was looking only at her work and he said nothing to distract her. "It is true," she continued. "I know this about him even from start. Lean forward." She dropped his arm and he leaned forward in his chair and a moment later her hands were at the back of his neck, rubbing between his hair and the collar of his shirt, around his neck, across his chest. "But I love him anyway."

"I know you do."

"He thinks sometimes he is only one to make sacrifice but I leave everything too. He forgets there are others. This thing we do is for children, I think, so they grow up here and not in Ukraine where it is too much difficult to make life."

She passed the lotion bottle to him over his shoulder and he reached up and took it from her.

"You should do face and legs too," she said. "This I cannot do."

He nodded and squeezed the bottle into his hand and began to spread the fluid across his face.

She turned from him and peered out toward the ocean and after a moment she said, "Look at Petruso."

He looked up to where Peter and the two children ran back and forth in the surf, laughing.

"What do you see there?" she said.

"A very happy man."

"Yes, because he maybe gets better job."

"And because he's here with you and the kids."

"Not so much that," she said. "More for job."

"That can be an important thing."

She sat next to him in the folding chair and then reached back and opened the cooler. "Beer?" she said.

He nodded and she handed him one and then opened one for herself and they sat without speaking for a long moment, both drinking, lost in whatever thoughts they each had in the twinned separateness of their lives.

"I know it is important," she said at last. "He is a man. I know that work at Target is not for him. It is not what he is meant to do here. I know this."

"It's a shit job for anyone."

"Yes, I know it's shitty job."

He looked at her and smiled.

"Shitty job," she said again. She looked at him but she was not smiling. "But how does job only make him happy. Everything else is same. What if he does not get this job? What happens then?"

"I don't know. He keeps looking for another job."

"He does not even look for this job. You make this happen. If he is unhappy then why does he not keep looking for new job? Anyway, he was not so happy at Golosiiv. He says he was so happy at Golosiiv but he is not scientist so he is complaining always there. He remembers different than I remember."

Keith sat and watched the surf. Peter had jumped backwards into the water and the children were following him out in silence. He waved to them and Luda waved back. "Be careful!" she yelled. He waved again and turned his attention back to the children.

"I don't know what to say," Keith said.

"I know there's no answer to question."

There was a pause. The children were up to their waists in the water and Peter dove underneath for a moment and reappeared slightly farther out. The children set to splashing themselves in the surf, their tiny bodies bobbing up and down in rhythm to the waves.

"He's lucky to have you," he said.

"I know that," she said quickly.

He smiled and this time she smiled back at him and he actually laughed and she too broke into a kind of giggle. "I guess we know where you stand," he said.

She blushed. "Well," she said, shrugging, "what do I say?"

He chuckled again. Then: "He knows that."

"Does he?"

"Yes."

"I do not think he does."

He paused and then said, "I think he's figuring it out."

She sipped her beer and he did the same. After a moment she said, "I wonder what happens if he does not get job. He goes crazy and drunk and passes out somewhere because he loves another girl maybe."

Keith was silent.

"I know he has crush on Starbucks girl," she said. "I am not stupid wife."

Again, he said nothing.

"I let it pass. I love him," she said, "but he can be idiot sometimes."

"Shit," he said, "can't we all?"

"Not like men. I apologize for saying, but men are idiots."

He smiled. "Well, that's probably true."

"Make mountain out of molehill always."

"Yeah, there's some of that."

"Too much," she said.

"Yes."

"And your wife, she leaves you for someone else?"

He did not answer.

"I apologize," Luda said. "I should not ask these personal questions."

"No, it's not that," he said. "I don't know. I don't know if it was specifically for someone else or just for other stuff. She had an affair while we were married."

"Oh," she said. "I did not know this."

"Well, you do now," he said.

"I'm sorry."

"It doesn't matter now. She's gone and that's how it is."

"You love her still maybe?"

"I don't think so," he said. "I don't even remember that feeling at all now."

"You love her when you were married?"

"I must have."

"It does not make sense to love someone and then stop," she said. "What does it mean that human beings can do this?"

"It doesn't mean anything."

"It should," she said. "And your daughter too. Too much to lose at one time."

"Feels that way."

"You pray for daughter maybe?"

"Not really."

"No?"

He shook his head.

"I pray for you both then."

"Good," he said.

"You think of her?"

"All the time."

"Good thoughts?"

"Sure," he said. "And some regrets." Quiet. The beach shushing them. Peter and the children in the surf. "The last conversation I had with her was an argument."

"What kind of argument?"

"She was brilliant at math but she wasn't doing anything with it. It was disappointing."

"She was disappointing to you."

"Yeah, she was disappointing to me. She was spending her time cheerleading and hanging out with her boyfriend. I don't know. It didn't make sense to me. Still doesn't."

"Did it make sense to her?"

"Apparently," he said. "But she's gifted. Was, I mean."

"Gift for astronaut work?"

"Maybe," he said. "Mathematics. She was gifted at math. I mean probably genius-level gifted."

"Yes, but why this gift?"

"I don't know. She got some of what I have, I guess."

"No," Luda said. "I don't mean this question." She paused and then said, "This good thing with numbers. You say it is like gift but then you do not think it is like gift."

"Yes, I do."

"No," she stopped again. "My English is not good. Not clear." Again a pause. Then she said, "Gift is when you give something or you get something. This is not gift she has."

He was silent for a moment and then he said, "Why not?"

"Because she has no choice. This is just how she is."

He looked over at her. He knew he would have told anyone else to drop the topic entirely—even Eriksson—but for some reason he was willing to listen to Luda's commentary. He did not know why this was so, but it was. "I don't know if there's a difference," he said. "You have a talent and you use it. That's how it works."

"That is how it works for you," Luda said. "Maybe not for your daughter."

"That's how it works for everyone," he said. "Anyway, she worked hard at other stuff. Cheerleading and she had good grades. All A's. But I just wanted her to really be great. She had that in her."

"She sounds great already."

"She was," he said. "Shit, I don't even know what I'm talking about. None of that matters now."

"If it matters to you then it matters. You're the father."

"It was never enough for me. That's the goddamned truth. It was just never enough. I wanted her to be better. All the time." Something had collapsed inside of him and his eyes were welling with tears. "What a goddamn idiot I was," he said.

Luda did not respond, sitting quietly, sipping at her beer. The ocean rolled in and streamed out again. Rolled in. Streamed out. After a moment she said, "You have other good memories, though. Not just argument and disappointment."

He breathed deeply and slowly. When he regained himself he said, "Yeah," and his voice broke and he was silent once again. He could feel her hand, his daughter's tiny hand, curling into his own. God how much he wanted those days back. And every day to come after.

The sea rolled in far below them.

"This is good," she said.

He was quiet. They both were. He tried to quiet the tears but they came nonetheless, running down his cheeks.

"I'm sorry," she said.

"It's fine," he muttered, smearing the tears across his face. "Shit."

"Everything changes. This is life."

"I guess." He sipped at his beer again.

"Girls love their fathers always," she said. "My father work for Russian government and everyone hate him for this. But I love him. Maybe he is good man. Maybe he is bad man. I don't know. I love him always."

There was a slight breeze off the sea that came in gentle puffs and ruffled at the shade umbrellas. "I wish I could have made her happy," he said at last. "Before it was too late."

"She decides what is happy for her, not for you."

"Maybe," he said.

"Stop with maybe. You and Peter are same. Both never happy here and now. Only looking for the next thing to do. You don't even know where you are and what you have."

The children were taking turns climbing on their father's shoulders in the low surf, Peter's body jumping up out of the water and the children flying backwards, laughing, into the waves.

"What do you want from your life?" Luda said.

Keith sat and watched them in the ocean. All three of them laughing, their voices rising out of the static hiss of the water as it rolled in gentle waves against the sand. "I used to be able to answer that," he said.

"You forget. Everyone forget sometimes. Peter forgets for years. But then you remember."

He was silent, his beer cold and wet in his hand. "I wanted to go back to work. Now I don't even know."

"You go back to work then," she said.

"It's complicated."

"You talk to me of complicated?" She did not smile and there was an edge to her voice. "I leave my whole country to come here. What is complicated for your work? This makes mountain of molehill again."

Far out at the horizon the colors matched so that there was a continuous field of blue from earth to sky.

"I'm sorry," he said. "I didn't mean to make you mad."

Her hand fluttered in his direction as if brushing him off and so he said nothing more.

After a time Peter called up to them from the surf: "You two come!" He waved to them and Luda waved back.

"You know what I want, Astronaut Keith Corcoran?" she said at last. "Right now what I want?"

He turned to look at her and she smiled at him and their eyes met. "This," she said and she continued to look at him but her hand extended out toward the sea, her husband and the two children out there in the surf at the edge of an ocean that stretched out forever to a horizon that was no horizon.

"Come!" Peter called to them, to her.

She looked back to the surf. "OK," she called back. The wind blew the dark hair from her face and she smiled, the sun on her skin, on her body. She sat forward and pulled the T-shirt over her head and pulled down her shorts, standing there before him in her bathing suit, her body smooth and curved and he looked from the shape of her to her face where it floated above him in the sunlight. "This is what I choose," she said to him. She smiled. "Not what I have to do, but what I choose. Is that not what we have?"

He squinted up at her, into the brightness of the sun, the beautiful dark eclipse of her face. Then she turned and walked down toward the water, her form straight and tall and the curve of her hips and the black of her bathing suit, her skin the color of snow. She tiptoed into the sea slowly and Peter thrashed out of the water to meet her there like some thick-bodied oceanic god come out of the coral to meet his goddess at last, and he held her hands in his and drew her into the water slowly, the children leaping around them in a circle, jumping into and out of the water, returning to the beach, then to the water again.

The day had become warmer and after a time he indeed drew a towel around himself and changed into the swimming trunks Peter had brought for him and removed his shirt and lathered the remainder of his body with sunscreen. He stood for a moment contemplating the sea and then adjusted the shade umbrella. "Come in, Keith Corcoran," Peter called to him.

"Soon," he called back. Peter waved to him. Luda's head bobbed from farther out in the ocean, then disappeared under the surface, reappeared again, the children crawling about on the sand like crabs. After a moment, they came running up the beach and rummaged in one of the bags for some plastic pails and shovels.

"We dig," Marko said to him.

"Good idea," Keith said. "The tide is coming in."

"Good," Marko said.

They both ran back down to the surf and sat just a few feet above the line of foam where the sand was yet dry and began to dig.

Keith turned his phone back on and after it was done powering up it vibrated and he looked at the screen. Eight missed calls, seven from various numbers at Houston and one number that came through as "unknown." He dialed his voice mail. There were only two messages, the first from Jim Mullins, asking him to call back with a sense of urgency that was surprising: "Keith, I really, really need to hear from you right away. Right away. Please. As soon as you get this, please call." He wondered momentarily what the emergency could be, thought that they were moving the things out his office and somehow needed his authorization to do so. Then he skipped to the next message.

"Chip, Eriksson here," the message began, the voice a conspiratorial whisper. "Listen, I don't know where you are, but we need you here at Houston right now. I'm serious. Call me right away. Or Mullins. Get here right now. It's important."

There were no more messages and Keith clicked the phone off and set it quietly on the blanket in the sand and sat looking at it, the beer still in his hand. Then he set that too on the blanket and looked at them both as if they might hold some secret message that he could decode if only he stared long enough.

Out at sea, Peter bobbed in the water, Luda nearby, the two children on the beach now, digging their hole in the sand with pieces of drift-wood. Everything had grown silent, the surf continuing to roll in but only as some distant faded hush.

He looked up at the sky. The burning sun above them all, its motion as if it were rotating around the earth. And then he could see himself in the Destiny Module again, the planet scrolling below him through the round porthole window, his head clear and his eyes bright and shining as he watched the blue swirl of an ocean that he knew was this ocean and was somehow also this moment, because everything else had dissolved: the measurement of distance in units of time or light or space or via some other methodology he did not know. There was no future. There was only where he had been and where he was now, and such locations were not measurable by any method but that of humanity itself.

"Astronaut Keith Corcoran!" Peter called to him.

He looked again toward the water, not moving now, frozen in his borrowed black-and-white trunks, barefoot on the multicolored beach blanket. In his imagination he could see the white shining stripes of pure blazing light where they came raining through that same blue dome of the distant atmosphere, the tiny shards of ice and dust and rock flashing to the infinite trembling moment that is this one and is already gone, and he could see where that blinding arc would become the flash of impact against the distant non-horizon of the ocean and the sky as the sea vaporized around the burning mass and then Peter and Luda and the children and the others along the beach, and everyone on Earth in their cars on the road and in parking lots, and looking through the windows of the megastores, and at Starbucks, and even the workers tenting his empty house, and those building a new empty house at the end of the cul-de-sac, and Jennifer and Nicole and Walter Jensen, and yes even Barb: all looking briefly and finally toward the sea, toward that still soundless flash, and wondering. He could feel another set of eyes too, staring from some other place he could neither see nor recognize and he said her name but of course she did not answer him and never would. And then the flat slap of the explosion.

Before him the incoming surf had filled the children's sand hole and they screamed and began digging in earnest. He walked toward the water and when he reached the children he squatted next to them, turning briefly to look back up the beach, back to the umbrellas and chairs above the high-tide line and then returning his attention to the hole they had dug in the sand, its basin filled with chocolate brown water as Marko and Nadia dragged their plastic pails through it, babbling incoherently in a language Keith would never understand.

The driftwood paddles they had used to begin the pit were still there in the sand and he reached for one and began to build up a wall on the ocean side of the pit and the children watched him for a moment and then turned their attention to the same task.

I tell you now: There are no epiphanies. The place where you sit reading these words is the same place you have always been, your life ever-arrowing to the moment that is this moment and this one. And this. An infinite set spiraling in brightness, without magnitude, cardinality, sum, or number.

The water hissed up the beach.

"Here comes the tide," he said. And so it came.

Acknowledgments

Many fine and patient individuals contributed valuable information during the research phase of this novel, amongst them Anthony Barcellos, Ph.D.; Scott Bonnel, MFT; Kristine and Major Scott Dunning, USAF; Kim Failor, Ph.D.; NASA Astronaut Ron Garan; J. Matthew Gerken; Dale Hayashida, PharmD.; Shane Lipscomb; and Shi-Wen Young, Ph.D. Any and all inaccuracies or misrepresentations herein are mine alone. Warm thanks to those who read and commented, sometimes on many different drafts: Lois Ann Abraham, Katie Henderson Adams, Michael Angelone, Kate Johnson, Jason Sinclair Long, Jefferson Pitcher, Jason Roberts, Harold Schneider, Nat Sobel, Karin Stevens, and especially to Michael Spurgeon, without whom I likely would not have begun writing this novel at all.

Eleanor Jackson was instrumental in many, many ways, offering a sympathetic and critical read and being the book's champion when it needed championing. Thanks to the book's copy editor Miranda Ottewell, and warm appreciation to everyone at Bloomsbury, in

Acknowledgments

particular Nate Knaebel, Rachel Mannheimer, and especially the book's editor, Anton Mueller, who helped me put it in its final form. To all: my gratitude.

But most of all, I would like to thank my family for their continuous patience and understanding and my wife for her help in shaping this character and this novel.

A Note on the Author

Christian Kiefer earned his Ph.D. in American literature from the University of California, Davis, and is on the English faculty of American River College in Sacramento. His poetry has appeared in various national journals, including *Antioch Review* and *Santa Monica Review*. He is an accomplished songwriter and recording artist and lives in the hill country northeast of Sacramento with his wife and five sons.